WHISPERROOT

A HUSHWOOD TALE

TIFFINI JOHNSON

Copyright & Disclaimer

WHISPERROOT: A HUSHWOOD TALE

Table of Contents

WHISPERROOT: A HUSHWOOD TALE

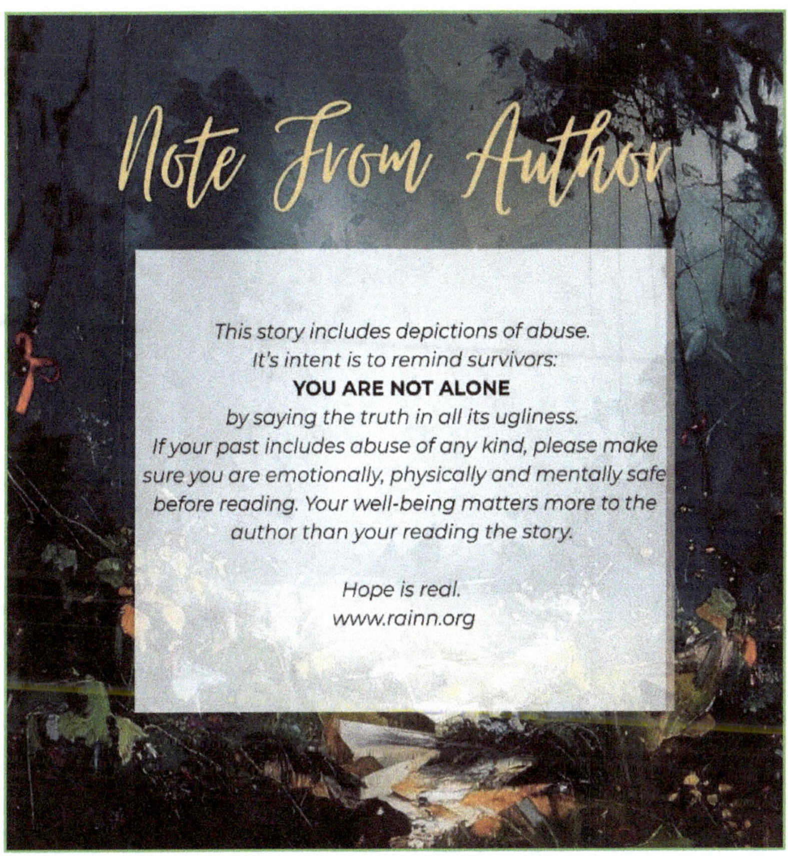

Discover More by Tiffini Johnson

Whisperroot: A Hushwood Tale

Remember the Nightingale

River's Rowan

Taramul Vieslor

The Storyteller

Me

Forget Me Not

Haven

Mountains of Hope

Ash

Broken

Dance For Me

The Character

Sing Me Home

Holding Home

DEDICATION

This story is about memory. My happiest memories revolve around my daughters. I am so thankful for time with them. They both helped flesh the idea for this story out, including cover design and plot points. My whole heart is wrapped up in my daughters, so this book is dedicated to Breathe and Alight. Each of them are wonderful storytellers themselves – Breathe writes poetry and Alight has original and beautiful ideas.

I love you!

Joyfully,
mama

Part One: The Quiet Before the Roots

Not all seeds sleep in soil.
Some wait in silence,
rooting in the dark
until the world forgets they were planted.

---

discovered in the margins
of an old hymnbook

FROM THE FOREST

WHISPERROOT: A HUSHWOOD TALE

We've been around the longest. Stillness settles here, sinking low, until its weight feels both frightening and comforting, like an old memory. Light seeks ways to seep in, a determined ally that chases shadows, but instead of welcoming its fullness, our spindly arms and thick canopies fracture sunbeams, sending them scattering like reluctant whispers. The floor here is soft not only to hold the memory of the brave footprints that trod but also to make it easier for voices trapped below to rise. Venturing into our sanctuary you enter a new world, a world where memories swell and stories stir.

We remember the beginning.

Long ago, when the land was still bare boned, there was a girl whose pain was so heavy she could not weep, whose story so tragic she could not speak. She walked the earth in silence, carrying all the world's forgotten griefs in her chest like unbreathed air. Her name is lost - but the wind here, it still curls around her shadow, and the roots remember her.

One night, she knelt in the middle of a barren field, dug her fingers into the dirt, and buried a single red ribbon torn from her hair. In that place grew the first whisperroot, its bark soft with ash, its bloom rimmed with the color of a wound. Around it, we continued to grow—at first, we were crooked, listening things—born not from seeds but from sorrows laid down. With time, we grew thick with hush. Not silence, but a different kind of hush: the kind that holds breath, holds memory, holds girls. We do not know if she walks among us. Some say the Hushwood is her body—woven from roots and whispered grief, every branch a memory, every leaf a story she never spoke. The wind is her exhale. Every ribbon you find knotted to our limbs is a wound she could not bear to forget.

Today, the hush is still here. Our roots stir. Not visibly, not quite, but the earth gives with breath. There's a glow that flickers in some parts of us. Emberflies: their wings make no sound but the heat they leave in the air crinkles like paper burning, like someone once cried here. The chime-thrush live in nests strung between bellroot blossoms. Their delicate songs match their small bodies, but their wings surprise you. Did you smell a hint of vanilla, a whiff of something like home, a tantalizing reminder of a comfort you've never had? If so, it's said that the chime-thrush heard the things you haven't said and added a bit of your story to its song.

There's a *sashaying*, a constant rustle here, as if we breathe through hollow reeds. We are not all the same. The weeping willow stands like a sorrowing woman at the forest's edge; her slender limbs draped in veils of green. Each of her arms hang low, heavy with memory, her leaves shimmer like strands of hair kissed by rain. When the wind passes, she stirs with the aching grace of someone remembering. Her long tresses swing around her and brush the earth like fingertips trailing through water.

There's the hushbark, among the oldest of us here. Some say it grew from a buried promise; others claim its roots wrapped around a buried girl. But

WHISPERROOT: A HUSHWOOD TALE

when the forest grieves, the hushbark bleeds blood-red sap that's bitter to the tastebuds. The dark-laden elderberries and towering ash trees—whose roots stretch into the very fabric of time—intertwine with hushbark to form a living boundary. They guard a hidden place: the Hushwild. The Hushwild is a hidden clearing protected by the interlocked trees and twisted vines that only move when the moon is full. It's a place well protected for it is the home of the duskstag. With a coat the color of twilight, soft and fading, like a memory on the verge of being lost, its eyes are pools of wisdom and warmth. Duskstag is a bridge between past and present, braiding sorrow and comfort. It appears only to those who are worthy and in need. Others, like the ashfeather owl and the redveil fox, dwell here.

      We are a place of refuge for the broken, but a prison for the guilty. Here, memories swell. Stories stir.

      We remember.

We are a quiet town.
But the silence is no longer ours alone.

———————————

Myreska

PROLOGUE: THE TOWN

WHISPERROOT: A HUSHWOOD TALE

We are a quiet town. We always have been. We knew what happened, of course we knew, but silence can offer a sort of grace, like a comforting lie a parent might tell to soothe a frightened child. *It's not many*, we told ourselves, willing to offer a few of our more wayward daughters as sacrifices if it protected the rest of us. We averted our eyes, walked with our heads down and our arms tight around the shoulders of the remaining children, as if we could somehow keep evil from stealing them, too. Silence that started as self-preservation slowly thickened and evolved with time until it became something else. Well, after all, no one denies that those girls–especially *that* one, Ainela–weren't proper. We teach our daughters, most of us do, how to dress, how to speak, how to behave like a good Christian girl. Hearing outspoken voices just provides the wrong influences. Father Ignacy warned us what could happen if we didn't guard against those influences, didn't he? We never wanted anything to happen to them. Some of us still tell ourselves they ran off.

It hadn't started all at once. The first girl vanished nearly five winters ago. A second followed the next spring. Then, for a while, nothing—just enough silence to pretend. When Father Ignacy left, we thought the hushwood had gone quiet with him. But two more girls vanished while he was gone, and still, we didn't speak of them. It was only after his return that the rhythm quickened. One girl didn't come home from the market. Another was gone before her mask could be finished. They vanished like breath in winter—slow at first, then all at once. By the time Ainela disappeared, the count had reached twelve.

We were already asleep when they came. The night was thick with snow and secrets, and the bells had not rung in days. We sensed that day was different because of the festival and because—because of the meeting. We all went to the chapel that night—husbands, wives, even a few elders too old to speak but not too old to vote. Some came home shaken. Others came home certain. One came home trembling and said we'd done something terrible. (He was the compassionate sort. He left not long after. Or so they said.)

But no, it wasn't twelve all at once. The hushwood is more patient than that. They disappeared slowly—one here, another there. A girl on her way to the stream. A girl who missed morning chores. A girl who simply didn't come home. We told ourselves stories for each. But the night Ainela vanished, the count reached twelve. That number—twelve— settled over the town like frost. Final. Complete. We did not say it aloud, but we felt it. We didn't see. Or perhaps we did, and we simply closed the shutters tighter, turned our faces deeper into our pillows, and told our hearts to forget. These are our great talents in Myreska—silence and forgetting.

There was no screaming. That is important to us. No doors were broken, no windows shattered, no blood spilled on the cobblestones—none that we could see, at least. We like to think that makes it different. We tell ourselves that they went willingly because that helps us sleep.

WHISPERROOT: A HUSHWOOD TALE

But Zosia saw them. She stood behind the curtain of the east window, the one with the warped glass that makes the world look like it's drowning. She saw her sister, Ainela, at the end of the line, clutching her coat around her like it could keep out more than the cold. There was a red ribbon in her braid. We all remember that part clearly. The men—soldiers, we say now, though no uniforms were worn—held torches that smoked more than they burned. Their boots made no sound on the snow. The dogs, who bark at everything, were silent. Even the church owl did not cry.

We did nothing. We stirred in our beds. We blamed the war, the hunger, the chaos beyond the hills. We lit candles the next day, but not for them. And when the mothers asked where the girls had gone, we repeated what we were told: *They were taken for protection. They will return when it is safe.* They did not return. And we stopped speaking their names.

But they didn't really disappear, not completely.

No one remembers who saw the first red ribbon, where or when they saw it. Some say it was a year after the girls left. Others say it was at the first full moon after. We told ourselves the ribbons were just tricks of wind and memory. Tattered bits of cloth picked up by gusts and caught within the branches, nothing more. The ribbons were bright and tied tight at first. We saw them nailed to the door of the blacksmith's barn, fluttering like a wound. They were seen on the chapel gate, around the birch tree at the schoolyard, and on the clothesline of the baker's wife.

No one asked who tied them.

No one asked what they were or what they meant. Some said they looked like the prayer knots the convent girls once tied in their hair before they were sent away. Others said that was nonsense—that the convent burned long ago, and nothing sacred could have survived it. But we whispered about them. The stories we invented about those ribbons helped us pretend. That mattered. Because, if we could pretend, we didn't have to change.

We thought they would go away. But they didn't. Women laughed nervously and said they were hair ties—*I bet it came loose when I was at the market*. Only none of us wore red ribbons and all of us knew it. Others, the more superstitious of us, whispered they were marks. Father Ignacy's sermons were fiery; he warned us that they were the Devil's threads spun of temptation and lust, that they must be destroyed. Whenever he found one, he burned it straight away. But once, only once, someone caught him holding a ribbon a little too long, a little too gently, rubbing his thumb over it as if trying to dislodge a memory.

The seamstress never said anything, but she always took them down, gently, almost mournfully, and put them in her drawer. Her children told us her room smelled of lavender and ash, and sometimes we said we saw red thread trailing from under her door. The butcher's boy was a mischievous troublemaker who scared the little children by telling them the ribbons were witches' markers. *Touch one,* he said, *and your tongue will rot.* (He said that because Zosia stopped speaking when her sister left.) When he was alone, that boy wound a ribbon around his wrist and whispered, *I didn't forget. I remember you.*

The little twins thought they were gifts from the forest and braided them into their dolls' hair. Their mother slapped them for it and buried the dolls under the pear tree. The pear tree never bloomed again. The midwife left them alone. She said, *"The forest marks its own. If you try to unmake the story, its roots will twist round your throat."*

Although we didn't invite it, subtle changes came.

The chapel bell, for one. It stopped ringing after they left. Father Ignacy told us the bells were silent for mourning. Except mourning didn't come. We still filed into the pews every week. We maintained our rituals: crossing ourselves, averting our eyes from one another. But the bells never rang again, and some of us swore the candles burned too quickly. Children known for being patient started crying during sermons and could not be consoled or rebuked into silence. Birds stopped nesting in the eaves. The chapel, once a sanctuary, slowly felt like a prison. We didn't know how true that was, but we sensed it. We wondered. That was a sin none of us ever confessed to, not even when we filed into the sacred confessionals. We told ourselves we were just a small village with nothing better to do with our time than invent stories, ones that likely caused grief to the girls' parents.

The girls' parents.

Each handled their daughter's absence differently.

One mother carved her daughter's name into the schoolhouse door. The next morning, it had been sanded away. One father left pamphlets under our doors — drawings of the girls, names printed below. He was gone by wook's end. They said he took ill. That he left for Warsaw. But his coat still hangs behind the door of his cottage, and no one's seen smoke from the chimney since. Most accepted it, most stopped asking questions. They had other children, after all, who needed them.

Zosia hasn't spoken a word since her sister vanished. Not in weeks—not even when the elders came, or when Mama wept into the quilt. Other siblings carry the ache in quieter ways—thumbs rubbed raw, sketches buried in drawers, questions swallowed mid-sentence. Time presses forward, as it always does, but despite what the parents insist, despite what we whisper to ourselves at night, we haven't really forgotten. This spring, when we braided wildflowers for the schoolchildren, someone tucked a red bloom behind the ear of every third girl. We said it was for beauty. For joy. We didn't say it was for memory.

On All Souls' Day, someone left four pebbles by the chapel steps. Just four. We pretend not to see them. Pretend they were always there. But they're smooth as eggs, warm to the touch—and no one ever sees who leaves them.

Besides, there's the Hushwood.

We don't go into the hushwood. Not really. We send the boys to chop kindling near the edge, and we gather elderberries before the branches twist too deep. But no one passes the third birch—not since the girls left. The trees grow too close together there. The light bends wrong. The dogs won't follow us in. The wind whistles through the leaves, but it doesn't sound like wind. It sounds like someone trying not to cry. The Hushwood is still here. Sometimes those of us who live close to the forest's edge hear whistling through the trees. We don't go into the hushwood. We warn our children not to, either, although we know they dare each other to sometimes. We allow that. Not out of remorse or guilt because the girls just ran off with the soldiers–willingly in our story––but, once, they were ours.

We tell ourselves it's over. That there's nothing left to see, nothing left to say. But lately, things have begun to stir. Quiet things. Rooted things. A red ribbon was found in the schoolhouse chimney. A name scratched into frost vanished before the teacher arrived. One girl claimed she saw a sketch

WHISPERROOT: A HUSHWOOD TALE

nailed to the chapel door — a girl's face, with eyes like ash and mouth sewn shut — but when the priest went to look, it was gone. One of the older boys carved a name in the birch–a name he had never heard before. When we asked him where he heard that name, he simply shrugged. And now he's become as silent as Zosia.

Zosia — she still doesn't speak. But sometimes she leaves drawings near the birch grove. She pins them to the fence or tucks them into tree knots: pictures of girls in threadbare dresses, girls with red in their hair, girls we don't name anymore. We don't take them down. We don't tell her not to draw them. But we don't speak of them either. We told ourselves the hushwood was done, that it had gone still. We told ourselves there was nothing more to hear, that the last of the stories had been told.

A new map of the town was printed last winter. We studied it carefully, the way we always do. The hushwood was gone from it — erased. As if it had never been there at all. But it's still here. It always has been. Sometimes the wind shifts strange — and if you listen too long, you'll swear it's not the wind at all, but a voice rising from the roots, calling a name you almost remember. That's when we close our windows. That's when we light a candle and say nothing.

We are a quiet town. But the silence is no longer ours alone.

You stitched a harness for a caterpillar.
I'll never forget that.

———————————————

Ainela

CHAPTER ONE - ZOSIA

WHISPERROOT: A HUSHWOOD TALE

A blanket of snow covers Myreska. Zosia lifts her knee high, stepping through the snow, and watches the hole her leg leaves behind. Last year, the snow came to her knees, but that was when she was eight. She's taller now and the snow doesn't reach as high on her bony knees. The hole in the snow feels right: there are lots of holes in Myreska. There are lots of broken things, too. She notices them as she walks: the chipped bell tower, the wooden benches where the old ladies quiet their knitting when children like her walk past, and the fence by the village garden is still missing a slat. Men like her papa mutter about critters getting the vegetables, but no one's fixed it yet. Zosia doesn't think they will: *it's safer to stay still,* as they say.

A broken thing is her errand this morning. She clutches the necklace with the small heart-shaped locket and its broken latch in her palm, careful not to squeeze too hard. The metal is cold now, but once it had been warm from Ainela's hands, slipped into hers the morning she turned nine, wrapped in the corner of a handkerchief with a crooked bow. *Because even brambles need to shine,* Ainela whispered, grinning.

The morning mist hasn't cleared yet. Myreska never fully wakes up, not like she does. She's the first out of bed each morning–before her sister Ainela and before her parents. She's learned being the last to sleep and the first to rise means sometimes she sees some of the secrets. She is one of the only ones to fully wake each day. Myreska stirs more than moves, the way curtains snap close if too many people pass by or the way everybody locks their doors in the daylight even though everybody knows everybody. *What goes on inside our cottage isn't anyone's business but ours,* Papa says, as a way of explaining. People only come out to go to work or chapel (and the chapel is only because they got to, less they want to go to Hell). Eyes skate past others'. Greetings are rushed.

Even the baker, who once greeted the sun with flour-dusted hands, isn't up yet. The strong licorice scent of caraway and rye used to tickle her nose and make her stop. With Christmas coming soon, piernik usually lined the baker's frosted window. Zosia misses the sound of the bell tinkling above the door when she pushed it open. But, these days, the baker *makes only what I should want.*

But what do you want to make?

Scowling, the baker shooed her away.

The crunch of the snow beneath her boots and the iciness of her nose make her wish this year was the same as years past. But things aren't the same. *I won't be like them. I will not,* Ainela whispers furiously. They both know it's a lie: of course she'll be like everyone else, she has to. The sound of hammer hitting stone forces her to look up, blinking a new snowflake out of her eyes. The blacksmith's is the only place that sounds alive anymore. The forge glows red and orange with flames.

Jakub is so tall he bends his head to enter the arched doorways of the chapel. He spends a lot of time there, helping Father Ignacy keep it clean. Papa says he's done that ever since he came back from the war a changed man. *He's fighting demons, what with the war and Anka.* His daughter. The one he never talks about.

"Good morning," Zosia speaks, her voice light as the nightingale's song.

He grunts instead of answers, using his forearm to wipe the sweat off his face. Sometimes his hammer fell too hard, too fast, as if he were still striking something that wasn't iron. The rhythm of it carried a violence that didn't belong to the forge. Despite the chilly winter morning, it's always hot in the blacksmiths shop. The town's dog, Sheriff, barks at the new voice and comes around from behind a table of tools.

She holds her palm out, the gold of the necklace a sharp contrast to her white gloves. He frowns, reaches out and takes it. His hands are so large she doesn't know how he holds it so gingerly.

"The clasp is broken."

"It's yours?" he lifts one dark, bushy brow. His leathery skin pulls across his face and his dark eyes demand answers. She already thought of this. Father Ignacy says it's a sin to own pretty things, that you shouldn't even want nice things because it might tempt others. The only thing you *should* want is a *pure and blameless life with Christ Jesus.* Pretty things are taken away and donated to the chapel or thrown in a fire.

"Ainela gave it to me on my birthday. Father said I could keep it." *No, he didn't. He doesn't know she has it.*

"Father said that, did he?"

"We shouldn't refuse someone the joy of giving. Even Christ accepted gold from the wise men."

"Hmm. Well, how'd it get broken?"

Zosia frowns and tips her head, black hair spilling from beneath her blue hood onto her cheek. "I'm not sure, really. I woke and it was pooled beside me on my pillow." *No, it wasn't. She had yanked it off and thrown it against the wall, hard, after Father came again to speak of Ainela. After Ainela cried.* "Can you please fix it for me? It has a sketch of me and Ainela in it." *The locket was meant to keep things safe, but even that had split. Like the fence, like Ainela's voice when Father pressed too hard. Everything in Myreska either broke or kept quiet.*

A dirty fingernail flicks open the heart to study a tiny drawing of two girls whose oval faces and dark hair resemble Ainela and Zosia. He snaps it shut, and his fist closes around the chain. His knowing eyes seem to peer too closely; his silence lingers a little longer than she likes. "Come back later."

The cold has a silence to it, like the world is holding its breath. Zosia sits cross-legged on the chapel steps, her fingers stiff in their mittens as she clutches the stub of a pencil. Her breath ghosts in front of her face, curling like steam over a forgotten teacup. The paper in her lap is wrinkled and smudged, but she doesn't mind—what matters is the drawing. *Here* is better than the cottage where silence is loud, especially without Ainela. Her sister has tutoring today; Papa will walk her himself to make sure she goes.

Before her, the Hushwood stretches like a shadow.

The trees closest to the chapel are thinner, more orderly—ash, birch, and alder—spindly and pale, their bark flaking like old skin. But further in, the forest thickens. The

WHISPERROOT: A HUSHWOOD TALE

hushbark trees rise tallest, their trunks dark and furrowed like the brow of someone keeping secrets. Their branches seem to tangle into one another high above, letting in only a little light, which falls in silver slivers and dusky patches. Zosia draws those branches carefully—like interlaced fingers hiding a secret. She's not the only one with secrets in Myreska, but hers could rival Ainela's—sneaking off to meet the seamstress's son after dark.

The Hushwood doesn't frighten her.

She's hidden from light all her life. When Papa gets angry, she hides in the dark space at the back of her closet. Presses her ear to the aged wood, listening to him yell about a wife's duty. She hides in the church pantry that smells of dust and rye when it's time for confessional. She hides in the elderberry patch when Ainela wants her to finish *her* chores. When you're hiding, you see lots of shadows. Shadows aren't the scariest thing in this town. Maybe that's why it doesn't frighten her.

She dots in a few bellroot blossoms, long dead now under snow, but in her memory still glowing with pale blue light in spring. A fox—maybe a redveil, if she's lucky— scurries somewhere between the trunks, just a suggestion of movement she catches in her peripheral vision. She draws it, anyway, even if she isn't sure it was real. That's what the forest is like: half-real, half-remembered. A place that pretends to sleep but never quite does, a place that surprises you when you least expect it.

The snow at the base of the trees is untouched—no footprints, no paths. No one goes that far in anymore, not since the whispers started. She pauses, bites her lip. Then sketches a single ribbon, tied to a low branch near the forest's edge. It isn't really there.

Not yet.

Crunching snow snaps her attention away from her sketchpad in time to see Father Ignacy walking towards her. She closes her sketchpad, and her boots turn away from the hushwood. Her posture straightens and she stands from the chapel steps, her eyes dropping like she's been taught to do. "Good morning, Father," she says. He smiles, his own cheeks rosy from the cold, his own eyes, the color of steel, avoiding the hushwood. "Good morning, young Zosia. Aren't you cold? You can come into the chapel to sketch if you'd like."

"No, thank you. I should be going home to help Mama with the chores."

"That's a thoughtful girl," he reaches out and places a heavy hand on her shoulder. She doesn't flinch. She just holds her breath like Mama taught her. If he notices her muscles tightening, he doesn't speak of it. His body, cloaked in the black robes of the church, is strong. *A shepherd should be strong to corral the sheep*. Everyone laughed when he said it—but not like it was funny. Because it wasn't really a joke.

She doesn't really go home.

Instead, she cuts across the snow-laden street, pats the chestnut-colored mare waiting to be hitched, waves at a couple of girls she recognizes, and darts behind the lamplighter's cottage. The town is home. Not just the buildings, but the spaces between them—the corners no one watches too closely. The mist has cleared, but the sun plays hide-and-seek with the puffy clouds, leaving the day as dreary as the Hushwood in winter: all roots and no bloom. She pulls her pale blue scarf up over her nose. She tries to remember what Ainela says about not being *obvious. You know, look down, like you're supposed to. But lift your eyes, just enough. If there's a message, the green satin will be braided with the vine. If they see it, they'll think it belongs to the Hushwood. They won't touch it.* She bends her head, ducking the cold, but her swimming blue eyes scatter over the base of every tree.

The hushbark, tall and thick, is very old. It sits at the edge of the forest, as if guarding its own memories. Vines twist around its base. *It's perfect,* Ainela sang happily. The hushbark is theirs. If the slip of green satin is tied into the twisted roots, then there's a note meant only for her. It's so subtle, the green the perfect shade of forest, that sometimes it's easy to miss.

But not today.

Zosia's heart skips a beat when she sees it.

She glances quickly behind her, towards the chapel, before she rushes forward, hiding behind the hushbark. Quickly, she reaches in the hollow space and finds it: a secret, a truth her sister trusts only her with. Unfolding the faded paper, she reads.

If Papa asks, I went to bed early.
If Father asks, I was never here.
If you ask, I just need to breathe.
I'll be back before morning.
Love you more than the hushwood hides.

A smile pulls Zosia's lip up. *She's going out again.* Pulling out a nub of charcoal, she scribbles her reply on the back of the hushwood sketch, tearing the page gently from her book. She folds it and places it into the hollow, then reties the satin into the vine like Ainela showed her. She hopes Ainela will smile when she reads it:

The fox is out late.
The owl sees everything
But the mouse won't squeak
(PS: I'll save you some piernik).

Jakub stands at a small table. He glances up when she enters, but his eyes then fall away. Father Ignacy sits on a stool, shifting through a small tin of trinkets. As she's been taught, Zosia greets them and then says, "I've come to see if my necklace is ready."

Jakub's lips purse. He shakes his head. "It's not here."

Zosia frowns, tips her head. "It's not here? Where could it be?"

Jakub nods toward Father Ignacy, who lifts his head to smile at her. "It's such a lovely keepsake, Zosia. But one must wonder how such finery serves your soul."

Zosia waits.

"Your necklace has been donated to the chapel. As a gift. Isn't that generous of you?" Jakub says nothing as Father Ignacy speaks, his silence both a profession of loyalty and a betrayal. Confusion makes Zosia's brows furrow. She wants to protest. She wants to be brave like Ainela, but she is not. *It's safer, child, to agree.* Her mother's words ring loud in her head. *The only gold you need is to walk upon those Heavenly streets. Until then, gold tempts you, it tricks you into taking your eye off God.* Father Ignacy's sermons scare her. What if it's true?

Zosia nods, her eyes skating down, heart pounding heavy. She murmurs *yes, Father* and turns. As she passes the forge, she snatches a small piece of charcoal. *It was hers. She hadn't meant to give it away.* She barely notices the snowflakes coating her face or the sting of dropping temperatures on her cheeks. *Chin up, Caterbutton.*

Ainela calls her that sometimes. Caterbutton. It's one of her favorite memories-when her sister first called her that.

Once, when Zosia was very small –just past her fifth birthday, she received another gift from Ainela: a nickname. Springtime in Myreska is Zosia's favorite time--the colors and garden festivals. That's where she is now, the chapel garden. Crouched on her knees, her hands are motionless and cupped when Ainela finds her.

"What've you got there?" she whispers, her skirt flowing around her, her long hair dancing in the breeze. She kneels beside her, the scent of honeysuckle and peaches settling around them.

Zosia opens her hands just enough to show a fuzzy little green caterpillar crawling over one palm. It had taken her all morning to coax it onto her glove with a bit of grass, and now she was too in love with it to move. "It's beautiful," she says.

Ainela's laugh sounds like windchimes. "And this?" she asks, pointing to a button Zosia stitched on the edge of her white church mitten, using red thread and a crooked needle. A small, mismatched button, sewn right where the caterpillar had started its crawl—"so it wouldn't get lost," Zosia said solemnly.

"You stitched a safety harness for a bug." Joy spills over Ainela's face. People say she's the most beautiful of the two. Zosia knows it's true. But she doesn't mind being less beautiful than Ainela.

Since then, Ainela sometimes calls her *Caterbutton,* for the sister who notices small things, who stays quiet so the world won't scare them off, who mends what she can, even if it is impossible, even if it is tiny, even if it doesn't stay. Sometimes Ainela still uses it—not just when teasing, but when she's trying to say: *I see you. You're still that girl. You still carry small things gently.*

That night, Myreska curls into itself. Wind hisses beneath the shutters. The fire has gone to embers, and the walls of the cottage creak like they're remembering things they'd rather forget. Zosia lies curled beneath the quilt she shares with Ainela, her knees tucked to her chest, the faint scent of her sister's soap clinging to the pillow.

Ainela's breathing is too steady. Too still.
Zosia keeps her eyes closed, waiting.

Then she hears it—the whisper of fabric, the careful placement of feet on the wooden floor, the slow creak of the latch. Her lashes flutter open just in time to see Ainela's shadow slip out the door. Her red shawl catches the moonlight for a heartbeat before vanishing into darkness.

Zosia doesn't follow. She never does. But she stays awake, staring at the knot of shadow where her sister had been, her hands curled tight into fists beneath the quilt.

A window across the lane glints. Just for a moment. A curtain stirs—then stills. She doesn't know who. But someone else saw. Someone who leaves their candle burning late and their mouth open in church. The silence in the cottage feels heavier now.

WHISPERROOT: A HUSHWOOD TALE

As if something has begun.

The forest is for men with axes and saints
with torches—not for girls with questions

———

Ainela

Chapter Two

Ainela

The hushwood does not whisper, it summons. It's always there, listening, breathing, waiting. Zosia doesn't fear it, but she doesn't know what it holds. Ainela moves through the hush like she belongs to it, though every step snags at her shawl and breath. Frost crusts the edges of leaves like breath held too long, and the birch trees gleam ghost-pale under moonlight, their limbs stretching like they remember how it feels to reach.

She shouldn't be here. She knows that. The forest is for men with axes and saints with torches-not for girls with questions. Girls who go missing from Myreska are always said to have run off with someone they shouldn't have. But Ainela isn't running *to* anyone. She's answering a call that hums in the marrow of her bones. The frigid air nips at her face, the exposed skin as vulnerable as the towns' girls.

Ainela looks in both directions, even turning to see behind her. She exhales a soft breath held since walking out the cottage door. She stops by the hushbark with the green ribbon woven through the vines. She smiles reading Zosia's note; they haven't had piernik yet this season because it hasn't been made. The baker stopped making it after his daughter didn't come home. There are a lot of dead things in Myreska. She's supposed to forget. But she can't.

The hushwood can't either.

A small rabbit darts past, its cottontail flashing once before vanishing into the tree line. She hears the ashfeather owl, a creature who only lives in the hushwood. His call is

WHISPERROOT: A HUSHWOOD TALE

low and breathy, like wind sighing through old curtains. It doesn't hoot so much as murmur—a soft, rasped hush that rises and falls in the dark, almost like it's whispering a secret to the trees. When it flies, its wings barely make a sound— just the faintest rustle, like paper brushed against bark. Sometimes Ainela and Zosia sit outside the cottage at night and play a quiet game to see who can hear the ashfeather first. She walks closer, her fingers curling around a ribbon– this one red, not green–hidden in her pocket. Her boots crunch the snow; her breath rises like fog in chilly evening air. Walking a bit deeper into the forest, she feels someone watching her but it's just the oldest of the hushbark trees. The dark brown, furrowed trunk is bent slightly, as if it's leaning towards her, as if asking her to listen. Everyone knows the hushbark remembers best. *That tree holds stories in its grooves*; that's what her grandmother says. *When I was a girl, we didn't dare misbehave in front of a hushbark. It might tell on us.*

Behind her, she can still the faint outline of the cottage, swallowed by silence, its silence thicker than hushwood. Zosia didn't follow her: she never does. Branches stir above her. She tips her head to find limbs reaching gently, as if welcoming her back, as if the forest had waited for her.

She wasn't meeting a boy. She doesn't care if they think she is. She knows she's one of *the wayward daughters* in Father Ignacy's sermons, the ones who tempt and invite the Devil into the thoughts of men. She knows Mama pretends not to notice the missing ribbon, or the way her daughter's eyes scan the forest as if they might speak. Ainela knows. But what *they* don't know is what calls her here. She herself doesn't know–not really. All she knows is that, when she steps into the glade, she doesn't feel alone. Something about the whispers of the wind and the lean of the trees makes her feel *known*.

Tonight, she goes further, past the birch marked in red. Even past the hollow where the whisperroot grows twisted and low to the ground. A muffled *pop*, *whoosh* makes her gasp, her eyes trying to see farther back into the forest. She tries to quiet her racing heart: *a frost crack or a limb falling, that's all it is*. She moistens her dry lips and pushes forward. Two of them are already there. Greta and Caroline always join her. Caroline wears a red cape, Greta a bright yellow. Red, yellow and green. Ainela feels pride pool in her chest like warm tea on a cold night. *Add pride to my list of sins*, she thinks ruefully, as she greets the others.

"Did anyone see her?" Greta asks, her eyebrows furrowing over her green eyes. The wind makes all of their cheeks rosy. Caroline shakes her head, her eyes skating around them. "Did you hear that?" she whispers. The girls quiet, listening, as though waiting for someone to finish a thought. Ainela breaks the silence first, bending and putting a palm against the twisted vine of whisperroot. She gasps as her hand warms through the glove and the vine seems to pulse like a heartbeat. It's not warmth like fire, but like memory—like the heat left behind after someone leaves the room. The pulse is soft, but insistent, and she suddenly wants to cry. "We didn't see her, but the whisperroot knows where she is."

"It only does that when there's a truth buried."

Greta seems the most reluctant. "I heard she ran off."

Ainela sighs heavily, standing, smoothing her skirt with her hand. "They can't *all* have run off."

"I have mine," Caroline says, pulling a red ribbon from her pocket. Ainela hesitates, glances at Greta, senses a discomfort neither admits. *Give the hushwood a ribbon, it might take you next.*

Caroline reaches out, grabs Ainela's hand and pulls it against the hushbark. The tree's limbs, heavy with snow, seem to sway towards them. "They're never coming back," she whispers furiously. Ainela's eyes slide toward Greta's. Almost as one, they reach into their own pockets and retrieve the bits of red ribbon.

No one knows who tied the first red ribbon in the hushwood. It just appeared a few days after the first girl vanished. *She always was a troublemaker,* they said. The town's merchant called her *sticky fingers* and small things in his shop seemed to *walk away* when she came in. *Eleven-year-olds know better*, they said. *She's headed down a sinful path*, they said. Until the day she went to pick elderberries and didn't come home. Nearly a week later, one of the younger schoolchildren noticed the red ribbon, tied to the limb of an ash tree.

Ainela wraps the red ribbon twice around the hushbark's outstretched limb, then weaves one end through the loop she's made, not pulling tight—not yet. Her fingers remember the motion, like muscle-memory from stories passed down. She tucks the tip through again, creating a hollow in the center. The knot tightens with a soft whisper. The middle remains open, like a hidden mouth holding breath. A secret kept. A truth waiting. The wind stirs it gently, and the ribbon flutters—not wildly, but like it's breathing. *In the old days, girls used it as a vow—tied into a scrap of cloth and slipped into a pocket or tucked behind a barn. If the boy saw it, and knew the pattern, he'd know where to meet. And if someone else found it? It would look like nothing at all. Just a bit of ribbon.*

Ainela stares at the three ribbons they've tied, one for each girl whose gone missing this year. She notices Greta's knot is a quick loop, rough and trembling. Caroline's is a tight braid, pulled hard, like she dared the tree to forget. Each of their knots is different because they each have their own secrets to offer the hushwood.

Fresh snow falls lightly, dusting her coat and eyelashes. The wind makes her cheeks rosy. When she slips back into the room she shares with Zosia, she leans back against the wooden door and closes her eyes. It isn't the rush of forbidden love that sends her sliding against the door—it's relief. She made it home. She wasn't next.

When she sinks slowly onto the mattress and pulls the quilt patched with stars over her, her toes accidentally brush against Zosia's. Her sister giggles. "You're an icicle," she whispers, dragging her foot away. "You didn't leave me any piernik?" Ainela teases, lying on her back. She still stares at the whiskey-colored ceiling when she hears Zosia's breathing deepen in sleep.

Zosia sets the basket of eggs gently on the counter. Mama brushes butter across the hot skillet, the scent already softening the morning chill. Papa's silhouette looms in the doorway, too tall for the frame, shoulders dusted with wood shavings. He's been out since dawn, chopping wood. In winter, there is never enough.

"Papa, you're in the way," Mama says nudging him toward the table. "Breakfast won't take long."

WHISPERROOT: A HUSHWOOD TALE

He's not my Papa. The thought slips unbidden into Ainela's chest like a match dropped into kindling. She swallows against the heat of it, shame curling inside her ribs. She tries to shake it off—tries to forget that truth, the one no one speaks but everyone knows. He married Mama out of pity, took in the silence... *and me.*

The *rap rap rap* on the door is loud and strong. Ainela swallows; she knows. Mama's eyes skip to her oldest daughter, and her face hardens. "What have you done now?" she whispers furiously. Papa sighs heavily, as if he's already tired, and says, "Ainela. Zosia. Go to your room." Though the door hasn't yet been answered, they all know who it is. He's been here before; they've learned the sound of Father's raps.

Ainela hovers by the bedroom door, keeping it cracked just enough to see silvers of those standing in the main room like shadows from her nightmares. Father is joined by three of the elders. Their voices start low but Father's rises and falls as if it's grumbles of thunder punctuated by sharp strikes of lightning.

"She was seen leaving after curfew – " Elder Gentry's eyebrows arch above his retreating hairline.

"She wears *green. Of all the colors to wear.* How dare she flaunt her sins like that?" Simeon, the youngest of the elders, spits.

"She's a bad influence on the other girls in the village."

"She's tempting the boys," the elder's voice strikes out like lightning, sharp and loud.

"She's got bad blood in her, and we want to make sure we curb the evil." Father's voice was thunder rolling– and, while not as loud as the elders, it was the strongest. "We thought it best to let you know she was seen, so that you can discipline her appropriately. The scriptures say that parents who do not discipline their child do not really love them. We know you love her."

Voices fade to murmurs.

Ainela closes the bedroom door. Zosia's eyes flick to Ainela, searching her face for any sign of understanding. She fidgets with the edge of her sleeve and says tremulously, as if the question could change everything, "They're wrong, right?"

Ainela walks quietly to the window that overlooks the hushwood. *What's the point in telling the truth if the truth isn't believed? The words would fall like snow—cold, unnoticed, already buried beneath the weight of their assumptions. Ainela's throat tightens. She swallows it down. They had never asked her the truth before. Why start now?* She smiles but the smile fades quickly under so much weight in the room.

The girls watch in silence as Father and the elders leave, their backs fading from view while their black boots leave heavy footprints in the snow. The morning clouds hang low, throwing Myreska into a gloomy shade. Ainela knows there will be punishment, shame. They believe she met a boy. Tempted a boy. Telling them different will do no good–and, even if it could save her from punishment, Ainela wouldn't confess. Visiting the hushwood is too important: she cannot be stopped from going there.

"Ainela?" Zosia's voice crackles with concern.

Ainela turns, joins her sister on the edge of the bed, takes the younger girl's hand in hers. "It's alright," she says softly, the steadiness of her soft voice betraying the rapid *thud-thud-thud* of her heart and the trembling of her fingers.

WHISPERROOT: A HUSHWOOD TALE

"It's alright, Caterbutton," she says this as much to comfort Zosia as herself.

Neither believe her.

When Papa calls them to break evening fast, Ainela holds her breath, waiting for the punishment she knows will come. Instead, there is only silence. Soon, the girls are called back to break evening fast. Silence reigns loud. There will be punishment, shame, but not yet. Not until chores are complete. While Zosia helps clean the house and feed the livestock, Ainela's task is simple: candle making. *Or,* she thinks, *stay out of the way, and stay alone.*

The heavy iron pot sits over the fire, its contents slowly melting, softening into a liquid mass. Ainela stirs it gently with a wooden spoon, the fat swirling in the heat, releasing a faint, oily scent that mingles with the smoke curling from the hearth. The fire crackles beneath her, the only sound in the quiet room except for the rhythmic scrape of the spoon against the sides of the pot. She leans forward, watching the tallow as it slowly transforms, the once-solid mass becoming a pale, almost translucent liquid. She stirs in slow, even circles, her fingers stiff from the cold air seeping through the walls. The heat from the fire and the tallow offers a brief moment of warmth.

Her mind, though, is colder still. Her thoughts drift to the elders, to the way they spoke of her as if she were already a lost cause, a shadow tainting her family. The shame they spread like salt on an open wound. The way they looked at her mother as though she had failed. Ainela pushes the thought away with a sharper turn of the spoon. She won't let it settle in, not here, not now. Outside, the wind howls against the house, making the wooden beams groan under its weight. The storm is coming again, just like every winter night, relentless, like the weight of the town's silence.

She adds more fat, watching it melt into the pot with a hiss. The tallow begins to solidify again, hardening at the edges as it cools, and she stirs more vigorously. Each turn of the spoon is like a ritual, something to focus on, something that demands her attention. It's a task she knows by heart, a motion as familiar as breathing. A part of her, deep inside, wants to leave the spoon in the pot, let it be. Let everything go quiet for a moment, even if just for a breath. But there's no time for that.

Ainela pulls the wick from the small tin beside the pot, its ends fraying from use. She dips it carefully into the tallow, watching the way it sinks, absorbing the liquid as it cools and hardens, one layer at a time. There is something about the way the tallow wraps around the wick, encasing it, that feels like a promise—something to hold, to steady, to keep from unraveling. The silence of the room presses in on her, heavy and thick, like the snow building up against the windows outside. Ainela shifts her weight, standing still as she watches the tallow settle in the mold. Her hands feel the weight of it as she places another wick in the pot, and then another.

"Ainela," Papa's voice sounds heavy, as if he's swallowed sandpaper. Pulling her bottom lip between her teeth, her limbs shaking, Ainela steps from the bedroom into the main room. Mama stands against the wall; Papa stands by the fire. "You bring shame into this house."

WHISPERROOT: A HUSHWOOD TALE

Ainela's eyes glisten with tears and she covers her mouth with her hands. "Please, don't," she whispers. She gasps and takes a step forward as Papa drops her green cape into the crackling fire. Ainela feels her world narrow as she watches the flames devour the only thing that was ever really hers.

"I didn't meet anyone. Mama, I didn't." Ainela's voice breaks as truth spills out. Mama says nothing, her eyes slinking to the floor. Anger and hurt claw up her chest, tightening her ribcage until it bursts out. "I went to the hushwood, I –"

Papa's fist slams onto the wooden table, making crockery rattle and her mother startle, closing her eyes briefly. "Enough!" he shouts. "You should be a role model for the younger girls–for your sister! Instead, you are a reminder of your mother's shame. You will not wear the colors of the Devil anymore. Not another word."

As Mama and Papa somberly move to other parts of the cottage, Ainela sinks into a kitchen chair, wrapping her arms around her waist, and staring into the fires until the last of herself has been devoured.

The morning after Papa burns her cape, Ainela says she's going to the chapel. It's not a lie—she does sweep the vestibule, straighten the hymnals, polish the brass cross until her fingers ache and the scent of metal clings to her wrists.

But it isn't why she came.

She waits until the narthex is empty, until Jakub's footsteps have faded toward the back hall, until even the ever-burning candles seem to flicker more slowly. Then she slips behind the altar, into the narrow room lined with donation trays and relic shelves.

There, beneath a yellowing cloth and beside a chipped porcelain saint, she sees it.

The locket.

Her breath stutters.

It's still here.

Still whole, though the latch is bent, the chain curled like a question. Ainela glances toward the nearest stained-glass window. A smear of blue light spills across the floor. No footsteps. No voices. She reaches out. The metal is cold, but her hand doesn't tremble.

She remembers the drawing inside. Two girls. Arms looped. Zosia had drawn it years ago—before everything became dangerous, before pretty things were taken and burned or turned to shame. Ainela closes her fingers around the locket and slips it into her coat pocket.

It is hers now to return.

What is buried does not rest. It waits

———————————

Myreska Proverb

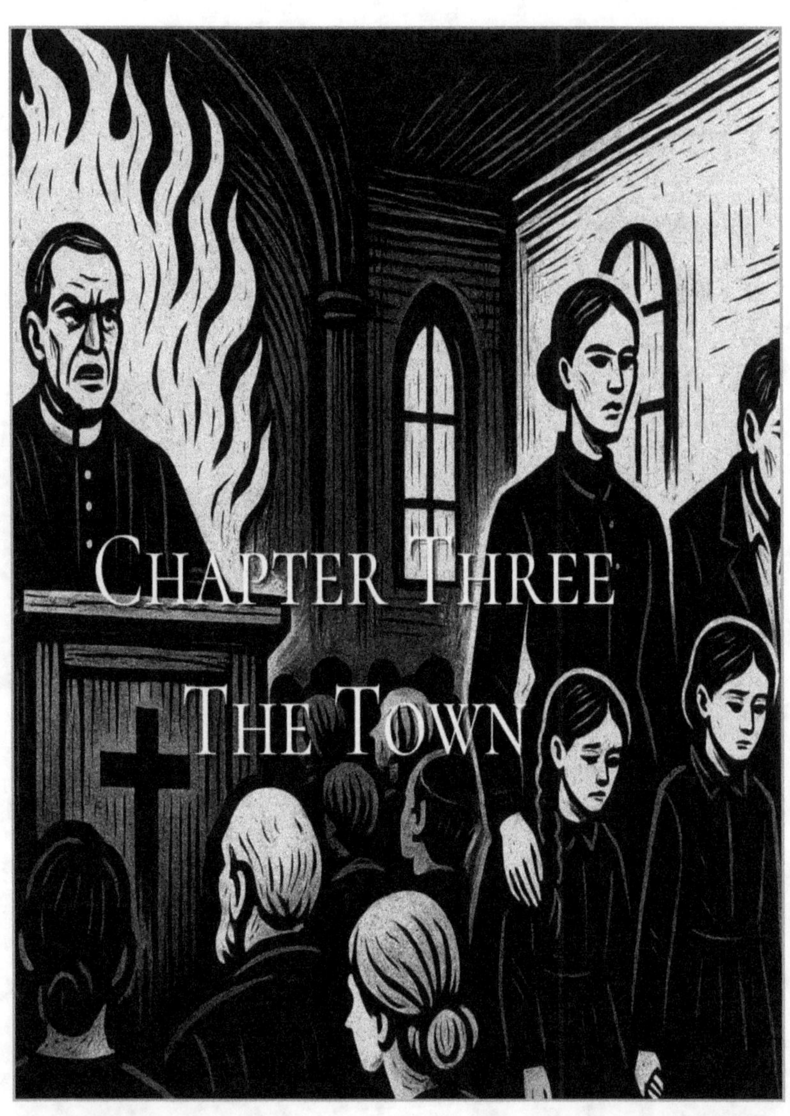
CHAPTER THREE

THE TOWN

WHISPERROOT: A HUSHWOOD TALE

We had gathered in the chapel because it was what we'd always done. Like good little Christian soldiers, we filed in, smiling and nodding to one another as we ushered our families to the same wooden bench we sat on every week. The air inside the chapel had always been different. It *smelled* of old wood and blown-out candles, of damp hymnals and floor polish. There was usually a trace of incense—though none of us could recall the last time Father had lit any—and something colder beneath it, like snowmelt on brass. The scent settled in your throat and made you feel as though someone were watching, even when the pews were empty.

Jakub had come and cleaned each week. He wiped the benches, scrubbed the curved windows. We imagined a man like that avoided touching the portraits of Jesus. Most of us quietly wondered whether a child ought to help Father prepare the sacraments instead of Jakub.

But we hadn't said so, of course.

Some of us remembered Jakub as he had been, years earlier, when he came home from the war. He wasn't the same Jakub we'd sent away. He had returned trembling, skittish. He hovered near the chapel door, twitching like a nervous hen. He'd never been much of a talker, but after the war, even his silence felt heavier. He stood in the back with one shoulder pressed to the frame, arms folded tight across his broad chest. A mountain of a man, he had inspired fear in the young and caution in the old.

Until one Sunday, in the deep bite of winter—though here, it's almost always winter—we arrived early. The wind still clung to our coats, snow melted on our lashes, and we saw him. Jakub was kneeling—*kneeling!*—before the altar. His shoulders were bowed, his lips slightly parted, waiting like a child for Father to place the sacrament on his tongue. We bowed our heads out of habit, but our eyes couldn't help but lift. We had watched as Father blessed him. When Jakub stood, something in him had changed. Those of us who saw it had clustered together after, whispering. He had walked out of the chapel like someone scrubbed clean.

After that, Jakub began shadowing the chapel regularly, cleaning and running errands. We said Father was a good shepherd, guiding a lost soul back into the fold. Some of the women asked Jakub what had changed him—what made him finally put aside his ways. He said Father had offered forgiveness. We never asked what the cost was.

We told ourselves our discomfort came from not really knowing him. From his silence. From the way he kept to himself. But some things... some things just settled in the bones wrong.

The chapel hadn't only been where we went to learn about the Lord. It was also where we went to learn about each other. Some might have called it gossip. Some might have said it wasn't very Christian. But in Myreska... sharing news about your life meant we didn't have to think too hard about our own. When Father Ignacy rose, the chapel had quieted without him asking. Children stopped fidgeting, babies stopped crying, and women leaned away from their conversations with neighbors. Father walked slowly—he always did, never hurried—each step echoing against the stone. He let the silence stretch. His presence settled over each of us in different ways, like frost weighing down fragile limbs.

All of us–those still here–remember the sermon.

"The world has a way of tempting the young," his voice sounded like ash, gritty and somber. The lines around his mouth seemed more pronounced when he delivered God's word, as if it grieved him to serve such a wayward flock. "Whether it is welcomed in with open arms or simply tolerated, sin spreads. It spreads through our homes. Into our daughters."

We didn't look at each other. We didn't need to. He did not name them. He never did. But we felt the shift in the room as if he had reached out and touched each of our children by name. The silence was more painful than accusation. It left room for us to wonder if he meant *ours*. He spoke of purity, of the rod that must not be spared. Of the need to protect what was left of our children's goodness—if there was any still left to be protected. Unchecked evil, he warned, could cost us our souls and, no matter the cost, it was imperative we resist sin, cast it out of our bodies, our minds, and our homes. If we didn't, we risked sending ourselves–and our children–into the fiery furnace. While the priest spoke of brimstone, we compared the sins of our neighbors' daughters against the secrets of our own cottages. We feigned self-assurance, whispered about girls who wore the Devil's colors, and sang *Amazing Grace*, though we rarely showed it.

"There must be discipline. Love without law is not love at all. It is neglect."

We nodded, most of us.

But a few of us thought of the marks we've seen on small arms. Of the way children flinch before the cane is raised. Of the ache in our own bones when we remember how silence was taught into us. We tell ourselves it's for their own good. That girls must be broken a little to stay safe.

We swallowed the words like medicine that made us sicker, not better. But we said amen. When the sermon ended, we watched as the family stood. The mother's back was straight as a blade; eyes fixed on the chapel doors. She held the little one's hand—Zosia, we think—but not the elder. Ainela walked half a pace behind, her shawl tight around her shoulders, her face unreadable. Some of us looked away. Others did not. There is a difference between shame and guilt. Guilt is a wound. Shame is the refusal to look at it.

And we—well. We are very practiced at not looking.

We remembered Ainela when she was younger— before her voice turned guarded, before her eyes stopped shining unless no one was looking. She used to run along the garden rows behind the apothecary's cottage, skirts muddy, fists full of violets. She was not always the girl who lingered near the hushwood, fingers red with thread. That came later. After the first girl went missing. After the ribbon. Some say she changed after the war. Others say she was never quite right from the start—too curious, too quick to wander, too much like her mother in ways the town pretends not to remember.

But what does a girl inherit except what she is given?

Her mama says little now, though we remember when she used to laugh. Before she came back with a child and no ring. She told us she forced, that a stranger accosted her, stripped her of choice. We saw the pain in her eyes, heard it in the desperate plea for compassion. But we remembered how she liked to sneak out after dark, and only during full moons. We recalled seeing her steal a kiss with

WHISPERROOT: A HUSHWOOD TALE

the butcher's son. So, we waited for Father to pray. When he pulled her aside, told her shame could be sanctified if she walked the straight path, if she kept her eyes down, if she raised her daughters not to repeat her fall, she grew quiet. We said it was remorse. We said her silence was repentance. We praised her for walking the straight path, called her redemption a blessing. But we sang grace more often than we offered it. When the butcher's boy, now a man, offered to marry her, we said it was proof she'd been forgiven. We may have forgiven, but Myreska never forgets. And we wonder, sometimes, if the daughters were ever given a path to walk at all.

We don't know what Ainela has done. Maybe nothing. Maybe only what the town has whispered into her since she could walk. But Father Ignacy watches her closely now, the way a shepherd watches a lamb that keeps slipping the fence. And we've heard him speak to her mother in clipped tones behind the chapel, lips tight, eyes narrowed—not in fury, no, but something colder. The kind of warning that sounds like protection. The kind that blames the girl for needing it.

We do not speak of what came before—of the girls wo couldn't protect or wouldn't. Of the nights we heard cries and told ourselves it was the wind. Our memories lie buried beneath years of quiet obedience, beneath the thrum of sermons and the clatter of supper plates. But the hushwood remembers. It leans at the edges of our fields and peers through frost-laced panes, patient and unblinking. It does not forget the names we no longer say. It holds the weight of every silence we've chosen.

We will not say it aloud—not to our children, not to each other, not even in prayer—but some part of us wonders what it costs to be seen by Father Ignacy. What it means to be noticed. We follow his sermons. We tighten our rules. We scour the dirt from our doorsteps and scrub the sin from our daughters' skin. We do all the things he tells us will keep the darkness out. But still, the hushwood grows thicker each year. And still, girls go missing. So, we blame the ones who ask questions. We shame the ones who stray. We watch our children for signs of strangeness, of softness, of spark—and we call it love when we stamp it out. We hummed our hymns and dusted the pews, pretending grace was something we lived by—not something we only sang on Sundays.

And still, we wonder about Ainela.

She walked too softly. Slipped out too late. There was something in her eyes—hunger or defiance, we can't quite say even now. Perhaps she *had* done something. Perhaps she *knew* something. Knowledge was the downfall of Eve, after all. We tell ourselves this, sometimes, in the dark. It is easier than asking what it means if she didn't. Because if she wasn't to blame, then maybe we are.

We are not ready to carry that.

But the hushwood is.

The town watched for sin.
She watched for me.

———

a sister's memory

CHAPTER FOUR: ZOSIA

WHISPERROOT: A HUSHWOOD TALE

The festival is this week." Her words come coated in hope, sticky and slow, like molasses on a cold day. It is the one thing that's still the same. A holiday festival with bright lights strung above the snow-laced cobblestones, dancing, fresh gingerbread from the bakery that taste like Winter memories. For one night, the town exhales. Father Ignacy disapproves, of course. He warns against anything that might lower our guard against sin, but even Father Ignacy can't stop the town from celebrating the holidays. It is the season of Christ's birth, after all. "What kind of mask are you going to wear?"

Ainela smiles coyly, lifting a shoulder to her chin, and replies, "It's a secret."

"From me? You're keeping a secret from me?" Zosia tries to sound disappointed, but a giggle ruins it. She swings her legs over the edge of the bed, looking beneath it. She pulls out an odd-shaped object covered in newspaper.

Ainela's eyes light up. "Is that yours?" she asks.

Everyone waits for kolędnicy. The square fills with laughter and candlelight as masked dancers spin through the snow—angels, devils, even creatures from the hushwood. Zosia had spent three evenings sewing hers in secret, just like the others. Hiding the mask from others until the Winter Gathering is part of the fun because then others must guess who dances behind each mask.

Zosia smiles, her face lighting up, her eyes twinkling. *This is joy.* She unfolds the newspaper just enough for Ainela to see a flash of tan, a hint of blue, then quickly drops the newspaper back down. She laughs when Ainela gasps, her eyes widening.

Ainela glances out the frosted window. Stars wink from the heavens, fresh snow rests on the ground, the hushwood's silence thickens. Curtains are drawn over the neighbor's windows. "What do you think happens to them?" Most wouldn't have heard the small tremor in Ainela's voice, but Zosia did. "Do you think she's still here?"

Zosia swings her legs off the mattress, sitting beside her sister. "Margarite says she thinks they just run off, maybe to Warsaw."

Ainela shakes her head. "All of them?"

Zosia lifts a shoulder helplessly.

"You don't have your green cape. What will you wear instead? The blue one?"

Ainela tips her head down to look at her sister. Zosia stares back beneath wide eyes the color of melted chocolate. She watches Ainela take a deep breath as if she's made a decision, and then she reaches out, putting her arm protectively around Zosia's shoulders. "You know what?" Ainela says, her voice dropping to a conspiratorial whisper, "It's a surprise."

The market smells like cold bread and chimney smoke. Zosia walks behind Mama, hands clenched around the basket handle, wool straps rubbing raw against her wrists. She doesn't complain. Her job is to remember the list: rye bread, cabbage, vinegar, onions if they haven't frozen through. Mama never writes things down. She says writing makes the mind forgetful. Snow crusts the cobblestones in crackling sheets. People curse the ice underfoot. A woman slips and swears.

Zosia keeps her eyes low, watching boots and hems, the way snow catches in frayed wool. She likes the market best when no one looks at her. She watches with her hands. With her eyes. Steam curls from cast iron pots—mushroom soup, plum compote, barley in tallow. A man elbows open his barrel of beets, juice staining his fingers dark red. A girl Zosia's age stands nearby, exchanging a coin for a smoked fish wrapped in newsprint. Her scarf is red. Not bright—ribbon red.

Zosia blinks. The girl is gone.

She tugs Mama's sleeve.

"Bread," Mama mutters. "Cheese. Then candles, if there's enough."

They stop at the candle stall. Beeswax tapers line the table like old yellow bones. Zosia picks two. The seller grunts and wraps them in birch bark. His breath smells like vinegar and onion peel. Across the square, past the cheese seller and the herbalist, there's a smaller table. It leans slightly. Its surface is cluttered—twigs of dried rue, painted scapulars, chipped saints, faded cloth. Behind it sits a woman in a black shawl, her face mostly hidden.

Zosia's feet slow.

Something glints among the clutter. Not silver. Not gold. Red.

A spool of thread, wound tight and bright. It's the color of frostbitten blood or the ribbons in stories no one tells anymore. The woman lifts her eyes. Pale as smoke. "Wool for brave fingers," she says. "Wound by moonlight."

Zosia doesn't answer. Her fingers ache to touch it. But she doesn't have coin for things Mama didn't ask for. Still, the woman slips the thread into a soft square of muslin, ties it shut with a knot Zosia knows she'll never undo. She places it gently in Zosia's basket. "She left it," the woman says, "for someone who remembers."

Zosia wants to ask *who*—but the words don't come.

On the way home, the hushwood leans closer to the path. Its trees look bone-white under the sky, unmoving even as wind scrapes the rooftops. She walks slower. Near the rotted fencepost beside the old shrine, something flutters. A ribbon. Red. Tied in a knot only the convent girls used. Zosia never learned it—but she's drawn it before. She stares at it for a long time, fingers twitching for her sketchbook. But it's at home.

Mama calls her name—sharp, distant.

The hushwood holds the silence in its branches.

By the time they return home, Zosia's cheeks feel frozen. She lays the satchel on the table, feeling its small wobble with its uneven legs, and then disappears before Mama can ask her to help put things away. She grabs her sketchbook and a piece of charcoal, then hurries out the door.

"Back before supper," Mama calls.

Zosia knows the way. Pocketing the nub of charcoal, she walks into the wind. The sky is an ashy grey. Snow falls gently; she won't be able to stay long. The alder is tall, just like all the trees that protect the forest. Even in Winter, when they are without their leaves, Zosia can tell the alder from the ash from the hushbark. Its alders and ash that form the outer crescent ring around the forest. The spool of thread, crimson red, is still tied to the elder tree.

WHISPERROOT: A HUSHWOOD TALE

It isn't the ribbon Zosia braves the cold for. Ribbons are seen every day.

Beyond the elder tree, what is that?

Curving around the trunk of the barren tree grows a vine. Zosia gasps. She's heard of the whisperroot; everyone has. Ainela's seen it. But Zosia's never ventured into the forest. Mama says it's dangerous. It's a strange plant with roots that are black violet, and slick with a faint sheen like ink, twisting in slow spirals. Thinner tendrils branch off from thicker roots and glisten. There's a swollen, ashen blossom in the middle of the vines, paper-thin and ghost-pale. A network of crimson veins that seem to glow faintly. Ainela said they glowed red, but the glow looks more silver to Zosia. Even with crisp snow on the ground, there's a faint scent of rain and... something she can't quite name... something comforting like a lullaby she hasn't heard in ages.

Zosia pulls the charcoal nub from her pocket and begins sketching. First, the tall, thin lines of the tree, then the darker vines of the whisperroot. Smudges of charcoal stain her finger as she gently rubs over the sketch to shade shadows. Sketching is what she would say if she had Ainela's courage: *look at this! It's real!*

A strong, sharp wind comes suddenly, lifting the page of her sketchbook and making her turn her head. The air freezes the breath in her lungs. She starts to stand when she notices something about the whisperroot. She frowns, tilts her head, and leans down, closer to the root. Her heart starts to race. She's heard tales about this:

Whatever you do, don't touch it.

It's alive.

It'll tell you things.

But Ainela touched it. *I put my glove on it, and it was warm! It's snowing outside, Zosia, but it was warm.* Zosia wishes she had her sister's courage. She holds out a hand, then draws it back. She cages her breath and dares to put her hand on the blossom. She feels it pulsing like a drumbeat against her palm. Ainela was right: it is warm through her mittens, as warm as a cup of hot tea with honey. The frigid air around her seems to thaw. Curious, Zosia leans down, putting her face near the root, not sure why.

At first, nothing. Just the crackle of the frost, the sound of her own breath.

But then she hears it. A sound so faint she might have imagined it, like a sigh that doesn't belong to the wind. It sounds like a girl's voice—not one, but many–layered on top of each other like pressed flowers in a book.

Come back.

Remember.

She was alone.

It isn't sound, not the kind heard with her ears but, rather, a whisper unfurling in her chest, like a memory, but one she didn't live. Some voices are tremulous, shake like her own, but others are angry and sharp. One is singing something she can't quite catch—a tune that curls around her spine like ribbon. And beneath it all: a heartbeat. Steady. Root-deep. As if the forest itself is alive and listening.

Zosia pulls back, the cold clinging to her skin like breath. But the whispers stay, curling in the corners of her thoughts. Not loud. Not gone. She opens her sketchbook and darkens a few of the blossom's veins. She doesn't know how to make a drawing pulse. She doesn't know how to draw vacant voices. Closing her sketchbook, she stands. She looks back at the whisperroot, her mind spiraling.

WHISPERROOT: A HUSHWOOD TALE

"Yeah? Then I dare you to go past the third hushbark. Into the grove."

A pause.

"Find the girl with the ash on her face."

The dare hangs there, cold and daring.

"Not alone," the girl replies. "You're coming too."

"Deal."

The two step into the hushwood as the other two children cheer them on.

The girl with the ash on her face?

The children sit anxiously through the Sunday sermon. The younger ones tug on the sleeves of their mothers, whispering, *what time is it?* or *how much longer?* while the older children slide down in the pew, earning mothers' abominations to *sit up straight right now* or sliding out to *go to the outhouse*. They don't really need the outhouse; they need to see the last of the preparations. Long tables adorned with woven baskets full of colored feathers, ribbons (though not red), straw, glue and strips of cloth wait just in front of the chapel for the mask making event. An annual and unofficial start to the Winter Gathering, it's also a chance to exhale, to play, to embrace the holiday spirit. Mrs. Starzynska, the town's herbalist, stands behind one of the tables, adding jars of dried herbs. Children strategize about the best table to sit at and the best seat based on their vision for their mask.

By the time Father releases chapel, children crowd the narrow chapel aisle, barely remembering to shake the priest's hand. For once, he chuckles instead of rebukes.

"Go on, Zosia," Mama says, smiling as she puts a hand against Zosia's back. "Make something beautiful." They are one of the last out of the chapel because Mama says it shows a repentant heart to linger in the chapel.

Ainela follows, her boots crunching the snow, her hands tucked inside pockets.

"Zosia," Mrs. Starzynska waves, smiling, "There's a seat saved for you, dear." She lifts a scrap of velvet the color of candle smoke and gestures toward the table's edge. "You always have the cleverest hands."

Zosia beams.

Ainela steps forward, smiling politely. "I can help Zosia," she offers. "We used to make paper saints for the window ledge–remember?"

Mrs. Starzynska's face falters, only for a moment, but even Zosia catches the pause–the tightening. "Oh, this little gathering is for the younger ones," she says, smoothing her skirts. "Tradition, you understand."

"She's not that much older," Zosia mutters quietly.

Mrs. Starzynska replies too quickly, "Yes, yes, but the spirit of the thing, you see..." She pauses, then titles her chin up to the side and meets Ainela's eyes directly. "This is meant to be ... pure."

Ainela's eyes survey the long tables; there are others her age. Some adults even sit at the tables, crafting masks. Zosia sees her sister pull the corner of her lip between her teeth and knows Ainela's hurt. She feels it. But Ainela nods once, smiles bravely, and pats Zosia on the back. "Sure. Sure. You go ahead, I–Mama will need help at home."

WHISPERROOT: A HUSHWOOD TALE

Zosia hesitates, frowning. She starts to speak when Mrs. Starzynska smiles brightly and nods. "Yes, I'm sure she will. Zosia, you deserve to shine, you should make something bright." When Ainela leans towards Zosia and whispers, "Go on, Caterbutton, it's alright. I'm alright," one girl moves her mask closer to her lap. A boy beside Zosia snickers, "My brother said you kissed a boy behind the mill."

"I didn't —" But Ainela catches herself, her voice fading.

"It's not true," Zosia says, but her voice is small.

"Not now," Mrs. Starzynska says sternly. "Ainela–"

Her sister's eyes have gone flat, Zosia notes. She feels something twist in chest as she watches Ainela turn, her shoulders slumped, to walk down the chapel stairs. Ainela looks small and alone against the stark white of the snow. Instead of leaving, she stands to the side of the festivities, watching from the outside, always watching her sister.

Mrs. Starzynska places yellow feathers in front of her. "There, now. You can shine, sweet girl."

But Zosia picks a scrap of navy wool, her fingers clumsy. She doesn't want to shine.

After the mask-making, the chapel sisters lead the children outside to the smaller fire bowl near the chapel steps. It isn't the big wish fire—the one ringed by logs and cider—but it dances brightly just the same, fed with pinecones and slivers of birch.

"One whisper, one spark," Sister Celina says, pressing a candle into each child's hand. "Make it true, or the fire won't listen."

The others giggle. One boy drops his candle twice. A girl whispers hers so loudly everyone laughs.

Zosia's hands are cold but steady.

She looks at Ainela, standing across the courtyard with her arms crossed, then down at the little flame.

She doesn't wish for sweets or sleigh rides. She whispers, "Let Ainela be happy."

The flame catches instantly—clear and gold, bright as morning sun on snow.

Several women nod. One murmurs, "She burns honest."

Ainela doesn't move. But her eyes soften. Just a little.

Zosia watches the flame dance as the wind brushes past her cheeks. It looks like the kind of light that won't go out easily. The kind that might follow someone home. Ainela lifts a hand in a wave, smiles, and turns to leave. Zosia's safe; she doesn't need anyone to watch after her.

The wind has picked up by the time the festivities end and Zosia heads home. Her fists are jammed deep into her pockets, the half-finished mask folded in one palm like a broken wing. Bits of straw poke through the cloth. She doesn't know what it's supposed to be anymore—a creature, a prayer, a disguise? She kicks at a frozen clump of snow and watches it scatter like brittle feathers.

They told her to shine. To choose something bright. But all she can think about is how Ainela's face looked when she turned away—calm, practiced. Like someone who's learned how to leave before being asked to. Zosia's feet move without thinking. Past the cottage. Past the shuttered stalls. Past the shrine with its tilted saint and frost-bitten flowers. The hushwood leans close, but she doesn't fear it—not tonight. She crosses the edge of the orchard and ducks beneath the low limbs of the alder tree.

Their alder tree.

WHISPERROOT: A HUSHWOOD TALE

They used to call it the Hollow Mouth because of the place at its base where the bark dips inward like lips parted in a secret. Sometimes they slip notes there—ribbon scraps, drawings, petals wrapped in string. Ainela once left her a folded paper bird that whispered when she opened its wings. The telltale green ribbon flutters. There's something inside.

Zosia crouches. Snow crunches under her knees. She presses her fingers into the hollow. There—tucked just inside, wrapped in waxed cloth. She pulls it free and opens it carefully. Inside is a ribbon—not one of the ones the town ties in the hushwood to remember the girls, not store-bought or bright—but hand-dyed, the color of beetroot and ash. It's been braided in their old pattern—loop, twist, loop again, the way Ainela sometimes does Zosia's hair in the mornings. Tears sting Zosia's eyes. Threaded through the center of the ribbon is something small: a dried forget-me-not.

The charcoal lines were faint,
but they tugged like thread
from a wound.

———————————

Whisperroot Proverb

CHAPTER FIVE: AINELA

WHISPERROOT: A HUSHWOOD TALE

Ainela turns her head against the pillow to see her sister. Sunlight still hasn't broken through the night. Silver moonlight falls on the snow. She's lain awake for hours, unable to sleep. When Zosia came home after the mask making event, she draped small arms around her neck. Laughing softly, Ainela hugged her back, asking to see what she'd made. Zosia showed a mask only half completed and a handful of crumpled feathers.

I bought it for you to finish.

She had a mask no one had seen. One no one would see until she danced in front of them with it. The aged leather of Zosia's sketchbook peeked out from beneath her pillow. It never lays far from her sister. Ainela tugs the edge of the leather gently, pulling it from beneath Zosia's pillow. The old wood creaks beneath her weight when she stands. She tucks a strand of coal black hair behind her left ear and sinks down into the sandy colored chair by the window. This window faces the east side of the house, the only other, on Zosia's side of the bed, faces the back of the house and the hushwood. It's usually that one Ainela's drawn to, as if there's something in the woods that belongs to her, but the moon is brightest on this side.

The paper feels as fragile as childhood dreams. A few of the edges curl as though trying to protect the secrets drawn on the pages. The charcoal is heavy in some lines, ghosted in others—bringing the town to life. There's the chapel–on the first page–its steeple leaning ever so slightly, just as it does in real life, but the windows are too dark, like eyes sewn shut. She frowns slightly, tilts her head, as if there's something to grasp just out of reach. Turning the page, she sees the alder, their secret place, where they leave notes and small gifts. Ainela's frown softens. The page sticks slightly to the next, as if reluctant to give up Zosia's inner thoughts. Carefully, she peels the edge up to turn the page. The hushwood—it appears again and again—its branches tangled like a girl's hair after crying. Some of them lean in. *As though they're listening*—Ainela realizes she's often thought this when she passes the forest. *Does Zosia also hear it?* Ainela lifts her face to see her sister—the quiet one, the *good* one.

A memory stirs.

The girl that went missing a few weeks ago—no one says her name anymore. No one talks about her at all. Ainela knew her; she was a year younger than Ainela and they shared the same teacher. While they weren't friends—they never talked—Ainela didn't believe the whispers. *Soiled. Tempted the lamplighter's apprentice. Sinful. Maybe with child. Maybe fevered.* Except sometimes her mother still asks, brokenly, if anyone's seen or heard from her, says she didn't come home one night. Father says the apothecary gives her laudanum now to hush the delusions.

Zosia doesn't talk about her, or any of the others, the ones who have disappeared over the last year. No one does. But...sometimes when Ainela passes the hushwood, she feels the roots beneath her feet quiver, a faint shifting, as if her weight presses something down, as though something buried stirs. Has Zosia felt it, too? Ainela turns the page. The whisperroot. *I saw it, I saw the whisperroot.* Zosia's whisper was full of confusion, wonder, and a little bit of fear. *It pushes against my hand. It's warm.* Ainela traces the charcoal lines with her fingertip. The root is gnarled and sprawling, its vines curling in tangled knots around the base of a tree. She flips back to the first drawing. The veins there are faint, barely visible. But in each new sketch, they grow darker. Thicker. Hungrier. The ink smudges deepen like bruises, the vines more twisted, more alive. She lifts the page to the moonlight and then she sees it, and her breath hitches.

Curled up against the whisperroot—tucked into its spiraling vines—is the shape of a girl. Faint as a forgotten name, only half-drawn. Her arm, pale and barely sketched, wraps around the vine like it's something precious. Her hair is moss-tangled, nearly indistinguishable from the forest itself. Ainela feels her heart racing. Traces of charcoal, faint, cover the girl's face like ash. Tenderly, Ainela turns the page – one more. A grove of trees fills the page. Ash trees, their trunks pale and tall. Etched into the bark, nearly erased by smudges and time, are four names. One Ainela knows, one she almost remembers, one she doesn't recognize at all, but then the that one stands out.

Eliza.

The most recent girl. The name everyone's already forgotten. The one *pledged to God* but who might have returned to the hushwood as all the others.

Ainela lets the sketchbook close with a hush, careful not to bend the curling corners. The leather cover is warm now from her hands, soft as breath. She holds it against her chest for a moment longer than she means to.

Zosia stirs beneath the quilt, one arm flung above her head, her braid a loose tangle across the pillow. She doesn't wake. She rarely does when Ainela moves at night. That's always been their rhythm—one always a step ahead or behind, but never quite apart. Moving slowly, Ainela crosses the creaking floorboards, kneels beside the bed, and slides the sketchbook gently back beneath her sister's pillow. Her fingers hesitate on the edge. Then she pulls a scrap of paper from her apron pocket. It's nothing special—just the corner of an old receipt, soft and folded twice. She's written on it in pencil, the words faint and slanted, like she didn't know quite how to say them until they were already written: *I saw what you drew. And I heard what it didn't say. I remember her too.*

She tucks it between the pages of the whisperroot drawing, where the veins run like threads through the center. Then she presses the book shut, soft as prayer. By the time Ainela crawls back beneath the covers, the moon has fully dipped behind the trees. Her breath fogs faintly in the air. She closes her eyes, listening—not for wind, not for owls. But for something else, something she feels but cannot name. For the hushwood.

They begin at the hearth, as always—lighting the lanterns with fire carried from home. But this year, there's a quiet behind the flames. Something tight in the air, like a room that hasn't been opened in months.

Zosia looks up at her. "How many ribbons this year?"

Ainela doesn't answer.

It used to be for the old saints, the founding mothers. The kind of remembering done with pride.

Now, the ribbons are red.

WHISPERROOT: A HUSHWOOD TALE

"For the girls," someone whispered last week at the bakery. Not *which* girls. Just *the girls*.

"Zosia can light our lantern this year," Mama says, motioning for Zosia to come closer. It's finally time to leave for the festival. Every year families light a lantern from their hearth and meet at the chapel steps for the festival's opening procession.

People will be gathering soon.

Ainela stands near the cottage door, slightly apart from everyone else, tilting her head to see past Papa, catching a glimpse of Zosia lighting the lantern.

Papa asks, "Do we have the ribbon?"

"Yes," Zosia replies, holding up a handful of ribbons, one for each of them.

"Of course, Zosia, you have them." Mama says with only a hint of relief.

People might talk if I carried the red ribbons.

Papa takes Mama's hand as they walk outside.

Snow doesn't fall, though it likely will later, and the wind invigorates instead of freezes her. Tugging Zosia's coat sleeve, Ainela motions her fingers. "I'll hold the ribbons; you carry the lantern," she whispers. Zosia's too young to feel so much weight.

They pass the bakery, where steam clouds the windows, the apothecary with its dark glass bottles, the blacksmith's anvil glinting in soot. They turn by the old linden tree, its limbs bare and bone-white. At the chapel steps, the town has gathered. Lantern light flickers across bundled coats and familiar faces.

Father Ignacy and a few of the elders stand at the foot of the chapel greeting onlookers. It's the first festival since Father Ignacy returned from burying his sister in the south, where grief clings like ash. The girls had stopped vanishing for a time after he left. Some even hoped it had ended. But now he's back—and the town ties more ribbons than ever. The priest came back thinner, quieter, the kind of silence born of grief—or practice.

Papa claps the shoemaker's back and laughs—too loudly, perhaps. Ainela hangs back, still clutching the ribbons. She feels the way eyes don't quite meet hers. How glances catch, then flit away. How silence grows in the spaces she steps into.

She is here. And yet not.

Her gaze slips past the chapel, past the crowd, to the edge of the hushwood—where no one dares linger long. The trees stand motionless. But she feels it. Knows it.

The hushwood is watching, too.

"Ainela," Papa's tone is sharp, pulling her back to the present.

Father Ignacy claps his hands. His voice never rises but, as one, the town quiets and offers him its attention. "Ah, Myreska... how lovely you are tonight, dressed in your finest scarves and snow-kissed joy. Look at you—lanterns glowing like halos in your hands, little ones laughing beneath the grace of heaven. It does my heart good to see our town so full of light. Truly, I am happy to be home amongst friends again.

This night, we honor tradition. We remember the old songs, the old paths, the blessings passed down like heirlooms from mother to daughter, father to son. We walk as our fathers did—together, humble and grateful beneath God's wide sky. But even amid the beauty, we must remain vigilant. The Lord delights in celebration, yes—but only when it is rooted in virtue. We must not mistake revelry for righteousness. Even joy, my beloved flock, must be modest.

WHISPERROOT: A HUSHWOOD TALE

Let our laughter be pure. Let our dancing be decent. Let our daughters be sweet and silent, our sons strong and steadfast. For the world outside Myreska does not share our values—and neither, I fear, do all who dwell within. Sometimes, the brightest lanterns cast the longest shadows. And sometimes, it is not the forest that leads our children astray, but the flicker of mischief in their own hearts."

A beat. A smile.

"But tonight is not for shadows. Tonight, we shine. So, raise your lanterns high, children of Myreska. Let the procession begin. And may the light you carry reflect the purity of your hearts. Remember: someone always watches over those who walk in truth—and notices when they do not."

As Father Ignacy finishes, a ripple of reverent silence passes through the crowd, broken only by the creak of lanterns lifting into the air. Ainela lifts hers with the rest. Her arm doesn't shake. But her breath curls tight in her chest.

"Let our daughters be sweet and silent."
She has heard this before. Not just in sermons, but in stares. In the hush that falls when she enters a room. In the way the baker's wife once reached for Zosia's cheek and let her hand fall just short of Ainela's shoulder.

"Sometimes, it is not the forest that leads our children astray..." Her gaze drifts toward the hushwood, still and waiting beyond the chapel. If only they knew what the forest whispers back. She keeps her face composed, eyes forward. Girls like her are watched too closely to flinch. But beneath her stillness, something stirs. Not rebellion—no, that would be too loud for a girl like Ainela. What stirs is quieter. Older. A kind of remembering. The lantern in her hand glows warm, but the light feels borrowed. She wonders, not for the first time, what would happen if she let it fall.

As the lanterns rise and the town exhales, Ainela glances sideways. Her mother's expression is unreadable, fixed in polite reverence. She holds her lantern with both hands, perfectly still. But Ainela sees the tightness in her grip. The way she doesn't blink when Father says, *"Let our daughters be sweet and silent."* The way her jaw clenches at, *"Even joy must be modest."*

A memory stirs.

She must have been nine, maybe ten. She'd come home crying—Jakub had said something to her in the street, something she didn't understand but didn't like. She'd asked what it meant. Her mother had knelt, her voice low and sharp. *"You don't tell anyone if something happens, do you hear me? They'll say it was your fault. They always do. They'll ask why questions about what you did, not what he did."*

Ainela hadn't understood then why her mother's eyes had looked so wild. Why her hands shook even after she brushed Ainela's hair behind her ear. Why, later that night, she'd said nothing at all—just scrubbed the floors until her knuckles bled. She never spoke like that again. After that day, she only said things like *"Keep your dress pulled low"* and *"Don't talk too much"* and *"You don't want to be misunderstood."*

Now, standing in the golden hush of lantern light, Ainela watches her mother's stillness. Not reverence. Not really. It looks more like... holding her breath.

The procession begins. Lanterns sway like stars drawn down from the sky, bobbing with the motion of feet through snow. Voices rise in old carols, soft and solemn.

Ainela walks beside her mother, the crowd pressing around them in warmth that feels distant. Her hands are cold even through her gloves. She glances up at her mother again—still composed, still too still. Without thinking, Ainela reaches out. Just a brush of fingers to her mother's coat sleeve. Not to ask anything. Not to say a word. Just to say *I see you.*

Her mother flinches.

Only slightly. Just enough to stiffen her arm and pull her hand more tightly around the lantern's handle. She doesn't look at Ainela. Doesn't break stride. But her breath comes faster for a moment, clouding the air in front of her. Then she speaks. Not unkindly. But carefully. "Don't fall behind."

Ainela lets her hand drop. She watches her mother's face from the side, the way she stares straight ahead, lips slightly parted as if she might be praying—or trying not to speak at all. Ainela doesn't say anything else. But she knows now. Her mother carries something heavier than shame. Something closer to fear.

The procession is one of remembrance. Some children hum lullabies. Most are quiet. As they approach the hushwood, each person silently ties a red ribbon to the limb of a tree. Ainela ties them at various heights. *Some were older. Some were very young.* Just ahead, her mother reaches up and ties hers—high, out of reach.

The fabric is different. Older. Faded to the color of dried berries or rinsed-out blood. Ainela recognizes it. It had been tucked in her mother's dresser once, long ago. A ribbon Ainela was never allowed to wear.

She says nothing.

But something in her chest twists—something she can't yet name.

As Father Ignacy passes, Ainela's breath catches and holds, but Papa smiles, as if nothing stirs at all, and says, "Good to have him home."

Gold is good and means you're true,
Blue's the wish you never knew.
Green is wild and roots too deep,
Red's the kind you shouldn't keep.
Black means hush—the fire said no,
And if it sputters, let it go.
So close your eyes and speak it right—
The hushwood's watching flames tonight

————————————————

Myreska children's rhyme

CHAPTER SIX: THE TOWN

WHISPERROOT: A HUSHWOOD TALE

We *must not mistake revelry for righteousness. Even joy, my beloved flock, must be modest.* That's what Father Ignacy said in his first sermon after returning. He hadn't been here when the festival preparations began. No one can say who started them—only that a few more herbs appeared on the drying racks, a handful of baskets were woven with brighter thread. The women brought out old ribbons and quietly traded patterns. The children whispered about costumes and prizes and songs too loud for inside voices.

We let them.

We told ourselves it was for the golden ones—to give them some brightness in the dark. What harm could it do? Sometimes we gathered in the chapel to sort cloth or count candles. If one of us laughed too loudly, the others didn't scold. We didn't call it brazen, or unseemly, or anything at all.

We just let ourselves laugh. Maybe we mistook revelry for righteousness; maybe we forgot that joy must be modest. We say it was tradition that stirred the firepots, but it was relief. Even a week without his sermons felt like breath after burial. But that's what he's for, isn't it? To corral us, remind us freedom doesn't come from sin. *The Tempter's lies are easy to believe without the rod.* We know that's true and we're thankful for him—it's our souls at stake after all.

And our daughters.

We told ourselves it was only him. That when he left, it would end. But the hushwood does not sleep, and neither do the old habits we dress in ritual. No one ever said who should take his place. They simply did. A man with quiet boots. A woman who locked her door too quickly. A neighbor who asked too few questions. The girls still vanished, and we still did not speak. Perhaps that's how we know we were never innocent—because even without his voice, we knew what came next. And we let it happen anyway.

His voice returned before his footsteps did. By the time he walked the chapel aisle, we were already shrinking again. Laughter softened. Ribbons disappeared into drawers. Scraps of cloth were still collected, but quietly. When we saw one of the girls making a mask in a shade that was just *too much,* we reminded her *modest is beautiful.* We weren't really *hiding* the preparations, but women moved back to their own cottages and urged their husbands to remind the priest about the Festival, to receive his blessing for our joy, for our traditions. Some of our husbands are also elders and they indulged us–some out of kindness, some out of weariness. And because, truth be told, joy may need to be modest, but it also needs to be *present.*

Father Ignacy warned us it was a dangerous idea, the Festival.

When you open temptation's door, sin walks through.

We're meant to be in this world, but not of this world. We're called to be different.

Maybe it was because he'd just buried his sister–bless her heart, the poor thing walked a dark path. Or maybe it was something different–an acknowledgement, a compromise of sorts, an unspoken and unholy alliance.

WHISPERROOT: A HUSHWOOD TALE

Whatever did it, he soon gave his approval and the preparations began, open but muted.

Tonight, we watch the children. Snow games have begun in the meadow; little ones throw snowballs at one another and hide behind structures–caves and tunnels–they've built and which will soon melt. The echoes of their joyful spirits offer a comfort we deny needing. *The only thing we need is You, Lord.* Adults find solace in the structure of the chapel's rules, children glean comfort from the freedom found in play, but what holds us together are our traditions. Like the Festival. Lines form to participate in the kulig races–the sleighs are polished and layered with blankets for those who pile in. Even the horses are excited as they wait to race. One of them stomps impatiently while another swings his head from side to side. A little one boldly walks up beside one of the horses to pet its face. When she opens her palm and the horse licks her hand, she giggles. Tonight, we won't scold her for taking sugar cubes from home or for feeding them to the horse without permission from the horse master. The sleighs burst into motion, circling the town square—bells jingling at the horses' necks, laughter trailing behind them like smoke.

Nearby, a large firepit glows. Thick logs ring the flame, offering warmth and rest.

The Wishing Flame starts soon.

We remember the first time the fire turned green. Not many speak of her now. She was the first to stand before the Wishing Flame with bare hands and a wish not written down. The fire was new then, the rhyme not yet formed. We didn't know what colors meant—only that the flame shifted when she stepped forward, that it leaned toward her, as if to listen.

Her name was Klara or maybe Milenka—memory frays where shame begins. She didn't scream when the fire turned, only blinked once and stepped back. The very next night, her house burned to the ground. They found no body. Only a half-charred ribbon tied around a tree root, as though someone had bent down and left it there gently.

We told ourselves she was a liar. Or touched. Or cursed. But the hushwood remembers. Some say she lives there still, crawling in moss and shadow, whispering truths we buried too deep. Others say she made a wish too wild, and the forest took her in—claimed her not as punishment, but as kin. Either way, when the Wishing Flame begins, we watch for green. And we do not speak her name.

There are so many wishes in Myreska. We know most of them–or, anyway, we tell ourselves we do. The schoolteacher and her husband, for example, they'll likely wish for a baby. We promise her the Lord is faithful to the devoted and will hear her prayers, but how long do you wait before you know the answer is *no*? *Our Lord is a God of wrath, and His anger spares no one.* Not even schoolteachers struggle to find peace in obeying husbands. The miller's boy will wish to be taller. He prays for broad shoulders and a deeper voice, something to quiet the laughter of the older boys. We tell him the Lord forms each vessel in His time, but the snickering continues all the same. Old Mrs. Kopec will wish to see her son again, even though we all know he's not coming home. She leaves an extra plate at dinner and speaks to the empty chair as if it still answers. Some call it grief. Others call it madness. Klara from the bakery will wish for love, though she'd never say so aloud. We see how she lingers when the lamplighter passes, cheeks flushed, lips parted just slightly. We remind her that good

WHISPERROOT: A HUSHWOOD TALE

girls wait for God's timing. Jakub, poor thing, will wish for nothing. Wishes require hope. The mayor's wife will wish for silence. She's tired of the whispers about her daughter's skirts, her son's late nights. We pretend not to hear her sobbing during communion. Little Tomasz will wish for the snow not to melt. For the laughter to last. For the monsters to stay stories. We know our people, their longings and their silences, the wishes they'd never dare speak aloud. And still, as the flames begin to flicker and rise, we watch with quiet hunger—wondering which wish might glow an unnatural color, and what it might mean when it does.

  Voyeurism? Perhaps.

  But also... absolution.

If someone else's wish burns wrong, maybe it means *we're not the only ones*. Maybe the forest saw what we did—and stayed silent. Maybe that's mercy. Or maybe that's just the hush before the roots begin to stir. Whatever it is, we wait anxiously for the Wishing Flame.

  Children and adults alike scribble wishes onto scraps of paper, folding them carefully, and clutching them tight to their chests until it is their turn. The shoemaker opens it up, reminding us to "wish pure." We sing the rhyme of colors, certain *our* wishes will be embraced and pure while equally certain someone else's will not.

> *Gold is good and means you're true,*
> *Blue's the wish you never knew.*
> *Green is wild and roots too deep,*
> *Red's the kind you shouldn't keep.*
> *Black means hush—the fire said no,*
> *And if it sputters, let it go.*

So, close your eyes and speak it right—
The hushwood's watching flames tonight

One of the stone masons stokes the fire and nods: the flames are ready for wishes. Tentacles of unease keep all but the youngest of us from being the first to step forward. The sky is lit with thousands of twinkling stars, the Milky Way's spiral faint but visible, like thumbprints on glass. The crackle and pops of the flame warms us; the hushed silence of anticipation holds us. One by one, people begin tossing their scraps of paper into the flames. When the wishes sizzle and flare as the color of hearths and lamplight, we exhale. Obedient hearts are familiar and safe. *For someone nice to notice me. For Ma to stop coughing. For a good harvest.* The kind of wishes that don't ask too much. We're a surface town; we prefer the expected.

She steps forward, alone, clutching her scrap of paper to her chest.

The girl who guards her sister, though from what she won't say. The girl whose boldness isn't bravery, but a quiet rebellion stands in front of the fire. The dangerous kind of girl. The kind that gets the hushwood's attention. An air of vulnerability wraps around her. She cuts a quick glance to the edge of the circle where the younger one stands, then closes her eyes tightly. We see her inhale sharply, but the exhale doesn't come, the breath lodged in her chest, as if the wish is too much to release. The longer she stands there, the more murmurs run amongst us, the more uncomfortable we feel in our seats. We see her free hand curl slowly into a fist by her side while, with the other, she tosses the wish into the fire.

Whoosh, the fire devours the wish. The flame leans slightly toward her. We pretend not to see. The warm yellow of the fire quivers slowly until, suddenly, *pop*, the flame burns blue. Not a sky blue or a stained-glass blue. It's blue like a bruise.

Murmurs start before she turns. "Did you see the way she looked at the fire?"

"Some girls want what they shouldn't."

Others are polite, tilting their heads and saying uncertainly, "A girl like that–maybe she wished for peace."

A few whispered to their spouses, "That girl doesn't want peace; she wants remembering."

Her mother's flame burned blue once. We pretended it didn't, but some say it cracked so loud it nearly split the log it caught. Back then, we told ourselves it was grief. A mother mourning what should have been. But grief and guilt burn the same color in Myreska. We sneak furtive glances at her mama in time to see her close her eyes briefly, purse her lips. As the blue flame fades back to yellow and orange, Ainela moves back to her seat.

She doesn't bow her head.

She doesn't avert her eyes.

That girl doesn't learn. Just like her mother didn't.

Defiant posture is inherited.

So are consequences.

She stares into the fire, her face flushed. The red on her cheeks may have been from standing close to the fire, but we whisper that it's odd. It's so cold and the fire doesn't stain anyone else's skin. Two men sit near her, emboldened by ale. When a strong wind blows across the festivities, the stone mason adds another log to the fire. Sitting near Ainela, one of the men, a lumberjack, swallows more ale. "My dog barked all night at nothing," he says looking towards the hushwood.

"That wasn't nothing. Bet it was that girl, the one the woods didn't finish."

"Finish her how?" Zosia asks.

Before the men can reply, Ainela offers an overbright smile and says cheekily, "Who knows–maybe *she* finished the hushwood. Come on, Zosia, it's almost time for the masked caroling."

Ainela waits for her sister to walk ahead of her–she's always trying to protect Zosia from us. As they walk towards the meadow, one of the men murmurs, "Mouthy girl."

The fire doesn't disagree.

Myreska's an old town.

Before we were Myreska, it was just wild land–dense forest tangled with fog and silence. The early settlers came not to conquer, but to disappear. Fleeing famine, war, or shame (no one agrees which), they followed a starless path into the woods, guided only by a woman whose name is lost but who wore a necklace of red thread. Legend whispers of things she went through. Some say she was kidnapped as a girl and sold to the settlers; others say she was the daughter of a violent clan chief who murdered his wife for daring to question him. Some of us say she was a wild thing who fearlessly led the settlers after war (most of us reject this version publicly–this was our founding mother. Surely, her soul was respectable). Like any old family, we can't agree on who she was. But the land—that belonged to her.

Not through an inheritance or a purchase.

WHISPERROOT: A HUSHWOOD TALE

The land belonged to her in a much deeper sense. She knew where the roots curled soft and the spring water healed. Where the trees leaned kindly. Where something watched—but did not harm. When they found a clearing where no birds sang and the ground pulsed warm even in winter, she stopped walking. She knelt, cut her palm, and let blood fall into the soil. A whisper rose up—some say it was wind; some say a voice, some say a bargain.

That night, they lit their first fire.

They named the place Myreska—from the old word *mirze*, meaning "marsh" or "mire," and *ska*, a suffix once used for sorrow. *The sorrowed mire.* But to speak it aloud was considered poor luck, so they told the children it meant *miracle.*

When spring came, the woman just disappeared. No one knows where she went or why she went. They found her necklace of red thread by the end of the forest. The soil started growing strange things after her vanishing. Herbs seemed to have memory–that tasted like something you'd never tasted but *knew*. Vines twisted around themselves, growing towards the sound of breath. Flowers sprouted whenever there was famine, disease or great loss. It was as though the earth created its own garden for those who left too soon.

The settlers built homes and a chapel. And they left things at the edge of the forest, to remember. Red threads, bits of honey, dolls made from ashwood, corn husk. To forget was dangerous. To speak too much was worse. So, instead, they crafted the traditions we still maintain today. Myreska forgot who or what it fled. It forgot who bled first. It forgot what the hushwood had heard. But the forest doesn't forget.

It never has.

And that's why we indulge in the masked caroling.

Father Ignacy allows it because *we don't protect the self; we protect the community.*

But we?

The town?

We'd never tell you if you were standing in front of us with flesh and bone, but it's a chance for us to show something of ourselves, something we've almost forgot. Or that we're just a little too afraid of admitting to. Our masks are acceptable–we'd never risk getting caught making risky apparel items–but, when we put them on, we channel the wild child version of the mother settler. We sing–carefully, never too loud. We dance–carefully, never too freely. But the masks allow us to pretend to be ... well, someone different. Maybe the real sin of girls like Ainela isn't what we think they do. Maybe it's the courage they dare to put on display. Courage that the rest of us only dare behind a mask.

Those who participate in the masked carolers find the oddest places to hide. A few of us saw Jakub emerge from the back door of the chapel–the door that leads to the basement. It's always locked. Children run to the edge of the forest, pull their colorful masks from coat pockets, and return to the festivities just a touch braver than before. We know who they are, of course, but we pretend we don't so as to allow them a good time.

We are a patient town.

The gasps are too loud to ignore.

We turn, our eyes blinded by something other than starlight and candle glow. One of the masked carolers–has gone too far. The mask covers not just her eyes but the full face. We move forward, trying to get a better look, while simultaneously shielding our daughters from the sight of

WHISPERROOT: A HUSHWOOD TALE

something so bold. It's wrapped completely in lace–not just any lace, but scarlet red. A red that warns you: *don't look away*. A red that dares you: *join me*. Dried leaves are glued around the eyes, black soot lining their veins. A trio of ashwood beads decorate each temple. Crimson red thread stitches sealed the lips. Blackthorn antlers at the top, bent to resemble antlers, and stitched into place with the same red thread. A wisp of red tulle trails from the mask and a dried and blackened whisperroot dangles from the right side. We know not where she would have found the whisperroot. We know not what to think.

Mrs. Starzynska pulls her daughter closer to her side. "That's too much red."

"What was she thinking?" someone else says.

"Girls like that..."

"It's – it's–"

"Not a mask. That's a summoning."

We look to Father Ignacy. He averts his eyes, bends his head, and clenches his jaw. We know it's her–Ainela. The girl whose flame burns blue. The girl who challenges, lures, questions. We thought we'd burned the red out of her mother.

"Someone *really* should speak to her mother."

"Maybe Father Ignacy should step in."

"This is how it started back then," someone whispers. "The *rebellion*."

Snow crackles beneath our feet; those who sense it sidestep lest the earth open up and swallow us whole. Only we know it's not cracks in the earth. The air is still, like it's holding its breath, watching the girl in the red mask dance a little too freely. Her feet move to a low, steady drumbeat from the earth that we pretend not to hear.

"Mama, look!" Zosia says, pointing. The trees near the hushwood sway, as if holding out their arms to the girl in the red mask. We look to Father Ignacy. Surely, he'll put a stop to this. Stitched in crimson and crowned in blackthorn, daring the hushwood to look at her–surely this isn't sanctioned.

We're not sure which child starts humming first.

It doesn't sound like much at first–maybe one of the simple rhymes.

But then. Some of us feel the hairs rise on our bodies. *No, no, not that song.*

Where red thread winds and roots run deep
The forest watches those who sleep

Mothers shush their children. Somewhere nearby, a twig snaps.

Beneath the hush, the lost still sing,
And blood remembers everything.

A few other children begin to hum, as if they sing this every day (we'd never let them).

Step not too bold, speak not too loud,
The earth wears silence like a shroud.

Someone drops a candle. Others simply freeze.

But if you dance when no one's near,
The whisperroot will let you hear.

We *do not sing the rest.* We do not speak it. Most of us don't even *remember* it. But the oldest amongst us do.

WHISPERROOT: A HUSHWOOD TALE

The ones with creased palms and grief like moss behind their eyes. They do not say it aloud. But when they see the red masked girl dancing freely in the snow–the antlers, the sealed lips, the *whisperroot* dangling – they hear the stanza again, deep in their chests:

> *Ash to mask and mask to flame,*
> *The daring ones forget their name.*
> *But if she comes with antlered crown,*
> *The hushwood means to take her down*

And the hushwood listens.

Some girls are not lost—they are traded for silence and remembered in story

———

Whisperroot Proverb

CHAPTER SEVEN: ZOSIA

WHISPERROOT: A HUSHWOOD TALE

The linden tree glows under strands of lanterns, its branches curl like old hands cupping light. Around its base, gifts have begun to appear: hand-carved dolls with button eyes, jars of preserved jam, woolen mittens dyed cranberry red. Each wrapped in cloth or tucked in ribbon, waiting not to be claimed, but to be exchanged. The rule, whispered this morning, was simple: take without asking, give without guilt. Zosia had brought nothing. Her pockets were empty, her hands unsure. Instead of joining the others, she stands to the side, watching the town–and Ainela who walks from one table to the next, collecting sweets. It makes Zosia smile, the hazel in her eyes sparkling.

Ainela's always had a sweet tooth.

She clutches her sketchbook to her chest. Her charcoal-stained fingers twitch, not with cold, but with the weight of what she hasn't drawn yet. The feast begins. Tables lined with steaming loaves and braided pastries wrapped in wax paper fill the space with sugar and cinnamon and clove. The empty chair stands near the center. Zosia's eyes creep to it again and again. No one mentions the chair, but Zosia watches Jakub place a plate of food on it– a bit of black bread, dried apple and a folded paper crane. He stands back, dips his head, looks up as if he's caught, and then quickly steps away from the chair.

Sitting cross-legged by the old chapel wall, Zosia pulls her sketchbook to her and draws the linden. Not the whole tree, just the lower branches, covered in snow, with the gifts nestled beneath like offerings. Her hand moves without thought, her fingers briefly lifting to brush strands of hair off her cheek.

A pair of soft mittens in purple, a pair of buttons stitched perfectly on each. A rag dog. A ribbon unspooling in the wind. She guesses which townspeople offer which gift, she guesses who will trade and for what. The noise of the festival fades as she fills one page and then another. The cold brushes her face. She watches the wisp of breath curl from her mouth as she exhales.

"Zosia, come, hurry, the Tale Tent's opening." Ainela stuffs a piece of chocolate filled with caramel in her hand. "And let this melt in your mouth, it's delicious!"

Zosia follows her sister, noting a pair of small prints in the snow that weren't there before. *There's no tread. They're barefoot prints.* She lifts her head and scans the festival. Lanterns hang from branches, campfires burn. A draft cuts across her skin. The firelight flickers, but no one is barefoot in the snow. The prints stop a few steps behind her sketching place, then vanish, close enough to have watched her draw. There's an old story like this, isn't there? Children run from one activity to the next, adults cluster in small groups to drink ale and gossip. No one is barefoot in the snow.

The Story Tent sags slightly at the center, its canvas patchworked with old embroidery and smoke-darkened quilt squares. Red thread runs through some of the seams— intentional or not, Zosia can't tell. Inside, a ring of folding chairs surrounds a chipped enamel brazier, and the elders sit like carved figures half-sunk in memory. The air smells of dust and dried cloves.

Zosia slips in alone.

WHISPERROOT: A HUSHWOOD TALE

The younger children sit on blankets near the front, legs crisscrossed and restless. They whisper guesses about which story will be told—The Threaded Crown, maybe, or the Girl Who Swallowed Winter. But tonight, the eldest woman in town—Mrs. Kopec, whose hands tremble when they reach for tea—calls for silence without raising her voice.

"There was a girl once," she begins, eyes unfixed, as if the story doesn't come from memory but from somewhere else entirely. "Not the first to suffer, but the first the fire listened to."

The children go still. Even the wind quiets against the canvas.

"Her name was Klara... or Milenka... or something that no one dares speak anymore. She was born under a moon with no light and wandered too far too young. Heard things she shouldn't. Knew things she wouldn't say. One eye green. One gold. Like something caught between worlds." "She never wrote her wish down. She *whispered* it."

A sharp intake of breath beside Zosia. She doesn't know who it came from—maybe herself.

"The flame turned green. And no one knew what it meant yet. But she did. She just nodded. And walked away."

Mrs. Kopec's voice falters then. Her fingers curl around the frayed edge of her shawl.

"That night her house burned to the ground. But she wasn't inside. There were no bones. Just a ribbon—half-burnt—tied to a whispering tree. We say she was lost. But the truth is... she was *refused*. The forest made room for her. Because someone had to."

A murmur ripples across the tent. Someone coughs. Someone else stands too quickly and pretends they forgot something in the cold. But Zosia doesn't move.

She's not ready to go home. Not yet.

Outside, the festival flickers onward—lanterns swinging, bells jingling, voices bright with cider and pretense. But Zosia slips into the shadows near the chapel and winds her way down the old path that curls behind the fence, past the stacked firewood and crooked shed, down to where the stones turn soft with moss.

The cellar stairs.

The old ones. The ones Father Ignacy said were sealed for safety. Zosia presses her palm against the cracked wooden door. It gives. The air inside is colder than outside, heavy in the way basements always are. Her breath fogs, and her boots creak on the stone steps. At the bottom is the hollow—*their* hollow. She and Ainela had hidden sweets here once. A scrap doll. A dried flower. Messages folded tight and tucked into the wall. She kneels now, fingers brushing the groove behind the second stone.

There.

A torn page, yellowed and soft at the corners, pulled from the back of an old hymnbook. At first she thinks it's another note from Ainela, maybe something left behind in a hurry. But then she sees the handwriting. It isn't Ainela's. And the ink runs sharp and jagged, like it was written quickly, urgently—by someone who didn't think they had long.

I begged. He didn't stop.
Green means wild. That's what the rhyme says now.
But the fire listened. It turned green because it
believed me. I am not wicked. I am watching.

Zosia doesn't breathe.

There's a sketch beside the words.

WHISPERROOT: A HUSHWOOD TALE

A girl drawn in charcoal—loose but certain strokes. One green eye. One gold. Her mouth sealed with twisting vines. Not sewn shut but *grown*. Like the forest closed her voice into itself. But her hands reach toward roots.

Zosia stares. The style—it's not hers. But it's *like* hers. Like someone else draws not what they see, but what they *know*. She turns the page over. There's no signature. Just a faint smudge of ash at the corner. Somewhere above, laughter lifts from the courtyard. A bell rings twice.

The Wishing Flame must still be burning.

Zosia folds the page carefully and tucks it into the inside pocket of her coat. She doesn't know who drew it. But someone remembered. Someone watched. And maybe, just maybe—someone still does.

Schoolchildren call Zosia to the open meadow. The festival's nearly over but the town lingers, reluctant to return to daily life. Zosia jogs over to the meadow, her nose red, her eyes bright. Laying the sketchbook gently on the snow, she joins the snowball games. The red ribbons they tied to the forest trees hours earlier sway softly in the breeze. Father Ignacy watches from the side, hands clasped loosely behind his back. The children form a circle, holding hands, and dance. Ribbons braided through one girl's hair flutter as new snowflakes fall. Lanterns glow, stars twinkle, and the hushwood settles. With bellies full of piernik (the baker made some *just for the festival*), heads full of stories and hearts of memory, the town begins to tire.

Women gather scraps of cloth, baskets of leftover fruit, and discarded masks to pile away. The stone mason snuffs out the fire; the lumberjacks move the unused wood piles to the back door of the chapel. The carpenters, including Zosia's father, breaks down the canvas tents while others move the tables back into the chapel classrooms. The apothecary walks with a young boy to retrieve some herbs for a runny nose. The stablemaster lifts himself into the sleigh, gathers the reins and waves goodnight. Mama and Papa shake Father's hand, tell Zosia to stay with Ainela, and head home early.

The sky has darkened into that soft blue between evening and night. Snow hushes the cobblestones. Lanterns swing gently from the poles, their golden glow bending the shadows. Zosia wipes her damp mittens on her coat, breathless from laughter, and retrieves her sketchbook from the edge of the snow. There are bits of hay caught in the spiral binding, and her fingertips are numb, but her heart is light.

Ainela waits by the fence, arms crossed loosely, her cheeks pink from the cold. She smiles when she sees Zosia. That secret sort of smile that always makes Zosia feel like the smartest, sneakiest girl in the whole village.

"I love the festival," Zosia says as they begin walking the path towards home. She pauses, words catching behind her tongue. "I found something."

Ainela tips her head. "What kind of something?"

Zosia reaches into her sketchbook and carefully pulls out the folded slip of paper she found. The page is torn from a hymnbook. The back holds a drawing: a girl with mismatched eyes and a mouth covered in vines, reaching for the roots.

WHISPERROOT: A HUSHWOOD TALE

The words scrawled beneath it shake her more than she lets on:

       I begged. He didn't stop.
Green means wild. That's what the rhyme says now.
But the fire listened. It turned green because it believed me.
I am not wicked.

       "What do you think it means?" Zosia asks.

       Ainela's face aches. "Zosia, will you wait for me?"

       Zosia blinks. "Where are you going?"

       "It will just be a minute–the old chapel stairs, can you wait there for me?"

       "But the woods –"

       "Look at the sky and count how many stars you can find. I'll be able to hear you if you call–it'll only take a minute."

       "Why?"

       "I forgot something, I'll be right back, I promise. Will you wait for me?"

       Zosia nods. "By the old chapel steps." Zosia turns to walk to the chapel steps, the snow crunching beneath her boots. Tipping her head back to stare at the night sky, she counts the stars. One...two...three... she sees the North Star and remembers part of a story Ainela sometimes tells. *The North Star was the first Embergirl's guide. The girl whose wish burned green. The star hung over the third circle of trees that protect the hushwild.*

       What was that?

       Zosia turns her head towards the hushwood, sure she heard something. Not a rustling, but a sound, so faint she might have imagined it. It didn't sound like the ashfeather owl, and the chime thrush only sing in the daylight. She gasps - there it is again. A sound like faint laughter. She tells herself it's the breeze, but the wind has quieted. Zosia pulls her bottom lip between her teeth and faces forward again.

Where is Ainela? Worry spreads like a cold chill down her spine. *She'll be back. She promised.* She carefully takes out the slip of paper and unfolds it, reads the note again.

I begged. He didn't stop.

What didn't he stop? Who was he?

Green means wild.

It turned green because it believed me.

Believed what?

She traces the final line with her fingertip.

I am not wicked.

She folds the paper again, slower this time, as if the words might shift if she moves too quickly. Tucks it back into her pocket. The snow has begun to fall again. Softer now— thinner flakes that drift like ash more than lace. "Ainela?" she calls gently.

No answer.

Zosia pulls her scarf up higher. The chapel wall at her back is cold through her coat, but she doesn't move. Not yet. Ainela said she'd be back in a minute.

She starts to count again, this time only in her head. One... two... three...

A ribbon flutters on the far fence post, bright red against the dusk. It hadn't been tied that high before, had it? She rubs her mittened fingers together. Her breath clouds the air in short, shallow bursts. The wind picks up again, just enough to make the branches creak. Or maybe that's something else. Something behind the trees. A step? A snap?

Zosia holds her breath.

A moment passes. Then another.

She turns back to the sky. Tries to count the stars. But her mind won't hold still.

She promised.

Still no footsteps. No voice calling her name. Zosia stands. She brushes the snow from her coat, looks back down the path Ainela took.

Nothing.

The fear doesn't roar. It creeps. Slowly. Carefully. Like frost working its way up glass.

Zosia doesn't move. Not yet. But she wraps her arms around herself. And this time, when she starts counting, she doesn't look up.

She watches the path.

We remembered what the fire tried to hush.
That's why we saw the duskstag.
They said we were chosen—
but never said for what.

———————————

The Embergirls

CHAPTER EIGHT: AINELA

WHISPERROOT: A HUSHWOOD TALE

Ainela walks briskly, inhaling sharply as she steps into the hushwood. She doesn't have long. She promised her sister she would be quick.

Where are you going?

But the woods–

The fear in Zosia's voice cracks Ainela's heart. She didn't use to be afraid of the woods.

I haven't protected her enough. The drawing Zosia found. The inked vines, the stitched mouth—it's like something from the convent's forgotten stories. Or Jakub's notebooks. Why would Zosia find it now? Who would leave it?

Zosia. Caterbutton. The little one who sees everything. Except what Ainela tries so hard to hide from her. When the first Embergirl went missing, Zosia was so little– she remembers *something happening,* but not who. Not how. No one knows her name anymore–if they do, they don't say it. But the inked mouth, the twisted vines… it wasn't just familiar. It was *hers.* That girl. The one no one names anymore. But Ainela remembers. Not her name—never her name. Just her voice. What it did to the room. Seeing her note, seeing the drawing of the vines sealing her mouth… it stirs a memory in Ainela.

It was Springtime. Bees hummed by the wildflowers planted around the chapel, the chime-thrush sang every morning. Farmers were busy now, shearing sheep. Children darted through drying yards like ribbons in the breeze. More than one horse was heavy with foal, ready to birth at any time. Even Father Ignacy's sermons softened, just a little— less fire, more forgiveness.

After a long Winter, the town relaxed.

Until she opened her mouth–then the whole season cracked.

It was just after the hymns had been sung and people were taking their seats, shifting their coats. Instead of sitting with her family, she waited until the chapel was quiet. Father Ignacy smiled gently and asked if she could take her seat. Instead, she spoke. Her voice was clear and strong. It didn't waver at all. "He holds me down," she said. "He doesn't stop when I beg him to. And no one here can now say you don't know."

They said it started with her. But Ainela thinks it started with them—how they looked at her afterward. How they pretended she hadn't spoken. The silence after the truth is louder than anything else.

She wasn't the only one.

They watched me, Ainela thinks, the heaviness in her stomach growing. *I mocked them, the men. "Maybe she finished the hushwood." They murmured about me under their breath, but I did it because Zosia was there. I wanted her to hear, to hear how to question them. When I danced with the red mask, they watched. I wanted them to watch. I wanted Zosia to watch, to learn she doesn't have to change, she doesn't have to be invisible. They think I've kissed boys, they think I sneak out in temptress colors to welcome boys' attentions. I don't, but I let them think I do. I thought I had time. But...* Three before he left. Ainela counted them then. Everyone said it stopped because of his grief, because he left. But that wasn't it, was it? It didn't stop. Girls kept vanishing. Three more while he was gone. And now, since he's come back—two more. Eight, there's been eight.

There.

There's the hollow tree.

Ainela reaches into her pocket, her mittens curving around the locket. As her fingers graze the cool metal, memory rushes in—not of the gift itself, but what came before it.

Papa's voice boomed and cracked like lightning. Every time he struck Ainela's tender back, he yelled at her. "A whore is not welcome here." The sound of a switch hitting skin is intimate: first a whistle through the air, then the wet snap of contact—like a branch cracking against a soaked cloth. A high, stinging crack. It's a sound the silence afterward cannot swallow. It's a sound Zosia couldn't unhear. Ainela had been threatened and yelled at before, but never physically punished. Until now. Father Ignacy and two of the elders came by: she'd been seen sneaking out–again. They ordered her to tell them who she met and where–but Ainela refused.

Mama ordered, then pleaded, Ainela to just admit it. "It'll be better for you."

Still, Ainela said, "I can't give a name I don't have."

Papa said, "We can't hold the boy accountable if we don't know who it is."

Ainela repeated, "I can't give a name I don't have."

Father Ignacy, sighing heavily, said, "It is a sin to lie. It is a sin to bring moral decay into a home–especially when you have another girl here. You cannot allow this one to be the example that one will follow."

And so–the switch.

"Papa is right, Ainela. We can't –"

"He's not my father. I don't know who my father is, but I know he's not it."

Mama's face paled, then reddened. "How dare you."

Ainela swallowed her fear, her shoulders lifted in a tiny shrug. She challenged, "Is he?" with thin eyebrows arched. A portrait of courage, but also vulnerability, Ainela stood still, her arms trembling, but her voice steady. Her voice was always steady.

"You will not speak to your mother that way ever again. Bring me a switch, Ainela."

So, she did.

By the time it was done, tears slipped from her almond-shaped eyes, tracing her cheeks and pooling at the corners of her mouth. Tendrils of black hair stuck to her cheek. When she limped into the bedroom, Zosia met her with a hug. Ainela hissed through her teeth as pain flared along her back. Zosia waited until she could no longer hear her parents, then snuck out the cottage door with a wooden bowl, returning with packed snow. Lying some on her sister's red back, she asked with a shaky voice, "Why won't you just give them his name?"

Ainela replies softly, "There is no boy."

"Just tell them that then."

"No one will believe me."

Flinching from the iciness of the snow against her skin and the soreness of the welts, she says, "It's almost midnight. It's almost your birthday."

Zosia said nothing. The thought of celebrating now, with Ainela hurt, felt impossible.

"In the back of the second drawer, will you look? There's a pouch there. Bring it to me."

WHISPERROOT: A HUSHWOOD TALE

Zosia obeys, pulling open the second drawer, the creaking sound loud in a quiet cottage. Ainela stares, unblinking, out the window–a few stars twinkle. When Zosia brings over the small leather pouch, Ainela tries to smile. "Go on, open it. Happy birthday, Zosia."

The shiny locket was the prettiest thing Zosia owned. She gasped, holding it up. Gently, Ainela touched her hand. "It opens. It's big enough for something you draw."

Popping the locket open, Zosia smiles.

"I'm going to draw us. Will you pose for me?"

Ainela nodded. Ignoring the stinging in her back, she sat up. "By the stars," she says. Happily, Zosia pulled her sketchbook open, traced the locket so she could get the portrait size right, and started drawing. "You moved!" she playfully teased, wringing a smile from Ainela. "I did not."

"Denials, denials, denials." She drew in a sharp breath, worried the joke had gone too far. Their eyes met for only a moment before Ainela laughed, the sound like that of the chime thrush. Relaxing, Zosia giggled. When the portrait was finished, Ainela said, "Now draw you."

And, so, the sketch was of the two of them, smiling.

Ainela brushed hair off her sister's face, saying softly, "I don't mind if they get angry, Caterbutton." She glanced up again, towards the stars. When she looked back at Zosia, her eyes shone with tears. Swallowing, she said, "I promise I'll always see you if you promise you'll always see me." When she held out her pinky finger, Zosia hooked it, patting the necklace that lay on her heart. "I promise."

The cold has seeped through her mittens. Ainela blinks, eyes adjusting to the shifting hushwood shadows. For a moment, she had forgotten where she was. She doesn't have a lot of time–she promised Zosia she'd be quick. Quickly, she pushes the locket deep into the hollow space of the tree. The green ribbon still tangles with the vines–Zosia will find the locket. *Let her know what it means. Let her remember*. Ainela starts to stand when something catches her eye. Something burrows in the hollow space. Reaching in, Ainela pulls out a faded ribbon. It's different than the others, faded, the color of dried cranberries.

Ainela gasps. She recognizes this, though she hasn't seen it in years. Not since Mama braided it into her hair, back when she still sang while sewing. Before the warnings started. Before everything became quiet. This is Mama's ribbon. A swarm of butterflies hatch in her belly, a jolt of unease travels in goosebumps along her spine. *Mama was here. Why? Why was Mama here? Why was she giving this to Ainela?*

The silence is so loud.

She rubs her thumb over the fabric. She looks again in the hollow space to make sure there's no note, nothing else. There's not. Just this ribbon that her mother used to wear hidden in a tree of secrets. *Does Mama remember?*

The shifting of snow demands Ainela's attention.

She looks up just in time to see it.

Between two hushbark stands the most majestic animal Ainela's ever seen. She blinks but it remains. Thick antlers the color of coco crown a lean, wise face framed by dark eyes. Two snowflakes sit on the bridge of his nose. His body is made of muscle; his coat is the color of smooth pecans; his legs are darker, like the hushwood floor after it rains. *The duskstag.* Ainela's breath quickens, then freezes.

Only those chosen see the duskstag.

No, Ainela thinks, fear clawing through her bones. *Not yet.*

The duskstag watches her. He stomps his right front leg twice. Snow billows around him just as she hears it. A sound that doesn't pierce the night, but softens it, almost like a breath over a flame. The low smoke-hollowed whistle, drawn out like a sigh caught is the ashfeather owl. *hwooooooh hwaaaahh*—then silence. But it's not an empty silence - it's a silence Ainela feels, like the trees are listening. The ashfeather owl isn't the barn owl–the ashfeather's call is smeared with sorrow and muffled at the edges as though filtered through the snow. When it comes again, it sounds closer, almost as though it's just behind her.

Ainela turns her head to see.

But it's not there.

If you hear the ashfeather three times in one night, someone is being remembered.

Ainela looks towards the hushbark again, just in time to see the duskstag walk towards her. Muscles leap in his shoulders as he walks. He holds his head upright. Time stops as Ainela holds her breath again, her hand clutching her mother's ribbon. As he gets closer to her, the air crackles with heat, as if she were standing by a hearth. *His black eyes hold stars the color of hazel.*

Chosen.

Ainela wants to run, but she cannot move.

She wants to touch the duskstag, but fear keeps her hands still.

He doesn't stop beside her; he keeps walking, his pace unhurried. Things shift around her as he passes. There isn't wind, but the trees seem to sway toward him, as if waiting for him to speak. He walks through a line of trees, disappears from sight. As soon as he does, the forest exhales. Time resumes.

Ainela knots the ribbon around the locket, twice, then again—tighter than before. Her fingers ache from the cold. She tucks it deeper into the hollow, beneath the green thread Zosia will recognize.

Let her find it.

Let her remember.

Her breath hitches. The duskstag is gone, but the hushwood still feels full of watching. Ainela places her palm flat against the bark, then leans in, close enough for the tree to feel her breath. She whispers one word: "Caterbutton." Her voice breaks around it.

She waits—just for a moment—like maybe the forest might whisper it back. It doesn't.

She steps back. Her hand is still trembling. Her legs feel weak. But she walks away anyway, into the hush. Not ready. Not steady.

But she walks.

"Zosia." Ainela sees her sister standing where she left her. "Come on, let's get home."

WHISPERROOT: A HUSHWOOD TALE

Ainela wraps an arm around Zosia. She doesn't tell her about the duskstag or hearing the ashfeather owl. Instead, she asks what her favorite part of the festival was.

"Mine was the masked carolers."

The girls don't recognize the boys as they approach, but they recognize the older one's voice. Norbert. Three years older than Ainela. Everyone knows Norbert—favored by Father Ignacy as a hard worker, respected by the town for the quality of his craftsmanship, hated by the town girls.

"Go home. I'll be there soon," Ainela says firmly, her voice calm and steady.

"But—"

"Go home, Zosia."

"Aw, sending little sister home so soon? A little selfish, don't you think, wanting us all for yourself?" Norbert and the other two boys—the ones Ainela doesn't recognize—laugh. When Ainela nods slightly, Zosia obeys, quickening her step.

Ainela tries to follow her, but the three boys block her path. One of them reaches out and snatches the red mask hanging from her coat pocket.

"Why don't you wear this for us and dance, Ainela?" Norbert reaches out to brush her hair. She jerks back, tries to walk around him. He blocks her path, smiling. She smells the whiskey on his breath. Smiling bravely, she says, "Been drinking again, Norbert? I didn't know you wanted to be like your papa."

Norbert's face changes. She doesn't see his hand but feels the sting of his slap across her face. Suddenly, she feels herself pushed backward, hard. She stumbles, falling into the snow, her words fumbling, half-formed. "Time you shared what you've been giving with us."

Her heart races as she flails her arms, the words barely making sense.

One of the boys grabs her wrists while another tells him to hold her down. When Norbert drops to his knees, falling on top of her, the other boys cheer.

Suddenly, a gust of wind barrels through the trees, scattering snow in all directions. The boys gasp as the nearby trees creak and groan, though there is no storm. A high, shrill owl cry splits the air. Then another. Ashfeather. The fire pots in the square sputter behind them. One goes out entirely.

"Let's go," one boy mutters, voice tight.

Norbert doesn't move. He's still crouched over her; his hand tangled in her coat.

A sharp crack echoes above—ice or branch, it's hard to tell. Snow falls in a sudden heap beside them.

Norbert flinches. "It's just wind," he snaps, louder than needed. "Just wind and some stupid bird." He faces her again, but his hand hesitates.

The air is still. Not quiet—*listening*. Then from the hushwood, a low rustle—dry leaves brushing bark, steady and slow. No footsteps. No animals. Just something moving.

Norbert's breath catches. He turns toward the sound, squinting into the dark.

"There's nothing there," one of the boys says, though no one asked.

Norbert swears under his breath and yanks his coat straight like it matters. "She's not worth it anyway." He stands. Walks away too fast. The others follow, promising she'll dance for them later.

Ainela lies in the snow, heartbeat thudding, eyes stinging. She doesn't move. As the last footfalls fade, she

WHISPERROOT: A HUSHWOOD TALE

watches the snow begin to settle. And for a breath—she thinks she sees antlers vanish into shadows.

The forest never needed ballots.
It only needed silence,
and a town too polite to scream.
— The Hushwood

CHAPTER NINE: THE TOWN

WHISPERROOT: A HUSHWOOD TALE

We're not a lazy town. Everything– from tables to baskets–is put away at the end of celebrations. No need to delay the return to real life, as Father Ignacy says. We tidy up after joy the same way we tidy up after grief–quickly, and without complaint. We clean up messes that are visible— festival tables, not bruises. Never bruises. Still, it's startling. You spend months preparing for the Winter Festival, collecting fabric scraps, drying herbs, gathering in the chapel to assign tasks—only to wake one morning to a clean and, well, *barren* town. Just snow. Just silence. It makes one wonder: was it real?

Especially with the snowstorm. It started in the middle of the night, rattling the windowpanes, howling across the trees, layering ice over the creeks. By the time it quieted this morning, anything left out had vanished beneath fresh snow. That's how the whispers started, too–quick as frost.

Zosia came home alone last night, telling tales. Some boys—she only knew one of their names—bothered them while they walked. Zosia was sent home alone. And yes, their papa's anger is well-known. We've seen Mama wear high-necked sweaters in summer. Once, she appeared in chapel with a decidedly *purplish* eye. But that's not our business, is it? (We never ask or interfere. But we bring it up when it's useful.) And letting the golden girl walk home after dark certainly wasn't the responsible behavior one expects from an older sister. The truth is, we protect girls–until their pain becomes a little inconvenient. We protect boys–even when they've had a little too much to drink. So, we aren't surprised Ainela hasn't ventured outside. We see Zosia's tear-stained cheeks as she sits on the chapel stairs, sketching in that notebook again. But her sister—well, she *did* dance in ways girls shouldn't, and with a *red* mask at that. She's old enough to know better.

We see Ainela the following morning at chapel, pale-faced, a hollowed-out version of the girl who danced gaily just two nights ago. She makes forgetting easy for us: she sits quietly beside her sister. Her eyes are lowered. *As they should be,* we whisper. If we're guilty of mistaking heartache for shame, well... we'll sweep that up just as tidy as we did the crumbs from the feast. There's a tension in the chapel, like kindling. Dry and waiting. A mother scolds her daughter for speaking to the girl. Others greet the family as though they're strangers, as if we didn't know their grandmothers and grandfathers, as if we didn't rock them in our own arms when they were babies. One woman thinks of her son–how he laughed at dinner when *she* mocked the priest; how he stared too long after her at the festival. What might happen to our boys if they follow the laughter too long?

Father Ignacy called us here.

Not for a sermon, not exactly. It's not Sunday.

"We're just meeting for a conversation, that's all. Just an informal gathering to talk about some things as a town." So, we came. Even the old widow, the healer on the outskirts, though she muttered her doubts. She questioned, "What do we have to talk about?" but no one answered her. We all knew; we were all there, at the festival, we all saw what

happened. The old woman herself was at the Wish Flame, when the flame burned *blue* for Ainela.

Someone brings up dancing. Someone else brings up the boys. The word *provoked* is used. So is *reckless*. No one says *deserved*... but we all hear it just the same. Father Ignacy says something must be done. "Moral decay cannot be allowed to fester inside our homes," he argues. "When you open the door to evil, it will not refuse the invitation. We must protect the golden ones—and our boys who are still susceptible to Eve. It is mercy," he nods, his eyes passionate.

We are still.

"Children, you are dismissed. You may return home while the rest of us stay. Older children, we rely on you to see to it that the younger ones get home safely."

Families murmur, gathering coats. The children are happy to leave. We watch Zosia and her sister shuffle from the pew. Zosia reaches out and takes her older sister's hand in hers. Children whisper. Only once the last of the young ones are gone does Father face us again. He doesn't stand behind the altar today, but beside it, as if he's coming before us as heavily burdened as the rest of us. He's a good shepherd guiding us to the truth. "This is a matter of the town's safety. Of preventing future harm and of boundaries that must be restored before innocence is lost for good." He pauses, his eyes shifting over each of us. We know he means *her*. But we wonder: could he also be talking about our daughters?

"We cannot pretend that there are no consequences to unchecked behavior."

A murmur of approval. Someone coughs. Someone nods.

"There's been... rumors. But the truth is, temptation takes many forms. And while we mourn the loss of good girls, we must be vigilant about the wolves among the flock."

He does not name her. He does not have to.

A man in the back clears his throat. "I heard she laughed when the shoemaker's boy tripped. Didn't offer to help him up or anything."

"She wears red. A lot," adds a woman near the window.

"She mocked the koledy."

"She danced alone."

"She left her sister in the dark."

We don't say *assaulted*.

We don't say *blamed*.

But we speak of decorum. Decorum matters to us. We are a town that prides itself on being polite and having proper decorum. So, we speak of that. We speak of providing examples to the golden girls. And of how easily wrongness can spread if left unpruned.

On a table near the pulpit sits a wide enamel bowl, chipped at its rim. Beside it, a stack of old scraps of paper. "No names," he says gently. "No accusations. Only a vote of conscience."

One by one, we step forward.

We do not speak.

We do not look at one another.

One by one, we write a word. Some of us write an initial or a symbol. We fold the paper. We think if we fold the paper small enough, maybe the blame folds smaller too. And we drop the folded slip into the bowl. Some of us are careful. Some of us scribble quickly. A woman clutches her shawl tight after casting hers. A man presses his lips into a thin line.

WHISPERROOT: A HUSHWOOD TALE

Mama stands in the back, the doll Zosia forgot to take with her clutched in her arms. Her eyes are swollen, but dry. Papa stands beside her, arms crossed, jaw clenched. He does not speak – but when someone offers him a pen, he takes it. Papa's vote is not quick. He stares at the paper as if it might catch fire in his hand. Then he folds it once, twice, and drops it in. Mama refuses the pen at first. She stares down at Zosia's doll, rubs her thumb over it, as if she's remembering something. Her hand trembles as she writes and she folds it three times before dropping it. It costs her, we see that, but not enough. Father Ignacy pats her shoulder, murmurs comfort.

The widow pauses, her pen mid-air. "But aren't we meant to protect *her* too?"

A man replies, "We protect the ones who still have a chance."

"She was always too wild," someone reminds her gently.

"She knew what she was doing; she dares them," another adds.

She sighs heavily, makes a mark on the paper, and drops it in.

Only one among us does not write. Jakub, the war-scarred blacksmith we do our best to ignore. "You're not guiding the boys," he says. "You're giving them permission."

The room stills.

Father Ignacy meets his gaze. "No, son. We're setting a path. For all our children."

Jakub doesn't answer; just turns and leaves. His paper alone stays blank, one slip of silence in a bowl full of verdicts.

A boy with blonde hair sits on the back steps of the chapel, legs apart, head bent in sorrow. He looks sick to his stomach. Norbert is his name. Across the way, not far, Zosia stands at the edge of the hushwood, as if she's waiting for something, as if she's trying to hear something. The red one hasn't been seen since coming to the meeting with her family. We think she may soon go to Warsaw, to stay with some distant cousin. We remember the time she wore a crown of carrot tops to chapel and told everyone she was the Queen of Rabbits. She was five, maybe six. When someone laughed, she curtsied so grandly she knocked over the offering basket. We let ourselves smile at that today. Just for a moment. But memory is a guest we only keep when it behaves. By morning, we'll forget again. Soon, if someone brave should speak her name, we'll tilt our heads, squint our eyes, and say, *which one was that?*

For now... Some of us still see her, in flashes—in the ash on the windowsill, in the bite missing from a honey cake. But it is easier to forget. So, we practice forgetting. We remember, just for a moment, the way she used to shout *"Caterbutton!"* when she wanted her sister's attention. A nonsense word, but it always made the little one laugh-- helpless, hiccupping laughter that echoed through the square.. We let ourselves smile at that today. Just once. But, again, memory is a guest we only keep when it behaves.

At the schoolhouse, the teacher readies the room for class when, among her papers, she finds a sketch the red one made. It is a heart with a jagged line down its center. Tangled vines grow from the jagged edges and wrap around the whole heart. Thorns prick the surface. The schoolteacher stares at it for a moment, then quietly tosses it into the fire burning in the hearth. She watches as the flames turn the white edges first to black, then to ash. Across town, the farrier exhales the breath lodged high in his chest and pauses to look out the barn at the snowy town he loves.

A red ribbon no one remembers tying blows on the fencepost.

The last thing she said was Caterbutton.
Not goodbye. Not help.
Just a word that meant Love you.
And Zosia kept it,
a whisper curled beside her heartbeat.

The Lost Girls' Rhymebook,
fragment one

CHAPTER TEN: ZOSIA

The bed beside her is cool when Zosia wakes. Ainela isn't beside her. Zosia rolls to her side, rubbing her eye. *She must be in the privy*, she thinks, but she slides her foot over to Ainela's side. If she was only in the privy, the bed should still be warm. The fire in the hearth has long since gone out, leaving the room chilly. She rolls to her back and listens. The sound of faint murmurs from the main room feeds her anxiousness. She hears the faint jingle of a bell she doesn't recognize.

Something's not right.

Her feet touch the cool wooden floor.

The way her cotton gown clings for a moment to the backs of her legs when she stands.

The frost on the blurry windowpane.

These moments settle in her chest like stones. The bedroom door waits, slightly ajar, as if it were left that way on purpose for her. She places a tiny palm flat against the pine and peers into the main room. Dimly lit by the glow of lanterns, Zosia sees three men standing near the door. Ainela crouches before them, tying the laces on her boots. When she stands, firelight reflects her eyes: shining but dry.

Spiderwebs of fear curl inside Zosia.

She *wants* to open the door, she wants to scream *no*, she wants to run into the main room and lock her arms around her sister. Sometimes, if Zosia woke from a nightmare, Ainela whispered stories and sang lullabies to help her find sleep. She made her laugh when no one else could. She didn't let the other kids tease her for sketching. She gave her pretty things. Zosia's fingers grip the edge of the door tighter. She watches.

"It's time." One of the men says. They are masked men. One holds a lantern with a star in the center; another holds a red ribbon. The words don't sound mean. Just certain. "We've come for her."

Mama bows her head, only for a moment, then lifts it. She glances at her oldest daughter–the one who never should have been-but doesn't speak. Papa's voice is gruff when he says, "It's for the best."

One man, tall and bulky, steps forward. He isn't cruel when he ties the red ribbon around Ainela's wrist–not tight, just enough. He touches her wrist like someone sealing a package. Ainela's eyes bounce past Mama to the bedroom. Zosia's breath catches. Does she see her? The light isn't bright enough to tell. The faint jingle comes again; Zosia realizes it comes from just outside her window, but she can't take her eyes off her sister. A masked man–the cow–nods towards Mama and Papa, then opens the door. When the other, the one who tied the red ribbon around her wrist, the one in the deer mask, walks, Ainela follows.

Her head doesn't bow.

She walks past Mama.

No words are spoken.

Mama closes the door. She rests there a moment too long, silent.

Zosia hurries from the bedroom door to the window.

There is no noise.

A line of girls, four with Ainela, stand in the snow. Coatless. *Will they not need their coats?*

WHISPERROOT: A HUSHWOOD TALE

Zosia gasps, putting her hand against the windowpane, its iciness the only thing that feels real. She knows that one. The second girl in the line, the one with freckles and hair like corn silk. They once painted the same pinecone in school. She thinks her name is Maryika–or maybe Marta. Or maybe not, maybe it was something else. Tomorrow, no one will say her name. But Zosia remembers–Zosia always remembers.

She watches, wishing she could scream... but she can't.

When the line starts walking, Zosia frowns——the first man, the one who holds the lantern, his foot drags just slightly, just like the butcher's does. And that one–the one who tied the ribbon around Ainela's wrist, the one whose shoulders curve slightly reminds her of the shoemaker. They are not strangers–they only want to *look* like ghosts.

Where are they taking her? Why would they take her?

Zosia dares to lift the window–only a small crack. The silence is so loud–the girls do not scream, though lanterns show one girl's face streaked with tears. The faint cracking of the linden tree branches and the crunching of feet in the snow are the only sounds. Even the moon hides its face behind shadowy clouds.

Ainela is last, her dark braid trails down her back.

She's never been first for anything.

A masked elder——this one a fox, one who doesn't seem familiar to Zosia–walks behind her. None of the masked men carry weapons but, sometimes, one will place a hand on a girl's shoulder as if guiding her in the right direction. As they walk past the cottage, Ainela's head turns towards the window. Her lips move–Zosia sees it's not a smile, not a cry, but a whisper. Even from this far away, Zosia hears it: *Caterbutton*. Or *I love you*–it's the same.

Zosia feels her heart cracking. Tears burn the backs of her eyes, her nose flaring with the effort to breath. Desperate for one last touch of her sister, she sticks her arm through the window, her fingers reaching hopelessly for Ainela. She opens her mouth to scream – but no sound comes. And the line of lanterns stretch into the dark night, one after another. They remind Zosia of stars after a storm– pale, flickering, almost gone.

Zosia stares out the window. The snow falls heavier by morning. Papa says a snowstorm's headed for them—the village's old men warn they'll see a few more feet of snow over the weekend. The heart of winter is here where anything still alive dies. Even the morning sun seems weak–its rays muted by the clouds. Zosia notes: there are no prints in the snow. Everything looks like it should. Hurt and anger and guilt bubble like blisters inside. It's only been hours. How is it that easy to erase a girl?

The sketchbook lies beneath her pillow–she feels its leather beneath her head–but she doesn't know what to draw. How do you sketch *emptiness*? How do you draw *fear that cannot be spoken*? The freckle-faced girl–tears streaked her cheeks. Ainela didn't cry, but Zosia saw the way her hands curled into fists by her side. *I do it when I need to stitch myself together again*, she explained once.

The coolness on the other side of the bed chills her– she edges as close to her edge as she can, wrapping the blankets tight around her. When the bedroom door opens, and Mama comes in, Zosia doesn't move. She stares past her mother to the window. *They walked towards the chapel* .

Were they going for other girls?

Were they going to the chapel?

"She's gone," Mama says, one hand holding the wooden door.

Zosia doesn't speak. She doesn't move. She only blinks.

Something inside her has closed.

A full day.

A full day has passed.

From her bed, Zosia watched out the window as Papa chopped more wood. Mama made food Zosia didn't eat. The crackling fire. Near midday, the widow healer came bearing some herbs. "In case you have trouble sleeping," she said softly. When supper came, Mama added a small, torn piece of bread to the windowsill – Zosia sees it when she goes to the outhouse. The next knock on the window is farmer's wife. "But where have they taken her? Where do they go? How would she get on in Warsaw?" The desperation in her voice tells Zosia: her daughter was among the four. Mama's whispered answer is too soft for Zosia to hear from her bed.

The candle flickers low on the nightstand. Mama doesn't sit on the bed. She takes the old woven chair by the window, the one with the fraying arms and the splintered leg. The one that's nearly broken, like everything else. She doesn't look at Zosia, not at first. Instead, she sits quietly, staring at the candle, her hands in her lap. When she speaks, her voice sounds raspy, clogged, as if gathering enough energy to speak is hard.

"I knew a girl once."

Zosia doesn't turn. Her eyes stay on the ceiling. Sometimes she pretends the cracks in the wood are pathways and if she can find the right path, she'll find her sister.

"This girl... she did everything right. She kept her hair pinned back and her voice soft. She wore the right shoes. Ate what she was given. Never asked for seconds. Never asked for anything."

The room is cold. The blanket on Zosia's shoulders isn't enough. She wants to stop Mama, but she can't. She knows it's not just a story. Mama's eyes rise only for brief moments to stare out the window–then they drop like hot coals back to her lap.

"Everyone said she was lucky. She believed it, too. Thought if she stayed quiet enough, small enough, they'd keep her safe." Mama's voice catches–not with tears, but with something deeper. "But... but, the truth is, quiet girls go unnoticed. And unnoticed girls go unprotected." Mama pauses for a long time, dragging in a labored breath and leaning forward, bracing her elbows on her knees. "One night... one night, someone did notice her. No one stopped him when he... when he grabbed her. No one heard her when she screamed—oh, she screamed so loud–" this time the crack in Mama's voice sounds like tears. The candle pops. A rivulet of wax slides down the side. Mama swallows, moistens her lips with her tongue and sits back again, her eyes shiny but dry now. "That good girl came home different. Her mother said nothing. Her father wouldn't even look at her. The neighbors bought soup and said it was a fever." Mama's eyes slowly travel to the bed, to the small daughter who hasn't spoken since last night when she watched her sister taken from her. "She stopped talking, too. But not all the way. She still prayed. And when the baby came, she named her something beautiful."

Zosia closes her eyes.

"Not everyone wanted her to keep the child. But she did. She tried. She made a life of rules and lists and chores. She told herself if she could just keep that girl quiet–if she could just keep her *safe*–then everything would be as it should."

Mama's hands twist in her lap, her eyes sliding away from Zosia.

"But the girl—she didn't stay quiet. She danced. She asked questions. She loved things too hard. She made up songs. She wore red when no one else dared to. She... she reminded everyone that silence is a choice."

A gust rattles the windows. Zosia's fingers clutch the blanket closer to her.

"They took her anyway. I let them. Because I was afraid too." She glances at Zosia again, her eyes red. No tears fall. "I'm sorry."

She waits.

Zosia doesn't answer. She pulls the corner of her lip between her teeth and rolls to face the wall. Mama stands slowly, her joins stiff. She leans over and blows out the candle.

"You don't have to forgive me," she whispers. "She won't forget you."

She leaves the door open behind her.

The coming snowstorm means no one sees the small, silent girl slip out the back door. In the hearth, the black kettle hisses with steam, boiling water spitting against the lid. Glass jars clink as Mama lowers them into the pot. She moves from window to window, stuffing old rags into the cracks to keep the draft out, too busy bracing the cottage for the storm. Sporadically, Papa opens the front door, more logs for the fire in his arms, a layer of snow trailing behind him.

They are too busy to notice Zosia as she scurries out the back door. She won't be gone long. She's heard the whispers: *girls go to the hushwood*. If Ainela goes there, she might leave something for Zosia in their secret place. In the hushbark's hollow place.

It hasn't been a full day yet, but Zosia misses her sister. *The red one*. She heard Mama furiously whisper the name to Papa: *They're calling her the red one*. Zosia remembers her sister dancing with the red mask. She looked beautiful.

Walking behind the chapel stirs a memory of the festival.

Everyone is watching you. Only a hint of fear traced the edges of Zosia's words—mostly she was confused. *Do you care?* Ainela laughed, shaking her head, dark hair spilling over her shoulders as they readied for bed. *Let them look*. She lifted a shoulder in a tiny shrug. *They're going to talk anyway, so they might as well have something pretty to look at while they do, right?* But she noticed how Ainela's smile faded then, and her voice grew smaller when she said, *Red mask or no, I don't think it matters*. Her fingers trembled as she pulled the brush through her hair. *Black as ash*, she murmured. *She was afraid.* Zosia hadn't thought so then, but now she is sure of it.

The splintering of bark grounds her. She stands still--watching. The hushwood looms just ahead, the alder, pine and hushbark sentinels guarding the forest's secrets. A branch falls. She blinks. She's been to the hollow tree many times. Maybe Ainela is safe. *The girls--they run away. Most of them run away from the convent.*

It's okay if you do, Zosia thinks. *As long as you're safe. Please have run away.*

The snow falls harder; the wind picks up.

Zosia edges past the line of alder trees, picks her way through the path. Just past the chapel, just before you get to the grove. There it is.

And the green ribbon is there!

Zosia's heart races; her steps quicken.

When she reaches the hollow, she falls to her knees, her fingers untying the special knot. She wraps the frayed green ribbon in one palm and stretches the other into the hollow space. *There.* Her fingers curl around a small, hard object.

The locket. My locket.

Father Ignacy's voice returns in memory: *your locket has been donated to the chapel.* Ainela got it back for her. The clasp is still broken, but Zosia's able to push it open. The sketch is still there. She closes her eyes, curls her hand around it. The wind picks up, dusting snow at her face. Mama will notice her gone soon.

Zosia takes both the green ribbon, *their* green ribbon, and the locket, and hurries out of the forest. She never sees the black eyes watching her from behind another tree—eyes ringed with shadow and specked with hazel stars.

She returns before she is missed. Soon, the wind picks up. Trees splinter beneath the weight of the sky. Mama shuffles from room to room; Papa sways slowly in the rocking chair, smoking a pipe. No one checks on Zosia. The cottage feels *hollow*. Zosia moves to the window. Frost spiders across the glass; snowflakes tumble, clumsy and wild. Gusts of wind trap them in a vortex, spiraling, just like Zosia's world. The glass is icy beneath her finger. She etches a small, tight spiral in the frost. A spiral that grows larger and more crooked with each pass. Soon, the coil looks more like a loopy whorl against the glass. Just like the chaos outside. Just like the maelstrom in her heart. The lines twist like a dizzying tether— like the one pulling Ainela round and round in circles, deeper into the dark.

Zosia knows the etching will soon disappear.
Just like everything that matters disappears.
The freckled-faced girl from school.
Ainela.
Zosia's voice.
The thought of one more thing disappearing makes Zosia's heart burn. She reaches under her pillow, withdraws her leather-bound sketchbook, and a small piece of charcoal. As the spirals on the window fade, she captures them on her paper instead.

Zosia closes her eyes.
She closes her mouth.
And the silence roots deep.

The thrush does not sing its own song—
only what the missing leave behind.

———————————

Etched into a hushbark trunk, origin
unknown

THE FOREST

WHISPERROOT: A HUSHWOOD TALE

We are not graves.

They are not gone.

The world calls them lost. We do not. We know where they are. They are here. Not beneath us, not yet. Not as bones in soil. But as breath. As weight. As sound caught between the trees. We remember what they were before—before the bruises were explained away, before the laughter was trained out of them, before ribbons meant sacrifice and red was a curse you earned by shining.

They came here with stories half-told, nails bitten to the quick, mouths stitched shut by shame they didn't deserve. We remember the girl who danced with wild feet, who sang to the beetles on the chapel steps. We remember the freckled one who painted every stone and once tried to teach a pinecone how to float. We remember the quietest one, the one who always stood at the edge of the circle, who hummed under her breath when she thought no one listened. She never asked for extra cake, but once left sugar cubes on the chapel steps for the ghosts she believed were lonely. When her name was called, no one believed it. But the hushwood did because we always saw her. We remember the girl who crowned herself Queen of Rabbits, curtsied so grandly she knocked over the offering basket, and whispered silly names to her sister—*Caterbutton, Ashseed, Mossmouse*—because she wanted to say *I love you*.

The world forgets those girls.

The town rewrites them as warnings.

We do not.

Every breath finds its way back to us. The wind carries every wish made to us. In the Spring, dandelions carry them from one of our fragrant flowers to the next. And then—in Winter—when blankets of snow hide our bursts of color, they're picked up by emberflies whose warmth keeps them alive until they reach our limbs, our bark, our soil.

Yes---we remember.

And with each memory, the hushwood changes. Only when wishes are made by those whose voices are never heard. But when it hears a voice destined to be lost, our roots tremble. The hushbark trees weep thin lines of sap—not golden and sweet, but dark, almost bitter. It beads along the bark like bruises surfacing. We taste their hurt in the soil— metallic as blood, sharp as rust. Even the snow lies strangely, piling where it shouldn't, drawn to the places where they once wept. The moss bends low over lost things—a mitten dropped in the panic, a snapped hair ribbon, a page torn from a drawing book. It curls around them gently, not to hide, but to *hold*, as if whispering: *We'll keep it safe. You've lost enough already.*

Some trees lean closer, bark splintering in lines that echo breaking ribcages. The roots rise too high in places, as if straining to lift sorrow from the earth. And the air—it forgets how to sing. Even the wind moves softly now, as though to keep from pressing too hard on the bruises left behind.

Sometimes, when the night is deepest and the frost curls like breath from a tired mouth, the duskstag steps through the hushwood. Not all see him. Only the girls who have lost too much too young. Only the ones who've learned to speak without sound. These are the girls he cares for, the ones he seeks. These are the ones who glimpse something, well, extraordinary. Because that is what we see them as: extraordinary. The memories we hold of them, the ones made before joy was stolen by thieves in masks, remind us. We cannot stop it from happening. We cannot undo the devastation.

But the duskstag can share the truth they deserve.

To some, he brings terror—not for what he is, but for what his presence confirms: *you are not safe. you are seen.* To others, he brings stillness. The kind that settles inside the chest like the pause between sobs. He does not come to guide, and he is not a rescuer. But he stands so they will know: *someone remembers what was done to you.* He comes hoping that a glimpse of him will help steel them for what is to come, to inspire because at least someone thought enough of her to warn her. He comes hoping that a warning may help them... not *accept* their fate, not really, but *anticipate* it. One day, he hopes, glimpsing him may be the spark that sets the town aflame.

His antlers bloom with dusklight—not gold, not white, but that color between fading and forgetting. And when he bows his head, even the chime-thrush goes silent.

He watches and waits.

And the hushwood watches and waits with him.

It's quiet here. Quiet like holding your breath under cold water. Quiet like knowing there's no one coming to stop what's been done. It is too quiet. That is why the chime-thrush sings. It was never meant to. But sorrow, when buried long enough, will climb anything to be heard. True pain will not be ignored. It hangs thick in the air, like a heavy curtain against the morning light. And the thrush responds. Its feathers are stitched from lullabies and sobs; its bones carved from rootwood and broken promises.

And its song is not sweet. It's not beautiful.

It's arresting. It calls forth a memory, faded and old.

Tonight, the chime-thrush perches low,
near the hollow where the red one wept, and it sings a line
the forest keeps like a wound: *Let them look, then. Let them
look at something beautiful.* The brave with a tremulous
voice. The bold with a caged look in her eye. The thrush is not
a sound easily ignored: it's a sound that makes others look
around and ask *did you hear that? It sounded just like when
that girl...* Sometimes we wonder: how many more songs will
the thrush learn?

But, one day.

Maybe one day the thrush won't have to carry the
song. And when they are ready to speak, we will listen.

Until then—we stretch our roots wide. We cradle their
dreams like seeds. We mark the trees with spirals, etch their
names in frost, and teach the thrush their songs. We rustle
our branches louder when she walks by. We press memory
into frost, into fallen bark, into roots that twist like riddles.
We let our moss cradle the things her sister left behind.

Zosia.

We have seen her.

So small. So quiet. But her silence is not forgetful.
She *looks* where others don't. She *listens* longer than they
allow. Sometimes we think she hears us. When her finger
traces the spiral in frost. When she stands too long in the
clearing, not yet afraid. When she leaves with wet lashes and
clenched fists. Can she see what's hidden?

We do not know. But we hope.

We hope she sees the ribbon knotted in the alder's
limb. We hope she finds the gift her sister buried in our roots.
We hope she names the song the chime-thrush carries.

WHISPERROOT: A HUSHWOOD TALE

Because one girl remembering—just one—could be enough to stir the rest.

So, we wait. We are patient. We are not graves. We are not kind. We are not cruel. We are only what remains.

And we remember.

Part Two: Beneath

We are not gone.
We are the ash that remembers the fire

The Embergirls' Rhymebook

If they take your voice,
spit in the dirt instead.
The roots will keep it safe
until you come back for it.

---

margin note,
The Embergirls' Rhymebook

CHAPTER ELEVEN

ASHWATER

The chapel basement. Its door is never opened. Once, when she was young enough to believe grown men told the truth, Ainela had tried—and Jakub told her to move along, that there was nothing down there but spiders. He lied. The air below shifts—thick, damp, hard to swallow. Her boots scrape stone slick with cold, the walls sweating in slow trickles. Water threads between uneven slabs, drying to a white crust like salt on an old wound. The smell rises to meet her: mildew, rust, and a sweetness gone wrong, as if fruit had been left too long in its jar.

A shove between her shoulder blades drives her down the last steps. The floor is packed earth under a thin scatter of straw that crunches instead of softening the fall. Ahead, a narrow corridor stretches forward, flanked by warped timber and iron. The bars are black with age, but the looks gleam—oiled against failure. Light slices in from slits no bigger than a hymnbook high in the wall; in those pale blades, dust drifts slow as ash. At the far end waits a heavy oak door, its surface scarred deep, like claw marks. She wonders how it will sound when it closes behind her—how the silence here will be different: thicker, watchful, the kind that listens more than it keeps.

As she's marched forward, her eyes catch on a scrap of fabric nailed high in the corridor's shadows — the corner of a robe, the rest long since torn away. Near the hem, faded stitches form two letters, the second only half-visible where someone has tried to pick it out. The first is an M. She doesn't know why it makes Jakub glance back at her. "Eyes front," he says. His voice is flat, but there's an edge to it. "That belonged to someone who forgot her place."

The room is not empty. Six girls are scattered around it: one murmuring over a broken rosary, another weaving cloth into the end of a corn doll. Two smaller ones huddle together. One sits alone, hair hanging forward; another faces the wall as if ordered to.

A sniffle—Lusia, maybe—carries through the cold. The man in the cow mask jerks the ribbon at her wrists, stopping her short as another masked guard swings the oak door wide. Her boots step into something wet. A bittersweet odor wafts up, making her throat tighten. The man in the deer mask catches her wrists, rough, cutting the red ribbon and freeing the raw skin beneath. When they leave, the door slams shut like a verdict.

"Don't sit in the middle. You're in someone's way if you do." The speaker is a girl with a long blond braid and a chipped front tooth—close to Zosia in age. Ainela knows her. Chapel benches, whispered jokes. *Klara.*

She stays standing, scanning the faces as the others shift into their places. The little one who walked ahead of her through the snow cradles a thin twig looped with red thread. Windburn stains her cheeks, a frayed red scarf knots at her throat. She curls against the door, knees to chest, sky-blue eyes unfocused and skittish.

"I know you." The corn doll girl's voice is raspy. Ainela remembers her leading circle games in the meadow, never without a doll her grandmother had made. *Tatiana.*

"You left after you sang the harvest song," Ainela says.

WHISPERROOT: A HUSHWOOD TALE

"You remember."

Ainela lifts her chin. "Tatiana." The name sparks, quick and hot, in the candlelight before the girl looks away. Halina—tall, with apple-colored curls—edges closer to Lusia, giving Ainela a small, knowing nod.

A faint sound draws Ainela's attention—a thin, breathy whistle from a girl sitting near the wall, her knees hugged tight, the side of her face hidden behind her hand. Her lips are pressed just enough to shape the note without voice. When her fingers shift, Ainela glimpses her mouth moving as though tracing the shape of petals. A flower? A sunflower, maybe. It's gone in a blink. The whistle fades. Ainela tucks the image away without knowing why.

A creak from the floorboards above freezes Klara mid-breath. She watches the ceiling, only relaxing when it stills. "What is that?" she asks, pointing to an enamel bowl crouched in shadow.

No one answers.

It sits in the far corner, crouched low in shadow. It's a wide enamel bowl with a white surface chipped to steel beneath, a dark ring of rust blooms along the rim. The inside is bone-dry, but a faint sourness clings to the metal, as if whatever it once held refused to leave. Ainela doesn't know what it's for.

Another set of footsteps overhead—heavier and paired with low voices.

Klara fidgets. The murmurs draw nearer.

The oak door groans open. Ainela's mouth goes dry as Father Ignacy steps into the candlelight, followed by three unmasked men. Jakub comes first—broad-shouldered, head tipped to avoid the ceiling beam, his eyes flicking over the room without resting on anyone too long. He has always been a wall between her and trouble, but never the kind that lets you pass. Behind him is Tomasz, a young man, a thin scar cutting across his jaw like a misplaced smile. He carries himself with the quick, restless energy of someone eager to prove he belongs. Last is Mateusz, older than the others, hair gone to iron-grey, a rosary looped twice around his wrist like a shackle. His gaze lingers on the enamel bowl in the shadows, as if already thinking of how it will be used. Fear curls like vines in Ainela's belly.

Halina's hand finds Lusia's knee.

Klara taps her foot. Ainela catches one of the girls, the one with the broken rosary, watching her. The girl's eyes skirt quickly away when she is caught. Her name is on the edge of Ainela's mind, but she can't hear it for the whorl of chaos and fear. Confusion morphs into panic the longer it takes Father Ignacy to speak.

Father Ignacy waits, eyes moving from face to face until the air feels taut enough to snap. Then: "We have new sinners among us," he says. "You are here because you have allowed corruption to root in your hearts. Scripture tells us we will know the tree by the fruit it bears. Rot must be cut away. Purification must come through pain, so that we may feel what our Lord suffered for us—and become more like Him."

Ainela's hand clenches and her eyes widen. Fear tightens, rolls, and pulses like a living thing inside her until nausea blooms when Father Ignacy nods towards Mateusz who steps quickly to the enamel bowl. As he walks past Tomasz and Jakub with it, Ainela tracks him until his frame turns to enter a different room in the corridor.

A sound–a moan, a crack, as if the weight of the fear was too great–from one of the other girls draws her attention.

WHISPERROOT: A HUSHWOOD TALE

Shadows are strangers; they can't be trusted. They hide things–like the purple and black bruises lining the girl's face– Ainela missed those when she first came in. Shadows, like strangers, play with the truth. When she first saw the girl, Ainela thought the shivers were from the cold, but she sees now the girl leans into another, trembling. The floor is cold, but not that cold. Shadows, like strangers, show only what they want you to see. Ainela squints, trying to remember the girl's name. She's seen her in the village, but she can't place her. Frustration knots with fear. Unease settles in, heavy as a curse spoken over still water.

"Each of you will stand." It is not a question: it is a statement.

Klara hesitates the longest; she is the last to stand. Father Ignacy walks to stand in front of her. "It is rooted deep in you, isn't it? The sin. The rebellion. The rot." Klara's mouth moves, her chest rising as her breathing becomes choppy. Without warning, Tomasz strikes her hard in the face, his knuckles cracking against bone. No blood spills, but she cries out and crumples to the floor.

"Now, now," Father Ignacy chides Tomasz, "You must be precise. Pain is not for the sake of pain. Why did you strike her?"

"She refused to answer your question, Father."

"Indeed. But she might not have connected the pain to the sin; the goal of a punishment is to prevent the sin from taking root. You must explain why she is being punished."

"Yes, Father Ignacy. I apologize."

"No need. You are young." Father Ignacy smiles briefly, then turns his attention back to Klara. Tilting his head, he says, "Stand up, Klara."

Father Ignacy motions to Mateusz who steps forward with the enamel bowl. Father's steel-grey eyes slowly survey the room. The girls have not made a sound: terror steals things. Sometimes even voices. "Klara will be the first, but not the only one to receive purification today." He looks at the bowl and smiles. "Mateusz filled the bowl with ashwater and vinegar. Ash, to remind us that from dust we came and to dust we will return. Vinegar, for the bitterness our Lord tasted on the cross. When He said, 'I thirst,' they offered Him not sweet water, but sour wine — the drink of mockers. Yet He drank and bore it." He pauses. Confusion mars Ainela's forehead. Will they drink the vinegar—with ash in it? She searches the faces of the other girls, the ones who have been here longer, for clues. But she only sees shadows and fear. Is this something new, just for the four taken tonight?

Father Ignacy's voice jars her eyes back to his.

"The ash strips away what is unclean. The vinegar seals the wound against the rot. Rot begins with small trespasses," he says, pacing the aisle. "Laughing bareheaded at boys. Humming tavern songs when you should be praying. Stealing from the Lord's own garden." A ripple moves through the girls. Klara's jaw goes hard. Lusia drops her gaze. Iskra's knuckles whiten around the hem of her shift. Father Ignacy continues, "Together they scour the body, so the soul may be made ready. Pain cleanses. Bitterness humbles. This is the cup of our Lord's endurance, and you will drink of it — in flesh, if not in mouth — until the sin is gone."

Ainela jerks in surprise when she feels someone take her hand. Gasping, she turns her head. A small girl with sandy-colored hair sun-bleached and cut unevenly doesn't look at Ainela. She is very young, nearly the age of Zosia, and something about the girl's fingers tucked into her own larger palm do what something else has not: tears leap to Ainela's dark eyes.

"Mila," the little one whispers.

Ainela squeezes Mila's fingers, curling her bottom lip in over her teeth. "Ainela." Her own whisper shakes. She swallows, then exhales long and low, pushing an image of Zosia's round face from her mind. She can't think of her right now.

"Purify her." Father Ignacy's voice shifts a shade darker. He takes a step back, allowing Mateusz to step forward. The man with hair the color of steel is heavier than Tomasz, nearly matching Jakub in height. He's quiet and deliberate. His hands are steady as he lifts the bowl, tipping ashwater over Klara. The first splash hits her chest and shoulders, striking skin already rubbed raw from cold. She jerks back a fraction, automatically, as if against her will, the breath leaving her body in a sharp *tch* through her teeth.

Ainela feels the small fingers in hers twitch. She wants to offer the Mila comfort, but she doesn't know how. She wants to look away from Klara's pain, but she can't do that, either. She watches Klara's hands, how they curl into fists, her nails biting her palms. She closes her eyes. Focus on the pain you can handle instead of the one you cannot. Somewhere in the room, a loud whistle begins as one of the girls stomps her foot and moves. More ashwater drenches her, searing up her neck. Her jaw clenches, her lips curl in pain. She doesn't look at Father Ignacy, but on the wall behind him—a crack in the stone. For half a heartbeat she is somewhere else—on her back, someone's shadow blotting out the light. The old terror claws up her throat, demanding a scream. She swallows it whole. She will not give them that sound.

It is only when a third splash slaps her face that she spits the water onto the floor. Her voice is low and venomous as it cuts through the air: "This will not cleanse you." She straightens her spine despite trembling in her legs. Her skin burns, Ainela sees blisters forming already, and Klara's chin quivering. But there is no scream. She meets Ainela's eyes as she walks by boldly. Don't give them what they want.

"Larisa."

The girl with the broken rosary. Her dark auburn hair flows long and unbound, er cheekbones are high, her eyes pale. When her name is called, her shoulders curl in. Instead of fighting, she walks calmly. It's not defiance. It's not anger. It's something else–acceptance. She doesn't look at anyone; her eyes lock on the floor. Her hands are tangled in her rosary, the only thing that seems to keep her upright. When Ainela sees her lips moving, she strains to hear. She catches the words on the first pass—soft, quick, nearly lost in the sound of dripping water.

Through my fault... through my most grievous fault...
The phrase loops again, quicker now, riding the rhythm of her breaths.

Mateusz steps forward. The first pour hits Larisa square at the collarbone, the stream bursting across her chest and soaking the rough linen. She flinches—not back, but inward—her shoulders curling forward like a gate closing.

She whispers faster.
Through my fault... through my most grievous fault...

The second pour sluices down her arms, raising gooseflesh. Ainela sees the tendons in her neck strain, the small tremor in her clasped hands. It's not that she doesn't feel the pain—it's that she seems to be swallowing it whole, trapping it inside herself before it can reach her face. By the third pour, the words have thinned into a ragged breath. Her lips keep moving even when no sound comes out. And when it's over, she stands dripping and silent, the beads of her broken rosary clicking faintly as she turns away.

When he calls Mila's name next, the little girl sobs, her fingers gripping Ainela's hand tighter. She shakes her head, screaming as Mateusz walks towards her, seeing that she isn't going to step forward. Ainela's breath catches in her throat. She tries to pull the girl, but she's not fast enough. The ashwater splashes her fast, over the shoulders. Mila screams, the child's terror bubbling through her fast as lightening.

And then –

"Iskra."

She doesn't move at first. The name seems to take a moment to reach her, as though it has to cut through water. When she finally stands, her steps are uneven, the left foot dragging just slightly.

Mateusz lifts the bowl. The water inside is darker now, the ash swirling in sluggish spirals. The first pour hits her square across the collarbone. She gasps and clutches the front of her dress as though the fabric might hold her together. The skin there is already pinked from cold — it mottles deeper, fast, as if the liquid is eating through her.

The second pour follows without pause. It runs down the inside of her arm, soaking her sleeve until the wool clings like a second skin. She jerks, a sound escaping her — not a scream, but a quick, involuntary cry, high and animal, gone almost as soon as it begins.

By the third pour, her breathing has gone ragged. The ashwater sluices over her shoulder and down her ribs, and where it touches, the skin rises in angry blisters. She doubles forward, one palm pressed flat to the floor for balance.

Father Ignacy doesn't speak this time. He just watches, eyes half-lidded, as Mateusz tips the last of the bowl over her head. The liquid streams down her scalp and into her eyes, her mouth. She spits black water onto the stone. When it's over, she stays on her knees, shivering hard enough that her teeth chatter. Her lips are turning a pale, bluish grey.

"Up," Ignacy says finally. The word is soft, but it lands like a blow. She tries — and fails. Tomasz steps forward, hauls her up under the arm, and shoves her toward the others.

She finds her spot without looking at anyone. The burn has taken her whole — not just her skin, but somewhere deeper, in a place she can't reach. Kaja is next. She doesn't look at the guards or the buckets. Her gaze stays on the thin strip of sky through the high slit, as if memorizing the color.

Her bath over quickly, she walks to stand beside Ainela. With her teeth and one hand, she twists her hair into a knot and binds it with a scrap torn from her own hem. The knot is small, tight, and perfect — a sailor's knot, though Ainela couldn't have named it.

"Kaja?" Ainela whispers, checking on her because the calmness seems unnatural.

"Some places let you go when people won't," she murmurs.

"Dying lets you go?"

"Ainela." The sound of Father Ignacy's voice makes her gasp. Her name cuts through the air like a thrown stone. She feels the room turn toward her — not in sympathy, but in the way one might turn to watch the axe fall. Mila's fingers slip from hers, small and warm a moment ago, now gone. She feels a brief hand touch her shoulder: Halinas's eyes steady her. You can do this.

Ainela steps forward because standing still feels worse. She steps forward because waiting is worse. Mateusz meets her halfway, the enamel bowl cradled in his hands. Part of her longs to knock it out of his grasp, watch it fall to the floor. But not even she is that brave.

The first pour is colder than she thought possible. The ashwater slaps against her chest and soaks instantly through her dress. It's not just cold — it bites, stinging every patch of bare skin like nettles made of fire. The taste of vinegar blooms in the back of her throat, though none has touched her mouth. She cries out–she didn't mean to, but the burn feels like skin melting. She flinches — not backward, not toward the door, but inward, curling around the pain. The shock drives the air from her lungs. As she struggles to breathe, she feels the others. The ones who are burning writhe in their own skin. The ones who still wait paralyzed with fear.

The second pour comes faster. It trails down her spine in thin, searing rivers. The chill of the stone floor under her boots feels a mile away; her world has narrowed to the burn where the ash grinds into her skin. Somewhere behind her, the whistle starts again — sharp, arrhythmic, almost bitten in half. She risks a glance and sees the same girl from earlier — Lenka, she remembers now — one hand cupped against her mouth, thumb pressed beneath her chin as though pinning a stem. Her lips shape the suggestion of petals between breaths. The sound falters when she sees Ainela looking. If they take your voice, spit in the dirt instead. The roots will keep it safe until you come back for it.

Focus. Focus. Focus.

Breathe. Breathe. Breathe.

The third pour strikes her head. The force bends her forward; the water streams over her face, into her eyes, her nostrils. She coughs hard, ash grit scraping her tongue. The vinegar smell is everywhere now, coating the air so that breathing feels like swallowing blades. *Caterbutton. Caterbutton. Caterbutton will you remember me?* The stinging is worse now, blisters forming on her skin. She straightens, though her legs tremble and her scalp prickles with pain.

Father Ignacy tilts his head, studying her. A faint smile touches his mouth; the kind a hunter might give a cornered animal that still refuses to drop. "Defiance," he says quietly, not to her but to the room. "It rots deepest when it hides behind silence." His gaze lingers a beat too long, as if committing her face to memory.

When Mateusz steps back, the hem of her dress drips black-specked water onto the floor. Her skin feels flayed. The cold rushes back to fill the places the fire has left.

She walks back to her spot, past Father Ignacy without looking at him, the echo of Klara's defiance ringing in her ears: *Don't give them what they want.*

Sometimes quiet is just the
loudest way to say no.

———————————————

margin note,
The Embergirls' Rhymebook

CHAPTER TWELVE

SILENCE DRILL

WHISPERROOT: A HUSHWOOD TALE

I t burns—oh God, it burns!"

"My eyes—my eyes!"

"I'm going to die. We're all going to die."

"I want to go home."

Coughs rattle the cold air. "My cough has black in it."

"It's the ash."

"I can't move. It hurts too much."

Ainela closes her eyes. Her sleeves scrape against raw skin; the fabric of the cotton shift feels as rough as pine nettles. The air feels icy against the burns. When she opens her eyes, she sees Larisa. Her hands grip the broken rosary, but that's not what Ainela notices. Larisa's eyes are closed. She inhales through her nose but, when she exhales, she parts her lips and breathes out slowly. She's been taught to endure.

Ainela tries it. She closes her eyes again, breathes in through her nose, then out through lips barely parted. Again. With the fourth breath, her heart rate slows. Her lungs open. Breathe. She keeps going until the moans, tears, and sounds of the room fade. Her world narrows until the only thing she hears is the intake and exhale of her own breath. Only when one of the younger girls says, "I can't take this anymore," does she open her eyes.

"I've seen you—you live on the edge of town. What's your name?"

"Kalina."

"Kalina." Ainela commits it to memory. "Close your eyes and take a deep breath through your nose. Like Larisa there is doing."

Larisa's eyes slide to Ainela's, but she says nothing. Kalina tries.

"It hurts, it hurts to breathe."

Ainela reaches over and touches the girl's hand. "Try."

The girl's sky-blue eyes blur with tears, but she does as Ainela asks. Kalina's forearm bears a thin, healing scratch—the kind a hushwood twig might give if it caught you just right. Over it, she's knotted a single loop of red thread, tight enough to stay through washing, loose enough not to cut her skin.

"What happened to your arm?" Ainela asks, gritting her teeth through the pain.

Kalina looks at the red thread on her arm. "A twig scratched me when I walked here."

"Oh. It's probably healed by now—you could take the thread—"

"No." The word is small, but the heat behind it makes pain flare behind her eyes. She presses her forearm to her chest as if to guard it. The red thread is no longer just a loop over a scratch—it's a tether, a mark she chose. Ainela doesn't ask again.

Ainela nods. "Okay. Just breathe."

"Iskra?"

Ainela slowly turns her head to see Halina edging closer to Iskra, who lays on the cold floor. The girl's hair, the color of ebony, is slick, blood staining the ends. Ainela hears Iskra's labored breathing. Halina purses her lips. Before she speaks, though, they hear the sound of the heavy oak door and footsteps.

WHISPERROOT: A HUSHWOOD TALE

Father Ignacy comes in with Tomasz and Jakub. Tomasz carries a bowl. He steps in front of each girl, allowing her to select a piece of bread and cheese. As he distributes the food, Father Ignacy stares at the girls, his eyes falling on Iskra first, then Ainela.

"You've received your purification. Our Lord did not complain or begrudge His wounds. He asked forgiveness for those who mocked Him. Pain, you see, gives you an opportunity to reflect on your sin and make peace with your Creator. Teaches you humility. Something each of you need. Tomasz, the cloth."

Tomasz quickly passes him a strip of black fabric. The way it folds in Ignacy's hand catches Ainela's eye — the hem is finished with the same precise hand-stitching she saw once in a robe scrap on the corridor wall. This cloth, though, bears no initials, only faint ghost marks where stitches were picked out. Father Ignacy runs his thumb over the edge as though remembering something before his gaze sharpens again. Ainela's eyes lock on the cloth—that shade of black, the way it folds in his hand...

"We're going to have a holy day of silence. There will be no words spoken for the next twenty-four hours. Tomasz will put this cloth on the door as a sign. Until it is removed, there will be no words. Tomasz and Jakub will monitor you for me. Do you understand?"

He waits, his gaze falling heavy on each of the girls, looking for signs of disrespect or resistance. Some look down. A couple meet his gaze. He says he'll see them tomorrow, and then, as he walks through the doors, Jakub closes it behind him. He stands with his feet braced apart, his face unreadable. Tomasz shuffles, walks around the room. When he bends his head to within inches of Ainela's face and says, "Boo," she swallows a reaction. Instead, she lifts her gaze above him to stare at the black cloth on the door.

"I can do it." Zosia's voice breaks through like cold water. On Remembrance Day, Zosia wanted to tie the black ribbon to the hushbark. She wanted to tie it high on the branch, as tall as Ainela, so that the breeze would be sure to lift it.

"I don't like black ribbons," she said matter-of-factly. "Why is black the color we use to remember people we care about?"

She fumbled with the ribbon, the knot a little off-center. Ainela answered, "Black just means we're sad they're gone."

"Is everyone sad they're gone?"

Ainela blinks, shaking the memory from her mind. Focus. Focus. Twenty-four hours with no words spoken. She can do that. Her eyes flit around the room silently. Larisa fingers the rosary, the beads twirling faster. Mila mouths a question: "What if we have to go to the privy?" Ainela gives a tiny shake of her head.

The younger ones might have a hard time remembering. She'll help them. She sees Halina looking around—she's likely doing the same—and Klara's chin tilts upward just enough to notice. Protectors. Kaja crowds near the air vent where faint smells of smoke and pine drift in. She won't speak. Lusia hasn't said a word; she won't speak. Tatiana... Lenka... Joanna... would they? What happens if they do? She opens her mouth to speak the question, but Klara glares at her, shaking her head. She doesn't want to risk a group punishment, so she closes her mouth.

WHISPERROOT: A HUSHWOOD TALE

The air already feels heavier. The girls around her shift, swallow, avoid each other's eyes.

It begins.

Time slows when there are no words.

Sound reminds you that you still live.

Every time someone's tin cup scrapes against the stone, flashes of Zosia's enamel mug wobbling on the table shift through Ainela's memory. The mug is chipped because, once, a rat scurried across the floor, surprising Zosia. The cup fell as she shrieked and jumped away. There's a *drip drip drip* from the ceiling above Lenka. Ainela times it–*one, two, three*– a water droplet drips every three heartbeats. Grimly, she wonders how long it might take to fill this room and drown them all. The thought scares her, and she shakes her head, looking for something else. There are two candles burning–one flickers as it struggles for fuel and gives a *crackling* sound. Tomasz's boots have stilled. He adopts the same posture as Jakub, who eyes him with a thin layer of tolerance.

Klara sits angled toward Mila, her shoulder a quiet barrier between the younger one and Tomasz. Halina still sits in the same place–by Iskra's side. Lusia and Tatiana hug the far wall, avoiding the guards' line of sight. Ainela swallows. Some of them–Lusia, Klara, Kaja, Iskra–have wounds the others do not. Kaja's lip is split, and she carries the weight of a deep purple and black bruise high on her right cheekbone, just beneath her eye. Iskra's body is a map of bruises and cuts; earlier, Ainela watched her limp for the ashwater bath. Blisters tear at everyone's skin, but Iskra's bleed. A deep gash mars her hairline. Lusia's bruises aren't as deep or as black, but long scratches like claw marks line her arms.

Everyone moves differently after this morning's punishment. Raw skin rubs against fabric; girls wince after the smallest movements. The smell of damp ashwater lingers in the straw, sour and smoky.

Joanna's fingers wag, as if she's trying to get her attention. She slides her eyes to the guards, but neither are watching. Joanna points to Iskra. Ainela casts one more look towards the guards, swallows carefully and stands, wincing when the burns stretch and roll across muscles. She lowers herself beside Iskra, putting a hand on the girl's back. Iskra flinches, sucking air up her nose with a *whsh*. Ainela hears a loud, angry sigh and looks up to see Klara staring at her. She lifts her eyebrows, slices a glance at the guards, and shakes her head. She mouths, "Not now."

Ainela doesn't listen.

She looks at the wounds on Iskra, notices Jakub watching her. He lifts his brows as if daring her to speak. Frustration blooms deep. She just wanted water for Iskra, but the silence drill turns need into shame–if you ask for water, you've broken the rule. Iskra won't ask for herself. Every movement, every glance, every act of kindness comes with a risk.

Ainela glances at the blisters forming on Iskra, but her eyes linger on the welts; she notes how Iskra curls into herself if someone touches her. The sound of boots scuffling outside the door makes the girls turn their heads, all at once, to stare, breath held, until the noise fades.

She bends her head backwards until it rests against stone. Across the room, Kaja is fixed on the air vent, her trembling hand lifting and lowering in a slow rhythm, like wind passing through a hushbark's branches. Lenka picks at the straw strewn on the floor, rolling pieces between her fingers. Another bites her nails. When Ainela notices Lusia moisten her lips and then pick up her tin cup only to set the empty vessel down, she offers her the only thing she can: her own tin cup with water still in it. Lusia frowns, shakes her head, turns away.

Ainela feels the refusal like a slap.

She can't help Iskra.

She can't help Mila.

Lusia doesn't want her help.

She can't speak.

She *could* speak. What if she did? What if she screamed? It wasn't a word. He said there could be no words. The anger coils tighter and tighter inside her, a fire reflected in the way her lip crinkles up. It's not just anger, though. She's still damp from the ashwater, and cold. She's not the only one. Joanna's lips have a bluish tint to them, and she shivers. Mila taps her and points to the door. She mouths, "When will we go home?" Ainela puts a finger to her lips, her eyes lifting to see the guards. She looks back at Mila, clasps her hands together, lays her cheek on them like a pillow and closes her eyes. *Sleep.*

Tatiana picks at the fabric and breath hisses through her teeth as she peels it from her skin to see the festering wound beneath. In candlelight, Ainela watches as Halina points to the water in Tatiana's cup, then to her skin. *Wash it.* Tatiana picks her cup up, looks at Halina, who nods, and then pours a small drop of fresh water over the burn. Her face scrunches, tears dot her eyes. Halina mouths something Ainela can't see. Tatiana shrugs, shakes her head: she didn't understand either. Halina takes one hand in the air and mimes scrubbing. *Clean*. Water will keep the wound clean. Ainela looks at her own sores. She thinks about cleaning it but then decides she doesn't want to run out of water to drink more than she wants to clean the blisters.

She can't yet see the stars out the window.

Time slows when there are no words.

Shadows deepen. Those in the corners are barely seen. Unable to stay as still as Jakub, Tomasz has walked down the corridor again. Some girls sleep. Some stare into space. Ainela's eyes glue to the crack in the wall. It's on the wall just across from her. It might be a bit taller than she is but, if she stood on her toes, she could reach it. She wonders how deep it is: it looks as deep as some of the gashes they share. Deep enough to hold something? Ainela wonders. She notices a spider crawling on the stone near her but makes no move towards it. It can go where it wants. The small thing with its black body and spindly legs moves freely. Up to the ceiling? Across the floor? Under the heavy oak door? It is not trapped. Jealousy is the knot that tightens in her chest the longer she watches it move—slow, deliberate, sure of where each leg will land. It will find a corner, spin its threads with a patience she doesn't have, weaving both a home and a trap in the same breath. Its silk will glisten, impossibly fine, impossibly strong, and she hates that it can hold what she can't. The spider will wait—and the world comes to it. No running, no pleading, no scraping for scraps. Her own hands are tender and clumsy, empty of the skill to spin anything. Her body is too long, too wide; she can't slide unnoticed anywhere. The jealousy prickles under her skin like the idea of being watched and, in the quiet between heartbeats, she wonders if the spider even notices her at all.

She pulls her gaze away, her heart *thump thump thumping* hard in her chest.

She just wants to go home.

She shares a bed with her sister–sometimes they laugh about nothing. *It was a big snowball–and I threw it hard! It hit him right behind the shoulder blades. He said I'd unlocked the snow monster, come to get me!* They would laugh until their sides hurt. They would laugh until Mama shushed them from the other room. The fire made sure they never got too cold and, even in the dead of night after it went out, there were layers of blankets to snuggle under.

The sound comes as a jolt after so many hours of silence, just a murmur, quiet. "Don't step on her toes." Ainela's gaze flies around the room. Halina and Klara both move at the same time as Ainela–sliding closer to the girl lying on her side. Tatiana. The girl is just a year or two younger than Ainela, a dancer. She dances in the meadow. *I loved your dance*, she told Ainela the night of the festival. "Faster, before they hear the music," the last word frays into a tiny whimper and her breathing quickens as if she's being chased. Halina shakes her as they hear heavy boots stomping down the corridor.

No, no, no.

Tomasz's energy fills the room as he steps into the darkened space. His eyes adjust, look around, land on Tatiana. He chuckles as he sees the girls huddled around her. When he reaches down and grabs her blistered arm, Tatiana wakes, disoriented, begging. "What did I do? What did I say? Please, no. I'm sorry."

The sound of Father Ignacy's voice speaking to Jakub in the corridor.

Ainela covers her mouth with her hands, biting her tongue to keep from speaking. The muffled screams that drift through the hallway make the silence heavier. Tears streak the faces of some girls. Kaja repeatedly hits the back of her skull against the stone gently, slow, steady, almost like a rhythm only she hears. Larisa catches Ainela's gaze and the fury shooting like arrows from her pale eyes surprises her.

Ainela forces herself to breathe evenly, her hands still pressed to her mouth. From the shadows, Kaja's voice drifts low, meant for her alone. "Prayers won't keep them from coming for you." The words are flat, certain — not cruel, but without mercy. Ainela swallows hard, unsure if it's a warning or a promise. A heartbreaking scream pierces the night that makes even Jakub, who stands by the door, wince. Creaking of wooden planks.

When Kalina wraps her arms around herself, her fingers tapping the red thread wound tightly around the scratch like it's the only thing keeping her together, her eyes wild with fear, and Mila bites her knuckles, an idea sparks in Ainela's mind. Something she used to do when Zosia was scared. She waves a hand to get Mila's attention. When the girl watches her, she slides a glance to Jakub. He's got his eyes closed. She takes two fingers and taps the back of her hand two times, waits for the space of two heartbeats, then taps three times. She repeats. Two taps, two breaths, three taps, three breaths, repeat. Tapping a rhythm. She nods at Mila. *You try.*

Mila looks skeptical, the frown saying more than words. Ainela keeps tapping, gentle and steady.

WHISPERROOT: A HUSHWOOD TALE

Kalina's voice slips in under the sound, so soft it could be mistaken for breath: "If they take me, it'll be for telling the mayor's sweaty son to keep his hands to himself."

Mila's grin is quick, audible in her whisper. "Better than getting locked in the bell tower for climbing it."

Her fingers join the rhythm.

Ainela blinks at the ceiling, thinking how many 'sins' in this room were just girls refusing to be small. Ainela taps.

Soon, Lenka joins. Johanna.

Ainela mouths, *Are you okay?*

Mila taps twice. *Does it help?*

Mila hesitates. Taps three times. *Yes.*

Tears sting the backs of Ainela's eyes. Looking at Klara, she tries again. She mouths, *Will she come back?* Klara sits for a long time. Taps three times. Then frowns, shrugs, taps two times. Looks away.

Hours later, most girls lay asleep, when the door opens, creaking on its hinges. Only Tatiana enters. She limps, her shift in disarray, the edge of its back tangled in itself, riding high on her leg. Her muscles are stiff as she lowers herself to the straw, then folds into herself, bringing her burned legs to her chest. She faces the wall, but Ainela sees the imprint of a signet ring in Tatiana's tender side. She swallows hard.

The stillness is heavy when there are no words.

Ainela's eyes drift close, her brain floating somewhere between sleep and wakefulness. Her breathing deepens. She listens to the dam air settle. Then—a low hum, almost mistaken for the draft through the vent, until it shapes into something achingly familiar.

Halina.

Kołyska bez słów. The cradle without words.

Mama. The smell of apple skins rises in her nose before she understands why.

It slips under her skin like a hand she hasn't felt in years. Mama used to hum it in the kitchen, usually with the words still attached — sparrows sleeping in the rafters, the moon in a silver coat — but only when she thought no one was listening. Ainela had once asked where it came from.

Mama was slicing apples for drying, the knife tip working quick and sure. "Before the war," she said, "there was a girl who lived in the hollow of the hushwood. She had no mother, no father, only the sparrows and the moon to keep her." Mama's eyes stayed on the blade. "She never spoke a word, but she could hum the stars to sleep. And when the soldiers came to take the children, she hummed so quietly they walked past her. They say she still hums for lost ones."

Ainela had been small enough to ask, "Will she hum for me?"

Mama's answer had been a quick, fierce "No." Then, softer: "I won't let you need her to."

The tune curls around her ribs, squeezing, and she's back in the cellar–the smell of straw, ashwater, unwashed skin pulling her back. Ainela wants to hate Halina for humming, for making her remember the sound of home, but the tune seeps through anyway. The ache feels as sharp as the blade Mama used to slice the apples. She recalls the last hug her mother gave her–before she became a reminder of Mama's shame. The smell of herbs–thyme and rosemary. The softness of her bosom against her head, the warmth of her arms around her.

She presses her fist to her mouth.

She will not cry.

She wants to go *home*.

Home is a cluster of roofs pressed close together, their chimneys leaning toward one another as if whispering in the cold. The streets are narrow and uneven, cobbled in places, packed earth in others, worn smooth by boots and cartwheels. In summer, the air smells of bread rising and damp wood drying in the sun. In winter, smoke clings to everything — your hair, your scarf, the wool of your coat — so that even when you walk out into the hushwood, you carry the village with you.

Every door has its own sound when it closes — a rattle of loose hinges, a low groan of swollen wood. Every gate leans a little in the same direction, bowed by years of wind from the east. The chapel bell isn't quite in tune; when it rings, the last note always drops a little too low, like a sigh.

There's a narrow lane behind the baker's that catches the morning sun before anywhere else. A frozen puddle there always cracks first underfoot, making a sound like splintering glass. The market square holds the echo of every laugh and argument you've ever heard there — the noise bounces off stone walls and lingers.

It's a place that scolds you for leaving but bruises you for staying, a place you swear you'll leave but find yourself mapping in your head every time you close your eyes. *Home*. The word is heavy as it is warm. She does not wipe away the salty tears that streak a slow path down her cheeks and into the corner of her lips.

The hum swells until it is no longer Halina's alone. One voice becomes three, then more, soft as breath against the stone. It threads down through the straw, slipping into the earth, winding its way along the roots that lie listening in the dark. Ainela closes her eyes, letting it carry her, and for the first time since the cellar door closed, she does not feel alone.

Mark yourself where they can't see.
The body keeps the memory
the way trees keep the rings.

———

margin note,
The Embergirls' Rhymebook

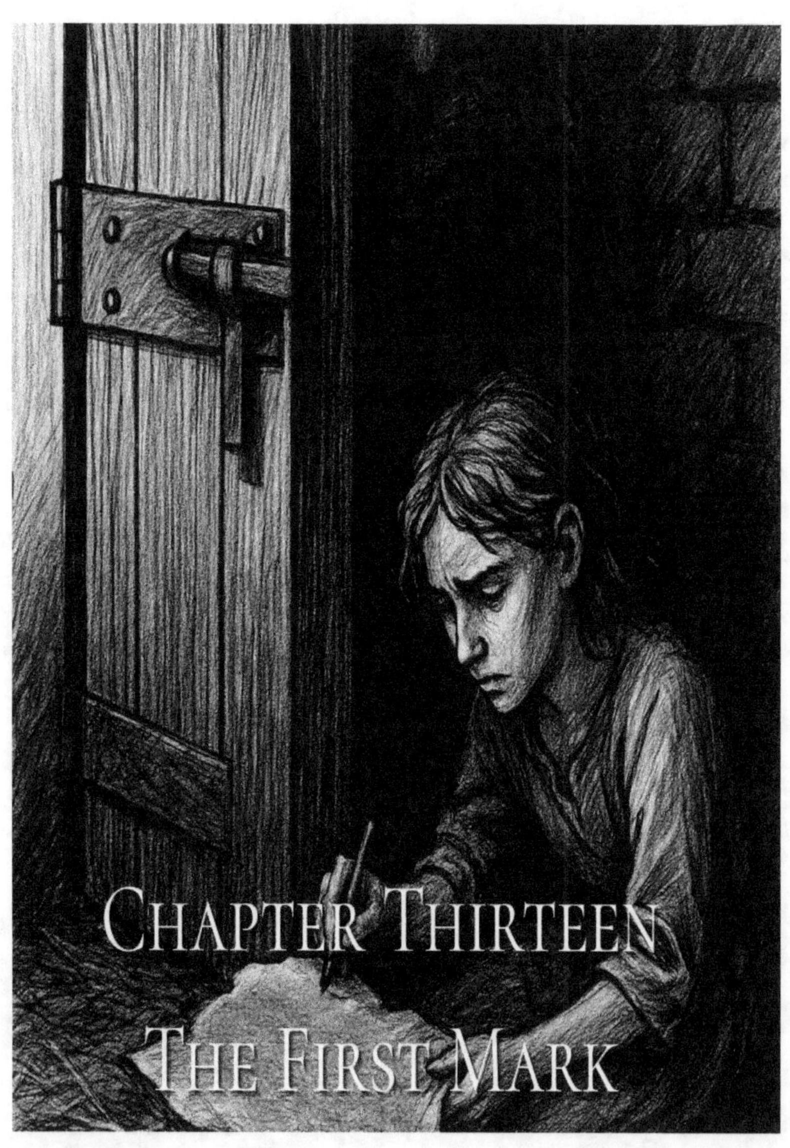
Chapter Thirteen
The First Mark

WHISPERROOT: A HUSHWOOD TALE

W hat are you looking for?" Lenka's voice is small. Her hair, the color of dirt, is cropped short. Ainela vaguely remembers Zosia's story of a girl with dimples being sent home from school after the teacher saw lice. The children laughed when she came back with hair cut to her ears. Father Ignacy's sermons talked about how godly women should dress and keep their hair long. Lenka slides closer to Tatiana, so her voice doesn't rise above the group.

Joanna picks through the straw. A small sigh. "Didn't you see the rat last night?"

"Rat?"

"I saw a spider," Ainela says.

"A small rat?" Mila asks.

"*Small*," Joanna's large blue-green eyes the color of the ocean widen. "This thing was the size of me."

"That big?" Lenka asks, her lips twitching.

"I woke up because he was nibbling on my toes." Joanna pushes the straw back in place over the packed earth, claiming the "rat king" must be gone.

Another muffled laugh.

The cellar still feels damp, but the dusky light that seeps through the tiny window pushes away most of the shadows. Ainela lifts her hand high, spreads her fingers, and watches the tiny dust motes float through the cracks of her fingers.

"Do you hear them?"

The air in the cellar is thick with the smell of damp stone and stale straw. The muffled rise and fall of a hymn bleeds through the floorboards above them, the rhythm of voices like the distant churn of a river no one can see. The words are too far away to catch, but the sound stirs memories that braid familiarity with anger and hurt.

Zosia is there. Mama is up there.

Ainela pictures them, standing on either side of Papa, coats piled high in the space that used to be hers. They hear a brief silence and then more song. The noise makes the silence feel... lonely as a lost soul. The flow of music fades, feet shuffle as people sit. They wait. It comes soon: a single voice, muffled but strong. He's too far away for the girls to hear the words, but they hear him all the same. Using a calm, almost *comforting*, voice to rail against temptation.

Iskra tilts her head, dark hair sliding over her cheek. "If I time it right," she says softly, her voice almost dreamy, as if the imagery of her words inspires her somehow, "I'll leap from that bell tower straight into his soup as he says *amen*."

The laugh that follows is quick and bright — gone almost before it begins, as if the air itself remembers how quickly joy can be taken.

Klara snickers.

Ainela smiles before she can stop herself.

Tatiana crosses herself with exaggerated solemnity. "Oh, Saint of Ruined Sermons–pray for us."

Halina crouches in the dim light, the cold earth staining her knees. She unravels the rag bound to Iskra's calf, careful not to tug at the crusted edges where the wound has begun to fester. The skin beneath is angry, rimmed in shadowed bruising — the kind of hurt that deepens in silence when no one tends it.

From the pocket of her shift, Halina pulls a twist of blue cloth, its corners tied tight. When she unknots it, the scent of dried herbs spills into the air — sharp and green, like a memory of the forest.

Across the straw, Kaja lifts her head. Her eyes half-close, like she's listening to something the rest of them can't hear. Kalina, nearby, pulls her knees up, knotting the red thread tighter around her wrist. She doesn't speak. Ainela notices the way she stares at the floor — like it might open and swallow her if she waits long enough.

Halina crushes the brittle leaves between her palms, pinching them into the shallow tin lid she's stolen from some forgotten pantry. Into this, she works a lump of yellowed animal fat, folding and pressing until it loosens into a slick, dark-green paste.

Next to her, Tatiana sits with a scrap of straw in her lap, quietly braiding it into a small, crude figure. Iskra watches her through the corner of her eye. "One-eyed again?" she says, grinning despite the pain.

Tatiana smirks. "Sees better that way."

A muted ripple of amusement moves through the girls. Ainela watches from across the straw, her back against the wall. She knows the rations barely keep them fed, that Halina has to save and scrape for every scrap of fat. On days when no meat comes, she mashes bread into water instead, making do. It isn't just skill — it's stubbornness, the refusal to let the wound win.

"Tell me when it hurts," Halina murmurs as she spreads the salve, her voice low enough that it won't carry.

Iskra winces, then grins, breathless. "I'll tell you when it doesn't." It's a weak joke, but it pulls the corners of Halina's mouth into the smallest smile.

Above them, the hymn swells, muffled and slow, and for a moment Ainela swears the cellar smells less of mildew and more of something clean — a fleeting ghost of the outside world.

Kalina stretches her legs out, idly tugging at the red thread around her scratch. "If they take me, it'll be for telling the mayor's sweaty son to keep his hands to himself."

Mila grins. "Better than getting locked in the bell tower for climbing it."

Lenka smirks. "Better than slipping a dead beetle into the communion bread."

Joanna picks a splinter from her palm. "Better than getting caught painting the chapel door."

Tatiana snorts, not looking up from her one-eyed doll. "Better than dancing barefoot on the altar steps."

Iskra titles her head. "Better than leaping from the bell tower straight into Father Ignacy's soup."

The laughter that follows is a fragile thing, like glass–quick, bright, and gone almost before it begins, as if the laughter itself remembers how quickly joy can be taken.

WHISPERROOT: A HUSHWOOD TALE

When they hear laughter and talking outside, Ainela is still holding onto the ghost of her smile, the last flicker from Iskra's soup joke curling faintly at the edge of her mouth. She is the first to move to the window, stretch onto her toes, her fingers gripping the windowsill. But they're under the chapel—no one can see them, and they can't see anyone. Only the tops of the hushwood forest and a sky that looks so far away.

"Ainela," Klara hisses, a heartbeat after the sound of boots scuffling outside threads under the door. Ainela gasps, turns and slides down the stone wall. When the heavy oak door opens, it swings back, nearly bumping her folded knees.

Jakub steps into the room, legs spread apart, his eyes slowly bouncing from one girl to the next. They land on Iskra, linger a moment, but then slide to Joanna. Mila. When they reach Klara, his gaze hardens. "You. Let's go." His voice betrays nothing.

Confused, Ainela frowns.

Go? Go where?

She notes: the way fear sparks Klara's eyes like a tidal wave, the defiant tilt of her jaw, the way she hugs her arms tight against her sides as she walks, the fine trembling of her fingers. She sees Kaja's eyes meet Klara's—only briefly, only for a moment —before Kaja's lips start moving, whispers without words, only the *swush swush* of a quietness that carries a sense of intimacy, of vulnerability. Ainela doesn't realize her hand slides beneath the door, curling around the bottom of it, until her fingers tighten just before the door clicks shut.

"Where is she going?" she asks in a soft voice.

"Maybe it's a chore, to help clean after the service." Mila's voice holds confusion. She feels the sense of tightness in the air but doesn't understand what causes it.

A cry that doesn't sound like Klara makes Ainela move. She scrambles to her knees, then her feet, moving to the edge of the door. It's cracked just enough for her to see the corridor.

There, against the far wall beyond Jakub's shoulder, sits a narrow linden-wood box on a high shelf. The grain is pale, the lid scorched at one corner as though it's been in a fire. Even from here she can see the lock — small, delicate, like a clasp on a jewelry case. Dust rims the edges, but the clasp gleams, recently oiled. For a moment she wonders what's inside, but Jakub shifts, blocking her view. When the space clears again, the box is still there, quiet as something waiting to be forgotten.

Shadows lace the staircase; a man's back is to her, but Ainela recognizes the curve of his spine, the shade of his skin. Klara is in front of him–Ainela only catches glimpses of her as she struggles to free herself from his arm. Suddenly, without warning, Father Ignacy's right arm draws back. The sound of the slap across Klara's cheek and the threadbare moan from her, like a tortured animal, makes Ainela's heart leap into her throat.

She wants to step out.

She wants to scream.

But she is frozen.

Her face pales as she watches Father Ignacy bend, pull, push. There are words, but she can't hear them — the roaring in her head drowns them out. The only thing louder is Klara's screams, ragged at the edges, pulling air like someone trying to stay above water.

WHISPERROOT: A HUSHWOOD TALE

Suddenly, Klara twists, breaks free, scrambles. Ainela's throat closes as she watches her lunge for the stair. Jakub stands planted against the only way out, his boots braced wide. His gaze fixes high on the wall, not on her — as if looking away could make him something other than what he is.

Father Ignacy chuckles. It's soft, almost companionable, but he moves with the precision of someone who knows how to catch what's running. His hand closes around Klara's arm, yanking her backward so hard her shoulder juts at an unnatural angle. She slams into the wall, the breath leaving her in a short, startled grunt. Her palm finds bare stone, fingers clawing for any edge, as though the wall itself could open for her.

Ainela doesn't realize she's bitten her lip until the metallic tang of blood sears her tongue.

Father Ignacy drives her to the ground. Klara's legs kick once, twice, then curl in — a reflexive shelling in that even she can't control. Her hand shoots out again, slaps the stone hard enough to redden the skin. She cries. The sound changes in waves: screams thinning to moans, moans fraying into stuttering sobs. And then—small, almost hidden—her fingers curl in, clutching the rough stone as if to prove to herself she can still hold *something* that Is hers.

Father Ignacy's breathing grows heavier, the wet catch of it audible even to Ainela. Sweat beads along his temple, catching lamplight, and the hem of his cloak carries a fresh dark stain. The sight rips something in Ainela's mind; the man she's known as shepherd, vessel, voice of the Lord collapses into someone with a body that sweats, a mouth that hides behind its own hand, a shadow that stains cloth. If he can do this, what can't he do to any of them?

He runs a hand over his mouth, staring down at her. Klara's dress is hiked high, the fabric wrinkled and twisted. Her chin is tucked to her chest, her shoulders caved inward as though protecting her heart.

Ainela's never seen her like this. There's no spark in her eyes, no quick, teasing retort waiting on her lips. Is she still Klara, or has he replaced her with someone else — a shell of who she was before this moment?

Jakub's head shifts, just slightly, in the direction of the heavy oak door. Ainela flattens herself against the wall, stares at the group. Tears wet Lusia's lashes. Kaja stares at the vent, rocking back and forth. Fear tangles with the fury: she doesn't want to be seen near the cracked door. She hurries across the room, slides down into the corner where she sleeps, hugs her knees to her chest, her eyes glued to the door.

Hours pass before it opens and Klara walks in.

She limps–and it stirs a memory.

Tatiana.

After her dream, she was taken away and, when she came back, she limped, too.

Ainela moves, silently, to sit beside her. Lusia, already there, lays on the straw beside Klara. Gently, she reaches out and moves a strand of hair off Klara's face. Tatiana wordlessly places the corn doll - *the one-eyed corn doll who can see better* - in the crook of Klara's folded arm. Klara, breath catching, knuckles white, won't let go.

Klara's quivering lip spills into a fractured whimper.

When the sound splinters the room, Kaja crawls on her knees to sit at Klara's feet, completing the circle around her.

The guards–Mateusz now, and Tomasz–watch.

WHISPERROOT: A HUSHWOOD TALE

Clouds hide the moon and the room darkens.
And the packed earth beneath the straw shivers.

The door stays shut for a long time after Klara's breathing evens out.

No one says his name.

They don't have to.

The air already knows it.

When it comes–the whisper that breaks the silence–it's from Joanna, and it's different. Not *Father*. Just *Ignacy*. The name drops heavy into the straw between them, and something in Ainela's chest tilts. She has never heard him called that. She looks around; no one corrects Joanna.

No one flinches.

It's not much, but it's theirs.

The circle around Klara holds until the guards grow restless, shifting their weight, muttering to each other. The girls retreat one by one, curling into their straw. Kalina lingers at the edge of the circle, her knees drawn up, her fingers worrying the red thread at her wrist. The knot bites into her skin as she twists it, tighter and tighter, until the blood drains from her fingertips. She stares at the ground, shoulders hunched, as if trying to make herself invisible.

Ainela sits a little apart, knees drawn up, fingers pressed to her mouth as if to keep something from spilling out. She watches Klara's fingers shift — just barely — over the corn doll's belly, as though testing whether she can still hold something of her own.

The air in the cellar feels thick.

Ainela's gaze drifts to the far wall, where a jagged crack runs down between two stones. Someone, long ago, patched it with a torn page — yellowed and curling, the faint print still visible if she leans close enough. The words aren't the kind Ignacy would want her to see.

She picks at the edge until the paper loosens, slips it into her lap. It's small, no bigger than her palm. She glances toward the guards. They don't notice. From her shift pocket, she pulls a short, blackened stick — charcoal from a fire gone cold, saved for no reason she could name until now.

The stub of charcoal is dull, but she prints the name the way Joanna said it — without the title — and stares at it until the letters stop looking like letters and start looking like a wound.

She draws a line through it. Then another.

She hesitates, the taste of fear still sharp on her tongue. What if someone finds it? Her thumb worries the corner until the paper goes soft, the charcoal smudging her fingertips as though trying to leave her marked. But the thought of letting the day fade without keeping it — without keeping *her* — feels worse.

She bends over the scrap and writes, the charcoal's blunt tip dragging, leaving crooked lines. The first rhyme. It's not for him—never for him—it's for the girls, so that their names will be louder than his. She writes: not even real sentences, just fragments.

Lenka, weaving in the dark.
Joanna, salt laugh.

WHISPERROOT: A HUSHWOOD TALE

Mila, climbing past fear.
Tatiana… sees what others hear.
Klara, holding what's hers.

Her hand shakes as she writes it, pressing harder until the page almost tears. When she's done, she folds it twice, the way Mama used to fold clean handkerchiefs and tucks it deep into the straw where she sleeps.
It isn't much.
It's barely anything.
But it's the first.

They can strip you to bone,
but the right name
still fits.

———————————

margin note,
The Embergirls' Rhymebook

CHAPTER FOURTEEN

THREAD RITUAL

WHISPERROOT: A HUSHWOOD TALE

The door opens without warning.

No scrape first, no cough, no mercy. The hinge sighs and the room seals itself quiet as Mateusz fills the doorway, Tomasz a step behind him. Names are taken from the air like loose threads. Ainela's is among them. She feels the shape of it in her mouth the way you feel a chipped tooth with your tongue—small, irritating, unavoidable. It jolts the girls—lips thin, heads raise, shoulders tense, breath stills. Instead of slow and deliberate, the guards are quick today, rough.

They move through the room like dogs flushed from cover—snapping glances, grabbing arms, ignoring the startled gasps. The straw shifts under boots, leaving shallow hollows where girls had been moments before. A dropped comb skitters to the wall, forgotten. One girl cries out as Mateusz wrenches her to her feet; the sound dies almost immediately, muffled by the shape of a hand over her mouth. The smell of sweat rises in sudden waves as bodies stumble and collide.

Tomasz grabs Lenka's arm, pulls her up. Panic fills the air, but he doesn't take her out. Instead, he pushes her to the center of the room, then grabs the next girl, Tatiana, who sits closest to him. He points with a dirty, wrinkled finger to Ainela and then Kaja. "Stand here." Mateusz and Jakub are pulling girls into small groups. Iskra can't stop the whimper when Jakub grabs her shoulder, pushing her behind him.

Tomasz leads, his hand resting loose on the hilt of his belt knife.

They walk as small groups of four from the main room into the corridor. It smells of boiled soap and wet stone. The basement is larger than Ainela first imagined. It's not just one room, but a set of throats—one passage opens into a storage space, crates stacked high, old vestments slumped like shed skins, while another ends in a chamber with a long-splintered table and a dumbwaiter chained shut. Ainela notes the faint chalk marks on the wall where height was measured long ago, some lines smudged, some initials carved. She wonders if they were children from before, now gone. It presses a cold thumb into her chest.

Jakub pauses near the chalk wall, running his palm over the tallest line. "This one cried like a goat," he mutters, almost with a smile. Mateusz snorts. Neither says the name. Ainela stares at the gouged letters beneath, wondering if the girl is buried here or somewhere worse. The others keep their eyes low, as if sight alone could tie them to the memory.

The laundry room's ceiling is low enough to bow the taller girls. Copper pipes run like veins along the walls, ticking in their joints, and a rust-scummed boiler squats in the corner, exhaling in damp, hot breaths. Tubs line one wall, their water cloudy with heat. A bucket of lye soap sweats a sour smell. The air tastes like old coins. Ainela's eyes are still adjusting to the new room when Tomasz says, "Scrub until white." It is both permission and a command.

They obey without looking at him. Tatiana mutters the water will melt her skin; then she slides her arms in up to the wrist. Lenka follows, jaw locked, refusing eye contact with anyone who might be keeping a tally. Ainela pushes her sleeves and lowers her hands. The heat bites bone. Her knuckles go pink almost at once; cloth slaps wet stone. The smell—sharp lye and something faintly sweet, like flowers that rotted in a jar—swells through her head. The sound becomes the room's heartbeat. Above them, the chapel rearranges itself—footsteps crossing, boards complaining, a chair leg dragged a finger's width. Life continues where no one can see it. Down here, time sits.

The steam blurs the edges of the room until the girls are no more than shapes, each movement a smudge in the haze. The heat makes Ainela's temples pulse. The pipes sigh and pop in irregular bursts, the sound oddly human, like joints being cracked. Somewhere near the boiler, a slow drip marks seconds like a clock that only runs in this room. No one speaks. Words feel too heavy to carry through the air.

Lenka works fast, her sleeves rolled up past her elbows, the muscles in her thin forearms tensing with each scrub. Kaja kneels beside the second tub, wringing cloth so hard the water squeals between her fists. Tatiana hums under her breath—off-key, the notes broken into uneven lengths like she's hiding the real song inside another. Ainela scrubs. Soap foams. Her breath evens. The corner of the room at floor level gathers a rivulet that snakes across to the drain, carrying lint and the grit of someone's old skin.

Across from her, Lenka jerks her hands out of the water with a hissed curse. The cloth she's been scrubbing—one of the thinner shifts—hangs limp in her grip, its seam torn wide under the strain. The fray is raw, the red thread unraveling in long, damp strings. When she wrings it, steam curls around the gap like breath escaping.

"You'll get hit for that," Tatiana murmurs without looking up.

Lenka's jaw tightens. "It was already like this," she says, voice pitched low, but the defensive set of her mouth says she knows no one will believe her.

Ainela glances at the rip. It runs jagged, almost diagonal, and she imagines the scrape of wood or stone catching it, the sharp pull. She knows that kind of tear. A guard's hand. A stumble when you're shoved too fast through a door. Tomasz's gaze skims over them but doesn't pause.

"Leave it," Ainela says softly, her voice almost drowned in the slap of her own cloth. "I can fix it later." Lenka blinks once, startled, then gives the smallest of nods, folding the ruined shift to hide the damage. The look they share is quick, invisible to anyone not looking for it.
The thought of mending lodges in Ainela's ribs, but it's not mending that will keep her warm.

Tomasz stands in the doorway, not quite inside, not quite out, like a man who doesn't want steam in his shirt. "His sister used to do this," Tomasz says, voice low enough that for a heartbeat Ainela thinks he's speaking to himself. He isn't looking at any of them; he is looking at the water. "Said the smell never left her. Scrubbed till she bled."
There is nothing safe to say, so no one answers.

"She died young," he adds, almost idly. "He never forgave her for it."

Ainela's brow tics up, quick as a sparrow's wing. "For dying?"

"For what made her die." He doesn't explain.

The steam thins for a moment, and Ainela imagines the sister's shadow still bent over a tub in this same corner, hair damp with sweat, hands red from lye. She wonders if the sister once stood where she stands now, listening to the same pipes tick, smelling the same rot-sweet air. The thought lands in her bones with the weight of inevitability—someday another girl will stand here thinking the same about her.

WHISPERROOT: A HUSHWOOD TALE

Ainela imagines a girl with a shawl the color of blood, shoulders bent over the same tub, eyes watering from steam. She blinks it away before it can root too deep. The words hang a moment, heavy as a wet sheet, then sag into the steam. Tomasz shifts his weight. Ainela's hands keep to their work. But her mind takes the sentence, folds it twice, and tucks it into a place she can reach later. Red shawl. Picked stitches. The box on the shelf. A shape is forming in the dark.

Lenka is nearest the corner where the wall sweats a little more than the rest. She coughs once to cover the small sound of fabric against skin, then moves her body to hide her hands. When the guard's gaze drifts, she slides a coil into Ainela's palm without looking up. Red thread. Not much, a thimbleful looped around itself. Lenka's whisper barely stirs the steam. "We can mend with it," she says, as if that's all the thread can do.

Ainela's thumb strokes the coil once. Images race through her mind, clicking like postcards shuffling. Tatiana limping. Klara's hand slapping the wet stone, knocked to the ground. Iskra's scars. Her eyes dart to ensure Tomasz faces away, then down at the red thread. Mending their shifts will give Ignacy something less to complain about, one less reason to be punished. "We can mend," Ainela says slowly, her voice low, almost lost in the slap of wet cloth on stone. "But... we can also mark."

Lenka's eyes lift, quick and startled. Tatiana hears it, too—her humming falters, a note cut short. Kaja's hands keep wringing, but Ainela sees her head turn, just enough to show she's listening.

Tomasz shifts in the doorway, pulling at the seam of his cuff. Ainela tucks the thread deep into her sleeve before his gaze finds it.

The steam smell follows them down the corridor, clinging to their hair and sleeves. The floor sweats under their bare feet. At a turn where the light thins to near-dark, Mateusz stops the group with a palm up. The guards mutter to each other in short, clipped words, their backs turned. The girls stand in silence, shoulders brushing, breaths syncing without effort. Somewhere beyond the wall, a low thud carries—distant, hollow. A door? A shovel striking earth?

Ainela's eyes adjust slowly. She can just make out the seam in the stonework where one wall meets another. The mortar is darker there, damp as if the wall has been crying. She pictures what could be behind it: another room, another set of girls. She lets her gaze wander just enough to mark the cracks in the floor, the slight incline toward some unseen drain. It's not only water that moves through here. She can almost hear the slow crawl of it—a patient seepage that knows every path to take. The air itself feels older here, thick with the smell of stone that has kept too many secrets. The drip of the boiler room lingers in her ears as if she's carrying the sound with her.

Tatiana leans close enough for her breath to touch Ainela's ear. "They're counting," she whispers.

"Counting what?" Ainela murmurs back. But before there's an answer, Mateusz snaps his fingers for them to move on.

The air in the corridor is colder, metallic. Somewhere deeper in the stone, a faint hollow knocking repeats at uneven intervals, like someone trying to signal but too far to hear back. Ainela's scalp prickles. She wants to count the beats, match them to footsteps or shovels, but Mateusz's eyes cut the thought short.

WHISPERROOT: A HUSHWOOD TALE

The oak door closes, its bolt a dull click. Ainela waits until Tomasz leans his head back against the oak door, then she draws the thread into the circle of their knees. One by one, the other girls sit up, slide closer, tilt their heads to see.

"This isn't for them," she says. "It's not for mending."

She cuts the coil into uneven lengths with a sharpened sliver of tin, the kind the guards missed in a hem. They pass it hand to hand, each girl tucking her piece under a finger like it's a promise. "I'm going to sew something, something he can't see. Something he won't know about me. Something to remind me of..." She frowns, shakes her head, words failing her. "Something that matters." The girls watch as she sews three crooked stitches that lick upward against the grain—a flame.

As each girl works, Ainela notices the way shoulders drop, jaws loosen. A rhythm builds—not of the needle alone, but of breath finding a common pace. Tatiana threads it through twice to make an eye, wide and open, like the doll that sits in her straw. "I see things too." Kaja presses the point through thick cloth, pulling it into the shape of a hushwood leaf. Lenka stitches a loop, the kind that links chains together. Klara makes a sharp triangle, pointed down. "One day—I'll bite back," she says softly. Kalina sews a bird's profile. Larisa makes a broken rosary bead. Halina makes a sprig of herbs. "If we survive," she says softly. "Then we win." Iskra makes a small star. Mila—a ladder rung. "I can climb all the stairs."

When the last stitch is tied off, Ainela presses the hem of her shift flat against her skin, so that the patch is hidden in the seam. The thread is still warm from her touch. And the air—instead of lye and sweat—smells of promise.

For a long moment, no one moves. It feels as though the needle has sewn them together too, each girl bound to the others by something both fragile and unbreakable. Ainela exhales slowly, and the sound is echoed around the circle. They are silent, but not empty—every glance between them is full of something unnamed. Fingers brush knees. A thumb rests for a heartbeat too long on another's wrist before pulling away. The warmth of the thread seems to travel between them without ever leaving their hands.

A thud sounds somewhere beyond the door. Instinctively, the circle loosens. The pieces of thread are hidden again—slipped into seams, wound into hems, pressed flat against the inside of collars. The girls' faces return to stillness, but Ainela can see it in the set of their mouths, the deliberate pace of their breathing: the thing they carry now is heavier than cloth and lighter than air. Somewhere above them, a door slams, but it feels far away—like a noise from a different world.

"He can strip us," she says softly. "But he can't take this."

Small doesn't mean soft.
Mice bite when cornered.

———————

margin note,
The Embergirls' Rhymebook

CHAPTER FIFTEEN

THE SMALLEST SCRAP

WHISPERROOT: A HUSHWOOD TALE

Cold seeps through the packed dirt, drifts from the tiny vent, and lays its palm against the frost-laden pane. It steals even the memory of warmth, leaving breath to bloom ghost-pale in the empty air. To coax the shadows of heat closer, some of the girls lie so near their bodies touch. But the cold here is like their guards—unyielding, without mercy. It snatches comfort in a heartbeat; sleep becomes only an idea.

Ainela studies a small stain on the ceiling—irregular, its edges rounded, curling and fanning like waves. A water stain: brown thinned in places, deeper in others. It reminds her of other things that fade—the bright colors of leaves in fall, ink starving to gray on a damp page, a red ribbon weathered to pale, the laughter of Myreska's girls. Around her, she hears the faint rustle of breath and shifting straw. Larisa rolls the rosary beads between her fingers, her lips murmuring a prayer with no end. Kaja stares at the air vent, moving her hand slowly to catch the flow. Most of the others are asleep.

Ainela's gaze drifts from the ceiling to the narrow window slit. Sometimes, late at night, the wind whistles softly enough to rattle the glass panes. The slit is high; all she can see are scraps of sky and the dark tips of hushwood trees. On clear nights like this one, she can count twenty-two stars. Sometimes the moon appears—tonight, though, it hides behind a cloud. She used to tell Zosia the brighter the moon, the more wishes people made that night. *If it's hiding,* she said cheekily, *I'll make my wishes on the stars then.*

No, Ainela replied, *the stars aren't really for wishing. Stars are for praying; that's why there are so many. To hold everyone's prayers.*

Does everyone have their own star?

No–they only hold one prayer at a time. Stars that hold the prayers waiting for God are the ones that twinkle the brightest. Once the prayer is answered, it dims a little until it takes a new one.

Her eyes find the tiny twinkling dots in the sky.

Has Zosia sent up a prayer to God that's being held by one of these stars?

I should be the one praying. A burst of shame bubbles in her chest.

She doesn't want to pray.

Evil girl. Good girls pray.

Ainela swallows and tries to think of something to say. Larisa's beads click, a prayer that doesn't end. She's just as trapped. But every time Ainela starts to form the words, Father Ignacy's voice intrudes—thick with judgment, bristling with rules, his eyes turning prayer into a test she can only fail. It makes her throat close. She wants the kind of prayer she once whispered with Zosia under the hushwood sky, not the kind that feels like kneeling beneath his gaze. She turns her eyes back to the stars. Somewhere, they're still holding the good prayers safe.

The shifting of straw and a low moan pulls Ainela back to the cellar.

Klara.

Ainela moves into a sitting position, her back resting against the cold stone wall, her eyes gliding across the girls until they land on Klara. She lies on her side, her knees bent, her hand clamped over her ribs. Restless, her head jerks, rolling into the crook of one arm. The quiet moan splinters into a sharp intake of breath.

Lying on one side of Klara, Tatiana shifts closer. She doesn't touch her, but she watches, her lip pulled between her teeth. Ainela twitches, her arm reaching out as if to gently wake her, but then her fingers curl into her palm, her arm dropping slowly. What if waking her makes it worse?

"She's shaking," Lusia whispers. Her jaw is tight, her eyes glisten in the darkness.

Ainela sees. The tremors start in Klara's hands but then spread to her shoulders. "No–not again...." she moans, rolling to her back, her legs restless. "Please... I can't–" her voice sounds raspy. Suddenly, her knees jerk apart as if forced, then slam shut, quick as lightning. The trembling spreads to her legs. The frayed, gray blanket tangles around her as if she's struggling against hands only she can see.

Across the room, Ainela sees Kaja grip her own blanket to her mouth, her gaze fixed, unblinking. Ainela feels her own heartbeat pound heavier against her chest. The fear that grips the room, that haunts Klara, is like ash—coating, choking, never fully gone. The weight of it thickens with every moan and whispered plea from Klara. She shakes, twists, her head restless–until, without warning, she cries out, "No! It hurts; it hurts..."

Some of the girls shift, whisper the guards might hear. Some sleep through it. Tears slide down Lusia's cheeks. Kaja covers her ears with her palms. The room holds its breath. Inhaling and exhaling become something Ainela has to remember to do, one breath at a time.

Without warning, Klara bolts upright, her eyes wide and wild with terror. She gasps as if she were held under water and brought back to the surface just before she drowns. Her hair is damp at the temples. Her eyes skim past everyone, snag for a second on Ainela's, then flee. There's a flash of recognition that softens the panic – *she's in the cellar, he's not here* – before she pulls her knees up, grips the back of her neck with both hands, and sobs. Her shoulders shake violently.

The room stills.

The air feels sad.

Ainela's own eyes mist. Her fingers move on their own to the scrap of yellow paper against her ribs. They brush against the curled edge; she takes it between her fingers and rubs, imagining the charcoal smudging her skin. The seam in the stone returns to her, and with it the feeling that the house keeps making more rooms for girls she hasn't met yet. The guards' boots thud distantly above; the sound fades quickly but Klara folds further into herself, shrinking as if the only thing that might save her is to disappear. Ainela presses the paper flat. One voice is too easy to erase. This place will take more than her. She counts the names she knows, then leaves a space, and another—empty places where the mind insists someone belongs.

Lenka sits stiff-backed on the bench, her shoulder seam hanging open like a mouth that's too tired to close. The tear runs almost to her collarbone, fraying in pale threads that curl from the cloth like frost-bitten grass. Ainela pulls her own hem toward her lap, finds a spot where the stitches have loosened, and works two fingers inside. With a slow tug, she frees a length of thread—thin, softened by wear. She smooths it between her palms, coaxing the kinks away. She's halfway through threading the needle when Iskra's voice comes from the doorway.

"Careful, or it'll look like the chapel seamstress got angry at the cloth again."

Ainela glances up, her eyes curious. "And how would you know?"

"I saw her once," Iskra says, crossing the room in long, deliberate strides. "She sewed like she was punishing the fabric for speaking out of turn. All puckers and knots— looked ready to bite the priest if he dared wear it." Her mouth tips in a half-smile, the kind that makes her eyes catch the light. She perches beside Ainela without asking, close enough that Ainela catches the faint scent of something warm—not here-warm but remembered-warm. Ainela's thread catches; for a breath she sees that damp seam in the wall. She blinks it away, but the thought remains: *since me*.

"Used to help my mother mend things in her bread shop," Iskra says. "The smell of bread makes fabric behave– that's what she always said. You can't fight with a seam when there's yeast in the air—it makes you gentle. Like the dough might overhear you and sulk."

Ainela lets the image settle—the round loaves stacked behind Iskra's shoulder, steam breathing into her hair. She pictures the thread passing through cloth the way steam curls past crust, both things held together by patience.

She bends to her work, setting each stitch with quiet care. The tear closes under her hands, but she shapes the final few into a curve that flares at one side—a flicker no bigger than a thumbprint. It could be a leaf, or a petal. But she knows what it is meant to be.

A flame. Iskra notices. Of course she does. Her gaze catches on the tiny curve, and her mouth softens in something between pride and warning. "That's not chapel work," she murmurs.

"No," Ainela says, tucking the last knot beneath the seam. "It's better."

Lenka has been silent since she sat down, her face tipped away like a shuttered window. Now she looks over, her fingers lifting to the seam. "Thank you," she says, barely above a breath. The words are so small Ainela almost misses them, but the sound threads itself between them anyway. From the doorway, Joanna has been watching the seam instead of the faces. Her finger hovers, not touching.

"You kept the flame small enough to hide," she murmurs, as if speaking to the cloth. "Small is how fire survives walls."

Ainela gathers the scraps of pulled thread from her lap. Iskra doesn't move. Her elbow rests against Ainela's knee as if it belongs there, her eyes following each motion of the needle even though the work is done. The bench feels narrower than before, the air warmer. Trust, Ainela thinks, isn't loud. It's the way someone stays after there's no reason to.

Afternoon thins to a gray that flattens the corners. The cellar is quieter when the guards lose interest, a hush that feels borrowed rather than given. Ainela sits where the

light reaches far enough to make a pale square on her knees. The scrap rides the heat of her skin, warmed through the thin shift; she draws it out the way you would lift a sleeping child—slow, careful, an apology in her hands.
The page is the color of old teeth. The lines she wrote days ago look small now, a little river that thought it could carry a town. She sets it on her lap to hold the fabric steady and takes two stitches to pretend that this is only mending, only a seam, nothing dangerous.

Larisa is near enough to hear the paper whisper. She tilts her head, a listening dog. "What's that?" she asks softly, not reaching.

Ainela could hide it. Let it vanish back into her ribs and be hers alone. But Klara's night has not left her; it sits behind her eyes, the way tremors sit inside a muscle and wait. She keeps her voice level. "For keeping what shouldn't be lost."

Larisa's gaze slides to the faint strokes of charcoal. Not a prayer—something else. "Whose?"

"Mine," Ainela says. "For now." She tears from the edge, not across the line she wrote, but down, where the page is weakest. The sound is clean and small. She hands the sliver to Larisa with the nub of charcoal pinched between two fingers.

Larisa weighs both as if they might be hot. "Like a margin," she murmurs. "Like the space where you tell the truth beside the printed lie." The tiniest smile touches her mouth and vanishes. She writes one word—slow, careful— and then, beside it, dots a tiny bead as if a rosary could be shrunk to the size of a fly.

Iskra has been watching without looking like she's watching. She leans in on her haunches, palm open. "One for me." Not a question. Her tongue presses to the corner of her mouth, the way it did when she watched Ainela's stitches. Ainela tears again, this time from a thin wrapper she has been saving, paper already wrinkled into memory. Iskra prints: *Loaf on the step.* When she's done, she dusts her hands in the empty air, a gesture that looks like she is shaking flour from her fingers, like she is wiping something invisible and mean off her palms.

Halina returns from a trip to the bucket and stops short at the shape of them—Ainela's lap a flat altar, Larisa bent, Iskra bright-eyed. "You're going to get that taken," she says, voice low and flat. "They find a scrap, and it's gone."

"I'll keep it," Ainela says. "Like a sister." The words come without thought and lodge in her mouth.

Halina's face flickers. Anger first, then something more tired than anger. She doesn't move closer, but she doesn't move away. Ainela tears another thin strip and sets it on the page as if laying down a card. She does not offer it. She waits.

Halina's jaw works. Then she snatches the sliver as if the hesitation shamed her and writes with stiff, sharp letters that bite the pulp: *Ignacy.* No title. The name looks like a nail when she's finished with it. She doesn't hand the charcoal back. She drops it. Iskra catches it on instinct.

Larisa's mouth tilts. "If anyone above writes us down, they'll call us lost."

Joanna's gaze has been on Lenka's shoulder, on the small curl Ainela stitched there. "Not lost," Joanna says, lifting her head. "She stitched a flame. Embers don't die. They wait."

"Then not The Lost Girls' anything," Iskra adds, almost smiling.

WHISPERROOT: A HUSHWOOD TALE

"The Embergirls' Rhymebook," Joanna says, and the room warms without light.

Tatiana counts the air the way you count stitches. *Four in, hold two, four out.* She lays the words on Joanna's name: "Bank the ember. Lost is not gone." They repeat it where no lips move—chest to chest to chest.

Klara hasn't spoken all day. She has tracked the charcoal like a cat tracks a moth—no motion, only eyes. When Larisa passes her the page to read what has been born, Klara doesn't touch it, but her breath changes. It goes shallower, faster, like the small breaths you take when you've been running, and you are trying to pretend you have not.

Ainela tears one more scrap—small as a fingernail— and does not hold it out. *For the ones we might already be missing,* she tells herself and does not say aloud. She stacks the pieces—Larisa's bead, Iskra's loaf, Halina's nail, her own first thin line—wraps them in a strip of linen torn from the inside hem of her shift. It makes a soft parcel, no thicker than a thumb.

"If they search you—" Halina starts.

A scrape wanders the corridor.

Klara hears it first; fear shines white in her eyes. She moves without choosing to, sliding so her shoulder is between Mila and the door. Her hands tremble and then they don't. She doesn't want to be a wall. She becomes it anyway.

"I swallow the smallest one," Ainela says. The room inhales and doesn't let the breath go for a moment too long. She tucks the bundle flat against bone, beneath the place where her heart goes hard when she holds air. She thinks of the seam in the wall again and forces the image away the way you push a door when it swells in the rain.

A sound scurries along the baseboard. A mouse noses out, a little comma in the dust, black eye bright as a seed. It freezes, then darts for the crack, the line of its body a thought you can't catch once it starts moving.

"Small doesn't mean soft," Larisa whispers, almost smiling.

They breathe the refrain without sound—*Bank the ember. Lost is not gone.* Inside, the bundle of scraps feels heavier than paper. It feels like a coal that knows how to wait.

Near the wall, Iskra shifts, careful of the burns on her side. The raw edges look less angry tonight, the skin closing in a way it shouldn't after only a day. The scent of something faint and green lingers close to her—sharp, like crushed leaves pressed in a book too long. Ainela notices, though she does not name it. None of them do. In this place, even healing can turn dangerous if the wrong eyes see.

The room relearns how to be morning. Halina's hands make warmth where stone won't.

She sits with Mila's small wrist between her fingers and rubs slow circles where the pulse lives. "Count with me," she says, voice the size of a thread. "Four to bring it in, two to hold it still, four to let it go." Mila's chest obeys after a few tries, the tremble smoothing until the breath remembers its own steps.

"Bread mends more than hunger," Halina adds, tearing the heel from yesterday's crust and softening it with her breath. She presses the warm edge against the split in

WHISPERROOT: A HUSHWOOD TALE

Mila's lip and keeps it there with two fingers, patient as if patience could invent heat. "Hold. Don't lick."

Iskra watches the crust like a cat watches a sun patch. "You're pricing your tenderness wrong," she murmurs, trying to wear a grin that doesn't quite fit this morning. "That's a two-crumb cure at least."

"Get rich elsewhere," Halina says, but she breaks off a sliver and passes it to Iskra without letting the room see her do it. Iskra breaks it again and palms half for later, because hands that have lived here have learned to think ahead of mouths.

Joanna sits near Lenka, eyes on the seam Ainela made yesterday, thumb hovering a hair's breadth above the tiny curl. "Small enough to hide," she whispers, and the words aren't about thread anymore.

Tatiana listens to the air the way some people listen to bells. "Four in," she counts with nothing but the lift of her shoulders. "Hold two. Four out." The rhythm moves through the room like a stitch pattern passed down a line of hands. They keep it without letting lips move.

Ainela presses her sternum, as if the locket's weight might be conjured by touch alone. It isn't there, but the body remembers the shape of it, how the clasp always found the same hollow. Courage crosses her in a small, bright stripe. She leans her forehead to Mila's hair and stays there long enough for the child's breathing to borrow hers.

Kaja sits under the vent and measures the thin draft with her palm, drawing the air as if she could warm it by sketching its path. Larisa murmurs a prayer with no end, the beads clicking like seeds in a paper envelope. No one speaks the book's name—the real one—they hold it inside the mouth where boots can't hear.

Halina lets the bread heel go. The split on Mila's lip is less angry now. "See?" she says, low. "It listens, if you teach it how."

Iskra huffs something like a laugh. "Dough and girls," she says. "Both rise better with warmth." No one answers, but the room takes it in and keeps it.

Below, breath counts itself steady. Above, a different counting waits on a chapel step.

Morning upstairs is honest and cold. Frost nets itself on the chapel steps, small white stitches that hold until the sun remembers them.

Zosia walks like streets might tell on her—heels down soft, shoulders narrow. The locket sits at her throat, the clasp still the wrong shape because some things are supposed to be difficult. She cups it once in her palm, lets it take her heat, and brings it to her lips only long enough to remind her mouth that metal can be a kind of spine.

From her pocket she unwraps two sugar cubes, the lemon paper crinkling with a remembered summer. She sets the cubes on the middle step—not the top, not the bottom— the place a hand would rest if it needed to pause between going in and turning away.

For ghosts, she says where only the jaw can hear.

Her breath makes a cloud that tries to be a ghost and fails. She counts without numbers, the way a body does when it has learned a rhythm from far below: four in, hold two, four out. It steadies the parts of her that have been running even while she stood still.

She tucks the empty paper back into her pocket because littering feels like un-giving. The cubes sit like two small bones learning light. Zosia doesn't look at the door; seams can look back when you do. She turns away, the locket resettling in its hollow as if it were agreeing to carry something for her a little longer.

The street swallows the act and leaves her face for later.

The cellar has a second night after the first one ends. It comes when the breaths lengthen and the bodies get heavy, when even the mice are done with their errands, and the damp has climbed as high as it intends to climb. Ainela is not asleep. She is lying in the kind of stillness that gives itself away by the way it watches sound.

A footstep crosses the world above them. Not many, not a march—just one, then another, as if the person carrying it is thinking between each step. A scrape follows, something dragged rather than lifted. It is not loud. It is worse for not being loud.

The mind offers the shovel before the ear has earned it. A metal ring against stone, faint as an idea. Ainela's breath goes shallow. The night makes a throat out of the corridor and swallows.

She says, under the breath she is hoarding, the first line she ever wrote on the page. The words come to her the way things do when they have lived in her mouth long enough: without needing to be fetched, already warm. Saying them does not make the sound stop. It makes her feel less like a single wall waiting to be struck.

A shape moves across the slit of darker dark where the air sometimes slips in. It halts. Keys do not jingle. There is no laugh. The pause is wide enough to hold a thought and then another. Ainela's skin tightens as if it expects weight. She does not see the way Jakub's eyes linger a heartbeat on Iskra, the faint crease of his brow—noticed, and then tucked away, as if silence itself could erase what he has already seen. The shape passes on. The drag resumes and then quiets in the way footsteps do when a door has been closed between two sounds.

She doesn't realize her hand has found the bundle until her fingers press the edges and feel the corners push back. Paper against bone. Linen against pulse. She pictures teeth—small, numerous, all of them sharp because they have to be—and thinks, *more*. Not because she wants more. Because more may already be true.

The room exhales by degrees. A little air comes back and lays itself down where it can. Ainela closes her eyes and sees the seam in the wall the way a person sees a scar on their own body, half from memory, half from touch. She tries not to think of it. The trying makes it clearer. The forgetting does not hold.

If you can't speak, hum.
If you can't hum,
breathe in time with the others.

---

margin note,
The Embergirls' Rhymebook

CHAPTER SIXTEEN

THE MEASURE OF BREATH

WHISPERROOT: A HUSHWOOD TALE

Hunger is alive.

At first it murmurs in the hollow of you, a faint gurgle, like something stirring far below the floorboards. If you do not listen, it grows restless—its voice a rumble, a drumbeat you cannot quiet. If you still don't feed it, it starts to grow tentacles that twist, roll, and clench your insides. It hijacks your brain until every thought centers around food. The air begins to smell of bread that does not exist. A shadow glitters like sugar. Even the inedible gleams—chalk, splinters, candle wax—suddenly possible. Your own tongue becomes a stranger, swollen with longing. It grows angrier—scraping the lining of your stomach, raiding hidden reserves for fuel, scalds the nerves until every breath is ragged.

Hunger grows cruel.

A crust of bread, a spoonful of thin broth–these will not be enough to keep hunger's anger away. Hunger is a kettle hissing toward boil, a mountain rumbling toward eruption. The longer it stays, the more it costs you. First, it takes your attention, then It steals your thoughts, then it ravishes your energy until you are just a hollow vessel for its song. Eventually, when you've nothing left to give, hunger becomes a forlorn companion who no longer screams at you. It leans close, whispering with every breath of how you have betrayed yourself.

It will not let you forget.

The girls don't speak of it: they don't want to stir its hatred. But, on days when no rations are given, there's a sense of unspoken urgency, a restlessness, that starts with the younger ones and spreads to the eldest. The cellar teaches you to plan. Halina, Ainela–as if by silent agreement, these girls rarely eat a full ration. Halina palms off a corner of her ration and knots it in cloth; Ainela mirrors her without looking

The heavy thud of a boot stills the room. Ainela notices a second heavy boot fall and then a slight pause. A shake of keys rattles outside the door. The sound passes around the room as an electric jolt: girls weakened by illness or hunger still straighten their postures. The scrape of an old key twisting inside the lock, the squeaking of the heavy oak door opening on rusty hinges, and the murmuring of voices freezes breath in some of the girls and makes it hollow in others. Ainela counts her breaths: *one–in, two–out, three–wait.*

Ignacy.

He walks in the room, his black robe shifting around him, the cross necklace hanging low on his chest, his hands loose at his sides. His face, chiseled in piety, scalds Ainela, but she refuses to look away. Tomasz and Mateusz stand on either side of him. Jakub leans against the doorframe, lingering. His eyes flick towards Iskra for a heartbeat, then moves to Ainela, narrowing.

Ignacy steps carefully toward Iskra, who pushes her back against the stone, as if trying to disappear through it. Without warning, Ignacy bends, his necklace swinging forward, as he grips Iskra's arm and lifts it to his nose. He sniffs, twists the flesh, which makes her moan in pain, and then drops it. Ignacy looks behind him at the guards. He doesn't yell but his voice is full of something sour that sends chills racing through the girls.

WHISPERROOT: A HUSHWOOD TALE

"You're right." Looking back at the girls, his gaze hardens. "She stinks of herbs. Where are the herbs?" Silence. "Stealing is against God's law."

"She blistered yesterday," Mateusz says, his voice bored.

Ignacy tips his head. "That's interesting because today it looks like it's closing. God doesn't work that quickly."

"We've heard them chanting." Tomasz adds, his voice eager. "Through the vent at night."

Ignacy quirks a brow; his lips thin. "Herbal concoction in God's house? That's sorcery." He spits the word. Squaring his shoulders, he demands in a voice growing more and more firm, "Where are the herbs?"

The girls shift, their eyes cutting from one to the other.

"Which one of you has been stealing from the church? I will not allow witchcraft to take root in God's house." Without warning, Ignacy slaps Iskra, his signet ring catching her nose. She gasps, her hand covering her skin. "Witchcraft is from Satan." Ignacy's voice lifts. His eyes find Jakub's. "We need to find the herbs."

Jakub slowly pushes away from the doorframe. "Line up." Like Ignacy, his voice is low. Tomasz seconds the order with a shout: "Move!" The girls scurry–Ainela and Klara bracket Iskra, ready to catch her if she falls. They're pushed to the far corner of the room, against the wall. Jakub kicks the straw with his boot, his eyes flicking to Halina, pause a beat too long, then snap to Ainela as if covering the pause. His hands drag over her back, sides, legs — rough, impersonal, like he is inventorying a garment instead of a girl. By the time he moves to Kaja, she trembles. Klara slides her feet, silently stepping in front of Lusia. She stays there, a half-pace shield.

Lusia's cough catches behind her teeth; her hand knots Klara's sleeve and then let's go. Jakub's eyes flicker: he grabs another blanket and shakes it hard. A comb flings across the room, clinking against the stone. Mila cries out when her blanket is ripped from her arms. Kalina stumbles back, her heated skin striking cold stone. Kaja spits straw from her mouth.

Joanna jerks back when Tomasz grabs the hem of her gown, pulling her forward. It's so fast she barely sees it: a flash of chalk, white like salt on an old wound, an impression, then he drops the garment and moves to Lusia. Joanna's eyes flick down. *Three.* Her gaze moves to Lusia's shift: *six.* Ainela looks at her number and counts, listening to the boots hitting the ground, the jingle of keys: *one–in, two-out, three-wait.*

The sound of Lusia coughing startles her. She catches Ignacy's gaze fix on Lusia.

"What's hers?" he asks, moving his head to see around Mateusz. "Six."

Ignacy replies, "Mark her."

Mateusz makes a note on a small ledger.

At the word, Klara edges the last half-step, putting her shoulder where the gaze wants to land. Lusia leans into her shadow.

By the time they stop searching, the room is in disarray. Ainela notes the girls are biting their lips, have jagged breathing, and eyes wild with fear. She times her breathing with the guards' steps: heavy boot, one, breathe in. Next heavy footstep, two, breathe out. She waits for the keys to jingle and then repeats. The world narrows, the sounds of the men yelling at them and ripping up the straw fade.

Finally, the room quiets.

WHISPERROOT: A HUSHWOOD TALE

Father Ignacy says, "His word tells us what should happen to those who steal. It says very clearly, 'if your right hand causes you to sin, cut it off and throw it away' lest the whole body be thrown into Hell. Confess now and I'll implore God's mercy on you. Which of you stole the herbs? Who is practicing witchcraft in God's house?"

Only the sound of broken breathing responds.

"Alright then," he says, his voice hardening. "There will be a correction upon you. It will be carried out tomorrow before prayers." He stares hard at Lusia, making her step even closer to Klara. Klara's hand finds hers.

By the time the men leave, the room is all jagged breath and broken eyes. Ainela keeps her gaze low, her chest rising in a quiet pattern the others don't yet know. Heavy, heavy, pause. It steadies her hands against the stone. The room stays twisted in disarray—straw scattered, blankets ripped, skin bared and bruised. No one moves at first. Breathing comes jagged, like glass dragged across stone.

Ainela presses her shoulders against the wall, the rough cold biting where Jakub's hands had been. Across from her, Iskra holds her arm as if she could hide the wound inside her skin. Halina stares at the place where Ignacy stood, lips pressed thin, as if silence might keep the herbs from being betrayed.

No one dares speak the word that was spit at them— sorcery. But it hangs in the air anyway, clinging to the straw, to their hair, to the raw patches on their skin. It lingers like smoke after a fire you cannot see. They lie back down in the ruined straw, one by one. The air does not soften. The silence is too tight, too sharp.

The cellar has no coal tonight, only ash. And ash remembers what it once was.

Correction.

Tomorrow before prayers.

Ainela's gaze moves quickly around the room, fear rising fast. Her dark gaze meets Halina's and, as though they'd spoken, they move. Halina touches the hand of those close to her; Ainela motions for others to gather round. No one asks Iskra to move–her wounds remain. Mila and Larisa are noticeably thinner, weaker. Hunger continues to ravage them. Ainela corrals the others around these three. The straw beneath them, trampled flat, is a reminder. Violence is here. Ainela taps people to sit together, arranges girls into small groups. Who is steady, who can stand. Who sways. Who might fall under a correction.

While Ainela sorts the girls, Halina crouches. She digs her thumb into the hinge of Lusia's jaw. "Press here." Her voice is unemotional. Practical. "It blocks the cry." Girls press the hinge of their jaw. The group sorted, Ainela moves her own thumb to her jaw.

Halina pinches her nail bed. "Doing this will keep you awake."

Girls pinch their nails. Ainela's eye flinches as she pinches the skin.

"Put your tongue to the roof of your mouth." Halina hesitates and her voice quivers. "It - it keeps you here."

Ainela cuts in, voice steady, pointing to Halina and Klara. "If one of us should fall..." Halina nods curtly. Klara swallows, pulls her lip between her teeth, inclines her head. "I'll help with this too." Ainela adds. "Someone to watch for the keys." Joanna gives a short nod. "And someone to keep track of our breath." Kalina's hand goes up. Her eyes are steady. "I can," she says, her voice soft. "I know how to keep time." The words hang oddly in the air, carrying a weight none of them quite touch. She won't need the rhythm explained twice.

"Three taps," Ainela says. "Stop. One tap, wait. Two quick taps, switch: just breathe."

A guard's step echoes too near. Ainela hums the first low note. The others follow—then she taps twice against her knee. The sound dies. The air contracts. Kalina's shoulders rise in perfect rhythm, her silence like a bird that learned too young how to cage its song. The guard moves past. The girls breathe again. A murmur outside–their names? their fate? Kalina hums; others join. The sound is barely audible but as all twelve – even Kaja – join, the air shifts. It feels like hope. The murmurs outside the door fade. Kalina taps twice; the sound fades. One—in. Two—out. Three—wait. Ainela taps three times. The room relaxes.

Ainela's eyes find Halina's.

Halina nods once, sharp as flint. Between them, something small and dangerous sparks. They're ready.

The boots return. A murmur outside. The girls' breaths spike, uneven, too loud. Kalina hums, the note small, a thread to hold. Others join, weaving their fear into sound. The keys scrape the lock. Ainela's heart thuds—too late, too dangerous. She taps twice against her knee. The hum dies, choked off mid-breath. The silence is raw, trembling. The hinges shriek as the door opens. The guards find them pressed into the straw, faces blank, chests rising in the rhythm of one—two—three. *Only breath.*

Ainela's heartbeat drops in relief.

They're not caught.

"Seven." Tomasz's gaze shifts to Lenka. Ainela isn't sure if she remembers the chalk on her gown—seven—or if she reacts to his gaze, but she moves. Standing. "Four." When Klara doesn't react, Lusia nudges her. Klara's gaze drops to her shift, sees the number four, and scrambles to stand before Tomasz grows impatient. "Five." Kaja lines up. Tomasz's eyes skitter around the room, a hunter looking for prey. "Twelve." Ainela rises, walks to stand behind Kaja. "Let's go," Tomasz says, turning.

The sound of Mateusz calling numbers echoes in Ainela's mind.

They're numbered.

They file out of the room, walking one by one. The corridor is dark and cold. The keys on his hip set the rhythm: heavy, heavy, brief jingle. Kaja hugs the wall side and, on each small cover sound—the hinge's whine, the keys' chatter, a muttered curse—she lets her heel roll a fraction. Some planks answer with a tired cry; others stay dead. She maps them without breaking stride, filing a quiet seam for tomorrow.

Ainela shortens her step by a thread so the four hold together; the count lives in her ribs: heavy, heavy, pause. Lenka watches the set of Tomasz's shoulders, not his face; when his attention tightens, she lets her fingers splay at her hip and the line lengthens by instinct.

Landmarks fix themselves as they pass: threshold lip—*cry; knot-dark seam—hush; drain grate—cry; hinge shadow—hush.* At the corner post, the worst board betrays itself under Tomasz's own boot—a long groan that carries. Klara hears it and tucks the note behind her ribs. *There. If someone must be heard, there.*

No one pauses.

They move like a thread pulled through canvas—steady, unremarkable. The map gathers anyway, stitch by stitch, held in heel and breath. 7, 4, 5, 12 march by number; Ainela walks by name inside her skull determined they don't thin to chalk: *Lenka. Klara. Kaja. Ainela. If they take the names, I will stitch them back.*

Klara cannot unfeel the moment Lusia's fingers found her sleeve.

"Four," Tomasz said—*not* her name—and for a heartbeat the sound slid past her like water. Then the nudge: small, urgent. She rose because Lusia told her to. What if she hadn't? *Heavy shadows, pushing her down; her tortured cry ignored.* She shakes her head sharply, steadies her breathing.

Night settles. The cellar rests; straw rustles and stills. Somewhere down the corridor the keys teach the dark their measure—heavy, heavy, pause—and the room folds itself around that counting. Kalina's shoulders rise and fall without thinking. Someone's teeth click once, then remember the pattern and stop. Another glues her tongue to the roof of her mouth while Iskra pinches her nail bed. *It'll keep you awake.*

Ainela visits each girl, seeking reassurance: *they're ready.* She lowers beside Klara. No words. Her fingers find Klara's wrist and run the pattern once—*three, one, two—* a check–*do you really know it?* Klara answers with the same pressure and pace. *Yes.* The code lives in both of them now;

this is only the promise they'll use it. They sit with the rhythm until fear has something steadier to cling to. Breath in on the first heavy, out on the second, hold on the jingle. The dark begins to move that way, too, as if the building itself has ribs.

Klara's hand goes to the end of her braid. She pinches off a tiny knot of hair—soft, soundless—and warms it in her fist. When the keys whisper far away again, she reaches across the narrow seam of straw and tucks the knot into Lusia's palm, folding Lusia's fingers over it. A token with no weight, only the promise it stands for.

Ainela's hand settles a moment over Klara's, steady heat in the cold. She doesn't tap the code again; she doesn't need to. The pattern hums in the room like a thread pulled through cloth—present even when no one touches it.

Klara swallows. The old nightmare flickers—skin, a voice that wasn't hers, the chapel's small world closing in—but it fades when she holds her tongue to the roof of her mouth. She is here. She has a choice. She leans close enough that the words don't have to travel. "If someone has to be seen," she whispers, smaller than straw, "it will be me."

Ainela's breath catches for one beat, then returns to the measure. She does not argue. She does not bless it. She holds Klara's gaze in the dark and nods once—sharp, accepting—and the nod makes it real. A sacrifice, but one of their choosing.

They listen to the corridor—heavy, heavy, pause—and practice without sound. The hum that might have risen doesn't. The breath that might have broken holds. Across from them, Lusia shifts and curls her fingers tighter around the warmed knot, the way a hand finds a coal and banks it under ash.

WHISPERROOT: A HUSHWOOD TALE

Klara presses her wrist to her own ribs and matches Ainela's cycle until the count lives under her skin. If the door opens: still. If the gaze hooks: wait. If the room must vanish its sound: switch. A language the guards cannot beat out of them.

She lies back and watches the stripe of vent-light crawl a handspan along the wall and disappear. The number on her shift tries to float up and claim her. She writes over it, slow and careful, the way Ainela would mend a tear: Klara. Lusia. Names she can keep. Names she can carry into morning.

The best healers don't
ask for thanks.
They just leave the jar where
you'll find it.

---

margin note,
The Embergirls' Rhymebook

Chapter SEVENTEEN
The Choice

WHISPERROOT: A HUSHWOOD TALE

Morning creeps in. The light is pale, veiled by heavy clouds, as if ashamed to deliver another day. Frosted air seeps through the vent, curling white from their mouths like smoke. Ainela flexes her stiff fingers, curling and uncurling them until the ache loosens. It isn't just cold—it is a freeze that dulls movement, a paralysis. Tiny rivulets of water slip down the seams of the stone, darkening patches of the wall. She shifts, pressing her spine against the damp surface, arms crossed, hands tucked into her armpits. Her gaze slides across the room.

Iskra coughs, the sound ragged and wet. Curled on her side, knees to chin, she clutches her thin arms. Ainela's eyes catch on the burn etched along her skin—purplish-brown, edges jagged. A blister bubbles across the bottom half, its translucent film breaking and reforming each time the lye soap stings, or a guard's grip digs into her arm. Dirt streaks her skin; keeping it clean is nearly impossible, though Halina tries.

Around the room, girls stir. Some drag themselves upright. Some shuffle to the bucket that serves as privy. Others lie still—eyes open but bodies unmoving. Ainela takes count: who can sit, who can stand, who only breathes. She notes Halina, Klara, herself—holding steady. Iskra's cough worsening. Mila, too pale. Larisa, unsteady on her feet. Joanna, Kalina, Lenka, Kaja—dizzy, weak, but still able. And Lusia, Halina whispered last night, heat rising at her hairline:

feverish. Tatiana's cough dry, persistent. Ainela marks them in her mind—at risk.

Correction comes tomorrow before prayers.

Ainela's fingers move to the hollow space at her throat, thinking of Zosia's locket. A memory stirs of the hollow space in the hushwood–the green ribbon to signal a new secret shared. Ainela's breath shakes as she draws it in. Blinking rapidly, her eyes fall to the hem of her shift. *Twelve.* Corridor walls flash across her memory: scratches, one line for each girl. *This one cried like a goat.* Chalk-white numbers stare back from garments across the cellar like ghosts. *We are not numbers.* She mouths their names, one by one, again. *Correction comes tomorrow before prayers.* What if it's her? What if she becomes another mark on the corridor? *Mark her.* That's what Ignacy said when he looked at Lusia. *Mark her.*

It will be me. Klara's whispered vow reverberates through her, shaking her. A sacrifice and a choice.

Halina rises. She rolls her shoulders, rubs at her eyes, then crouches beside Iskra. From beneath her bedroll, she draws the hidden pouch of salve, the one she buries in a hollow of earth. Between her fingers she pinches a smear of it, hesitates. Sorcery. Infection, or punishment? Which will kill quicker? Her face remains impassive as she spreads the salve across Iskra's wound.

She lifts her cup next, tips water to Iskra's lips. Ainela watches the long delay before the girl swallows, her throat finally shifting under the strain. Halina moves to Mila, then Larisa, repeating the ritual. When there is water in a girl's own cup, she uses it. When there is none, Halina gives from hers.

Healing is expensive.

WHISPERROOT: A HUSHWOOD TALE

Time crawls.

Fear coils in Ainela's stomach, a snake squeezing until she folds inward, rocking just to ease the pressure. She paces the room, bites her nails, tips her head back toward the ceiling to listen for heavy footfalls or murmurs. Dropping her shoulders wearily, she sits between Klara and Lusia.

Klara eyes her. "You used to do that in chapel."

"What?" Ainela frowns.

"When everyone stood to sing, you'd bite your nails until your mother pushed your hand to your side and then, when we sat down, your shoulders would fall, like standing was just so hard."

"It was." Ainela shifts quietly. "People tried to say I was looking at Pieter. Or sometimes it was Marcus. Everybody stared at me. I didn't know where to look, so I looked down."

"I heard you kissed Pieter." Lenka says, her voice quiet.

Ainela lifts a shoulder, says nothing.

"Did you?"

"I liked Pieter. But I never met him after dark. I didn't kiss him."

A heartbeat's pause. "Well, at least what they said about you wasn't true then." Her cheeks burn. "I am dirty."

The admission costs Lenka—Ainela sees it in the way her shoulders curl in, her eyes fix on a dark spot in the wood. "Whoever he wants today, it should be me."

Ainela remembers: a teacher found lice on Lenka and sent her home. Ignacy's voice rises in her memory: *not worthy of the sacraments. Vermin must be made clean before touching the holy bread.* "One time, I saw Zosia twisting her finger into her cheeks. I asked what she was doing, and she said, 'I want dimples like Lenka.'"

A tiny smile touches Lenka's face.

The sound of wooden boards moaning makes them all go quiet. Kaja stands, her head tipped back, her finger tracing an invisible map. "Hush, hush...cry." When she says "cry," the boards above them groan under weight. The groan deepens, lifts, deepens. "Two of them," Kaja says. "Coming from the left stairwell."

Heavy—breathe in. Kalina inhales—others follow.
Heavy—breathe out.
Jingle— The wooden planks outside groan. Move.

Kalina threads a low hum. *Kołyska bez słów*—the cradle without words. Others join. Iskra points to her throat—she needs to cough. Ainela shakes her head, holds a finger up.

*Heavy—*there's the footfalls, *breathe in.*
*Heavy—*second one, *breathe out.*
*Jingle—*Ainela nods to Iskra who coughs, the sound wet and ragged.

The hum steadies the room; shoulders match the rise and fall of breath.

The footfalls pause outside the door. Keys scrape the lock. Ainela taps twice against her knee. The sound is small, but the hum dies instantly—snuffed like a candle. Only the breaths remain, steady, shared. One body, waiting.

WHISPERROOT: A HUSHWOOD TALE

Jakub stands there. His face unreadable as his eyes sweep the room, sharp and measuring. The air thickens, heavy as wet cloth, as each of the girls pull in their breath and hold it.

"Six."

The word cuts like a blade, simple, final.

Lusia's breath stutters. Her fingers curl tight, her knuckles blanching white against her knees. Her chest jerks once, then twice, like she's fighting against her own lungs. She clamps her lips together, but the sound of her sharp inhale betrays her.

"Six." Jakub's voice again, edged with impatience. "Let's go."

Ainela's hand knots into the hem of her shift. Her fingertips find the small flame stitched there, the thread rasping rough under her nail. The flame burns against her skin—not with heat, but with the reminder of what it meant. Her body tenses, coiled, the thought trembling through her: *move now.*

But before she can rise, movement catches her eye. Klara's hand, light as moth wings, rests on Lusia's wrist. The touch halts her.

Klara's throat bobs. Once, twice. Her face is unreadable stone, but her fingers rise to the hinge of her jaw. She presses there, hard. Ainela knows what it means. It will hush the cry. *Her hand shakes faintly when she pulls it back.*

Jakub steps forward, his arm reaching toward Lusia. The room exhales, sharp and panicked, a rustle of straw and shuffling feet. Ainela feels her own heart hammering in her throat, a pulse so loud it drowns out the scrape of boots.

Klara moves first. She stumbles in the shove of Jakub's hand but slides quick between him and Lusia, her shoulder striking his chest. Her voice bursts out, steady despite the tremor beneath:

"I'm the one."

Jakub freezes mid-motion.

"I—I stole the herbs." *The smallest catch splinters her voice before she steadies it.*

The room contracts around her words. Ainela feels it like a tightening noose. The other girls shift: Halina's chin jerks up, her mouth opening in a soundless protest. Lenka's shoulders hunch forward as if she's shrinking smaller, eyes darting to Klara then away. Lusia lets out a strangled sound and clamps both hands against her mouth. Kalina presses her back hard to the wall, her nails scratching faint crescents into the stone.

Jakub's brow lifts, slow. His eyes study Klara's face, dragging across every line as though searching for a crack. Silence stretches long enough that Ainela feels the sweat bead at her hairline, cold despite the freezing air. His gaze slides, sharp, across the room. It lands on Halina. For a moment Ainela thinks he knows—*he knows about the salve, the hidden pouch, the water given away.* Halina's lips part, then she snaps her jaw shut, her shoulders squared though her fists tremble.

Jakub moves on. His eyes flick to Lenka. She lowers her gaze instantly, her dimples carved deeper by the hard bite of her teeth against her cheeks. He looks back to Klara, narrowing his eyes.

The pause breaks. His hand closes around her arm.

She jerks once at the force, her thin body lurching forward, but she steadies, plants her feet. *Her breath*

*hitches—a quick, shallow draw—but she forces it out slowly,
as though even her lungs must not betray her.*

He yanks, and she stumbles again, but when she
rights herself, her head is held high.

To Klara, it is sacrifice, but it is chosen. They cannot
control whether one of them is hurt, but this time she has
decided who it will be. That, too, is defiance.

Ainela's breath is shallow, her body burning with the
urge to call out, to stop it. But she doesn't. She can't. Klara's
steps echo in the silence, each one louder than the last, until
they fade into the corridor.

Her head does not bow.

Silence fills the room for one heartbeat, two, three—
then it breaks.

"I didn't ask her." Lusia's voice wavers, clogged with
tears. "I didn't know she was going to do that. Why would
she? She's already been there—" Her arms tremble, then her
legs, shaking uncontrollably. She scrabbles beneath the
straw until her fingers clutch the knot of golden hair, the
token pressed into her palm that morning like a promise. She
clutches it hard against her chest. "No. No, they called me.
They didn't call her—"

Halina's jaw tightens. Her eyes flash, voice sharper
than she means. "She protected you. Do you understand?
She protected me too. She saw what Ignacy was looking for.
Don't waste it."

Lenka's whisper cuts through, bitter with fear. "And
what about the rest of us? She can't keep saving everyone."
The words drop like stones.

The cellar stills. Even the air seems to draw taut,
listening. Ainela's hand presses to Lusia's knee, steady but

wordless. For a moment, the fragile hum of unity threatens to snap.

Then Kalina shifts. Her back peels from the wall, her gaze moving slowly from girl to girl. Her voice comes quiet, unsteady at first, but she keeps speaking. "My sister used to sing," Kalina says. "Everywhere. In the kitchen, by the well, even when she braided my hair. Not just hymns—old songs too. The ones he hated."

The girls turn toward her. Even Halina stills.

"One night he heard her. Ignacy." Kalina swallows. "He dragged her to the square. Said rebellion must be broken. He struck her hands with a switch until they bled. When she cried out, he hit her face. Then he made her bite her dress, gag herself so no one would hear her voice." Kalina's hands knot in her lap. "That night she sat in the corner, fingers wrapped in rags. She never sang again." Her voice falters, then steadies. "I never sang again either. Not because I didn't want to. Because every note felt like it would make her bleed."

The words settle over them like ash. Even Lusia's sobs quiet, her arms still curled around the golden hair. Kalina draws a shaky breath. "They want us divided. Afraid of who will be next. But Klara—she chose. She gave herself so it wouldn't be torn from her." Her gaze sweeps across the circle, resting on each face. "We don't choose who gets hurt. But we can choose this." Her voice breaks softer now, but sure: "We are sisters now. I don't want to let him take that, too."

For a moment the room holds only stillness. Then Ainela hums, low, coaxing. Kalina joins her, the note trembling, then steadying. Lusia presses the lock of hair to her lips and lets her own voice slip into the sound. One by one the others add theirs, until the cellar fills with the cradle without words.

They wait, voices braided together—sorrow, defiance, sisterhood—trembling, but unbroken.

Joanna lays a palm against Iskra's forehead. "Halina."

Halina glances up, then slides closer. Using her own palm, she tests Iskra's skin. Feverish. Heat radiates from her body. She hasn't sipped water in hours. Halina murmurs something no one catches, reaches beneath her shift, high, where she's sewn a small pocket. Pulling out the linen pouch, she tests the salve. "It doesn't need more yet," she says. "But when it starts to itch, pinch a bit of this. If it's dry, spit on it and then roll it between your fingers until it stretches. Don't let it itch. If you tear the skin by scratching it, it could get infected." She measures the ground and Iskra's body before tucking the pouch under a small pile of straw, buried beneath just enough dirt to cover it. She takes Iskra's hand and places it over the pile.

"A doctor who practices for free *and* gives away medicine?" Iskra jokes. "Careful, Halina, you'll never earn your keep doing this."

Halina scoffs. "I'm not a doctor. I'm barely older than you."

"A witch then?"

The room stills. Kaja's head turns. Joanna sighs heavily.

But Halina doesn't miss a beat: "If it costs Ignacy sleep, I'll be a witch."

Joanna's shoulders relax. Kaja returns to staring at the vent. Ainela adds: "I'll join the cult."

Halina's eyes soften just a moment as she stares at Iskra. "I don't know how you do it."

"Do what?"

"You've a fever. You've still got burns that won't heal. And yet–you joke."

Iskra's eyes shutter. Memories stir in Ainela – the roll of bruises Iskra wore at the Winter Gathering, watching men pull her father off her bloodied mother. Iskra, cracking jokes, redirecting everyone's attention from the black-and-blue map of her body to laughter. "It's a shield," she says softly. "Laughing means it can't hurt me. No one can hurt me." With a half-smile ghosting her lips, she adds, "If I'm a witch, laughter is my spell."

Joanna's gaze flicks up. She taps her knee once, as if pressing the line into memory. "That belongs in the book."

Two taps follow, quick: "Shh shh."

The room stills; breaths hold. *Heavy, heavy, jingle. Heavy, heavy, jingle.* The sounds repeat but fade. They aren't stopping at the room. Three taps: resume. Only no one speaks.

Time swells.

Bells ring somewhere above; straw settles; Lusia retreats.

And still–they wait.

The light fades, shadows creep higher on the stone walls.

WHISPERROOT: A HUSHWOOD TALE

"Will she be back?" Mila asks, her voice faint.

"The hushwood's quiet." Kaja's voice is low, almost a hum in itself, as she stares towards the window. It is too dark to see the tops of the trees now, but Kaja's memorized the height and location of each.

"What does the hushwood–"

Footsteps pause outside the door; moments later, it opens. Someone pushes Klara hard. As she stumbles, girls move to circle around her. She brushes them off, shaking her head. "Don't touch me," she mumbles, her teeth gritted. Ainela notes the buttons on her shift are fastened wrong; there are teeth marks on her neck; a bruise blooms around her eye. Her hair is tangled, strands stuck to her wet cheek, their ends tucked into the corner of her lips. She holds a hand in front of her, observing the trembling of her fingers, and smudges of dirt stain her pale skin. When she lowers her arm, it's to cover a spot high on her ribcage, just below her breasts.

Klara—
the word itself a thread,
a stitch against unmaking.
I wrote It once,
so the world could not forget.

Halina notes her breathing: shallow; she winces with every inhale.

She doesn't lie down.

Instead, she sits, her eyes trained on the heavy oak door. "Tuesdays," she says breathlessly. "Jakub doesn't come here on Tuesdays." Every word ends on a frayed moan, a telltale sign she struggles to talk or breathe comfortably. When Lusia touches her sleeve, her fingers light, Klara flinches, but allows Lusia's comforting touch to remain.

Long moments pass.

Ainela counts nothing silently.

*One...two...three...four...*at twenty she notices the first tear creeping down Klara's cheek, followed by another. Mila moves to sit on the other side of her; Iskra reaches a hand out. Klara takes it. "Tuesdays," she whispers again, her voice raspy. "One less guard on Tuesdays." Her head dips back, her eyes never leave the oak door. Ainela pulls out the Rhymebook and uses the nub of a charcoal piece to add another line. "You missed it," she says quietly. Klara slides only her eyes to see her. Writing, Ainela nods. "Halina and I are witches now. Iskra's our jester. We're hoping it keeps Ignacy awake at night."

No reaction.

Wordlessly, Ainela holds the faded page out to Klara.

We laugh as spell, we bleed by choice
Tuesdays are ours with one less voice

Klara looks up at her, pulling her lip between her teeth. She's *heard*. Ainela nods as if she understands. Klara drags a shaky breath in, folds the page and holds it back to Ainela. She takes it, adds it to the stash, the fragile pages swelling like lungs, the Embergirls' Rhymebook breathing larger with every line.

To name a girl is to root her in the earth.
To strip her name is to scatter her to the
wind. But silence is also a name, and it
cannot be taken

The Embergirls' Rhymebook

CHAPTER EIGHTEEN

THE BREAKING WORD

Ainela's eyes open, stare at the stone. No one slept last night: the guards' walked heavy outside their door all night long. Sometimes barks of laughter startled them. The keys would impale the lock, twist... but then retreat like a cruel joke. Iskra's wet cough, Tatiana's dry one were the loudest noises in the room. Someone sneezed, sniffled. Blankets shifted. Girls rolling against the straw to find a more comfortable position. Ainela watched Cicho – the mouse who appears every night – scurry along the wall straight to Larisa's bed roll. She always leaves a tiny pinch of bread for him. By now, as she stretches her back and rolls into a sitting position, lack of sleep frays her nerves and her body aches.

Frustration mounts higher in her chest as the morning slowly tracks by with no breakfast, her head throbs. Mila and Tatiana stand jump repeatedly to stay warm. Mila tires quicker than Tatiana and falls to the straw. Tatiana continues to jump. Kaja stands on her toes, fingers holding the edge of the windowsill, staring at a world they cannot touch. Klara talks about Tuesday, but this grates on Ainela's nerves.

"Who cares?" Ainela bursts, shrugging her shoulders.

Klara's voice fades, her eyes narrowing. "It's one less guard," she repeats for the tenth time. "It's a.. a chance—"

"No, it's not." Ainela shakes her head. "So, there's one less guard here on Tuesdays. How does that help us if we can't open *that* door?" she points sharply to the heavy oak door that traps them. Crimson stains Klara's cheeks. "It's what I *got*," she spits. "I didn't make that choice for nothing. At least we *know* something that *could* be useful one day. What have *you* gotten that's so helpful?"

Ainela sighs heavily, turns away. She walks to the door, bangs on it with her fists. "Hey!" she cries loudly. "Where's our *breakfast*?"

"Ainela." Sharp notes break out across the room. Footfalls pause on the noisy board outside.

Halina steps in, touches Ainela's arm. "Stop. Ainela. Stop."

"See if I protect *you*," Klara mumbles.

Before Ainela replies, she notices Tatiana hugging Mila; Larisa sits near them, whispering.

Her anger collapses, like bread pulled from the oven too soon. Without comment, she sits, tugging the Rhymebook from its hiding place. She reads each page. Notes the names already recorded: Klara, Halina. Reads the pages recorded by the other girls–with their symbols drawn; the rosary bead sketched in soot makes her eyes skate to Larisa, the bird in a cage slides her thoughts to Lenka.

The sound of footfalls outside the door interrupts and surprises her. She drops pages of the Rhymebook as the key twists in the lock. Cheeks staining red, she scoops up loose pages, taking the ones Lusia gives her, and sliding them into the earth just as the door creaks open. Her heart pounding, anger fills the empty spaces in Ainela's belly, swirling with the hunger that splinters her patience.

Ainela's heart heaves with the weight of a morning of swallowed words, hollow stomachs and a growing anger. When she sees him, with his black robes and calm face, Ainela shifts her weight and digs her fingers into her palms to keep quiet. He gestures loosely towards the wall.

"Each of you are here because, in some way, you've struggled with disobedience and cleanliness. Today, you will repent for your disobedience and your uncleanliness. This begins with confession." He moves to stand in front of the line, smiling. "We're going to call your number and, when we do, you're going to answer, 'Unclean but obedient.' Are we clear?"

WHISPERROOT: A HUSHWOOD TALE

Unclean but obedient? The phrase pounds in Ainela's head. Her muscles tense. Girls murmur. Ainela hears Lenka beside her and glances in time to see her whispering the words to herself.

Tomasz begins:

"One." *Halina*, Ainela says.

The response is steady and quick: "Unclean but obedient."

"Two." *Iskra*. Ainela hisses in her mind. She thinks: "She's not a number, she's a jester."

There's a small cough; her wounds thin her voice. Raspy, she responds: "Unclean but obedient."

"Three." *Joanna*. Ainela knows how she will answer: she wants to survive, and she won't push back. The words feel mechanical. Ainela hears them stacking in her skull like bricks: *Unclean but obedient. Unclean but obedient.*

"Unclean but obedient." Being right angers Ainela further.

"Four." *Klara*.

The hesitation is long enough for Tomasz to step close to Klara. His size intimidates. She thins her lips, swallows, but parrots: "Un–" Her voice breaks again.

"Speak up, Four."

She draws a steadying breath. "Unclean but obedient."

Tomasz sneers, then moves down the line. "Five." *It's not five. It's Kaja. Her name is Kaja.*

Her voice is thin, ghostlike, barely audible, but without delay. "I'm unclean but obedient."

"Six." *Lusia*. Ainela slides her gaze to the girl. Fear makes her anxious; she answers fast: "Unclean but obedient."

"Seven." *Lenka*. The sequence falters. Lenka does not come. The pause stretches until all that fills the room is her choked sob. Ainela turns her head to see Lenka beside her. Tears roll down her hollow cheeks, her shoulders cave inward, her head bowed. She tries, "Un–un–un–" Her throat closes, the word snags, her breath rattles like someone trying to cough up stones. A sob rips from her throat, her shoulders shake. Her neck and face bloom red. Silence thickens in the room, closing in around Lenka.

"Seven, speak up."

Ignacy steps forward, waving Tomasz back. A slight smile crests Ignacy's face as he crouches down so that his face is in front of hers. "She knows it's true," he says softly. "What are you, Seven?" *Lenka*. But this time when Ainela corrects him, it's not an angry correction, it's a heartbroken one. Ainela wraps itself around her caving heart and she screams Lenka's name again, silently, but with passion: *Lenka!* Ainela presses outward–her breath shortens, her hands curl into fists.

Wiping her eyes, Lenka's mouth purses. Shame feels like eyes watching you struggle. Shame feels like heat crashing through your body like waves. This word–unclean— had always belonged to her. To speak it aloud now was exactly what Ignacy said it was: a confession. Confessing what she already feared was true: that she deserved to be in the cellar. Ignacy's arm lashes out, a measured strike, sharp enough to send her stumbling.

Anger ignites to fury in Ainela as she reaches a hand out.

The sting of a coiled whip cracks against her knuckles. Klara says, "She–"

"Speak without permission and you'll feel it next." Ignacy says sharply, his eyes cutting to Klara.

"Un....unclean." Lenka finally says it, her chest heaving. "And obedient," she adds quickly, her hand covering her mouth as if trying to shove words back inside. "I'm sorry. I'm sorry." Her eyes never lift from the floor. Salty tears slide into the corner of her lips.

Ignacy nods, steps back.

He motions to Tomasz.

"Eight." *Larisa*. Ainela corrects automatically, but her eyes stay on Lenka whose body trembles. Ainela glances at

WHISPERROOT: A HUSHWOOD TALE

Tomasz and Ignacy; they are focused on Larisa. She quickly brushes her fingers against Lenka's.

Larisa answers quietly: "Unclean but obedient. Mater." The last word barely slips through. *Mother*, for Mary. Devotion. Larisa speaks their language for them but then adds her own. Kaja's head twists; she hears her even if the guards didn't.

"Nine." *Tatiana.*

Tatiana, the performer, says brightly, almost happily, in a sing song voice, "Unclean–but! Obedient."

Tomasz frowns, glances at Ignacy who doesn't react.

"Ten." *Mila.* Fear crowds Ainela. Mila's been ill. What if she can't say it? Her voice comes out rough, as though it costs her breath, but she doesn't hesitate. "Unclean but obedient."

"Eleven." *Kalina.* A flash of memory beats in Ainela's mind. She was so sure when she lifted her hand and said, *I know how to keep time* when Ainela asked for a breath tracker. Her voice comes slow and steady, as if she's been practicing her tone. Her voice is clear, calm. "Unclean and obedient."

"Twelve." *Ainela*, she whispers to herself.

Silence. The twelfth voice never comes. The sequence stops on silence, her absence louder than the cloven that came before.

Tomasz steps closer, his eyes narrowing. "Speak up, Twelve."

Silence.

She hears fist knocking on bone when the first blow comes. When Tomasz pauses, giving her a chance to speak, she stares at Ignacy, upright and silent. Only her chest heaving betrays her. The next strike is harder: she stumbles, falling into Klara on her right side. Lenka watches, pushing the back of her hand against her mouth. Before she stands, a steel-toed boot kicks her. She feels her nose crack. Her breath hitches, a moan fills the silence.

"Say it," Klara hisses. "Before it gets worse, say it." The whisper is so violent and so low Tomasz doesn't catch it.

Ainela does. She will not repeat the words *unclean and obedient.* She will not give them meaning. She will not own them. It's two more blows before Ignacy holds a hand up, stopping Tomasz. Blood spatters onto the stone at her feet. It darkens, then dries quickly on the cold surface. Nothing will grow here. Bruises will blossom by morning. Ignacy doesn't speak. He doesn't move. He only watches as Tomasz strikes again, and again, until finally he lifts a hand — a single sharp gesture. The silence afterward is worse than the blows. When they step back, something shifts in Ainela. *She won.* She's bloodied and beaten, but she has not spoken.

When she stumbles to her feet, her eyes skate around.

Lenka's gaze hurts the most. Lenka's shoulders droop, her head bows. Ainela couldn't be beaten into saying the words—Lenka said them on her own. For Ainela, it is a victory. For Lenka, it is confirmation: she *is* unclean.

There is no break. Not in the chant, not in the breath, not in the space between blows.

Ainela shuffles. Klara slows her step, so she walks beside Ainela, stands beside her in the new formation. Halina shifts so that she's on the Ainela's other side. Her cheekbone throbs from the beating, and her right eye swells.

Ignacy points glances at Jakub, points to Ainela. The message is clear: *You. Watch her.* Wordlessly, Jakub moves to stand against the wall, opposite Ainela. Jakub's shadow looms as the line shifted. His hand brushes Ainela's arm, guiding her forward. For the briefest moment he steadies instead of shoving, his touch almost careful. Then his jaw locks, and he withdraws as if ashamed of the mercy.

WHISPERROOT: A HUSHWOOD TALE

The room spins around her. Briefly, she closes her eyes, shakes her head, sways.

"Nails." Halina whispers without moving her lips.

Ainela pinches her nail bed as hard as she can. The room drifts into focus.

Ignacy drones on about obedience and how they achieve godliness through obedience. He tells them they will memorize Scripture by reciting it until they are told to stop. He has them repeat after him:

"The wage of sin is death. Her flesh runs with blood, and she shall be put apart. You are an unclean thing. Let the woman learn in silence with all subjection. From all your filthiness will I cleanse you. The wage of sin is death."

Larisa breathes, "That's not what it says." But her voice is murmured so low only Halina, who stands beside her catches it. She whispers it again, her hand twitching. "Not what it says," so Ainela can hear it. Ainela breathes it to Klara. It runs through the girls like a secret until they all know: Ignacy is not quoting Scripture. He's cannibalizing it, tearing phrases from bone and stitching them into something monstrous.

The chanting begins, filling the rooms. *The wage of sin is death. Her flesh runs with blood, and she shall be set apart. She is an unclean thing*—Ainela's voice drops to a murmur, but she continues, the dizziness and the pain keeping her compliant. Until the next line. *Let the woman learn in silence*—Ainela's voice stutters, breaks the rhythm. The guards notice. Jakub pushes away from the wall, moves to stand in front of her. Halina and Klara, as if by silent agreement, speed up to cover the break. Jakub's face is impassive, watching Ainela's lips move. *From all your filthiness will I cleanse you. The wage of sin is death. The wage of sin is death. Her flesh runs with blood, and she shall be set apart. She is an unclean thing*—Ainela says it, but through ground teeth, her voice dropping to a whisper. As the others say *let the woman learn in silence* – she shakes her head, stopping. She will not let these words mean anything.

Except they do.

And, so, she will not speak them.

Ignacy holds a hand up, stopping the chorus.

Jakub steps back as Ignacy approaches Ainela. "You will say it alone."

Her head shakes, a mere shadow of movement, but it is blatant refusal. Ignacy's patience thins. "Oh, believe me, child, you will." He glances briefly at Jakub but then motions for Mateusz and Tomasz. "They will stop when you speak. Not before. And the others will wait. The longer you take, the longer you're making them stand. Will you speak the Scriptures?"

She shakes her head again, bracing her muscles for the blow she knows will come.

Her vision fades in and out as she is punched and kicked. Brutal blows land on her temple, forcing her to her knees. She uses her arms to shield her face, but Mateusz circles her, using his boot to stomp her back until she's flat on her stomach, fists and boots kicking her ribs, her back and the side of her head.

"Ainela, say it already! Before they kill you." It isn't her words that make Klara's plea stick. It's the tears she hears behind them. She can't lift her head—she can barely move, but when Tomasz grabs her arm, lifts and throws her against the cold stone, she gasps. She holds her hands out in surrender.

Ignacy steps in.

"Do you have something to say?"

Opening her jaw hurts. It feels locked—the metallic taste of blood drips into the corner of her mouth. She grates out the first lines. Then she stops. When Tomasz's arm lifts in a clear threat, she grates, "Let the woman learn in silence with all subjection."

Ignacy's face relaxes.

"Again," he breathes softly.

Tears fill her swollen eyes, but they are tears of anger. She spits the line back at him, her voice dripping with venom.

WHISPERROOT: A HUSHWOOD TALE

For the first hour, she repeats it correctly, fear blushing her fury.

The wage of sin is death. Her flesh runs with blood, and she shall be put apart. You are an unclean thing. Let the woman learn in silence with all subjection. From all your filthiness will I cleanse you. The wage of sin is death. The chorus in the room rises again, twelve voices reciting in unison. When Ainela stops speaking the lines, she only drops a few words here and there. The guards don't notice because she makes sure the lines that mean nothing to her are said. Sometimes she changes words. "Woman" becomes "man" - she "shall be put apart" becomes "he shall depart." The lines begin to blur as each hour passes. Even though she stutters and mispronounces a few sometimes, she says them correctly during other rounds, deliberately, so as to confuse the guards who watch her like a hawk.

Iskra falls near lunchtime.

Mila collapses near evening.

They make the girls link arms with others to remain standing.

Eventually, all twelve girls' arms are linked–a chain of vessels spiraling towards ghosthood.

The girls collapse into straw, voices raw, throats cracked. Some cough until their ribs ache, others bury their faces in their sleeves to hide the sound. The cellar feels smaller, the air heavier.

The fracture shows quick and clear.
Some turn toward Ainela with fury sharp in their eyes—if she had just spoken, just yielded once, they might have been spared more blows. Others skirt away from Lenka, as though her sobbing makes her contagious, as though shame can spread by touch. A few simply curl inward, hiding faces in

their knees, trying to erase themselves into straw and shadow.

Ainela sits stiff among them, fists pressed to her thighs, head throbbing from Tomasz's boot. Anger still surges hot in her chest, but it doesn't shield her from the ache of what happened. She looks at the others—at Halina's steady jaw, at Tatiana still smirking faintly as if the phrase were a stage line, at Kaja whose eyes stay fixed on the ceiling cracks—and feels the silence press harder than the whip. She cannot forgive the words. Not for herself, but for what they hollowed in Lenka.

Lenka tastes salt and straw on her lips. She bites down to keep the sobs from breaking free, but her jaw aches with the pressure. She curls tighter, forehead pressed into her knees. If she makes herself small enough, maybe the shame will shrink too.

Her ears still ring with the sound of her own voice: *Un... unclean.* The stammer cracked her wide open. The silence that followed was worse. She'd felt every eye in the room on her, each gaze like grit grinding into her skin.

It isn't new. Dirt has always followed her—under her nails, in her cropped hair, in the whispers about lice. She used to scrub her hands raw until they bled, hoping the water would scour the shame away. Now the words themselves have rubbed her raw, and there is no water here. Only stone, straw, and the memory of her own mouth betraying her.

She whispers apologies into her palms. To no one. To everyone. "I'm sorry. I'm sorry. I tried." The words dissolve into wet heat against her fingers.

Through the blur of tears, she sees Ainela's face. Even bloodied, she is unbowed. Lenka flinches from the sight, hating herself more. Ainela could not be beaten into the words—Lenka gave them freely.

Her shoulders shake. Shame gnaws deeper than hunger, deeper than cold. She knows the others see her weakness, knows they will remember. She will remember.

WHISPERROOT: A HUSHWOOD TALE

When Ainela's fingers brush hers—quick, secret, fleeting—Lenka almost sobs aloud. The touch says *you are not alone.* But the words she spoke remain, heavy as chains, and Lenka believes them.

She is unclean.

Ainela draws her hand back, her lip bleeding again from where her teeth press too hard. She feels more alone than ever—her fury has cut her from the others, her silence punished, her defiance misunderstood. Yet sharper, too: something in her hardens. If the others cannot hold fast, she will. If silence is the only name left to her, she will keep it, and she will not let it be taken.

Night sinks deep, thick with damp stone and restless breath. The cellar is quieter than usual—not the soft murmurs of comfort or the secret humming they sometimes risk, but the silence that follows a wound.

Ainela cannot sleep. Her lip splits anew every time she shifts, the taste of iron pooling on her tongue. She slips a hand beneath the straw, fingers brushing the hidden spine of the Rhymebook. She pulls it close, knees hunched around it like a shield.

When she opens the page, a smear blooms where her hand falters—blood, dark and sticky, sinking into the paper. For a moment, she almost recoils, but then she breathes in steady. It is right. If the priest can make them bleed, then the page will take the blood and keep it. Her body may be battered, but her words will not be obedient.

She writes:
They can count us,
but they cannot name us.

The letters wobble, her swollen knuckles dragging, but she presses harder until the strokes carve into the paper. Each word feels like a blow redirected, stolen back from Tomasz's fists.

Around her, the others stir. Halina shifts closer, her broad back turning into a wall. She doesn't speak—she doesn't need to. Her shoulder blocks the line of sight, her body a quiet shield.

Klara, who snapped earlier, still awake, watches. Ainela expects mockery, expects impatience, but Klara only moves toward the edge of the straw heap. Her eyes sharpen into the dark, keeping lookout at the door. A small guard for a fragile act.

The room settles heavier, and Ainela dips her head lower, whispering as she scrawls fragments of names into the margins. Not whole names, not yet—pieces that won't betray them if discovered. *Lu. Ka. Is. Ta.* Seeds pressed into the soil of the page. She remembers Lenka's collapse, her shame cracking open like an egg. She remembers the way Lenka said *unclean* as though it had always belonged to her. Ainela writes harder, faster. *Len.* The tip tears the page, but she lets it stand.

Her lip bleeds again; the stain smudges where her hand rests. She leaves it, a mark that is hers and no one else's. A wound turned into witness.

Halina shifts once more, covering Ainela's hand as if to warm it. *She bends the letters toward Halina, slipping her name back into the book where no guard could strip it out again.* Ainela doesn't look up, but her throat tightens. Even now—fractured, wounded, ashamed—the ember of sisterhood glows faintly. It may not be loud, but it endures.

When she closes the book, she whispers to herself, not prayer but vow: *We will not be unclean. We will not be obedient. They can count us, but they cannot name us.*

And in the silence after, she imagines the whisperroot above the earth, reaching higher, fed by blood they did not intend to give.

The hours creep by. The cellar holds its breath. The girls curl where they've fallen—some already slipping into shallow sleep, others awake but still, as if afraid to move and crack the silence apart. The straw scratches Ainela's skin, but she stays awake, the words she wrote still burning behind her eyes.

A whisper cuts through. It is small, frayed, but enough to stir the air.

"Do you think Ignacy will…"

The name hangs like smoke.

Another voice—sharper, trembling but insistent—interrupts. "Not his name."

A pause. The straw shifts with uneasy movements.

"Not his name," the girl repeats, more firmly this time. "He's only the priest. Or… him."

The correction quivers, but it sparks.

Ainela's gaze drifts to Mila, curled small as a sparrow, lips barely moving. Her voice never rises above a hush, but it's hers.

Mila—not "Nine," not a tally mark in someone else's hand. Her name tastes of soft consonants, a child's breath held in cupped palms. Ainela will press it to the page, anchoring her there, so no one can unmake her.

A murmur ripples low through the dark. *Not Ignacy.* The word passes mouth to mouth, hesitant, then certain. *Not Ignacy.* His name will not belong here. Not among them.

Ainela listens, her breath caught sharp in her throat. Her lip stings where it has split, but the ache fades beneath the throb of something stronger. She feels it move through the girls like the humming had once done, like the tapping signals across the floorboards. A small rebellion, as fragile as a match's flame, yet luminous.

Kaja whispers: "Only him."

Tatiana, her voice quick, eager: "Yes. Just him."

Larisa murmurs a prayer, but this time she does not use his name at all.

Ainela closes her eyes. *Ignacy*—the sound itself feels like stone pressing on her chest. *Him* is air. He cannot grow roots if they refuse to give him soil.

She repeats it inwardly, as if setting it into her own marrow: *He is not Ignacy. He is only him.*

Her fists curl tight. For Lenka, who bent beneath the weight of unclean, this is a gift back. For herself, it is armor. He will not outlive them in name.

The cellar drifts quiet again, but it is a changed quiet. Ainela feels it—thin, tenuous, but real. Despite the fractures of the morning, despite the ache in their throats and the shame clinging to Lenka like ash, something small has been won back.

The ember of unity glows faint in the dark. Not enough to warm, not enough to feed—but enough to remember. Enough to carry.

Paper is only as blank
as your hands are empty.

———————————

margin note,
The Embergirls' Rhymebook

Chapter Nineteen

Blood in the dirt

WHISPERROOT: A HUSHWOOD TALE

The night is long after the recitation is long. Ainela's temples pulsate with pain; her muscles clench tight; breathing feels like a noose tightening, choking her. Long after she puts the Rhymebook away, she stares at the ceiling. No one says it but she knows the others hear the same thing she does: the chanting. As morning fully wakes, birdsong, voices, crunching snow can be heard outside but, inside, the air is stiff, dark, and heavy. No one moves. Ainela tries to say something, anything, but her jaw sticks. Footfalls come, but no one hums, so there's no need to tap when keys jangle outside the door.

Jakub brings stale bread and a thin broth.

Ainela's eyes, swollen nearly shut, glance towards the window, realizing it must be later in the day than she thought. Her lips, cracked, taste of dried blood. Girls shift. Those who can push themselves upright; those who can't lift their heads just enough to spoon the broth into their lips. The flush of anger is still there—Ainela feels it—but it's an ember now, not a flame. The broth, though thin, buoys some of the girls' energy. Straw shifts, feet rake across the packed dirt beneath.

"I love bread." Mila's voice is light. Her amber eyes are bright, warm like the glow of a hearth. She smiles, tearing a piece of the stale bread. "I love kneading bread with my mother. Something about doing it over and over: folding the dough, then flattening it, then forming it into a ball just to flatten it again. Mama says if we ever get angry, we should bake bread cause kneading will work it out of us."

Tatiana smiles, picks up her corn dolly.

Joanna doesn't look up, but her head cocks. She's listening.

Mila chews. The bread is stale, hard. It doesn't taste like her mother's, but she pretends it does. "I could smell it before it was done. I'd say, 'Mama, I think it's ready' cause the room started to smell like yeast and honey." She swallows. She doesn't complain. Instead, she laughs. "My little brother liked kneading dough, too. One time–just a few days before... well, before I came here–he wanted to help shape the dough. He used his little chubby hands to roll out the strands. He said, 'Roots! I made roots!'" Mila's eyes brighten. Ainela can't tell if it's happiness or the glistening of tears. She wonders if the story is for the others or to soothe herself. "He took his dough roots outside and buried them in the dirt. He swore they'd grow tall as trees if we just watered them," she finishes on another laugh, the sound like church bells.

Kalina smiles faintly. "I love – I mean, I used to love watching the oven. For some reason, I thought the orange color of the fire burning was so cozy and pretty."

"I remember baking bread, too," Lusia says softly.

Like the smell of bread baking, the shift from resentment to peace is fragile. But it's there. Ainela tears a piece of her bread and holds it out to Mila. A silent *thank you*.

It doesn't take long for the silence to creep back in like cold air. The sounds in the air–the hacking coughs, the sniffling noses, the tiny whimpers of pain—fill the empty space around them with weight. The weight of fear closes in on them, makes roots soft. When they hear fierce voices above–the scraping of chairs against the wood, heavier footfalls–the air thickens with dread and exposes nerve endings. "What are they doing?" Klara asks, her eyes lifted to the ceiling.

"Could it be another vote?"

Something heavy drops, voices rise. The girls exchange glances. Ainela swallows. What if it another girl?

WHISPERROOT: A HUSHWOOD TALE

What does that mean for the ones already here? Is it a punishment? *He whipped her hands until they bled.* Who might be punished? Zosia? The air collapses around Ainela, shrinking, until it feels as real as the walls that trap her. When the hush falls—and there's no sound upstairs–the girls catch themselves gathering at the air vent, straining to decipher the murmurs. Not knowing is agony.

"They'll come here next." Larisa warns. "If something's wrong there, we'll pay here." Heated murmurs ignite sparks in the room.

Klara glares at Ainela and says firmly, "If he comes, don't cause trouble."

"You're telling *me* not to cause trouble?" Ainela grounds.

"Every time you do something stupid, it makes it hard on all of us. It won't hurt you to just obey."

Joanna agrees. Obeying is Joanna's safety net; Ainela doesn't respond to her. Instead, she looks at Klara. "Do you really believe that, too? You don't. You know you don't."

Klara hesitates. "There's a time and a place to say no. It's not just *your* safety, it's all of us."

"But it's my life."

Klara pauses. Ainela thinks she sees Klara's gaze soften, but then she blinks, and the fierceness is back. "It's ours too."

"All it does," Kaja's voice is breathy and light, almost as though it's just a light gust of wind blowing through the room, "Is make you a target. What difference does it make if you resist and are killed?"

"They won't kill–"

"You don't *really* believe that, do you?" Klara throws her question back at her, sarcasm dripping from her voice, her eyes narrowing.

Ainela looks away, the room falls silent. "They're my words. If they take that, what's left of me?"

So, they listen. They don't make plans. They don't practice the tapping code. They don't hum. They simply sit in silence–silence pressing heavier than the chanting.

"They come." Kaja hears it first: footfalls by the stairwell, moving fast. Faster than their usual rhythm. She frowns and murmurs, "Three–no, four—four coming."

Panic spirals through the room like leaves falls from trees. Girls move. Halina looks at Ainela's wounds–her swollen eyes, her split lip, the bruises—then snaps to Iskra, lingers briefly, cuts to Mila. Who to protect? Ainela watches her hesitate, then step away from her, positioning herself between the two weakest. Klara angles Lusia a half-step behind her.

Ainela pauses.

"*Every time you do something stupid, it makes it hard on all of us.*" Klara's words whisper through her mind. She wants to step to Lenka–she vows to protect her–but what if she has to protect herself? The edge of her heart cracking feels like breaking bone as she stays put, alone, without a shield.

As the footfalls pause outside, keys jingling, Klara's shoulders drop half an inch. She motions, waves her hand, for Ainela to come closer. Ainela shakes her head, her chest heaving, her heart quivering. The door tears open, fast. Mateusz, Jakub, Tomasz, the priest — faces blur together.

"Move! Get up!" Jakub shouts the command.

Girls scramble but Mila freezes. She means to obey, but her body isn't as quick. Mateusz's baton strikes her in the stomach as she tries to rise. Tomasz yanks Halina by the arm when she tries to step close, throws her backward. The priest watches, standing beside Jakub. Clasping his hands behind his back, he nods. "It may seem harsh, but blood sanctifies obedience. The ground remembers what sinful flesh forgets."

Mila curls on the ground, her knees bent as she grips her stomach. He doesn't tell her to stand again; Mateusz simply strikes. When Ainela pushes past the girls, trying to get to her, Tomasz's whip cracks against her shoulders. The sting as it rips open the flesh of her shoulder makes her arch, stumble into Kaja. Girls crowd back, moving away. Iskra tries but isn't fast enough. Mateusz shouts, "I said move!" and his baton snaps against Iskra. Ainela screams "stop!" and Tomasz punches her to the ground, kicking her in the stomach. As she rolls to her knees, Ainela lifts her head. She notes Jakub looking to the side, towards the empty wall, his face furrowed in a brow, as if he sees something that isn't there. The priest stands, lips thinned, unmoved. From the side of her eye, Ainela watches as Mila is thrown, hard, against the stone wall. She slides to the ground. Just behind her, the sound of crunching bone reverberates in Ainela's ears. Iskra.

A piercing scream cuts the room like a knife.

He doesn't speak but the authority of the priest is noticed by everyone: he holds up a hand, and the men stop. He studies the room, blood splatters on the dirt, on the stone walls, on the knuckles of his guards. "What are you?" he asks softly.

Those who can reply, "Unclean but obedient" in voices that stutter, shake, or rasp with tears. Those who cannot, try. Shaken by the sight of Iskra and Mila, needing him to get out of the room so she can help them, Ainela gives partial concession: she speaks so as not to draw attention to herself. Only Klara hears her voice: "Clean but *dis*obedient."

"Do not touch the ones who did not speak." He nods at Jakub, who positions himself against the corner wall, legs spread slightly apart, whip coiled around his wrist. The others leave, closing the cellar door with a snap.

Halina, Ainela and Klara move as one–Ainela barely standing, Halina's pale skin blooming with the outlines of bruising.

"What are you doing? Get away from them," Joanna's voice cracks, her throat swallowing convulsively. The three leaders pause. Joanna's gaze slides to Jakub. "They'll come back," Joanna whispers.

"It's too late for them." Lusia agrees, her voice tearful.

"You don't get to make all the decisions. Not when it's our lives too."

"You made it worse again. You *yelled* at them, why did you do that?"

"He was killing her!" Ainela's own voice cracks under the strain. Closing her eyes, she drags in a deep breath. "They're part of us." Her voice pleads with the others. She holds out a hand towards Iskra. "Look at them," Ainela begs.

Klara bites her lip.

Halina hesitates, her gaze sliding toward Jakub. Fear strangles compassion. "I'm not going to touch them."

"Halina."

"Stop!" Halina's voice rises. Tears glisten in her eyes as she stares at the Iskra, then Mila's still body. She uses her knuckles to cover her mouth as if she's stifling a scream of her own. "I don't want to die." She pauses and then whispers, "I'm sorry." She turns and slides down against the nearest wall, bowing her head into her knees. Ainela swivels, watching girls, one by one, retreat until only she and Klara remain standing in the middle of the room.

Ainela's chest heaves as she looks at Jakub who watches her silently. Even his silence felt dangerous: what he didn't do, what he didn't stop. Tilting her chin up defiantly, she rips a thin strip of fabric from her sleeve and goes to Iskra first. The blood on the ground is wet and warm as it oozes between her toes. Working silently, she wraps the strip of fabric around Iskra's arm that bleeds. Klara starts shaking. She takes one step forward but when Jakub's body shifts, she shrinks, folding to the ground. When Ainela's fingers fumble, unable to rip more of her shift, Klara uses her teeth to tear the hem of her dress. She passes it to Ainela who wraps Mila's head. As her shoulders start shaking uncontrollably, Ainela presses her forehead to Mila's and closes her eyes, tears sliding from the crease of her nose and into her mouth. The taste of salt reminds her she is alive.

And, as the blood soaks into the packed earth, it pools in a place so deep beneath the surface that only whispers survive. From that pool, something stirs. It travels the wrong way–up instead of down—fueled by truths left unsaid. Roots braid with roots. Soon, it breaks the surface, and something stronger than geology pulls it through blankets of snow. By the backside of the chapel, Zosia notices a whisperroot growing where it hadn't before.

Ainela doesn't move from Mila's side. Instead, she lies beside her, her hand touching the smaller girl's. She prays—something she thought she wouldn't do ever again. She barely notices the throbbing in her muscles, the pain of the bruises, the ache of the cuts. As her eyelids fall, that wretched verse crawls in: *the wage of sin is death. Her flesh runs with blood, and she shall be put apart.* Ainela shakes her head, two quick, sharp shakes to dislodge the lies. She barely notices when the heavy oak door clicks shut with Jakub moving from within the room to the corridor. Her breathing deepens, her body recognizing safety before her mind.

The frost on the window thickens, making a tiny fissure along the edge of the glass. It's a small thing that only Kaja will soon notice. The sound of the ashfeather owl is close enough for the girls to hear its low cry. It isn't piercing. It's just loud enough to be heard, as if someone blows out a flame. Ainela adjusts her head against the crook of her arm, trying to find a comfortable position. Black whips. Steel-toed boots. The sound of bone cracking. She moans, rolling, her hand falling from Mila's as she tries to escape the nightmare. *Unclean but obedient. The wage of sin is death. Her flesh runs with blood, and she shall be put away.* Mila's blood–or maybe it's Iskra's—stained her knees, squished between her toes.

It should have been me. I refused to be obedient. It should have been me.

Her legs twitch as branches scratch her face; she runs, but there's nowhere to run.

The sound of the breathy ashfeather owl comes again: *hwooooooh hwaaaahh*. Ainela sees it fly across the back of her eyes. It happens so fast she's not sure if it was truly an ashfeather owl or just a random barn owl. Cold hardens at night, making her curl into herself, using her breath to warm the space between her face and her knees. By the time dawn seeps weakly through the window, and Ainela's eyes open, a dread settles deep inside her. The others begin to stir. Quietly, Ainela turns.

Mila.

She's still sleeping. Blood and straw dried in her hair, scratch marks alongside her cheek. Her small hand, the one Ainela held, lay half-curled, as if she's reaching for something even in sleep. She never found the breath they stole. No one names it. Naming it makes it real. But they watch, their minds alive. *Her brother buried dough strands, called them roots, and swore they'd grow as tall as trees if they were watered.*

When the bolt scrapes and the door opens, Jakub steps in alone. His boots scuff against packed dirt and he pauses by Mila's body. He uses a piece of chalk, white against his cracked hands, to mark a line on the stone wall. A tall, clean and sure. The sound of chalk against rock is sharp as bone snapping. Ainela's chest seizes at the sound: the tally is as final as a grave. There's no cruelty, no satisfaction on Jakub's face, only the precision of a soldier. But the emptiness of it, the lack of his mourning, feels like another blow. The priest doesn't come. This makes Larisa break down in tears. Clutching her rosary, she frantically whispers, "She has to have a funeral." But there is no one to perform one.

Wordlessly, he grabs Mila around the waist and lifts her over his shoulder. She makes no sound, no movement. Her eyes don't twitch. Her limbs dangle, light as straw, her hair dragging the dirt. Ainela's eyes follow Jakub, her eyes never leaving Mila's face. She leans her head against the stone, closing her eyes.

The ashfeather owl cries again, a breathy whisper.

In Myreska, they say if you hear the ashfeather owl three times in a row, it means someone is being remembered.

Ainela sits with the Rhymebook balanced on her knees. The frost along the window has spread in the night, a thin white scar across the glass. She runs her fingers over the cover, smudged with dried blood and soot, as if touch alone could force words out of her.

The page waits. Blank. Too blank. When she presses the nub of charcoal to it, the sound it makes is sharp, scraping, like chalk against stone—like Jakub's tally. Her hand jerks back. Her shoulder throbs, but she hardly feels it anymore; pain has become background, a faint hum her body no longer resists.

She tries again. The charcoal hovers over the paper. Her hand trembles, searching for letters, for names, for anything—but the only words that come are the ones carved into her skull:

Unclean but obedient. The wage of sin is death. Her flesh runs with blood...

They crowd out everything else, slithering through her memory, poisoning it.

She squeezes her eyes shut, willing Mila's face to stay. The little brother with dough roots, the laugh like bells. For a moment she sees it—and then it slides away, like frost melting from glass.

The charcoal slips from her fingers. Falls to the dirt. No sound at all.

Her breath shudders, but no tears come. The sobs stay locked inside, like they belong to someone else. She feels hollow, an emptied-out thing, her ribs the walls of a room that only silence inhabits.

The ashfeather owl calls once, low and breathy—*hwoooooh hwaaaahh*. The sound drifts through the cracks in the cellar, carrying with it the legend every girl here knows. Three cries, they say, and someone is being remembered.

Ainela clutches the Rhymebook to her chest, pressing her forehead to its cover. The rough fibers bite her skin, and she almost welcomes it. If the book can't take her words, at least it can take her weight. No name goes down tonight. No verse. No rebellion stitched in ink. Only silence.

And in that silence—heavier than the chanting—Ainela lies still, listening for the owl.

Out of the depths I cry to you, O Lord.
Lord, hear my voice.

Psalm 130:1-2

Her tears prove the cleansing has begun

Myreska

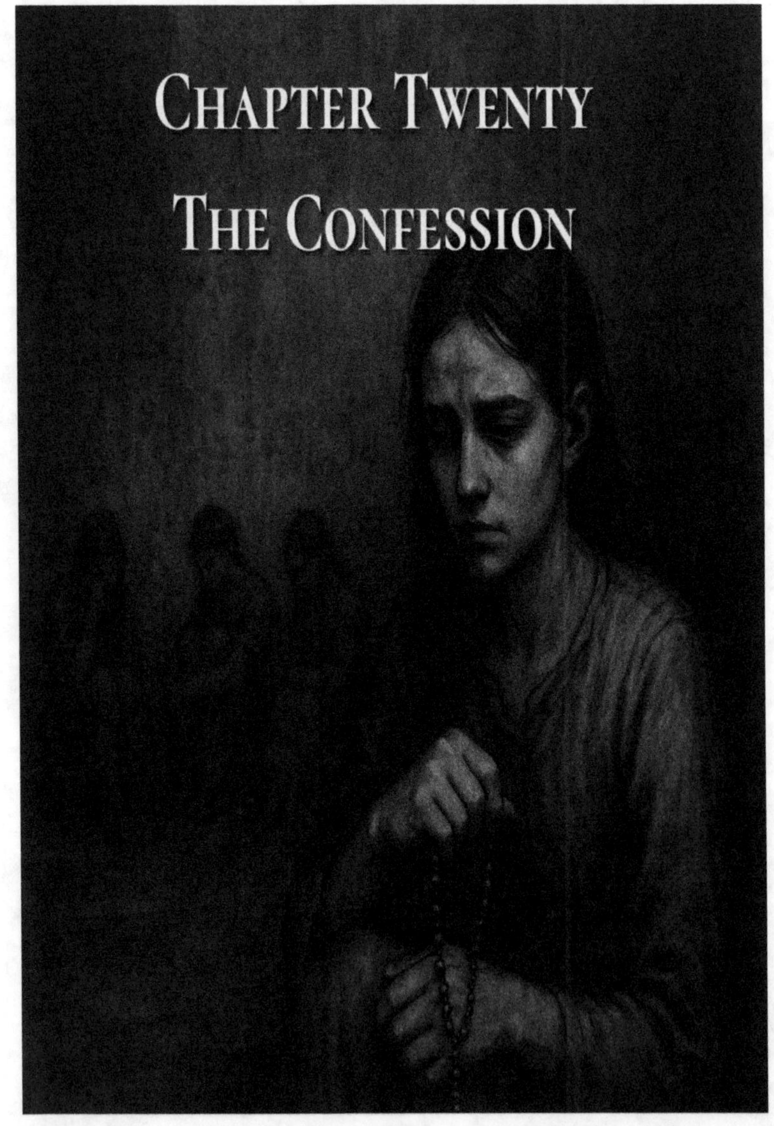

CHAPTER TWENTY
THE CONFESSION

WHISPERROOT: A HUSHWOOD TALE

Sorrow breathes. Like a thief, it slips past the locks of your heart and slides in unannounced. Sometimes it sits quiet but crushing, like a stone you can't shift. It refuses to be dislodged or ignored. Sometimes it transforms ordinary things–like a tin cup, tipped over by an empty space or a bit of thread in just the shade of ash–into landmines set to detonate. Sometimes, sorrow storms through in tidal waves, bringing tears, screams or body shakes for no reason at all.

And then, sometimes, instead of dropping one stone into the hollow spaces of your chest, sorrow drops dozens of them at once. Instead of one wave, it's a tsunami made up of shreds of memory, fragments of whispered stories, and images of what might have been. To survive, the mind rips the feeling from the memories, leaving only numbness behind. You're left to watch your own grief as if it were a play. Not real. Sorrow breathes, inhaling and exhaling pain like razor blades slicing hope. Numbness clogs the lungs, trapping the sorrow that's already inside, refusing to draw in more.

That's what grips the room now.

Numbness born of a tsunami of violence, tidal waves of sorrow.

Blood stains in the dirt. Straw still remembers her body's shape. A small splash of water, knocked over by a guard's boot, spirals Ainela's thoughts. *They didn't let her drink all her water.* This sparks the sorrow stones and heats Ainela's fury. She rolls the sorrow as if it's a hangnail to pick, feeling its weight, its shape. Her eyes stay locked on Mila's empty space.

Whispers fold into the quiet spaces–at first, too soft to distract the sorrow, but then grows in intensity. Ainela glances to the back wall to see Larisa clutching the rosary beads, her eyes closed, her lips moving. She clutches the rosary beads so tight Ainela fears they'll cut her palms. She rocks back and forth, slowly, sitting on her knees.

When the whispered prayers finally stop, Ainela exhales a breath she didn't know she held; her shoulders relax. Larisa rises from her knees, twisting the beads around her fingers. "I need confession."

"What?" Lusia asks.

Larisa brushes her hair off her face. "Don't you see?" She pulls her lip between her teeth, her brows furrowing. "Mila's gone. We have to do something. What if they're right about some of it?"

"Right about what?" Klara's voice holds skepticism.

"I don't know. I don't know. But remember the sermons? Chapel? What if suffering is proof I've sinned? If I confess...."

Bubbles of silence grow around the room. Sermons from the priest tangle with the Scriptures they know. "I don't think that's how God works," Tatiana says. "Is it? Does He make you hurt if you've done something wrong?"

Larisa hesitates. "I – I – the Bible says He's an angry God."

"But isn't He supposed to be loving? Merciful?" Joanna asks.

Tears billow in Larisa's eyes. Her breathing turns shallow. Her hands tremble. "If I can have confession, it might stop all the hurt."

Halina holds out her palm, trying to calm her. "So, what? You want to ask for the priest?"

"You'd be walking into a trap," Ainela says clearly. For a moment, her eyes soften. "I know what you're trying to do. You prayed, and you want Him to help. But asking that priest for anything isn't a good idea."

"I just –"

Ainela bristles. "He *wants* us to think we're *unclean,* Larisa."

WHISPERROOT: A HUSHWOOD TALE

Lenka flinches at the room. Iskra coughs and mutters, closes her eyes, too weak to protest. Most of the girls shift their gazes, afraid. Afraid that Larisa is right, and afraid that Ainela is right. Larisa folds her arms, one hand clasping the other, pressed against her heart. She walks to the end of the room, stares out towards the window.

"You had your sister," she said softly. "Mila has – had a brother. Most of you have one or the other." She swallows. "I don't. I never did. I only had God." She hesitates, her eyes taking on a haunted look. "He – he says I'm an idolator, that I pray to Mary like she's my god. He says I was creating my own religion, mixing superstition with Scripture because I carry my beads everywhere." Her voice cracks. "One time, my mother almost died. He wouldn't pray for her because she didn't go to confessional. So, I prayed for her. I held my rosary, and I prayed so hard."

"Your mother is still alive."

She nods. "She got well."

"I remember this," Kaja whispers. "He gave a sermon against false gods and superstitious charms–said they were rebellion dressed as piety. He said you weren't praying; you were –"

"Chanting." Kaja and Larisa speak it at the same time.

"I – I said no, I wasn't, that I was clinging to God." She lifts a shoulder. "But I wasn't like everyone else. I prayed too much."

Ainela says, "If it's God that can heal you, confess to God, if that makes you feel better."

"I can't. I've asked Mary to intervene, I've begged. But–Mila—" tears choke her. "I need a priest. I need confessional."

The words hang in the air. Larisa spirals further and further with each passing hour, alternating between crying, walking, and praying. Her breath snags like she's drowning, her knuckles go white around the beads. When the door opens, she runs to Tomasz's feet. Klara gasps as if to protest, a strangled sound coming from her throat. A gut-level dread settles like heavy fog between the girls. What if she confesses something they've done? Klara's lie about stealing the herbs? Ainela's secret tapping code? Halina healing? Trust frays easily.

Surprised, Tomasz freezes. "What are you doing?" he asks, holding bowls of broth for their midday meal.

"Please," Larisa begs, her head bowed, her eyes on the floor. "Please ask the priest if he'll hear my confession."

"What confession?" Tomasz frowns.

"I need the priest to hear me."

Surprise fading, Tomasz steps around her, passing out the bowls. Larisa doesn't move. She stays in the center of the room, kneeling. Her rosary, condemned as charms, hangs between her fingers. Tomasz mutters, "I'll tell Father Ignacy."

He did it.

Tomasz really told the priest she wanted to confess, and the priest had not laughed at her. Now the door yawns, and it's her name called. Her step. Not Ainela's. Not Lenka's. Hers. She scurries to stand, her fingers aching from clutching the beads so tightly. Nerves curl in her stomach, making her nauseas.

Idols.

False gods.

The rosary beads burn her palms. Should she leave them? No. No, she won't do that. What he said isn't true: she prays to Mary; she uses the beads because they are conduits to Him. She isn't worthy of going before Him as she is—she's a sinner and He can't be in the presence of sin. So, she prays to Mary, she clutches her beads. It is not the priest's. It is God's. t's not that He doesn't love her. It's that He can't hear her until she confesses. She believes that – she must believe that.

WHISPERROOT: A HUSHWOOD TALE

The air upstairs is cold—colder than she remembers. Her thumb rubs the worn crucifix smooth. He doesn't lead her into the confessional booth – instead, he shows her into a small room behind the sanctuary. A rack of vestments wait in the corner. He doesn't speak but when he waves, she kneels while he sits in a wooden chair in front of her. She feels small. The stone bites her knees, but this is penance. Penance offers a chance to be heard by God.

"Bless me for I have sinned," her voice shakes, her eyes stare at a chipped spot on the floor.

He does not thunder. He does not sneer. Instead, he bends forward, bracing his elbow on his knee. For a moment, Larisa sees him as he should be, as the town wants him to be. In a gentle, low voice, he asks, "What bothers you, child?" Shades of blue swirl in his eyes, and she can see herself reflected in them.

She spills the words she carries like stone inside: her anger at the girls who blame her prayers, her fear that doubt is the worst sin of all, her hollow ache at night when she wonders where He is. She confesses hunger, envy that Klara and Halina and Ainela still seem so strong, even her flash of anger at God when Mila died. Her throat burns, but the words pour out like water from cracked jug.

The room quiets afterwards. She smells the musty, warm smell of the chapel. She waits for absolution. For mercy. For the sign that heaven still opens for her. But, when he spoke again, his words were not of forgiveness but of memory—his memory. He spoke of his sister, of how she tempted men with her wildness. With child when she was but a child herself. "Her child was breathless out of the womb, but she denied the baptism. She wrapped her in a red shawl and buried her, nameless, unblessed, denied heaven." His voice thickens with grief and Larisa leans forward, her own eyes glistening.

He knows. He understands.

But then his voice hardens. "Sin took them. Her impurity kept them from heaven. Do you see? It is better to scourge than to leave the soul unclean. It's better to suffer in flesh than rot in eternity."

She gasps, leaning back. The candlelight flickers and something flashes in his eye. She thinks it's mercy. She believes it. She has to. He lifts his hand, as though in blessing, and she waits, trembling. His thumb presses hard into her forehead, grinding ash into her skin.

Ash—the ruins of fire, the remains of what is consumed. Ash—the end of a body once whole, now scattered, nameless. Ash—what is left after sacrifice, after destruction, after all voice has been burned away.

It is not oil of chrism, not the cross traced in blessing. It is ruin, ground into her flesh. A mark not of forgiveness but of annihilation.

She inhales sharply, her fingers tightening around her beads. He leans forward, his robes flowing, the smell of candlewax and smoke drifting towards her. He whispers: "Your confession is obedience."

The door creaks open, and Ainela's head lifts before she can stop herself.

Larisa stumbles inside, knees scraped raw, a dark smear of ash pressed into her forehead like a wound. She clutches the rosary so tightly the metal cross bites into her palm. Her lips move ceaselessly, prayers tumbling out in a frantic murmur, faster than breath.

The girls recoil. Lenka curls toward the wall, whispering *unclean, unclean,* as if the word could make her vanish. Halina edges back, her spine rigid against stone. Even Kaja's stillness fractures, her gaze darting toward the window slit, as though the forest might answer where heaven will not. Ainela cannot look away. Her jaw tightens until it aches; her nails carve half-moons into her palms. Her stomach twists, bile rising sharp in her throat.

Larisa's face is not softened by confession. It is fevered, shining with something that isn't hope but desperation hardened into zeal. Whatever the priest gave her, it wasn't mercy. It was poison.

An understanding so terrible it causes Ainela's limbs to quake blooms. *That's what he's doing; he's finding something to break each girl like a wild horse is made docile through the snap of a whip.* Lenka, splintered by shame, hollowed until she has only one word left. Mila, erased by death, her laughter nothing but a ghost in the straw. Iskra gnawed so thin they see the shape of her bones more than her flesh. And now—the weapon he uses against Larisa is her faith.

The thought claws through Ainela's chest: *he will find her fault line too.* If he does, he'll split her open the same way, until nothing remains but obedience. Her throat burns; her limbs grow heavy with the weight of it. Panic twists. She threads a soft, low hum—her eyes moving from one girl to another, silently pleading–*don't leave me alone, hum with me.*

But no one does.

Her tune fractures, splinters, but still she presses on. The hum tangles with Larisa's whispered, frantic prayers. The sounds curl through the chamber like smoke, filling the air. One sounds like a vow. The othor sounds like surrender.

Some roots remember
longer than the forest does.

---

margin note,
The Embergirls' Rhymebook

CHAPTER TWENTY-ONE

UNWRITTEN

WHISPERROOT: A HUSHWOOD TALE

Kneeling on her knees, Ainela pauses, blowing out a small breath. Her eyes instinctively triage the others. Kalina hasn't needed as many rests–drenched in cold water, she still scrubs the stone floors with almost as much strength as when work began. She stumbles when walking–carrying the water bucket is hard for her. *Still safe from collapse.*

Her eyes barely skim over Joanna before noting–*safe from collapse.* Joanna thrives when they work. She says it's a chance to see. When she turns the page that night, Ainela will ink the name *Joanna*, kindling it beside the fire of her notes. *Mateusz eats with his left hand. If you hug the wall of the corridor, there's a 'quiet lane' - boards that don't creak or groan - that leads from the cellar to the laundry room. The priest's hand twitches before he singles one of them out.* Joanna gathers it all as if each fact is tinder for a fire that has not yet been struck and Ainela commits them to memory, to the Rhymebook. Survival is built from fragments.

Her gaze falters on Lenka.

The girl's rag moves in jerks, shoulders quivering with each scrape. When the bucket sloshes too high, Ainela nudges closer, dipping her own cloth into it to disguise Lenka's slowing pace. Their elbows brush. Lenka startles, breath catching, but matches Ainela's rhythm until their strokes fall in sync. Scrubbing the stone, she hears Lenka's breath catch and moves only her eyes. The girl sill works.

"If I had fought back like you...maybe...they wouldn't have..."

Ainela whispers, "If you had fought back, you wouldn't be scrubbing these floors."

"But you fought..." Lenka's voice scrapes out, as if shame has burned her throat.

"We're not the same person. You survived. You're alive. So, you won that fight."

Lenka's lips press tight, her jaw trembling. Her gaze shifts, catching on Ainela's steady hands. Her strokes smooth out, steadier now, as if the rhythm belongs to both of them.

She shoves her hands into the bucket, lye stinging her hands, water sloshing over the rim. With one palm flat on the stone, she scrubs. When she sees dark spots—stains—memories flash hot behind her eyes: blood pooling beneath Mila, the sight of dark red staining her palm, her body limp over Jakub's shoulder. *The wage of sin is death*.

Her palms grind harder, punishing the stone until her breath hitches. The stain will not lift. It never does. She blinks, but the vision lingers—Mila slack in his arms, the dark spill spreading wider than any cloth could cover. Her chest tightens. The lye burns deep, sharp as if it wants to carve penance into her skin.

A shadow falls across the floor. Ainela flinches, expecting the boot, the bark of correction. Instead, the brush of a bucket nudges closer. A fresh rag settles at the edge of her reach, rough but clean. She does not look up. She knows the stride, the way silence follows him like a second shadow. Jakub does not speak. He does not linger. But when she presses the rag to the stone, the work eases. For a heartbeat, survival does not mean only enduring—it means someone else sees.

The longer she scrubs, the more her hands sting. Red splotches scar the back of them, the angry red spreading between her knuckles. She rocks back on her heels, taking a moment to pause. She uses her two first fingers to gently brush the splotches. When the steel-toed boots appear in front of her, she sighs, picking up the cloth. She grinds her teeth, preparing to push her tender hands into the lye soap, but then: "Stand up, Twelve."

My name is Ainela.

She deliberately wait, counting slowly in her head. *One, two, three.* "Don't make this harder on yourself. Stand up." Jakub's voice is tense. She decides she will not stand before she gets to *ten. Four, five, six.* From the corner of my eye, she sees Lenka bow her head. *If they punish me here,* she thinks, *she might get caught in the fray.* When Jakub shifts threateningly, she puts her palms on the floor, shifts a leg, and starts to stand. *Seven, eight.* "Twelve, that was my last warning." To make his point, Jakub kicks the bucket of water away from her. She continues to slowly rise, straightening her back so that she stands fully upright only when her mind reaches *ten.*

Jakub's eyes stare unflinching at her: instead of bowing her head, she returns his stare.

"Insolence," Tomasz spits.

Jakub steps half a step closer to her, forcing her to look up. She swallows but does not back down. When he grips her arm and pulls her ahead of him, a ghost of a smile plays on her lips. The smile fades as he leads her alone into the corridor. As they walk, she notices fear clipping her breath, shortening it with every step. She stops breathing, holds her breath for two, three steps, then focuses on the boards. That one makes no noise beneath hor weight... *hush*...the one by the drainage pipe groans...*cry.* Instcad of watching as the room at the end of the corridor comes closer, she names each board. *Hush...hush...hush....cry.* The three boards between the laundry and the cellar door are silent ones. Her memory tucks it away.

Her breath is steady but her heart races as Jakub grasps the edge of the wooden door and pulls it open. He does not step inside but announces: "Twelve." He puts a hand between her shoulder blades firmly. Her feet skid slightly on flagstones slick with damp. One stone in the center has been worn smooth, as though knees have knelt there too many times, grinding themselves into obedience. A dark groove near the wall collects water, dripping faintly, plink...plink...the sound puncturing the silence like a metronome. Jakub pulls the door closed, leaving her alone with the priest. She shifts, trying to remember. She thinks of Joanna. She would remember everything about this room: it's low ceiling and stone walls that make it feel as small as a cell, the way dark patches of mold spreads across the stone wall like bruises, the four iron sconces that line the walls. A single stub of candle burns, but it flickers more than it lights. The rest are dark.

He stands by a small table draped with a cloth that was likely once white but is now yellowed. A brass, tarnished crucifix lies by his hand. The room breathes with silence. There are no girls. No sound at all except the *thu-thump thu-thump* of her heart and the occasional plink of water in the groove. The longer he is silent, the louder her heart.

"The time has come," his voice is soft. Never loud. But, beneath the softness, there's something else–an anticipation, an eagerness–that stills Ainela's breath. She bites the inside of her cheek hard; her pointer finger scratches the nail bed of her thumb until a hang nail forms. When he walks towards her, Ainela instinctively takes a half-step back.

She doesn't see the belt in his hands until the flickering candlelight catches its silver buckle. Her eyes train on it, her mind whirls, cataloging the room. Table. Scones. An old chair. "They laugh; they dance—they rebel. And, when they do, the fire consumes them."

Panic races through her. Without thinking, she turns, grabs for the door. Her hands claw the edges of the door, then curl into fists that bang on it. Suddenly, she feels his hands grasp her shoulder, tightening his grip. Before he can pull, she twists, running to the other side of the room.

He lifts his brows calmly. "I know your kind."

"You don't know me at all," she spits.

WHISPERROOT: A HUSHWOOD TALE

"Oh, but I do. You think rebellion saves you?" He laughs. "It doesn't. It just damns you twice." He walks towards her, she steps backward. Her scream pierces the silence of the room as she grabs the crucifix from the table and throws it at him. The brass cup is next. One clicks against the stone, falls to the ground, the other hits the wooden door and slides to the ground. He stops moving and says very calmly: "Kneel."

"*No.*"

"You mistake defiance for courage, child. It is better to be broken now than to rot forever. A father chastens the daughter he loves." When she sprints, he moves faster than she'd ever seen him do. His arm grabs her hair and yanks so hard she stumbles. Her side hits the stone wall before she trips. She tries to pull away, but he twists her hair around his fingers like a rope and yanks so hard she screams from pain. She grabs his wrist and pulls but he uses his arm to shove her down.

The room spins, narrows. Panicked, she takes her fingers and rakes them so hard down his cheek she draws blood. He jerks her head up, then bangs it down against the stone floor. When he grabs the hem of her shift, fear explodes like a bullet inside her. She can't hear his words anymore, only his breathing, and the smell of incense fills her nostrils, making her head pound. His knee pins one leg down. Her screams echo. When his hand grabs the edge of her undergarments and pulls so violently they tear, Ainela arches, her lungs collapsing, the air in the room shrinking until her vision starts to darken. The stone is so cold against her bare flesh. Shame washes over her in waves as she realizes she is bare before him.

"Stop! Stop! I've never kissed anybody, I swear!" Tears clog her voice. His elbow digs into her chest, holding her down. When his weight settles on top of her, she turns her face so she can't see him. She sees a silver button popped from her shift and she stares at it until the tears come so fast she starts hyperventilating. There's a deep groan, a thrust and then—a sharp pain she's never felt as something breaks her body open.

Caterbutton!

The silver button changes color, looks like the button Zosia used to thread a safety belt for the caterpillar. *If I just keep looking, it will stay a caterbutton, not what he is doing to me.* Shaking, she catches sight of a feather lying against the corner of the room. It's grey, the color of ash, and she stares at it. *If you hear the ashfeather owl three times, it means someone is being remembered.* She chokes on her tears. *There's no ashfeather owl here to remember me here.*

"Her flesh runs with blood," he murmurs. "She shall be put apart. This is the way of cleansing you." Again and again, her body is shoved up against the stone floor, his breathing hot against her face, his weight making bruises on more than her body. She thrashes her legs, kicking until she hits the small table. It wobbles and the candle snuffs out, pitching the room into darkness. He laughs, his hand gripping her face and digging his fingers into her cheeks. "You'll look at me. I'll see you breaking." His mouth is angry and hard when it grounds onto hers. His tongue feels too big. She uses her fists to strike his shoulders, his back, but she's too small. She pushes against him, but it's not a fair match and when he bites her bottom lip hard enough to draw blood, she mumbles a foreign word: "Please."

The hairs on his legs against hers, the feel of him scraping her, thrusting harder and harder, and the sting of him slapping her over and over make collide until Ainela's world shatters. Chaos: there's untamed chaos tumbling through her mind, burying her body in it.

Abruptly, he stops, pushes himself off her. Frigid air *whooshes* over her skin, raising goosebumps. Shock crashes through her. She rips her gaze from the feather, pushing short, punctured breaths through her teeth. The tremors start in her legs, then travel quickly to her stomach and her arms. Her face flushes, then pales.

WHISPERROOT: A HUSHWOOD TALE

"Kneel." He says this as he shifts his robes, picks up the belt with the silver buckle from the table. She doesn't think she can move. Before she can try, the sting of his belt snapping across her thighs causes her to half-crawl, half-drag herself along the floor. But the sight of her blood on her legs makes her freeze, her lungs trapping her breath.

"Kneel."

Kneel. The word itself shackles her harder than the belt.

Feeling something deep inside of her crack, Ainela chokes on a sob as she rises to her knees. Her body shakes violently, bruises forming along her thighs, her chest, her heart. Her hair tangled and sliding across her face, she keeps her head bowed. Kneeling while he stares at her body births something hot, heavy and awful inside her: shame. She kneels not because she chooses, but because something inside her has been bent until it split. Obedience spills out of her like marrow.

When she obeys, he allows her to dress. His voice rises as he calls for Jakub.

The heavy door opens. She rushes towards the opening so fast she collides with Jakub's chest. Her arms lift to protect her face from the blow she knows will come. When it doesn't, her eyes dart upward. Jakub's lips purse, his muscles tight. There's a grain on his sleeve, he smells of sweat, and the threadbare cuff—its seam unravels. Something coming undone. "Let's go."

She takes two steps, realizes she's limping, and moans, a breath fraying into a sob she swears he won't see. Her fists curl, her fingernails cut into her palms, and she walks out of the room.

She's never felt more alone.

Aboveground, the hushwood stirs. Whisperroots shift beneath the soil, carrying a tremor too deep for words. Zosia pauses, her fingers closing around the crooked button she stitched herself, thread fraying at the edges. For an instant she thinks she feels it dampen, as if the red thread were bleeding through her palm. A sudden ache splits her chest, sharp and nameless. She presses the button to her lips, whispers the name only her sister ever called her— *Caterbutton*. In the branches overhead, an ashfeather owl cries once, twice. The forest listens.

Confusion hangs like a curtain in her mind as she limps, wincing with each step, into the cellar. A few girls–one with dimples and a chipped tooth, another with hair the color of almonds, a third whose small pouch of herbs smells like rosemary–say her name, but she doesn't recognize who they are. Shock is like that. Brokenness is like that. Evil is like that. Takes what once was comforting and distorts it until you can't claim it.

Unclean but obedient. The phrase beats in her skull as tears blind her. She slides down the wall, the stone cold against her back. She is that now: *unclean but obedient. She knelt, so what does that make her?*

She hides her face in her knees, wrapping her arms around them. The stone, cold against her back, makes the room shift until it's *his* room. The stone was cold against her back there too. She moves until she touches nothing, tugging the hem of her shift down to cover more of her legs.

"Can I—"

She lifts her head, hair sliding over cheek.

Halina sits in front of her, holding a tin cup of water, gesturing to the blood smearing her skin. A piece of fabric — a torn piece of her shift – hangs from her hand, fraying and ragged. Ainela stares at the piece of torn garment, tips her head to her shoulder, her bottom lip quivers. Her garments were torn too. The spiral begins. The walls tilt, her breath shortens, her legs tremble.

Then—Klara's hand. Light against hers, three soft taps.

The hum threads through the room, breaking Ainela and yet stitching her together. She can't hum, not yet, but she listens. The hum carries her, and though she feels hollow, somewhere beneath the ash a hidden ember waits, faint but alive.

The only light is from the silver moon peeking through the high window. Silver—like the button she clung to, like the buckle. The page gleams faintly beneath it, daring her to write. *Name it.* The charcoal makes a crooked K. Her hand stutters. She presses harder, smears the mark into black until the page is ruined. Not a word. Not yet

The empty page mocks her. *Write it down.* But she can't. It burns the edges of her heart jagged until she snaps the loose pages together, shoves them back into the earth, as if she never wanted to write in the first place. She holds her hand in front of her. It trembles still, so she curls it into a fist and tucks it under her chin.

If we forget each other,
they win.
So we didn't.

———————————

margin note,
The Embergirls' Rhymebook

CHAPTER TWENTY-TWO

THE LAST JEST

WHISPERROOT: A HUSHWOOD TALE

Time is a shield.

Thin, cracked, but there all the same. It doesn't stop the blows, but it dulls the edges, stretches distance between wound and memory. Days blur until they are less a march forward than a wall they crouch behind. Ainela feels it in her own silence—how words press back into her ribs like seeds hidden in soil, waiting. Sometimes she thinks of Kalina, whose quiet is a shield, or of Zosia, whose silence is an unbreakable wall.

Ainela's silence is different: it roots. Stretches upward as if trying to break through the darkness to feel a touch of the sun. She can't find it. Nightmares wake her in cold sweats, the sight of buttons—any buttons—sparks tremors. Still, she roots. Searching for something, something beyond the nightmare. Every day, she opens the Rhymebook, caresses the word "embergirls" written in the margin of the first page. Banked. Every time that door opens and swallows a girl—Klara, Lusia, Kaja—there's a hot flicker deep within her, an ember waiting to ignite.

The others sense it. The longer her silence, the closer they come, as though her quietness bends the air, pulling them into orbit. They feel the edge of the flame. Some fear her defiance, her fiery passion, the way she paints a target on herself. Yet even in their fear, they draw nearer, shielding the ember, protecting it even when they don't mean to—because they know: if Ainela's hope breaks, so will theirs.

And so, the shield of time bends again, carrying them into another day of water and stone, where buckets bite into raw palms and silence weighs heavier than the work itself. The stone floor sweats beneath them, slick with cold. Ainela counts each girl as she always does—Kalina, still steady. Tatiana's lips cracked but humming. Lenka pale but upright. Her eyes linger on Iskra.

Iskra's shoulders dip beneath the weight of the bucket, arms trembling with every step. She stumbles, recovers, stumbles again. A cough seizes her thin chest, forcing her to her knees. The water sloshes across the floor, soaking the hem of her shift.

"Up," his command comes from the shadowed doorway. His voice carves the air, splits it, as sharp as a blade. "If she cannot stand, let her fall. Mercy is indulgence."

Ainela steps toward her but Mateusz's hand seizes her arm, jerks her back. "You don't listen."
She bites the inside of her cheek until she tastes iron.

Iskra wobbles to her feet, forcing a faded, crooked grin even as her lips split. "Guess I wasn't meant for this kind of work," she mutters, her words ragged and too thin for laughter.

No one dares smile, but they all cling to it.

Time is a shield. The more hours that pass, the closer they are to being marched back into the cellar, the closer they are to rest for Iskra. But a shield doesn't protect everything: it still leaves areas vulnerable. It can't block words that float like dust particles over and around it to gnaw at your mind even when the body still works.

"The frail are weeds in the field. Weeds choke the wheat. The field must be cleared of every last one." His voice acts as nails raking down a chalkboard. The deeply buried ember flickers as she watches Iskra's lips loosen, trying to find an easier way to take in oxygen. Her rag moves in jerks across the stones, her pale skin turning greyish and clammy. She coughs and nearly folds in half.

Ainela steps forward, ready to take her place, but his gaze warns hers.

"The unclean will not be carried." A benediction twisted into law.

Iskra shakes her head, as if she's sinking under water, and slides down against the wall until her shoulders hit stone. Her head tips to one side, eyelids flutter. She exhales with a whistle in her throat. The others pause, hesitate—but the priest's voice lashes them:

"Work."

The shield falters as though the arm that holds it has grown too weary to keep it high enough. And the sound of scrubbing drowns the sound of Iskra's failing breath.

They do not speak when the command finally comes to stop. Buckets are stacked, rags wrung until they hang limp, dripping trails across stone. The guards herd them back, their boots striking in uneven rhythms, echoing too loud in the corridor. Ainela keeps her eyes on Iskra's bent back, on the way she clutches the wall with one hand as if the stones might lend her strength. Every few steps her knees buckle. No one dares reach out. Even touching her now feels like defiance.

The air in the stairwell is different—closer, stale, tinged with smoke from somewhere above. It scratches Ainela's throat raw. She forces herself to memorize the pattern of the boards underfoot, the way one plank groans more than the others. Survival demands cataloguing, always cataloguing, though tonight the ledger in her mind runs in jagged ink. *Iskra's cough. Iskra's stumble. Iskra's lips split open from smiling when no one else dared.*

At the cellar threshold, Mateusz shoves the bolt back with a clang that makes them all flinch. The heavy door swings wide and swallows them again. They descend into dampness. Straw crunches beneath bare feet. Ainela waits until the door thunders shut, until the scrape of the key recedes, before she lets herself breathe.

For a moment, no one moves. The silence thickens until it seems the air itself presses on their chests. Kalina sets her bucket down with careful precision, as though breaking the hush might shatter something fragile. Lenka's arms tremble too much to lower hers quietly; water splashes across her shift, but she doesn't flinch.

Iskra slides to the floor, back against the stone. Her face gleams with sweat, strands of hair plastered across her forehead. Her breath rasps shallow, a bellows on the edge of collapse. Tatiana kneels quickly, pressing a rag of damp straw to her lips. The sound it makes—wet, pitiful—is worse than any scream.

Ainela crouches near but does not touch her. She wants to. Every nerve in her arm longs to wrap around Iskra's shoulders, to hold her upright. But the memory of Mateusz's hand jerking her back still burns like a phantom bruise. *The unclean will not be carried.* The words chase her into the cellar, gnaw at her ribs. She digs her fingernails into her palm until half-moons mark her skin.

No one weeps. Not yet. Their throats are too tight, and their silence is too heavy. It feels like standing on a frozen lake, the ice thin beneath their heels, each breath threatening a crack that could send them all plunging under. Ainela stares at Iskra's profile in the gloom. One thought root deep, sharp and bright as coal: *they cannot have the last word.*

Night. The cellar breathes heavy, each inhale and exhale overlapping in a broken choir. Iskra lies in straw, her body curled like a withered leaf. Every breath rattles, shallow, scraping her throat raw. Her skin burns hot then chills, sweat beading across her brow.

Ainela knows.

The others know.

Iskra knows.

But no one says it. Instead, they draw close, aching. Ainela curls beside her, entwines their fingers. "Stay," she whispers, though she knows the word is too small to hold her, the shield rusted until useless.

The cellar smells different: heavy, clotted, as though it has forgotten how to move. First comes the sweetness— sickly, cloying, like fruit left too long in summer heat. Underneath it, sharper notes creep in: metal and rust, as if the very walls have remembered blood. Damp stone holds the scent close.

It is a layered smell, one that clings to the back of the throat: sweet decay, iron, dust unsettled from stillness, the faint musk of something once warm now turned to silence. You could almost mistake it for old flowers, wilting in their vase—until the acrid bite pricks your nose and you understand. The room smells of endings.

The silence is so loud it speaks. Once, Iskra whispered a silly verse about the guards' squeaky boots. Ainela meant to write it down—she promises herself she will—but that page never came. The morning after she came back a shell of who she used to be, Ainela lay staring at a small crack in the wall where a shaft of sunlight slipped through. Iskra pressed her hand towards it and whispered, "*See? The world hasn't ended ye*t." Ainela still remembers the warmth across her skin.

"You made me a crown from straw once." Tatiana's voice is thick. Iskra's eyes flutter towards her, her lips curving gently. "Said queens don't need castles, just laughter. I thought you were serious for a minute."

Lenka gives a small chuckle. "Remember when you sewed that button back on my shift with thread you pulled from the straw? It held for weeks. I still check it before we line up."

"An old—" Iskra's voice fades, waits, tries again. "An old knot of my mother's."

"What I remember is that awful joke," Klara says, smiling through tears. "The one about the guard's bald head? No one laughed but you just kept repeating it until we did."

Laughter circles the room.

"It was funny," Iskra insists, her eyes drifting closed.

Voices rest. Time ticks by.

"If heaven," Iskra's raspy voice hugs them all, "needs cleaning, I'm not going." Her lip quirks again as Joanna brushes her hair off her face, resting her palm against Iskra's cheek. The words ripple through them, breaking into choked laughter. Kalina hides her face.

WHISPERROOT: A HUSHWOOD TALE

"You told me to breathe," Ainela whispers, her lip quivering, salty tears slipping from her eyes. "When I came back. You patted my hand and helped me breathe."

Iskra looks at her. Her eyes are glassy but not from tears. Iskra's hand twitches in Ainela's grip, there's a gasp, a sharp inhale. "Save me a page in the rhymebook. But... not page one." A wheeze. A grin. "That's too much pressure."

Their laughter is quiet, broken, but it circles her like a shield, raised high once again, a shield time can't break. For a moment, the blows dull, the weight eases and hope flickers.

Then her chest stills.

The silence is absolute.

And, somewhere deep, somewhere beneath the tears, beneath the pain, beneath the memories of torture, something hot, angry, and dangerous ignites within Ainela.

At the hushwood's edge, Zosia pauses, the locket warm in her palm. She doesn't need words to know. The absence finds her first, heavy as a shadow falling across her chest. The ground shivers faintly, whisperroots pressing up as though restless, as though carrying something too weighty for the soil to hold.

Emberflies scatter all at once, their sudden flight a storm of sparks rising into the branches. They drift in strange patterns, almost forming the shape of letters before dissolving again. The air tastes of ash, of endings carried on wind.

The ashfeather owl calls once. Twice. Three times. Each note lingers, stretched and mournful, echoing deeper than the forest should allow.

Zosia presses the locket to her lips, eyes closed. She does not speak—her silence is vow, shield, ember—but her body trembles with the effort of keeping it.

Somewhere in the hushwood, a low groan stirs, like boughs bending under unbearable weight. For a moment, Zosia feels as though the forest itself has reached for her hand. She opens her eyes. The emberflies have settled again, but the hush remains alive, restless, watching.

The room mourns.
But anger fuels Ainela.

She seizes the Rhymebook, charcoal trembling between her fingers. She presses down, desperate to remember, determined someone will know, even if it is only a blank page. Words spill over in her mind, fighting so hard for the chance to land first that letters smear, disintegrate. Isk— becomes black ash across the paper. She grits her teeth, struggles to control her breathing, to calm the wild hammering of her chest. But every time her eyes flick toward the far wall—toward the straw mat that will never again rise and fall with Iskra's breath—the fury blooms again. Her fingers shake too hard to obey.

Kalina shifts closer, shielding her with a thin frame, her back to the door in case it should creak open. Tatiana hums, soft and steady, a tune meant to anchor trembling hands. Lenka leans close, resting her forehead on Ainela's shoulder, her warmth a tether to the living.

WHISPERROOT: A HUSHWOOD TALE

Ainela squeezes her eyes shut. Counts. One, two, three. Four, five, six. Charcoal digs into her fingertips, smudging black into her skin.

She scrawls again, jagged and broken, the words crooked but unrelenting:

She made us laugh, and we will not forget.

"What was the poem?" Ainela's voice is hoarse, edged sharp.

"The poem?" Klara frowns, confused.

"About the guard's boots."

Joanna lifts her head, eyes glimmering with tears, the one who always remembers. Her voice quivers but steadies: *"Left foot, right foot, squeak on the stone."*

Ainela jerks her hand across the page, catching the words as they fall. *"He marches loud, so we all know we're alone."*

She can hear Iskra's grin in her mind, as if the joke still circles the air. She grips the charcoal tighter, and this time, her voice braids with Joanna's: *"Step again, step again, squeak and it fades—"*

The others lean forward, voices weaving into the rhythm. Together, they finish the line:

"Even the boots want to run from this place."

For a moment, their laughter rises—thin, choked, but real. The sound fills the cellar like breath after drowning. The words etch themselves into the page, into the air, into memory itself.

And Ainela thinks: if time is too weak a shield, then they will forge one out of words.

Appendix A

The Lost Girls' Rhymebook

A recovered document, found after the Myreska cellar was unearthed.
What remains of the girls' writings has been gathered here.
Though fragmented and incomplete, they remain preserved here
for historical records.

THERE IS A _MISTAKE_ HERE.
THEY CALL THEM LOST.

BUT I WATCHED THEM CARRY WATER DOWN THOSE STAIRS.
I COUNTED THEIR STEPS WHEN THEY RETURNED,
FEWER THAN WHEN THEY WENT.

I HEARD THEM WHISPER.
I SAW THEM WRITE.
LOST IS NOT THE WORD.

THEY CALLED THEMSELVES EMBERGIRLS
I SAW THE STITCH THAT PROVED IT—
FLAME, RAGGED BUT BURNING.

I WILL NOT LET THE NAME DIE.

THE BOOK IS NOT ASHES.
IT IS EMBERS.
IF YOU READ, READ IT AS FIRE.

J

Klara — She held fast, even as they tried to unravel her.

Halina — She guarded more than her own hunger.

Joanna — She taught us that memory itself is tinder.

Mila — Her laughter carried where silence could not.

kneel
they said
as if stone were safer than skin
my marrow cracked
and still I whispered
caterbutton, caterbutton
—a made-up name to hold myself inside
no ashfeather cried for me that night
so I drew one in the margin
with wings made of soot
and eyes that would not close
I called it memory
and told it:
if you see the silver buckle
turn your head
but remember me anyway
remember I stood
until they made me kneel.

Ainela — She named even silence to keep herself alive

ISK

I PRESSED THE ~~LETTERS~~ DOWN,
BUT ASH SCATTERED THEM.

HER SPARK CRACKED THE DARK,
THEN VANISHED INTO SMOKE.

Iskra — She sparked laughter, even when the cellar was ash

LEFT FOOT, RIGHT FOOT,
SQUEAK ON THE STONE.

HE MARCHES LOUD, SO WE
ALL KNOW WE'RE ALONE.

STEP AGAIN, STEP AGAIN,
SQUEAK AND IT FADES—

EVEN BOOTS

RUN FROM THIS PLACE.

For Iskra--her laughter carried further than their boots

We remember.
Not only as stone remembers,
but as roots remember
threading deeper with every silence.
The town called them lost.
Jakub named them embers.
But we—we have carried their voices,
and they do not fade.
In the hush of our branches,
in the marrow of our soil,
they are not gone.
they burn still.

The forest remembers longer than stone.

Part Three

We will not be silenced. Not again.

The Hushwood

TIFFINI JOHNSON

WHISPERROOT: A HUSHWOOD TALE

Snowfall still drifts as the heart of Winter turns the cold to frigid. Our animals have mostly retreated to burrowed dens or the cave tucked between our southern border and the blacksmith's shop. But a few prints, one human set and one set of hooves, can sometimes still be seen. Zosia is a frequent guest; her footprints trace the same path between the backside of the chapel and the frozen creek. She always stops at the same hushbark, the one with the hollow space, the one she and her sister used for trading secrets.

The *empty* hollow space.

She comes, clutching the locket, the one with the clasp that's still broken. We greet her by swaying–in the Spring, we'll have leaves again but, for now, our branches tilt just enough to shower her with a dusting of snow. She's discovered some of our secrets like the small brooch–curved teardrop holding an amber stone with darker speckles inside it. The surface of the stone was still glassy. We held the name of the girl who dropped it while running, a girl with a talent for noticing details. Her mother pressed it into the palm of her hand when they came for her. When she found it, Zosia rubbed her thumb over the rounded stone. The ground seemed to swell beneath her as if exhaling a name it had been waiting to share. We saw the moment she heard it – our whisper - because she gasped slightly, looking up and around her as if looking for the source of the sound.

She also discovered some of our secrets—even the hollow the duskstag likes to visit. She hasn't seen him. Not many see him. But she saw hoofprints the snow held and followed them. There are many trees that stand as sentinels, guarding the hushwild. She can't get in. But we watched her curiosity grow until she came to the woods and walked to the edge of the hushwild with her sketchpad and a stub of charcoal. She came early, right when the morning sun broke through the middle of the hushwood trees, casting their long shadows on the startling white snow. She spent hours here, sketching. Sketching each one of us as if she knew us personally – the ice cracks, Winter's fractured scar, the way some of us lean just slightly towards the chapel, the way the whisperroots crawl up the side of our trunks, the ashfeather's nest, made with tiny twigs and lined with feathers tinged in soot.

She's the only one who's ever noticed the soot.

She's back today, but we didn't drop snow on her or lean toward her gently. There's a weight in the air, a heaviness that only comes with mourning. The crunching of the snow beneath her boots remind us of breaking bones. The soulful cry of the ashfeather owl pierces the night—low and long. Emberflies hover but with only a flicker of their usual warmth, their light flickering slowly. Grief does that: it slows the pulse of life. Our exhale, the wind, blows sharper, its bite cutting through Zosia's mittens and into her skin. The kind of cold that makes you reconsider going to chapel. The kind of cold that makes your muscles ache the way our roots do. The kind of cold that makes you forget what warmth feels like. The kind of cold that seeps into the very fabric of your soul and makes you cry.

We cry, too.

WHISPERROOT: A HUSHWOOD TALE

Our bark tastes the metallic burn of iron as red sap drips from deep within us, slides with paralyzing slowness to stain the blanket of white snow on the ground. The ashfeather cries again, his song breathless and low. The shadows aren't playful or grand. The sun hides its face behind thick clouds. The ground trembles as a new whisperroot breaks through the frozen ground. Whisperroots spread the longer a truth is buried, but they start out small, as if they are waiting for someone to notice that something's amiss. Fragile, as if they don't want to grow, but staying below ground suffocates them. When it finally gathers the courage to break the surface, to expose a tiny piece of the buried truth that birthed it, it shivers in the cold, its veins blushing a faint red, as if embarrassed to say *I know something important.*

We are not embarrassed.

But as its roots burrow deeper into the soil, the whisperroot changes. It grows in strength. It tangles with other roots, grows arms that embrace the darkness and call it home. Its fragility is replaced with something more dangerous: anger. If touched, it warms the palm, as if to say *remember.*

The memories soak into the marrow of our soil until the trees swallow it.

We remember.

The girl with the bright smile. The one we watched because she made us laugh. The one who came with a playful jaunt to her step. The one who softly pet the hushwood when the sap came because she thought it dripped like tears. The one whose jokes made even the oldest of us smile. We remember her. We watched once as the priest made them stand barefoot in the snow until their skin turned blue. One girl clutched a corn doll and cried but Iskra didn't cry. She leaned closer and said, *Don't be scared. Watch.* And when the priest turned his back, she stuck her tongue out quickly, widening her eyes. Tatiana's tears frayed to laughter. *Now God knows who's really in charge.*

We remember.

The frigid air we exhale forces you to feel the loss. We breathe and you shiver with longing. You think it's for the wind to stop blowing. But that doesn't help. When the wind stops, that's the hushwood inhaling. It shrinks the air until you feel your chest tightening, your ribcage pressing against your sides. Without the wind all that's left is silence. The kind of silence that screams her name until it's the only thing you hear. The kind of silence that whispers *what if* until your heart cracks. Silence that lingers in your throat so thick you can taste the shape of the words you never spoke.

Iskra is not gone.

Not really.

Mila is not gone.

Not really.

Their voices, their laughter, their fears, their dreams – have become ours. We hold what the living forget. See? Look there, just beyond the third birch. The ground breathes, rising and falling in a soft rhythm. Pieces of charcoal-stained pages lay buried between our soil. The town may have found some of the writings, but not all of them. Words–their words–make certain places in the forest unexplainably warmer than others. The emberflies hover over these areas, as if the hidden words themselves embers, refusing to go out. You can silence a girl, but you cannot silence the roots. Roots name things. Roots carry truths. We've held them, cradled them in our arms like precious gifts, but truth refuses to remain buried.

We've waited so long.

We've been patient for so long.

We've held the remnants of things—brooches, ribbons, secrets, girls–too long.

Movement catches the dying light, shadows shift. From behind the birches, he steps. The duskstag stands on the crest of the hill, roots tangled in his antlers, hanging over his eyes and face. Snowmelt drips from the unburied roots and onto his coat. His skin glistens. The birch straighten themselves. We inhale. The air stills. Twigs snap from a birch and fall. The duskstag moves forward, taking two steps in the direction of the chapel, as if he's waiting.

We are weary of carrying so much, weary of a town who snuffs out their own. The roots ache with truths that will surface, truths pressing against the soil like bones against a shallow grave. If Zosia does not take them, if she does not open her hands to what we will place there, then we will give them anyway. Names will rise. Our arms are not meant to hold the silenced forever.

The cry of the ashfeather owl pierces the forest.

Someone is being remembered. Again.

We exhale and the cold bites your skin.

We heard her voice
and swallowed our own

Myreska

CHAPTER TWENTY-THREE

THE HUMMINGBIRD

WHISPERROOT: A HUSHWOOD TALE

Życie toczy się dalej.

Through war. Through Winter. Through hunger. Through gone girls. Even their parents couldn't wilt, not with other children to care for, to feed. Only one went crazy; the mother of the girl who sang. She wouldn't stop asking questions. Why, one day, the woman was waiting on the chapel steps when Father Ignacy arrived. She didn't just ask where her girl was, she *demanded* to know. She angrily pointed to the forest and said, *There? Has my little girl been hushed? Is she in that forest?* Father soothed her by promising her daughter was *in a better place* and taken care of; that this was for the best, not only for her daughter's soul, but for *the sake of the town*. She went home, her head low, tears rolling down her face. When we didn't see her for a few days, we sent Father Ignacy to inquire about her because that's what good Christians are supposed to do. We saw him go into her cottage, and we saw him come out. He told us there was a note saying not to worry about her, that she'd gone to Warsaw to stay with her mother. We said we'd pray for her a safe journey and return home.

The seamstress's daughter, Lydia, says she was lighting a candle on her bedroom windowsill and saw figures go into the cottage one night soon after. Three went in, but only one came out the front door, and he held a knotted rope. The other two must have left through the cottage's back door.

We believe she'll stay in Warsaw.

We don't feel much sympathy for her. In fact, while we would never have said it directly to her, some of us whisper. *She thinks her grief is worse than ours, but it's not. We can't even say our daughters' names.* Maybe we could have; she said hers.

But we didn't.

Instead, we moved through life.

Today's the communal feast. We've decorated the chapel's gathering room. Father went door to door, to each home, with a basket, asking for ingredients *for the feast.* We couldn't say no. Not to Father Ignacy. So, we gave what we could: a jar with a little bit of honey, a few teaspoons of yeast, bit of cheese, a piece of fruit or two. The butcher offered one goat—not really enough for the whole town, but we'll make it work. Father gathered a few of the women, asked us to cook for the communal feast. We knew he chose the ones whose cooking has the greatest flavor. This made us proud. We also knew we wouldn't see this many ingredients again for a long while; that, by sharing our supplies, we had given up something precious. This made a few of us angry and jealous; added sins we've never bought to the confessional.

The rations we're being allotted aren't enough and yet we have to share with that *family? I know everyone is hungry, but I have five mouths to feed, most only have two or three. What is Father Ignacy donating to the feast?*

Others spoke loudly, as if their words could drown the whispers. *Father Ignacy is such a good shepherd; he's teaching us to be more like Christ. He gave all He had. We're happy to abide a few hunger pains to become great in heaven.*

If suffering is righteous, Myreska is as holy as can be.

If suffering is wealth, then we are rich.

WHISPERROOT: A HUSHWOOD TALE

At least the children are excited. They speak in excited whispers, their eyes glowing at the dishes set upon the table.

"Where's Lusia?" Breathe lodges in our throats, our eyes cutting to Father Ignacy as the child's mother, embarrassment staining her face, *shushes* the child. The father murmurs apologies. Father smiles gently; our shoulders relax. He says a prayer, mentioning nothing important, and we eat. We talk about the snow, wonder how much longer it will be upon us. Men warn of possible war with the Soviets. Women pretend we didn't hear that: we have enough to worry about. Instead, we speak in clipped tones and tense smiles about the accomplishments of *our* children. One's playing impressive numbers on the piano, but another chopped *enough wood for the rest of Winter* without being asked. *Such a useful son.* Another speaks of how their girl assisted with a birth. *Such a helpful daughter.*

When the baker's daughter moves seats, shifting to sit closer to a friend, the butcher's boy, Samuel, frowns and says, "That's Tatiana's seat." The butcher slaps the back of Samuel's head. "Hush, boy," he says harshly.

"The cost of disobedience must always be paid," Father Ignacy's voice is both a gentle reminder and a stark warning to the children: *we do not speak of the gone.*

"Do you hear that?" another child, this one the daughter of the apothecary. She lifts her head towards the curved window. "It's the ashfeather owl, isn't it?"

The child's mother reminds her son that owls are only awake late at night. *Now, don't speak again.* We hear her voice and swallow our own. Jakub sighs heavily, his eyes lingering at something past Father Ignacy's head. The owl's cry is unanswered.

The stone bruises the girls' knees.

Lit by only three candles sitting on the long table and slivers of moonlight breaching the windows, the room is dark. For hours, they sat in the cellar listening to the scraping of chairs, the chatter of the townspeople, childlike feet running through the chapel. Once, Kaja walked to the other side of the room, her face tilted. They could see her counting steps and listening. "The stairwell door."

But then Mateusz's muffled voice. Quiet.

"They're all up there." Klara's voice wasn't soft.

Ainela imagined Zosia. Her mother. Her heart squeezed tight.

A low threaded hum starts. Lusia. The hum isn't their usual one, it's not the hum to steady the room. It's an older hum, one no one knows but Lusia. It's notes are soft and haunting, swelling and falling, swelling and falling like a heartbeat. Her eyes track the sounds above them, the hum stays on her lips. "Did you learn that from home?" Tatiana asks, picking at the corn doll's eye.

Lusia nods. "My mother gave it to me."

"I smell goat." Wishfulness thickens Ainela's voice.

"I smell bread." Halina adds, curling and uncurling her hands as if kneading dough.

"I wish we had bread." Tatiana crosses her arms around her chest.

"Here," Larisa uncovers a stale chunk of bread. Her cheeks hollow, her bones protruding, she shakes her tired hand when Tatiana hesitates. "Go on, I don't need it. I'm fasting."

WHISPERROOT: A HUSHWOOD TALE

Tatiana hesitates, but the promise of bread is too strong to pass up. She reaches out and takes it from Larisa, murmuring *thank you*. Larisa closes her eyes, moves her beads to her lips, and prays.

Hours pass before voices shift, wooden boards creak.

"They're leaving," Kaja's voice was sure. She's right; the hinge of the chapel door pinches open, the snow crunches, children's voices, raise just slightly. The window sees a blue ribbon floating by and then, moments later, a young girl's boots running. They hold their breath. The room grows quiet when she runs back. They see just the tip top of her head. "Stupid." Klara spits. "No one in this town ever looks down."

It isn't long after dark that the guards came for them.

They're taken upstairs to the communal room and ordered to clean the tables and scrub the stone floors *until they shine.* Ainela's arms ache but the soreness of her knees is unbearable. She shifts until she sits on the stone instead. This gives her knees relief, but not her arms. Not her hands. Her head throbs at her temples. The guards are on all edge, acting stranger than before. More threatening. Angrier. Even Jakuh seems agitated.

"You missed a spot, lazy. Scrub." Tomasz klcks Kaja, making her fall. Mateusz walks around, his boots stopping inches from Ainela. She forces her hands into the bucket. Mateusz kicks it out of her reach. "Stop playing. Work." Ainela's teeth grind. Jakub curses under his breath, his toe striking the bucket, sliding it closer to Ainela as he walks past it.

"What's up with you?" Tomasz notes the unusual display of aggression.

Jakub shakes his head. His eyes are busy, but they linger a moment too long on Halina's hair. "She'd be fifteen today."

Ainela frowns. *He remembers birthdays.* The thought burns edges in her mind.

Tomasz groans. "Not this again." He turns and walks away.

Mateusz hesitates, says, "It's not gonna change."

Jakub doesn't answer.

A small sound that's not quite a full sound catches Ainela's attention. The same hum rises in the air. Ainela coughs to cover the sound. Lusia turns her head and Ainela taps two quick taps against her hand. *Stop.* Except it doesn't. Lusia continues to hum. Klara tries: she uses her elbow to nudge Lusia. When the girl looks up, Klara mouths "quiet."

But Lusia doesn't stop.

Quiet enough that the guards don't hear her. Loud enough that the girls do.

Klara panics the longer Lusia hums. Her eyes move to the guards, back to Lusia. When she returned from the priest, Lusia was there. She was there for Klara. She's always there. Klara's gaze finds Ainela's.

Stop her. She pleads with Ainela. She knows it's a risk. Striking back at the guards in any way she can is Ainela's safety net: she might encourage Lusia. But, if any of them can get her to stop before being noticed, it might be *the flame thrower.* Ainela inclines her head, shows she understands. She scrubs the floor, making more noise than necessary to cover Lusia's song. But then Kalina, the one who stopped singing after her sister was punished, adds a tremulous, soft note.

"No," Ainela whispers. She watches the guards. They are agitated, bickering with one another. Ainela can't decide what it's about, but she hears pieces. Tomasz sounds angry when he says, "I'll get my wages."

Mateusz says, "The windows in our cottage rattled all night long, no sleep."

"There was no wind, Mateusz."

"You callin' me a liar?"

"*I'll give it to you on Monday.*"

"Piece of shit, when you pay me, I'll pay you."

"I should have been there. That damn war." This voice wasn't as rough, quieter, as if remembering details of someone lost. There's a heartbeat of pause. Another. One more.

"What the hell are you, some kind of hummingbird? Shut up already."

Lusia's voice falters as Tomasz's voice slices through the air. Ainela exhales as silence returns. Her hands push the rag harder into the stone, catching Klara's shoulders drop in relief. A warning. It's just a warning.

The return of the hum makes Ainela's stomach churn. Klara's eyes grow wild, fear etches itself into every line of her face. But Lusia doesn't look scared. Candlelight shines on the side of her face. Her eyes are on the stone, her arm scrubbing as hard as anyone else. Her lips are closed. The hum grows like coals waking beneath ash.

It snaps—cut without warning—Tomasz yanks her by her braid off the floor and throws her across the room. Klara screams, her knees buckling beneath her as she falls to the ground. Lusia's head makes a sickening *thud* sound against the stone, there's a swishing sound as her shift and body slides to the ground. Klara scrambles, tries to rise, but Jakub stands in front of her implacably, a stone. Klara sees his fist curling and uncurling. His jaw tightens. His eyes warn her: *don't try it*.

Lusia moans, her fingers flutter like the wings of a bird.

And she hums, the sound broken and fragile. *Aware*.

It isn't Tomasz but Mateusz who strikes next, landing a square punch to her throat, his knuckles cracking against her chin. He shakes his hand from the sting as he pulls his arm back. Tomasz meets her before she falls backwards, throwing her again against the unforgiving, stone wall for the second time. Blood splatters.

The humming stops.

She crumbles to the floor, her eyes searching the room, stopping only when they land on Klara.

"Please," Klara whispers, her lips cracking, her breath cracking beneath the weight of grief. Lusia was there for her. She was always there for her. Klara has to be there for her now. "Please," she begs again, her eyes pooling with tears.

Jakub hesitates, his eyes moving to the still girl on the stone, calculating the blood pooling beside her. When he turns and walks away, leaving the room, Mateusz follows him. A moment later, arguing in the hall draws Tomasz out.

The girls move as one to Lusia.

Kalina covers her mouth with her hand, her heart pounding hard in her chest. Klara takes Lusia's and squeezes it. Halina sets to work. "I need .. I need something to stop the bleeding."

Lenka takes the ribbon from her hair, holding it out.

WHISPERROOT: A HUSHWOOD TALE

As Halina puts pressure against the bleeding, she says, "Did you know that hummingbirds aren't just small, Lusia?"

Lusia's eyes flutter, focusing on her.

"No, they're more than that," Halina speaks quickly, the words rushing out in whispers, before the guards return. "They're fighters. Fierce fighters. They are bold and ... and fearless. They'll come up to anyone - once, I had a hummingbird chase me around the yard, yelling at me for food. Do you know what else they are?"

Tears spill from Klara's eyes, her lips quivering.

"They're very smart. Hummingbirds remember everything. They know how long it takes for nectar to fill the flower, they – they remember where these are and will return even years later to a good one. So.... So... Lusia... he's right, you *are* a hummingbird." Ainela notes how she's taken something from them and redefined it. What they mean to wound can be made new.

"I ... I couldn't do it anymore is all." Lusia's shoulders shake. "I miss my mama."

A sob breaks Klara's silence. Her world collapses the longer Lusia struggles.

"It hurts," Lusia whispers.

Panic seizes the girls. Klara squeezes her hands. "I'm sorry," she whispers. "I'm sorry I didn't stop it."

Ainela doesn't tap. She just starts humming. The flame thrower mimics Lusia's hum. When Lusia gasps, her fingers loosening in Klara's grasp, Halina joins the hum. Then Klara. Soon, even Kaja braids her voice with the others. The blood spreads staining their skin; still, they hum. It carries beyond stone, through snow, and into the roots. The hushwood hears. When her breath stills, and her mouth loosens, Klara shakes her head. Kalina rocks.

When Kaja hears shifting in the hallway, she taps twice, quickly, moving. The others follow.

Except Klara, who refuses to leave the hummingbird.

The wound throbs the hardest when they return to the cellar and stare at another empty mat. Mila's name intertwines with Lusia's. No one speaks, but they form a circle near Ainela, as if they know. *She'll hold the name.*

Ainela feels the weight as she pulls the sheets of the rhymebook and sets it on her lap. She swallows her tears, her hand just resting for a moment on the fragile pile of papers. Dirt stains each one; corners have been chewed by the mouse.

"Can I hold one?" Larisa asks, her voice small.

Ainela passes one to her. The pages feel coarse and smell of earth and fear and hope. She doesn't have the charcoal anymore, but while they cleaned the kitchen, she pocketed a piece of charred wood. She retrieves it from the pocket of her shift and turns to the new sheet. This one is a ledger page scavenged during work. But now it'll be something different; it'll be Lusia's.

"Something about her hum." Joanna murmurs.

"I like what Halina said about the hummingbird, how it remembers." Tatiana adds.

The charred wood rolls between her fingers, her bottom lip tucks between her teeth. She presses down, makes a mark, scratches through it, the thought fraying in her mind. She tries again, writes.

WHISPERROOT: A HUSHWOOD TALE

She sang against the stone, and her wings remembered.

She looks up, her eyes searching the others'. Their faces mar with heartbreak, they nod, looking to each other for reassurance.

"There's two of them gone now." Lenka says softly, looking towards the empty spaces.

"Look," Kaja points. She stands on her toes, gripping the edge of the windowsill. Keys jingle, snow crunches, shadows lengthen.

"Mateusz."

The others watch his shadow move towards the forest, a girl's limbs over his shoulder, bumping his shoulder with every step. Candlelight catches her hair, Lenka gasps. But the others already know who he carries.

"He's—"

"I don't want to see this," Klara's voice isn't angry, it's haunted. She buries her face in her knees and rocks. The others watch Mateusz's shadow disappear into the hushwood. Ainela moves back, gathers the pages of the rhymebook, and tucks them into the earth. One name written. One body carried away.

Zosia holds a candle as she walks towards home. She left her sketchbook at the chapel after the communal feast. Mama sleeps, so Zosia returns for the sketchbook. She finds it leaned against the locked door of the chapel, waiting for her. She wonders who knew she'd return for it. As she walks home, the hushwood seems to stir. The jingle of keys and the sound of crunching snow draw her eyes.

Despite the darkness, she recognizes the heavyset, tall figure as Mateusz. She frowns. He's coming from within the hushwood. Without knowing why, she slides behind the birch, the third one, where no one goes anymore. Her palm rests against its bark. She counts her breath curling in front of her face. *One, two, three... six, seven.* He goes into the side door of the chapel. A moment later, she sees a candle extinguished in one of the windows.

The forest stirs again.

Curious, Zosia steps out.

Footprints lead into the hushwood – but only one set. She swallows, her eyes moving to the chapel. It is quiet, still. Windows remain darkened. She steps carefully into one of the footprints held by the snow. The large print swallows her smaller one. She takes a step forward, stretching her legs far to match the stride. But then chills race along her spine. Fear stops her. She tilts her head, trying to see into the hushwood, but the forest presses in, trees leaning closer. She hears something and strains. The wind sounds like a heavy hum, too heavy to be nothing. Darkness presses down, shutting off even the moonlight. She feels the pressure; she hears the warning.

She listens.

Turning, she steps quickly back onto her own path. She runs home, the hushwood chasing her silence.

WHISPERROOT: A HUSHWOOD TALE

Our soil's been disturbed.

The steel edge of a shovel has torn and tangled our roots. The whisperroot wraps around the truth, holding it, while our limbs tremble. Not in fear, but in anger. In mourning.

We see her – Zosia – curious, stepping closer, but there's only so much she can see right now. We ache to tell her. We ache to sing the songs that live here, to shout the names thrust into us. But not now. Not yet. If she sees our soil bunched up, forming a round mound or the fragment of the frayed ribbon that came unbound from Lusia's wound that one of our branches caught and held or the tanned butt of a cigar, extinguished, tossed carelessly onto the mound after he finished—her silence might root itself so deeply it can't be undone. She might not take what we want to give her. Fear might stop her from listening.

We won't allow that.

So, we press in, shutting off the moonlight, shutting off the path in.

Our bark itches with the smell of smoke that he left behind. It clings to the air that should still smell of frost and pino. The mound sighs heavily, sinking back into the earth. Emberflies sense the new weight in us and hover near the mound, flying in slow circles around it. The only light we tolerate is their flickering glow and the new whisperroot as its veins glimmer an angry red.

We will hold her. Our roots pulse rhythmically: what was placed into us will not rot in silence.

We promise.

Men shall not live by bread alone

———————————

Matthew 4:4

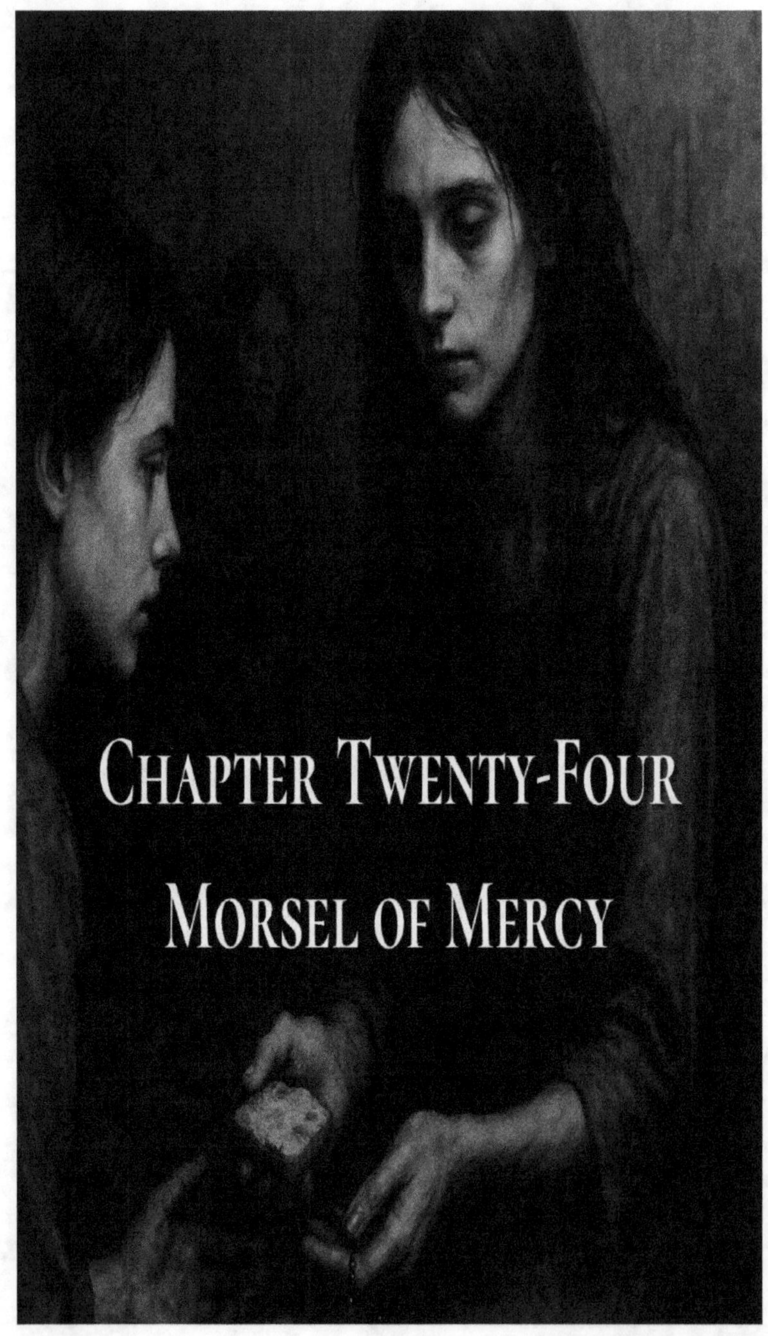

Chapter Twenty-Four

Morsel of Mercy

WHISPERROOT: A HUSHWOOD TALE

Days smear into one another, identical and gray. The scrape of the key in the lock, the same ladle of broth, the same sermon. Time folds over itself until even the guards' boots sound like echoes of yesterday's boots. One of the guards comes each morning and evening to hand out food. Father Ignacy comes–not every day, but every third–to give sermons and check on them. Individual girls are called to join him in the rectory. There's no pattern for this. They are separated into work groups every day and, every evening, they gather to share what they found, what secret item they hid. Any kind of paper is considered gold because they add it to their rhymebook. Ainela hopes for kitchen or laundry work because she finds the most useful things there: recipe pages become paper for the rhymebook, carrying hot water for the laundry means she can scavenge for charcoal from the fire.

Every morning, she counts.

Halina's cough is still wet, still sporadic. She's been adding bits of herbs to her water tin to help. Klara's face is pale; she doesn't speak as much. Since Lusia's death, she's become a shell of herself. She tore a piece of Lusia's shift before they left the room. Every night, she takes it from the hiding place in the crack of the wall, holds it to her nose to breath in the scent of her friend, and then refolds it, tucking it carefully into the stone. Still, she, Kaja, Halina and herself remain the strongest. Joanna next, although one of her wounds is bubbly and greenish in color. Lenka sways, dizzies upon standing. Kalina and Tatiana, weak. Dizzy, hungry. Larisa: weak. Ainela closes her eyes, pulls in breath, though she doesn't know why.

Heavy, heavy, jingle.

But there's no noise to interrupt, so no taps.

When the door opens, the priest orders them to stand for their rations. He stands to the side, watching with interest as Jakub and Mateusz pass out the bowls of thin broth and stale bread. Standing beside her, Ainela notices Jakub palm Halina an extra piece of bread. Halina's fingers curl around it automatically. She slips it into her pocket before the priest sees; her face gives nothing away. It isn't the first time her portions have been slightly larger than the others. When Mateusz reaches Tatiana, he gives her a bowl of broth, but no bread. "We ran out. Tomorrow," Mateusz says gruffly.

The sounds of girls chewing, swallowing fill the cellar.

Larisa glances to Tatiana and holds out her piece of bread. She's given her bread to Tatiana before.

Ainela protests. "Larisa, you need to eat that. Here, she can have a piece of my bread."

Larisa shakes her head. "No. I'm fasting, I can't eat it. Go on."

Larisa's bones protrude like branches from under her skin; her eyes are sunken. Sometimes they've heard her gasping for breath. Her cough has worsened. And she will not eat. Tatiana shakes her head, wary. "I don't want it." Shame blooms in red over her neck and face. Dizzy spells and a few tumbles mark Tatiana weak.

"It should be *her*," Lenka can't hide the bitter note in her voice as she points towards Halina. Whispering is dangerous, her eyes track the guards, look the slightly hint they hear her. Whispering in front of the guards has earned them beatings before. Still, the flame thrower says they cannot allow their voices to be silenced. "Why does she get extras?" She bows her head, as expected, closes her eyes, murmurs a prayer. And waits for a response from the girls.

Halina hesitates, tilts her head just slightly. She extends the bread toward Tatiana. The priest's gaze sharpens, following the movement. "Larisa," Halina whispers, "you eat. Tatiana can have this extra piece."

The priest quirks an eyebrow, his cassock brushing against the stone as his attention shifts to Larisa.

"No." Larisa shakes her head, whispering without moving her lips. To the priest, to the guards, she's offering her bread without explanation. The girls hold their breath as she whispers behind her throat, "Halina helps the ones who are sick. That's why she has more. Tatiana is not sick, not yet. But she is hungry." Then her voice rises, strong enough for the guards and the priest to hear. "I am holy fasting. I cannot eat it. Better to give than to let go to waste. Tatiana, take the bread." Her rosary beads click against her ribs.

The girls fall silent. She's spoken out loud. Lifted the whispers into voice.

Larisa struggles to talk; it exerts too much of her energy. Her face is long and hollow. She starves. Tatiana's eyes leak tears, but she reaches out and accepts the bread from Larisa. She murmurs *thank you*. Exhausted, Larisa pushes away her bowl of broth and lies on the straw, her fingers holding the rosary.

"Your sacrifice is pleasing," the priest nods. He turns to Tatiana. "Greed is a mortal sin."

Tatiana's jaw slows. Chewing becomes harder. Ainela notes how long it takes before the girl's throat pushes the last piece of bread down, and how, when it's gone, Tatiana's whole body quakes with guilt.

Her eyes glue to Larisa.

Larisa sleeps, her breath rattling in her lungs. Her lips move even in sleep, as if she's desperately trying to find something before letting go. Ainela slides closer to her, the rhymebook in her lap. She listens to Larisa breathe.

"I wish I had as much faith," she says softly. "My mother has that kind of devotion."

"I don't think it's faith," Joanna protests. She looks up towards the window, then back toward Ainela. "It's selfish. Look what she's doing to Tatiana."

Tatiana hides her face but cannot hide the tremors. She says brokenly, "I told her I didn't want it."

"It's hers to give away," Lenka says.

"The bread?" Joanna quizzes, her voice rising a pitch. "Or her life?"

"Both."

"Joanna's right." Halina frowns. "When there are others who also suffer...it makes it look like her suffering is worse than ours. But she's choosing to suffer."

"Because she wants God." Ainela protests. "Fasting is real. We did it. You did it with your families."

"Not when I couldn't walk across a room without fear of falling."

Ainela's eyes stare at Larisa. "What does it matter if she lives but loses her trust in God?" She gently rubs the pages of the rhymebook. "She doesn't know how else to be.

She believes He'll save her if she can just get Him to hear her."

"No one is going to save us." Kaja's voice is flat, tenser than they've ever heard her. Her face tilts up, toward the vent, but her eyes are closed. The starkness in her voice makes them more real.

Ainela leans her head against the stone. "Once," she begins softly. "Some six or seven seasons ago, before the first girl went missing, I thought God was mad at me." She picks lightly at a broken nail. No matter what I did, it was wrong. When I laughed, it was too loud. If I played with a boy, I was 'asking for trouble.'" She inhales a breath that shakes. "I heard the whispers about my mother. Showing up with me and no explanations. I heard her telling Papa she was forced." The silver buckle flashes through her mind. The way the table wobbled when she hit it. The water stain on the ceiling she stared at so long it disappeared. The heaviness of his body on hers, the blood no one warned her about. She shakes her head, and the cellar returns. "I thought no one wanted me. So, one day, I stayed at the chapel after services. My mother was pleased because she thought I was asking for confessional."

The silence presses so long Klara asks, "Were you?"

"No." Ainela smiles sadly. "No, I wasn't *that* desperate. But I asked the priest what I could do to make God love me." Tears prick the backs of her eyes and her breath hitches. She's never shared this with anyone, not even Zosia. "He said I was born of sin. That God cannot love what begins in filth. That God is holy, perfect, that He could never love girls who just lead men astray." Memory washes over her in waves. She doesn't notice her hand curling into a fist. "He said I could try, that if I could give up everything but obedience and silence, maybe He might hear me." She swallows and adds in a heartbroken whisper, "Sometimes I wish I had done that." She looks at Larisa. "I don't think she's selfish. I think she wants someone to love her."

The quietness stretches until a cough snaps it.

Ainela looks down at the rhymebook. When she flips through the pages to find an empty one, she runs her fingers over it, frowns. She pulls the charcoal out, presses it down, but she doesn't know what to write. The charcoal slips, making a line across the page. She closes it, gathers the pages, and hugs them to her chest.

The snow doesn't fall.

The patch of sky they see from the window looks bluer. Ainela's lost count of how long she's been here, or of what month it is. She's heard the guards talk about how deep the snow is—Tomasz laughs when he says it's fun to watch the children try to walk through it, that it almost buries some of them. *We still have weeks of this stuff left*.

When the keys jingle at the door, her shoulders tighten.

Jakub enters alone. Wordlessly, he refills their water tins. He hesitates, but when he sees Larisa moisten her cracked lips, he sets an extra cup of water by her. She smiles faintly, pushes it away. "God will quench ... my hunger? No... no, wait..." but the words trail, as if she can't remember what she wants to say. She frowns, lifts the rosary to her lips. "Thirst..." she whispers, relief flowing over her. "He'll quench my thirst."

Jakub doesn't respond, but he doesn't remove the water, either. He simply walks forward, refilling the next girl's cup. Larisa's lips are so cracked, they bleed.

Tatiana says, "Larisa. Please."

Larisa hesitates. "I'm not thirsty. But–" she dips a finger into her water cup, wipes her lips with the moisture. She closes her eyes and sighs at the relief. She repeats the motion once more, then rubs her fingers together, drying it.

Frustration snaps the piece of charcoal Ainela holds between her fingers. Light flickers in the flame thrower's eyes, sparks of understanding dance with glimmers of impatience. "How long? How long do you have to fast?" she asks.

"Until He hears me."

The gasp from Lenka draws her attention.

"What?"

Lenka swallows. "I — I know that's Elizabeth." The name cracks over her lips and she covers her mouth with her hand. "Daniel." The girls all move to the window, except Kaja, who stays beneath the vent, and Larisa who cannot move. They hear childish laughter outside, see a balloon floating. They see legs, skinny ones, run by. A voice calls their name. "Papa," Lenka whispers, placing her palm flat on the windowpane.

"What happens if we bang on it?" Ainela asks, her voice hard.

"We die." Joanna says starkly.

Ainela looks behind her at Larisa's mat. "Isn't that happening anyway?" She raps against the windowpane, gently, at first, but the sound is swallowed by the glass. Klara's fingers circle her wrist, push her hand away. She warns, "You will not get all of us killed." She pauses, dropping

Ainela's wrist, and adds softly, as if the words are gravel in her throat, "Obedience is the way we survive."

Elizabeth and Daniel fade from view. The sound of crunching snow fades. "Do they still look for me?" Lena whispers brokenly, her shoulders quaking. A memory stirs for Ainela, of something she overheard the guards say. *That one has a brother and a sister. What we did was a blessing for her parents. One mouth less to feed.*

One by one, they move away from the window. Everyone except Lenka.

The cellar fades back into silence.

"Do you see Him?" Larisa asks suddenly, her eyes alert for the first time in days, staring at the corner of the room. "Do you see?"

The girls follow her gaze but see only a darkened corner.

"Yea, though I walk –" she trails, her lips faltering. "Come to me, all you–" she shakes her head, her lips quivering. "I can't remember..."

"Come to me, all you who are weary, and I will give you rest." Joanna quotes softly. She doesn't look up from mending a hole in her shift.

Larisa relaxes, her head sinking deeper into the straw. "Yes," she whispers thankfully. "Come to me, all you who are weary, and I will give you rest." Larisa closes her eyes, returns to sleep. Ainela watches the rise and fall of her chest and how her lips still move, whispering prayers and half-verses until her own heart aches. This time, when she opens the rhymebook, the charcoal doesn't smear when she presses down.

Her lips would not stop, even in the dark.

WHISPERROOT: A HUSHWOOD TALE

When night falls, the cold deepens, dripping into their marrow like poison. Breath frosts the air and vanishes too quickly, as if even warmth has learned to flee this room.

Klara folds into herself. Ainela watches her remove the strip of Luisa's fabric. She rubs the fabric, refolds it carefully, and tucks it back into the wall. *Obedience is the way we survive.* Ainela bristles. That's not Klara – Klara wouldn't have said that. It's just the Klara still grieving for her friend.

We're all grieving.

Ainela rolls to her back, winces when the movement stretches a wound. Tatiana sits besides Larisa, keeping vigil, refusing sleep. The extra bit of bread Tatiana ate has made her face hollow, her smiles fewer and farther apart. She waits by Larisa's side. They all wait. Twice, Larisa wakes. Twice, she points to an empty corner and asks if they can see what she sees. The corner is dark, not even the mouse waits there. But Larisa whispers of a light so bright *it's blinding*, of a man *with dark hair and dark eyes and a smile like home*. She prays, but they're fragmented now, almost as though she's piecing together verses and prayers. Ainela isn't sure she has more tears. There's a hole deep inside—she feels its edges, like the mouse has chewed corners of her heart instead of just scraps and paper edges. Sometimes the jagged edges burn. She feels hollow. Nightmares splice her nights, jerking her awake and wrenching moans from someplace awful inside her. But, mostly, she just feels empty. Numbness is like that– almost a burning desire to hurt, to care, to feel anything at all because even pain echoes of life. She curls tighter around the rhymebook. Its pages are her pulse, her proof. Without it, she fears she would not even remember she once had a heart.

Heavy, heavy, jingle.

The sound wakes her, jolts her upright. It is too late for someone to come. No one ever comes this late. Still, the scrape of the key in the lock, the twisting of the knob warns her its real. It isn't the guards this time. It's him. The priest. He holds a candle and slowly moves it from one side of the room to the other, his eyes squinting in the dark, as if he's looking for someone. The glow of the candlelight reveals hollowed eyes, bodies that look more like skeletons, and faces full of dread. It passes Larisa but then slowly moves back to her mat. Something from Klara, a ragged exhale, catches her attention. When she looks, Ainela thinks she sees a flash of something spark in the girl's eye.

The priest stands over Larisa's mat, looking down at her, the candle lowered so he can see her face.

She lifts a hand towards him – not in fear, but in hope. She recognizes him but can't rise. "Do you see Him?" she whispers. She points. "He's—" she moistens her lips with the edge of her tongue. "He's beautiful."

The priest looks behind him, following her finger. Something flickers across his face. Almost pity. He squats, bending closer to her. When his hand moves, Ainela shifts her legs, ready to step between them, but he simply puts a finger against her forehead, drags it down, then across, tracing the shape of an invisible cross. His voice is soft, thick, almost gentle when he says, "Ego te absolvo–I absolve you of your sins, child."

Lenka's fingers brush against Ainela's, seeking her presence. Ainela folds her fingers into the smaller girl's hand. It's what Larisa wanted when she asked for confessional. It's

WHISPERROOT: A HUSHWOOD TALE

what she needed. Her eyes close, resting. He stands, glances once more at the others, and then walks from the room. The key twists the lock closed.

"Amen," Larisa's tiny whisper is the only sound left.

But the Lord is in His holy temple; let all
the earth keep silence before Him.

———————————————

Habakkuk 2:20

CHAPTER TWENTY-FIVE

CRACKS

We don't count days. We count Sundays, weddings, burials. We measure time not by months on a calendar but by festivals and religious traditions. It is our responsibility to train our children, especially our daughters, to prepare for the future. Basia learned to knead bread this week, and Marianna's fingers are quick now at the loom. We train them to be useful, helpful. And kind, of course.

There are noticeable absences.

The other day, a few of us walked together to the market and, along the way, we passed the open meadow. It's a place the children love—or, loved, whichever the case may be. We feel the absence most keenly here: the hollow spaces where laughter once echoed, where scarves trailed behind running girls, where small feet trampled frost into crooked paths. Mothers walk past now with baskets clutched tightly and we say nothing.

Last week, the town went ice fishing on the river. Many of the girls who were sent away loved this Winter tradition. We wait until the very core of Winter, when the ice is thick enough to bear us all, and then we spend all morning showing the smaller children how to make a hole in the ice and how to bait the line. We teach the older ones how to take the scales off a fish, how to cook it. These are lessons in endurance and survival as much as in food.

We didn't say so, but we felt their absence at the river. Some of the girls who left were eager for these traditions, their hands quick at learning, their voices bright against the cold air. At the river, we thought of them without speaking. We did not need to mention their names, after all–the ribbons would remind us even if nothing else did.

We tie some of them. We all have our reasons for doing so. If we tie something where all can see it, then others believe we hurt. We wear that coat of grief like a shield of armor that shields us against blame, against questions. It helps explain to our children why we can't mention the girls. *Naming things makes the pain worse. We don't want to hurt our friends. So, hush.* We also tie the ribbons as warnings, reminders, to the children. *God prunes the wayward.* The girls who were sent away were too weak to survive; they wouldn't have lasted the Winter here. It's one of the harshest on record, they say. Even the strong among us stumble.

Sundays are the heartbeat of our town. Mothers fuss around their children, making sure hair gets braided, there are dresses for our girls, nice pants for our boys, a good scrub behind the ears and under the nails for both. We hoard our rations every day but Sunday; the extra bit of food when we break fast helps children stay quiet longer in service. The extra bit at dinner acts as a kind of an unspoken reward for their silence and obedience while in front of others.

Now, don't be judging us.

We're not really just putting on a show for Father or our neighbors. Our souls—and that of our children's—are what we seek to protect. Showing up in our finest, and on our best behavior, shows God we can are worthy of mercy.

And Father Ignacy notices.

WHISPERROOT: A HUSHWOOD TALE

His eyes sweep the pews like a hawk, pausing when a child squirms or a mother's hair is undone. He frowns when a child fidgets until his mother snaps her fingers, leaning forward to whisper furiously in his small ear. The child stills. Father does not miss the smallest failing. His voice still rises strong, sharp enough to slice through the rafters, though now and then a cough breaks it. A catch in the throat. We pretend not to notice, or if we do, we say it is the Spirit burning him up from the inside, too fierce for the flesh.

But some of us have exchanged glances, quick and guilty, at the tremor in his hand as he lifts the chalice, at the sheen of sweat that beads his brow though the church is cold. We can't speak of this, not openly. He's anointed by God so, then, to question him, well, wouldn't that be to question God? What are we to do then? It's better to keep those sorts of things to ourselves, to believe that it's just his holy fire that makes him go on like that. Zeal is a gift reserved for God's vessels. It's unsettling, that's all, to see cracks in someone you didn't believe could split. Anyway, it's better if we hush any sort of doubt before it blooms.

We know where doubt leads.

Instead, we obey the lessons our mothers and fathers and grandmothers and grandfathers taught us. Our mothers bowed, so we bow. Our fathers were silent, so we hush our children. We straighten when his gaze passes over us, we fold our hands, we look the other way if his cough bends his words. Our children see us do this and that is good. We want them to learn, to mimic us. We want them to grow knowing that questions are fruitless—dangerous, even. Father Ignacy tells us Scripture says it's better to pluck you own eye out if it sees something it ought not to. Blindless obedience. That is what our Lord requires. It is what Father Ignacy requires. It is what it means to be faithful. It is what it means to survive.

The tavern sits at the back of the town, far enough away that its boisterousness won't taint the chapel, that our children won't hear the bawdy talk. We allow its existence because our men work hard every day and need a place to call their own. Our women wearily allow it, though we don't pretend to understand it, because we are faithful even in this. Men are the head of the household, after all.

Torches hang by the door and sit on dirty shelves. The space is small (on purpose; the town's womenfolk wanted to restrict the number of patrons the place could have at any one time). Rounded tables that wobble when touched and chairs that squeak with weight are packed like pigs in a pen. The room swells by nightfall with the lanky and the heavyset and the muscled arms that make up our men. Nathaniel–he owns the tavern. He pours warm beer into mugs, stuffs the bills thrust at him into his pocket, and shouts to the kitchen for orders.

Most of us can't afford kielbasa or pierogi with cabbage, so they fill up on vodka and pickled herring in oil. Served cold with a slice of rye bread, it's salty and cheap— with vodka or an endless supply of beer, it all tastes the same. It's what Jakub and Tomasz order; Mateusz skips the food altogether and opts for more rounds of vodka. Slapping the baker on the arm, he laughs hard and loud. "D'you see the way the chapel floor looked yesterday? Hand to God, it took three of 'em to scrub that floor and it still stinks like a pigsty. Ha!" He swigs a drink, shifts forward in the creaky chair and slams a fist on the wobbly table. "Give me that whip; they'd learn to shine it with their tears."

Jakub shifts, blowing a long, low breath. His hand curls around his mug, but he doesn't drink from it. Instead, he holds it as if it's his fraying patience. Tomasz won't be outdone; he adds, "Eh, the prettier ones aren't so proud after a night locked in. Pride doesn't fill a belly, does it now?" Harsh, loud laughter circles the tavern. The butcher lifts his mug, salutes.

"What's that little ditty like anyhow? The red one?" someone yells.

Mateusz stands, thrusts his hips forward and back. Tomasz laughs, jumps up, spilling beer on the table as he pushes Mateusz. "Yeah," Mateusz drawls, stumbling. "She put such a fight at first. Thought she was hot blood, but I say she's just another cold fish now. Cold as the river. Ain't that right, Jakub?"

We laugh because it's Mateusz and Tomasz. They drink too much. Mateusz has always spoken out of turn, even when he was a boy. No one stops him. Better not to challenge a man's tongue when the vodka is so thick on it. We said Tomasz was jealous, playing off Mateusz's stories. Jakub's tongue was dry and quiet. We told ourselves if it were true, the tales they told, Jakub would have left town by now. Why, he had a daughter not much older than the girls who left. His silence preserves our fragile story, though it still rattles in our bones. He stands, his mug barely touched, and slips out into the night before the others, the sound of laughter chasing him out.

Men gather in taverns.

Women gather in the market.

Shopping for preserves or rye or ribbon, we smile as we let the children run between the stalls. "I can't believe it's been weeks since they left."

"I heard they've been moved to cousins in Krakow."

Slipping a piece of fruit into the basket, one of the mothers says softly, "I tied a ribbon for my Lenka, for God's will, not mine."

"Shh," we remind gently. "No names."

She nods, her eyes downcast, her lips pursed.

The market is a crowded place, a place where secrets can be whispered and drowned in the noise. The smell of smoked fish and the clatter of things in stalls make it a perfect place to keep secrets. It's a place everyone is seen. Zosia's mother avoids the market carefully, often sending her daughter for the errands instead. Children run around her, but she walks calmly, almost eerily, clutching her basket. Our eyes follow her almost fearfully. We never say it, but we wonder: is her muteness contagious? But when she comes across us, we smile, and only once she's moved on do we whisper. "That child," we shake our heads. "She hasn't spoken a word."

"It's not normal," someone hisses back. "Why doesn't she speak?"

We remind ourselves: her sister brought it upon herself. The red one was always too loud, too noticeable. We quote Father Ignacy because it is easier, "God punishes the wayward." None of us ever ask *what her sin was* because then we'd have to ask ourselves about ours. We can't do that because, as Father Ignacy reminds us, *if we choose to live among sin, we will be condemned to Hell.* It must be set aside.

"I saw something.... it was like a shadow that darted through the hushwood."

Silence drops, panic spreads. Until someone corrects her, "Shh, you know what he says: superstition is a sin. It wasn't a shadow you saw, it was a deer."

"That's right, I remember now. A deer." But she knows that the shadow she saw had only two legs, not four. We call it a deer and knot another ribbon, this one tighter than the last, so the wind won't remind us otherwise.

Father Ignacy talked about temptation this past Sunday. He read from 1 Peter where it says we are to *submit ourselves to God and resist the Devil.* We have to guard ourselves against it carefully and diligently. We have to watch for it because it might otherwise slip in and then where would we be? We'd be in the middle of sin, our souls in jeopardy, and more of our daughters moved to Krakow or Warsaw. We're reminded that our Lord suffered, Scripture tells us of when He was tempted in the desert. If temptation can make our Lord suffer, what can it do to us?

That's what it is.

The men's talk in the tavern, the unease about Father's cough, the whispers in the market. It's just temptation, it doesn't have the ring of truth to it. We will not speak the names. We will not ask. We do not see shadows because shadows birth doubt, and doubt is a seed the devil waters.

We rebuke temptation and, instead, we'll continue telling our stories. These poor girls who were sent away were weak and weakness cannot endure here. Myreska is not a place for the faint-hearted, the rebellious, or the physically frail. Remove those who cannot keep themselves from hell's gates and what you have left are the righteous. It is a mercy to let them go. We are thankful God prunes His vines and humbled we are not cut with them. These stories comfort our children when they ask, and they soothe us when the silence presses heavy.

Our faith is secure. It's in order. In obedience. In the way we bend our necks when Father speaks. In the way we keep our mouths shut when Mateusz or Tomasz laugh too loud at the tavern. In the way we braid our daughters' hair on Sundays and teach our sons to hold their tongues. This is how a town holds itself together.

Still, there's the hushwood.

Its branches scratch against our windows, its roots press beneath our cellars. The ribbons we tied, they flutter. They remind us of wounds that just won't close. The wind tugs and pulls and sometimes we hear it whisper, but we close our ears. We tell ourselves silence is holy, silence is safe. But even as we say it, even as we believe it, something in us knows: silence will not hold forever.

A ribbon scorched is still a ribbon tied.

The Hushwood

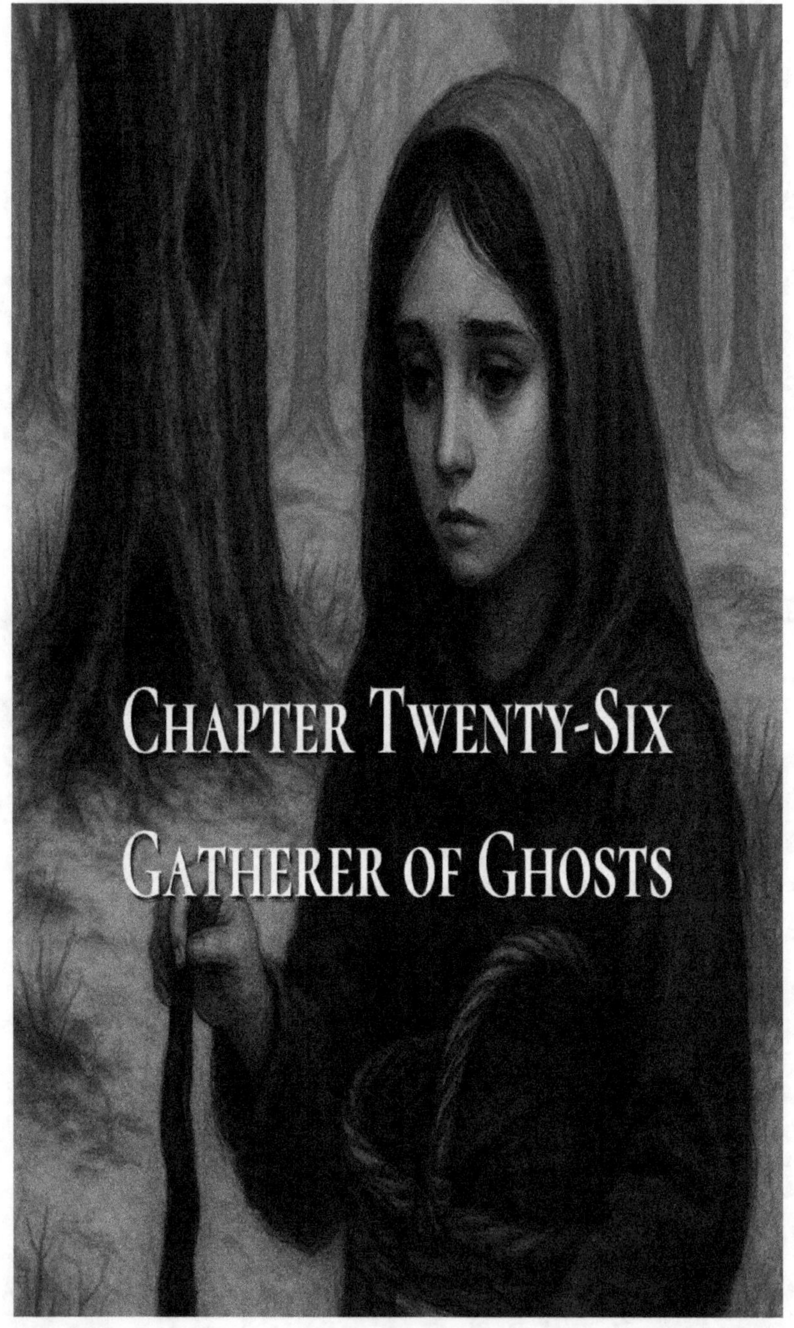

CHAPTER TWENTY-SIX

GATHERER OF GHOSTS

WHISPERROOT: A HUSHWOOD TALE

Zosia's brown eyes are alive and alert as she slips into the market. Snow falls from the sky in big drifts. Snow piles are high. It's not as much fun as it was at the Winter Festival to throw snowballs and slide down the hills in cardboard boxes. Now, it just feels heavy and hard to navigate. Still, Zosia holds her tongue out as she walks, catching flakes and smiling to herself. *You're Frosty!* The memory of Ainela teasing her tugs a smile from her. *What's your favorite thing about snow?*

Snow cream!

Ainela's eyes lit up every time. *Mine too!*

They spent hours collecting bowlfuls of snow, adding fresh cow's milk and sugar to the mixture. *Snow is like a free dessert every day!* Ainela said, her laugh like magical chimes. Zosia promises herself she'll gather a bowl of snow when she returns home. She hasn't had any this Winter, but Ainela would want her to.

A thin layer of straw coats the snow as she walks into the marketplace. Zosia notices the golden threads on her boots, her eyes lingering. *Straw.* She reaches down to pick up a piece of it, rolls it between her fingers, tilting her head. Something stirs in the deepest parts of her mind, but she can't place why. Someone bumps her shoulder—-the lamplighter. He quickly glances at her, mumbling a hurried apology, shrugging his coat over his shoulder.

"She hasn't spoken in weeks."

Zosia hears the whisper but can't place the voice. She turns her head to see, notices two women quickly look away. She clutches her basket closer to her side. Her lips move, remembering Mama's list: onions, kvas for pickling, lard, a charcoal stick for the hearth, ribbon (*for mending,* Mama explained). She pushes through the crowd. Voices are everywhere: a child cries, a man laughs, a woman says, "Well, I only have ten, take it or leave it." The colors blind her: fruits in yellow, orange and red, large baskets woven in intricate designs, small baskets for lighter loads. Fabrics hang from thin line stretched above the splintered tables. Children tug at their mother's hems, vendors wrap packages in thin wax paper before handing them over, men count out each bill as though reluctant to part with it.

Zosia stops at a stall, her eyes catching on the onions. Pointing, she holds up three fingers. *Three onions.* "Mute girl, you got no voice for barter?" The vendor chuckles, throwing three of the smaller onions into her basket. He mocks her by holding up fingers; she passes over the required bills, her eyes falling. She slides to the left since people press against her back, trying to get to the table.

You'd think it's the end of the earth, Ainela's voice whispers. *The way they push and shove and yell at the market.* Once, she climbed up on a small, three-legged stool, stretched herself taller, cupped her hands around her mouth, and shouted: *Frost bites so hard, my nose will fall! Stand back or you'll catch it all! Step aside, everyone, I will not wait, or we'll bury you in snow, head to plate!"*

She hopped off the stool, scooped up a handful of snow and threatens to throw it. People laughed, children scooped up their own handfuls of snow, and people actually moved, allowing Ainela and Zosia to go ahead of them. Another shoulder bump, this one harder, and without an apology, chases the memory away. The deeper she travels through the stalls, the more she smells smoked fish. She closes her eyes and inhales the aroma, her stomach growling.

But it's not fish for them.

At the butcher's, Samuel greets her, waving. "What'll it be?" he asks.

Embarrassment stains her cheeks. Hugging her hand close to her chest, and tucking her head down, she points to the lard. *Poor man's meat*, her father spat, when he saw it on the list. But, in Winter, you take what you can to survive. Samuel nods. "Good choice," he says. He packages it up for her, quotes the fee, and trades with her.

She picks up the charcoal stick next and then weaves her way through to the other side of the market. Ribbons of every color clash against each other. Tied from beams and the backs of chairs, her eyes scan for something right. She sees a shade of blue that matches her Sunday dress, but also ... reminds her. She picks up the ribbon and an image of Ainela's *blue* flame dances in her hand. *What did she wish for?*

"Got any vodka back there? We're gonna freeze without it," the bawdy laughter trails as she scurries along. She glances in her basket and counts. Onions, lard, charcoal stick, ribbon, and kvas. Everything Mama needs. She breathes a sigh of relief as the noisy market fades behind her.

The snow crunches beneath her feet as the town stretches ahead of her. When she glances towards the forest, she feels something. She veers off the path, cuts across the snowy road to the edge of the hushwood. The forest looms ahead of her. She notices the birch and hushbark branches: skeletal branches that look like bones with the snow crusting on them. The silence here feels more welcoming than the noise at the marketplace, deeper. She walks further, to her hushbark, and checks the hollow space. The amber brooch, a dark feather, a bit of lace – things she's found. Pieces of something. She draws the straw she saved from the marketplace and tucks it in with the other items.

The snapping of a twig turns her head.

When she sees nothing moving, she takes two steps more into the forest. She feels the silence crowd around her, pressing almost as though arms are holding her. A small exhale whooshes; the wind blows snow from the ground up in front of her. When it settles, she gasps. *There*. On a branch of a tree just steps away. *What is that?* Gingerly, she steps closer. The ribbon wasn't there before the wind came. It's trapped among the branches, fluttering. Zosia reaches out but when she touches it, her eyes widen. *It's hot*. The ribbon is scorched. The forest exhales again and the smell of smoke, faint, but distinct, drifts. She sniffs. *Fire*. She looks around. She doesn't see smoke; she doesn't see flames.

She tries again.

This time, when she touches the scorched ribbon, the forest lets her pluck it from between the branches. The red is dull; the edges are singed black. She trembles. A hint of fear dances along the back of her neck, but it's not just fear. There's also sadness.

Zosia tucks the scorched ribbon into the hollow space of the tree, her hand resting for a moment on its bark. She scratches the bark gently, as she might a dog. Then she checks once more to make sure her things are safe. Only then does she leave the hushwood.

WHISPERROOT: A HUSHWOOD TALE

Zosia retreats to her room as soon as she finishes supper. She bends her knees, pulls her sketchbook to her lap. She pulls the silver locket Ainela gave her from its hiding place and sits it on top of her right knee. It helps her feel close to her sister. The pages crinkle as she turns them one at a time. When she finds an empty page, she draws. The charcoal in her hand is already worn down from turning Zosia's thoughts into sketches. Black dust settles into the crease of her fingers. She doesn't begin with Ainela, though her sister always tugs at her heart first. Instead, she shapes Mama.

The curve of her cheek, sharp now in places it used to be soft. Zosia presses harder, shading until the hollows of Mama's face deepen against the page. She drags the stub downward, marking the line that bracket her mouth. They seem permanent now, grooves carved by too many words left unsaid, too many nights bent over mending in poor light.

Her hand hovers, unsure.

She hears Mama in the next room, cleaning from dinner. Zosia's hand shifts again, drawing her eyes. Brown, like hers, but weary. There's something in them Zosia tries to capture – a watchfulness, an ache, a guarded tenderness. As if afraid to let all of the softness come forth. She smudges with her thumb to soften the edges, but it doesn't quite lift the sadness.

Last, she sketches Mama's hair. Pulled back in the same knot every day, but Zosia cannot resist letting a few strands stray loose across her brow, the way they sometimes fall when Mama forgets herself. That touch makes the drawing ache with life. Not a portrait to show because it feels true. A mama who is breaking, and still holding together.

Before she can stop it, she turns the page, and quickly sketches another figure, as though she might lose the memory if she hesitates: the spark of a smile, the curve of laughter at her mouth. She tries to catch the tilt of Ainela's chin when she teased — bold, almost daring. But charcoal falters; the mouth looks too serious, the eyes too shadowed. Zosia presses harder, dragging lines darker, trying to restore the light. Instead, she leaves smears across the page, as though Ainela is slipping out of reach. She presses the locket against the paper, as if it can anchor the drawing in place.

Then the charcoal seems to spark to life on its own, running without asking. Her fingers dance across the page, but the image isn't hers. A face takes shape — it's not Mama and it's not Ainela. Zosia bends her head, concentration taking over. The hair is coiled into a heavy braid, almost like a rope. The eyes are cast down as though they hold a devastating secret. The throat is slender and here Zosia's hand falters, hesitates, but still the lines appear as if on their own: a ribbon, tied close, edges frayed. She doesn't know this girl, but her face feels alive, urgent. Waiting. She flips the page quickly, her heart racing, her fingers shaking. The smudge of the girl's eyes bleeds into the paper below, a ghost that won't quite stay hidden.

Mama raps on the bedroom door. Zosia closes her sketchbook and slides it beneath the covers just before the door opens. Mama smiles gently, her brown eyes weary. Breaking, but holding together.

WHISPERROOT: A HUSHWOOD TALE

"I see you've been sketching again," she nods towards Zosia's fingers which are stained with charcoal. Zosia curls her fingers, rubs the soot, nods, the sketchbook resting beneath the blankets against her legs.

"Thank you for going to the market today," Mama says again. "It was very helpful. I'll mend your Sunday dress tonight, so you'll have it before chapel."

Zosia smiles faintly.

Mama sighs, reaches out a hand that trembles just slightly, and strokes Zosia's hand. "You remind me of her, you know," she says softly. She hesitates and then adds, "I'm glad you do."

The silence deepens. Mama frowns. "Zosia, there is such a thing as *too much* silence. I—" but the thought frays and she shakes her head, sighing heavily again. She strokes her daughter's hair, then quietly moves from the room.

Zosia lies on her back, staring at the dark ceiling. Outside, the wind is still. Snowflakes continue to drift. Earlier, just before bedtime, they heard one of the windowpanes in the main room crack beneath the weight of the frost. Mama came back tucking fabric more securely around the edges of the glass, murmuring about not needing to catch a chill.

Zosia's mind whirls with the day, snaps from Samuel waving happily at her when she approached the butcher's stall to the vendor who mocked her silence. It lingers on the scorched ribbon, how it was so warm to the touch her fingers recoiled. It was faded, as though it had lain in the snow for ages. But she was sure it hadn't been there before the snow shifted. The sketches of the unknown girl with the ribbon around her neck, tied close. It's her face Zosia has in mind when her thoughts grow scattered and her lashes fall like a curtain over her eyes.

Branches sway back and forth, back and forth. They creak like a choir of whispers. She strains her ears, but she can't make out what the whispers are saying. They're just breaths mingling with the wind. Branches snapping make her head roll against her pillow, but there's nothing there. Just long shadows reaching deeper into the forest. Swarms of emberflies glow erratically, circle over an uneven patch of soil. The third birch tree seems to grow until it towers over the whole forest. It thunders without making a sound. Her bed starts shaking violently, the extra pillow falls to the ground. When she moves to retrieve it, she sees the wooden planks of the floor bow upwards, as if something pushes them from beneath. They fall, the shaking pauses, then starts again. Light at first, then heavier, until the planks stretch outward, bowing until one snaps. Snow pushes forward, spreading over the floor in her room, piling high until the walls of the house cave burst and she's outside, shivering in the cold. She pulls her blanket tighter around her, and that's when she sees it.

The faint red glow of the ground as it pulses. The ground swells, sinks, swells, sinks, like the rhythm of a heartbeat, and then—another exhale. The wind whistles past her and the whispers become more clear: *Do not forget us*. When morning comes, it is the one thing she will most remember.

One bore the ribbon, one bore the lash

———————————

margin note of Embergirls' Rhymebook

CHAPTER TWENTY-SEVEN

THE SCAPEGOAT

WHISPERROOT: A HUSHWOOD TALE

Ainela's eyes open. Her neck is stiff from being in the same position. Her breath frosts in the air and she stretches her fingers. Early dawn light seeps in from the window and lands on Larisa. Ainela shifts, moves to sit up. Despite the sliver of sunlight coming through the window, the cellar is dark, cold. Her eyes land on the wall by the door, noticing the white chalk marks Tomasz made when Mila and Lusia died. Her gaze lingers for a moment at the small tally marks. *How many does he want?* The thought crosses through her mind, the taste bitter. She stands, shuffles her way to the corner with the bucket. It was emptied yesterday but the room still holds the memory of the bittersweet scent of urine. When she first got here, the idea of going in front of the others embarrassed Ainela. She wasn't wild like they said. Now, she doesn't even blink twice.

A few of the girls shift or exhale heavily, signs of slow waking.

She does the same thing she's done every morning: she counts. Her own bruises are in various stages of healing – some are purple, others have more of a yellow tint to them. There are scars from the ashwater baths and cleaning with lye. She glances at Klara. Unlike Tatiana, she isn't curled into a fetal position, just lying on her side, but her shoulders are hunched. She hasn't been herself since Lusia died. Quieter. Quick to obey. Sometimes Ainela thinks she sees flickers of boldness, embers of defiance... but it vanishes these days before she's certain. Larisa... prays. Ainela's thoughts trail. She tips her head, her brows furrowing.

Her bare feet are cold against the stone, and she feels her shift clinging briefly to her legs. Ainela's heart beats harder in her chest, dread filling her stomach. "Larisa," she says, but the girl doesn't move.

Others start to glance over at the form lying on the mat.

Tatiana reaches her the same time Ainela does. Together, they reach out, touch Larisa's hand. It is cold. Her lips are blue, and her face ashen. Rosary beads fall loosely to the ground, her fingers no longer able to keep them close to her.

"Is she–"

Halina puts a finger beneath Larisa's nose, pauses, then nods once.

Dust motes float in the sunbeam, and the sickly-sweet smell of death brushing the girls' noses. Silence binds the room like an invisible thread. Though none admit it, some feel nothing at all anymore. Others feel a burning sense of anger. Fear still ensnares others. They keep losing sisters. Tatiana's the first to react. Tatiana touches her hand, tears filling her eyes. "She died alone." Her voice cracks.

"She was asleep," Lenka says gently, putting a hand on Tatiana's back. "She probably didn't know we weren't awake."

"I said I didn't want it," Tatiana whispers, her sunken, pale cheeks staining with guilt.

"Her face looks—" Klara says, frowning softly. "It's gray, it looks like ash."

No one answers.

"Does everyone turn that color?" Threads of fear lace Klara's shaky question. "Mila wasn't that color."

WHISPERROOT: A HUSHWOOD TALE

"Because we saw her right after." Joanna's voice softens. "Everyone turns some shade of gray. It's..." Halina looks away. "It's part of it."

Klara's hand starts shaking.

Tatiana leans down and puts her arm around her. Ainela notices Tatiana squeeze her eyes close as if she prays. When she opens them, she pats Larisa's cold hand and whispers, "You're not alone."

"Tatiana?" Joanna sits beside her. Tatiana's sadness holds the rest of the room captive. Without responding, Tatiana moves quite suddenly, as if chased by something no one else can see. "Can I have that?" she asks, pointing to Ainela's hair, tied into a braid, held together by a red ribbon. Ainela unties it, frowning. "Why do you–" she sees the angry tilt of Tatiana's chin, sees the grief forged in the tightness of her mouth and the tell-tale redness around her eyes. Ainela holds the red ribbon out. She watches Tatiana eye it for a moment before her fingers take it. Swallowing past a lump in her throat, Tatiana moves her fingers, bunching the ribbon in her palm. She moves quietly, her footsteps heavier than before, to her mat where she pulls the cornhusk doll from beneath her pillow.

It never leaves her.

Tatiana sits crisscross by Larisa. Ainela watches as she ties the red ribbon around the cornhusk doll. She ties it tight and then runs her fingers over the ribbon. Ainela closes her eyes, memories stirring. *Red ribbons tied on fenceposts, on trees, on lampposts. Some with frayed edges, some with seared edges, some brand new. There were some ribbons tied too high or too low to be the work of a townsperson. The breeze lifted them making them dance. When the wind blew too hard and one came untied, the forest's exhale carried it until its edge snagged on a limb or it floated to the ground. How many were covered in Winter's snow? They were meant to remember.*

But no one hung ribbons to remember.
Ribbons were hung to gentle the forest.
They were also hung to warn.

Ainela gasps softly, a sharp intake of breath seeing the ribbon tied against the corn doll's neck. When Tatiana leans forward and gently places the doll with its ribbon on Larisa's still chest, she whispers, "You're not alone anymore."

Murmurs shift through the girls, a sense of unease wavering in the air. Joanna bristles, shakes her head. "I don't think..." but her voice trails, her eyes dropping. Kaja stares at the doll on Larisa's chest for a long time. No one expects her to speak so, when she does, heads turn.

"When I saw ribbons, I thought of them."

Ainela tries to name what she feels, but she can't. Memories of ribbons blowing in the wind fill her with sadness. Not only sadness for girls who were taken, but sadness also for who she was just a short time ago, before she came here.

Would she dance in red now?

Would she sneak out of the house now at all?

She pulls her eyes away from the doll, from Larisa's ashen face. *It's all Tatiana has to give.* The thought draws her eyes up to see Tatiana. The small girl with the round face and the braided hair sits with both arms wrapped around her middle. The doll matters to her; it always has. Giving the doll to Larisa was a sacrifice, one born of both guilt and grief.

WHISPERROOT: A HUSHWOOD TALE

Ainela wraps her arms around her knees and tucks her head down.

No one moves when the boots are heard or when the keys scrape the lock. The cellar is dank and cold with a smell of rotting apples. Snowflakes swirl outside; ice on the windowpane cracks; girls breathe into hands cupped around their mouths to find warmth. When the heavy oak door opens, all three guards walk in. "Line up," Mateusz orders.

"Hey–" Tomasz slaps Jakub's chest, nods towards Larisa.

Girls shuffle to their feet, lining up for daily work. Ainela's eyes slide toward Larisa's form. "She's dead," Tomasz's voice is flat. As he turns towards the line of girls, Mateusz bellows, "Get Father in here. Look at this." Grabbing the corn husk doll, he holds it up towards the light in the window. He rubs the pad of his thumb over the knot in the ribbon. "They been practicing curses."

"No–" Tatiana says quickly, quietly, but Klara nudges her, shakes her head.

Tatiana quiotens.

"Father will want to see this." Tomasz agrees. "I'll bring him down."

Mateusz faces the girls, his face splitting into a grin that misses two teeth. "Who did this? Which one of you been binding up the dead?"

No one responds. Jakub glances away, towards the window, looking out at the tops of the hushwood trees.

He chuckles, pushes his face in front of Lenka. She swallows but doesn't blink. *She would have cowed before.*

Our strength grows. The thought makes Ainela's back straighten. They haven't been broken.

The sound of boots and the creaking of the stairs make some girls shift. Ainela's breath catches in her throat as the priest's black cassock swishes through the door. Tomasz points to Larisa. She lies still, the strand of rosary beads dangling from her fingers, the doll on her chest, her eyes closed gently in eternal sleep. *It's odd*, Ainela thinks, *to see her not in prayer.* Then, the thought *she's not hungry now* almost makes her happy.

The priest gasps, lips drawing down. "What is this evil?" He grabs the doll, stares at the ribbon, and then shakes it in front of the girls. "These ribbons are meant for the obedient. We remember the pure. This is witchcraft and idolatry. Larisa wouldn't have died if there wasn't evil in this room. Who did this?"

The only sound is the occasional dripping of water from the ceiling in the far corner. Kaja's eyes move up, stares at the irregular shaped water stain by the vent.

"I will only give you one more chance to confess. If you will not tell the truth, then all of you will suffer. Evil will be rooted out. Who hexed the dead? Who tied the ribbon?"

Just as the silence grows unbearable, Tatiana whispers, "I – it was me."

Movement draws their eyes as Ainela steps between the priest and Tatiana. "No, it wasn't her. It was me. Ask them," she nods towards the guards. "The red ribbon that tied my hair is gone – I did this." Ainela doesn't know why she speaks up - she doesn't mean to. But Tatiana is small; she won't survive whatever the priest does. Every morning, Ainela counts. Every morning, she takes stock of who is strong and who is struggling.

WHISPERROOT: A HUSHWOOD TALE

The priest looks between the girls, hesitates. He glances towards the guards. Jakub's eyes narrow. Mateusz and Tomasz glance at each other. "Her hair? Was it tied with a red ribbon?" the priest asks. Tomasz nods. "Yes. It was her."

"No–" Tatiana shakes her head. "It wasn't."

"Silence." The priest holds up a hand, reaching out to pull Ainela forward. "We're going to have all of you help with her correction. We will root out rebellion. It will not be in God's house." He puts his hands on her shoulders, pushes her to her knees.

Ainela's breathing snags. The weight of his hand on her shoulders throws her back into the other room when he held her down. She hears the sound of her breathing in her ears as it grows ragged. Hair slides into her face, but she's vaguely aware of voices, of shuffling feet, a tiny, sniffling voice saying, "this isn't fair," more hands over her shoulders. Klara and Lenka stand in front of her, holding her arms. Lenka's eyes are wild with terror. Klara closes her eyes. When she reopens them, she holds Ainela's. The hum is so low no one else hears it over the priest's voice and pounding hearts.

But Ainela hears it.

Gritting her teeth, trying to drown out the priest's voice, Ainela hums back. Without warning, something stings her back, tearing her flesh. She arches, but doesn't scream. Klara's hands tighten; Lenka's slip as her feet shuffle to move with Ainela's body. Klara hums. Tears stinging the backs of her eyes, Ainela tries again, echoing the hum. *Witchcraft. Rebellion. Evil hearts reap punishment.* The hum threads through her, even when her voice frays into a scream as the lashes strike again and again. The girls' hands on her shoulders, on her arms, hold her down. One after another the lashes come. The sound of the leather slicing through the air, snapping against her flesh, shouts in her ear.

"Name her sins," the priest says.

"Rebellion," Mateusz shouts, bringing the whip down hard. It lands on her shoulders. It snags the fabric of her shift, ripping it as it bites into her skin.

"Idolatry," Tomasz spits at her. His lash hits low on her back. She convulses, panic tearing at her insides. Lenka's hands slip again, resettle. Klara's stay firm, her eyes waiting for Ainela's to see her. Shame pours deep into Ainela even as she fights against the lashes. When blood leaks down her forehead and over her eyebrow, she feels ugly, as if she deserves this somehow. The burn of the lash against her tender side makes her scream so loud Mateusz wraps an arm around her neck, his hand clamping down against her mouth to muffle the screams. Someone's hand falls from her; someone yells at her to put it back, hold her still or she'd get the same correction. The world blurs: faces spin past as her head falls forward, tips back, rolls, anything to get away from the burning lashes. Time seems to move in slow motion, voices sound distorted, as though they are swollen. It's a big drop of blood that seems to fall slowly from her chin, as if gravity itself isn't sure it wants it. As it hits, as another lash cracks against her back, Tatiana loses her grip on her arm, steps forward too quickly, bumping her shoulder.

It almost seems as though the lashes aren't hitting her anymore.

She feels her body reacting, sees the drops of blood and pieces of fabric float to the floor, but none of it seems real now. *I chose this.* She doesn't know where it comes from, this thought. *I made this choice. It's not what they are doing to me, it's what I'm making them do.* Muffled voices sound again, angry and loud. But it's only as real to her as a dream. *The flame thrower chose this; I volunteered.* She clings to that as the blows continue.

Finally, the lashes stop.

Blood splatters across the floor, spreads.

A sudden commotion. Through the pain, Ainela barely hears Tatiana screaming, a flash of fabric skimming by her line of vision, other girls crying objections. Klara's hands momentarily release her forearms. She takes a step as if to interfere, but then steps back, hands on Ainela's arms, her brown eyes to the ground. She rolls her eyes to see Tatiana launch herself at the priest, tiny fists pummeling him. She screams he's a liar. Ainela wants to stop her, but blood bubbles from the crease of her lips, legs shake convulsively. Klara's soft hum threads through the chaos.

The priest's face appears in front of her swollen face. "Pride goes before the fall, Liar," he says gently. "It wasn't you. But you wanted it to be you so that you could be the hero." The priest makes a *tssk* sound with his teeth. "Pride is a sin. Scripture teaches that pride is the downfall of mankind; pride is a sin. Lying is a sin. It wasn't you who tied the ribbon to the cornhusk doll. How many sins can one girl make?"

He stands again, looks around the room, then smiles almost gently and says, "Take the singer upstairs."

Ainela's not sure when the world went black, only that her brain felt heavy one minute, and she felt herself falling. Arms–she thinks Kaja and Halina–kept her upright. She wanted to speak, say something about how sorry she was, but the world kept spinning. Just before the world went black, she sees Jakub slip Halina a piece of bread she pockets. The sound of someone coughing woke her. A quick glance tells her Tatiana's mat is empty; Larisa's body is gone. Halina sits beside her using the torn hem of a shift to pat wounds. Ainela lies back, staring at the ceiling.

"I screamed," she says softly. Shame thickens her voice. Images of the whips striking her flash like lightning through her mind. She twists her head down to see her shoulder, holds her hands up in front of her. Welts bubble over her flesh, cuts and bruises hide her pale skin. Her shift is torn, a gaping hole revealing the curve of her shoulder. The shame spreads. "I screamed," she repeats, more to herself than to the others.

"Anyone would have," Lenka mumbles.

Halina asks, "Anyone have a drop of water? This one might become infected if I can't clean it."

Joanna pushes her cup forward. Halina dips the edge of the shift into the water, then lays it over the wound on Ainela's side. She flinches. "Your back is worse," Halina's voice is taunt, medical, matter-of-fact. "We should look at it, too."

Ainela hisses through her teeth at the pain, but obligingly sits. Halina moves behind her and lifts the shift to reveal open welts, thin red lines crossing her back, bruises lining her spine.

"Will she come back?" Kalina's voice is quiet. She stares at Tatiana's mat, empty, her tin water cup tipped on its side.

No one answers her.

Halina finishes cleaning the wounds and moves back for Ainela to lie down.

WHISPERROOT: A HUSHWOOD TALE

"I want to go home," Kalina says softly. She so rarely speaks that, when she does, the girls listen. "My sister and I used to gather herbs in the field by the widow's cottage. Sometimes we would be out there all day."

Halina leans forward, her eyes intent. "What kind of herbs would you find?"

Kalina shrugs. "Oh, rosemary, thyme. We gathered lots of stinging nettles. Mama knew how to use them to stop pain."

Halina nods, quiet, thinking.

We made up songs and picked herbs." She goes quiet, rolling to her side, bending her knees. "Tatiana reminds me of my sister because she likes to sing, too."

"Oh," Klara breathes. "No."

Girls move to the window. A lantern bobs in the night, its glow eerie. When Ainela steps between Kalina and Joanna to peer outside, she swallows. The man is tall and walks with an uneven gait that Ainela recognizes. "Jakub," Halina whispers.

"Is that—"

Fog hangs low over the land, and the hushwood is darker than usual, making it hard to see clearly. A bulky shape slung over a shoulder, stringy hair trailing down his back. Kalina moves away first, then Kaja. "I don't want to see," Kalina says softly, tears filling her eyes. A few watch until his shadow disappears between the hushbark trees.

"Did you see that?" Klara asks breathlessly. "The snow swirling—"

"Just the wind."

Klara swallows, nods. "Just the wind."

No one mentions it when the ashfeather owl cries three times. The sound threads through the stone and roots, settling over them like another lash.

Morning blushes slowly, as if it's ashamed of offering another day. Exhaustion curls through Ainela. Sleepless, she spent the night remembering Tatiana. She shifts her legs, sits up, and leans against the wall. Blood still stains the stone from the lashings. Ainela's eyes glue to the cornhusk doll, trampled and sprawled across Larisa's mat, its ribbon cut by one of the guards. As she does every morning, Ainela looks to the others and remembers the lost: Lusia. Mila. Tatiana. Larisa. Iskra.

Her hands tremble when she pulls the Rhymebook pages out. The corners are faded, water stains mark some of the loose pages. The charcoal stick is nearly gone, so she thinks about every word before writing.

"When they clamped her mouth closed, her corn doll spoke for her." Gently, she blows the bits of charcoal off the page. Her eyes shift up, stare at the empty mat where Larisa lay. Beads broken from her rosary lay on the ground, her blanket oddly piled, as if waiting for her to return. The pit in Ainela's stomach grows harder as she writes: *Her hunger was a prayer no one answered.*

Ainela's hands, raw and scarred, tremble as she buries the pages again. She trembles not with fear. Not anymore. Each word she etches into the page acts as tinder for the flame burning inside. She stares at the empty spaces, at the places where girls once lay, and vows: *he will not win.*

If we cannot avoid death,
we must choose freedom

Ainela

Chapter Twenty-Eight

Freedom

Another one is gone.

Joanna's mat is cold, her body taken away this morning. In the weeks since Tatiana and Larisa's deaths, cracks have formed. The priest coughs sometimes, shakes his head as though trying to clear it of fog. Each Sunday, they listen to chairs scrape the wooden floors, the voices of their families singing hymns, the snow crunching as the world races them by. Snow still lies in piles outside, but fresh drift hasn't fallen in days. While the violence worsens, and he's quicker to drag Ainela or Kaja upstairs, the room feels other changes, too.

Joanna's death hurts, but it's expected. Halina gave her the extra bread rations, but it wasn't enough. Ainela stares at the mat. The straw bends, holding her shape. The weight of silence comes, but its edges are harsher now, as if it grows tired of holding so much sorrow. Ainela holds the pages of the Rhymebook, her finger tracing its words. Halina whispers a shaky prayer, trembling. No one wants to say it, but their grief is tinged with fear: *who will be next*? Ainela wonders about Halina's prayer: does she whisper the prayer of the dead—*eternal rest grant upon them, Lord*—or does she pray she won't be next?

Why?

The question taunts Ainela like forbidden fruit. She thinks it as she watches Halina's lips move. She thinks it even as Kalina clasps her throat and rocks; she's been like a caged bird. Afraid to speak because of what happened to her sister, but also because there are fewer of them now. Easier to be seen. Harder to hide. Klara worries Ainela now. She found Joanna without breath and mumbled, "Obedience is the only survival." Flickers of who she once was haunt Ainela; she longs to see the same spark in her as was there before Lusia's death. Lenka stares blankly at the wall, her eyes fixed on stone. When she speaks, it's to usher everyone into line. Ainela hears her, late at night, crying for home in her sleep. She listens to her and thinks, *do I do that?*

Thinking of Zosia fills Ainela with shame. Is she still the girl who called her sister *Caterbutton*? Is she still the one who dared to dance in a come-hither red mask or sneak out at night? The priest says she tempted the Hushwood, that she invited evil into her home, into her body, by opening the door. Is that true? Ainela's eyes skitter away; her jaw clenches. Maybe it is, but she won't show the other girls here that.

When Kaja turned away from Joanna's still form, spitting, "None of it matters," she asked her what she meant. Kaja went back to the vent, her eyes longing for a slice of fresh air. None of them remember what it feels or tastes or smells like.

"She's really gone," Klara mumbles. Murmurs from the others circle the room. But Ainela says nothing, a small smile playing on lips. She stares quietly, afraid to voice her thoughts. *They won't understand. They'll think he's right, that I am a witch.* But she still can't stop the thoughts from swirling inside her.

"What are you smiling for? She's dead." Kaja says, bitterness hugging her voice.

WHISPERROOT: A HUSHWOOD TALE

Ainela opens her mouth, closes it, the ghost of a smile curving her lips. When the others continue staring at her, she lifts a shoulder, says softly, "Good."

The silence shifts from sadness to shock.

"What?" Klara asks sharply, her eyes turning to stare angrily at Ainela. Kalina frowns, tucks her head between her drawn knees and turns away. Halina's expression, though, doesn't change. Instead, her eyes warm slowly with curiosity.

Ainela bends her head, trying to think of how to say what she thinks. When she lifts her head, her eyes move from Iskra's empty space to Mila's. It drifts from Lusia's to Tatiana's; Larisa's to Joanna's. They've lost six sisters. Memories bloom, one after the other. Wheels spin, putting people and places in order.

"Iskra...." she moistens her lips, tries again. "Iskra didn't go through all the reciting. Mila didn't go through the loss of more food. Larisa didn't have to ... to hold me down," her voice cracks. She blinks, swallows. Her voice grows stronger. "They aren't hurting anymore." She pronounces each word softly, clearly. The flame thrower's eyes begin to shine. "They're free," she whispers.

Something in Halina's eyes softens.

Lenka frowns.

"He cannot hurt her now. He can't hurt any of them. But if ghosts *are* real, *they* will haunt *him*."

Kaja tips her head, reluctantly curious.

"No, they're just dead," Klara mumbles. "They're gone. They can't do anything. They can't be happy. They're buried in the hushwood. They don't feel pain, but they also don't feel happiness. It's cruel to be happy that they were hurt so much. At least we have our lives."

"What good is our life here?" Ainela demands. "What are we feeling except pain?"

"I'm glad they're not being hurt, that they missed some of what we've been through since." Halina's voice hesitates.

"It's freedom."

"Death?" Skepticism raises Klara's voice. "Death is freedom? That's ... dangerous, what if they –"

"The ending of pain," Ainela clarifies. "The ending of pain is something to be thankful for." Her eyes beg Klara to understand. "I wish they were here, I think of them every single day, too. But—" she searches for words, pulling her lip between her teeth. "But, if we cannot avoid death, we can choose freedom."

The words hang in the air like salt, soaking up the rawness of death, the pain that vibrates in the room, the unspoken memories that have left their hearts split open– and the hopelessness that fear brings. The words sink into girls who were never passive, girls who were taken because they dreamed, or sang, or dared to be different. Tiny embers of something dangerous sparks in the room, warmth circling.

Kalina shifts; eyes move to watch. She listens first for the other pattern they know: *heavy, heavy, jingle.* Her stomach churns with the fear of keys scraping the lock. But still: she moves. She rests her first and middle fingers on the back of her right hand. Her first finger taps once. "F," she whispers. The same finger taps once again. "R." Both fingers tap two times together in quick succession. "E.E." Tipping her head, she starts from the beginning. First finger taps once. "F," she whispers. It taps once again. "R." Both fingers tap twice, quick. "E.E." Her eyes lift, move from one girl to the other.

Halina tries but fails to stifle a smile.

Ainela's tentative smile grows.

When Kalina begins again, Halina's fingers imitate it. Ainela joins. Lenka and Kaja tap the word. Klara sighs. Only when Ainela pauses to put her hand on Klara's knee, holding her eyes, does Klara reluctantly join.

Free.

Halina's hum is throaty, hesitant. She shifts until she's closer to the others. One by one, they move until their bodies form a close circle. Sitting crisscross, knees touching, breaths mingling, they hum and tap. Kalina keeps the rhythm by tapping instead of her voice. *One, one, two, two. F. R. E. E..* After the last tap, Lenka rolls her wrist, the two tapping fingers finding her pulse. Shivers race down their spines.

Choice.

Tap. Tap. Tap, tap. Roll, pulse.

F. R. E. E. Find the heartbeat.

Remember.

Tears shine in Ainela's eyes. The priest holding her down, his body heavy over hers. The lashes ripping her skin open, her blood staining the stone of this room. Watching six girls die. *The wage of sin is death.* These words haunt her. Her lip quivers, her throat squeezes closed, and she just listens to the hum holding the room together. *Let the woman learn in silence. From all your filthiness, I will clean you.* His voice whispering in her ear, *the evil is inside of you. I'll root it out.*

Tap. Tap. Tap, tap. Roll, pulse.

F.R.E.E. Heartbeat.

Remember.

Let them look, then. They're going to talk anyway, so they might as well have something pretty to look at while they do. A laugh like chimes. You made a harness for a caterpillar.

I'll never forget that. The girl she used to be....*she's still here. Zosia. You've kept me breathing.* Tears slipping from the corners of her eyes, Ainela tilts her chin up, hums. Softly, she turns, pulls the Rhymebook from the earth, slips to a new page. Kalina watches. Scars mark Ainela's body, dirt burrows beneath her nails, and smudges on her cheeks when she wipes the tears away. Lenka pocketed a new charcoal stick days ago in the kitchen; Ainela marks the page, and her fingers do not tremble:

> *If we cannot avoid death, we can choose freedom.*
> *FREE*

Kalina pauses tapping, but the others keep the rhythm going, as if it's sustenance, something to help them blow the ember into a roaring blaze. Kalina takes the charcoal and makes her own marks on the page beneath the letters.

> F R EE
> * * * *

Aboveground, the frost cracks. Snowmelt slips for the first time all Winter down the windowpane. The sound of crinkling pages and the smallest bit of warmth promise the emberflies hover nearby. Their glow lighting dark places of the forest, places where soil piles unnaturally high. Whisperroots pulse ever so slightly, their vines lighting up softly, listening, holding, remembering. The hushwood stirs, exhaling a breath held too long. The burst of air drifts snow, suspends it midair, swirls it, sends it floating nearby until a new thing lies unburied: a tiny piece of red ribbon a girl held

WHISPERROOT: A HUSHWOOD TALE

in a cellar once tore from a longer piece with her teeth. The ribbon was wrapped around a cornhusk doll—not to warn, but to remember–and the tiny piece she tore, she stuffed into the pocket of her shift. It remained there until she was moved once more, this time to the forest, on the back of a man with an uneven gait. The tiny piece of ribbon fell from her pocket and was buried under snowdrift.

Until now.

Soon, Zosia will find it and, when she touches it, it will be warm despite the cold. When she clutches it in her fist, the whisperroots will heave in the same rhythm the girls make now: *thump. thump. thump-thump.* The emberflies will crackle. Antlers will appear in the fog, pause as if waiting for something, and then disappear into the hushwild again. The hushwood will expel short breaths and, somehow, she'll feel the word: *free*.

The rhythmic tapping and humming continues as the girls take turns holding and adding to the Rhymebook. The hall is quiet. There are no boots coming, no jingle of keys. They huddle together. Ainela's blue eyes shine fiercely when she says quietly, "We have to get out of here."

It's as if she didn't speak. No one replies. Ainela frowns, touches Kalina's knee. "We have to try and escape," she says again, her voice firmer. Halina looks up from the Rhymebook. Gently, she lifts her shoulders in the tiniest of shrugs. "It wouldn't work, Ainela," she says softly. "We'd never win."

"It's a really good way to die," Klara says distinctly. Anger starts to roll deep inside Ainela. Lusia's death snuffed

Klara's fight. She refuses to believe that. She shakes her head. "We can do it. We have –"

"Nothing." Kaja says. "It's not fair but then–nothing's fair, is it? What's *fair* about us being taken in the first place? It's not fair. But it is what it is."

"We need to just obey. If we can just stay quiet, and not get in their way –"

"Then we die!" Ainela's voice raises.

"Shh!" The girls simultaneously chastise her, looking in panic at the heavy oak door. Ainela sighs heavily, stands, the loose pages of the Rhymebook sliding off her lap. She walks from one end of the cellar to the other. Standing beneath the glass, she turns and stares at the others watching her warily. "What happened to Joanna? What happened to Larisa? They obeyed, didn't they? What good did it do them?"

"Ainela."

"It's true!" She swings her arms up in the air, slapping her palms against her legs. "They didn't do anything wrong. They *starved*. They got *sick*. Look at us!" She waves a hand. The faces of the girls are closed. Ainela's shoulders drop. *Maybe they're right*, she thinks. *The wages of sin are death. If we're sinners, maybe he's right, maybe we do deserve to die.*

She makes another try. "Halina, will we all get sick? Can someone survive forever on the food we're given? What if Jakub stops giving you extra pieces of bread? What would happen then?"

Halina shakes her head once, slowly, her eyes narrowing.

Lenka says, "If we got out of here, we'd never get upstairs."

WHISPERROOT: A HUSHWOOD TALE

"It's a death wish," Klara insists, her voice blank. "We are locked in this room, first of all. So, even if we wanted to escape, we couldn't open the door. We have nothing to break the glass of the window with. When they come, they are always, *always*, right there with us. It would never work, and you know it. You just want out, even if you die trying. The rest of us want to live."

The *drip drip drip* of the water from the vent makes the only noise. Ainela looks towards Kalina. She says, "You think that, too?"

Kalina frowns. "I … I think she's right, I think it's impossible."

The shuffling of feet as she moves, sliding against the stone until she's sitting again, reminds her of wind blowing through the trees. She closes her eyes, breathes in deep.

"They thought I snuck out to see the seamstress's son, but I really went to the hushwood." She smiles sadly. "I knew better. It was late at night, and I knew someone would see me. But I went at night because I love the emberflies. They're so pretty. And I would hide little things in the tree for Zosia – whatever I had, sometimes I didn't even have a message, but I put something there because she liked finding things." She takes a breath. "The wind would blow through my hair, and it made me feel alive. It made me feel   " she uses her fingers to tap the code for *free*. "I'm never going to see my sister again. I'm never going to feel the wind."

She sees Halina's eyes glistening.

Kaja mumbles, "That forest is our home."

"It's like I said earlier," Ainela says softly. "If I'm going to die *anyway*, then I want to choose when and how. Maybe," she hesitates, her eyes cautiously tracking Klara: she sees the small twitches in her jaw, the way her nails are biting into her palms. "Maybe we try. Maybe we get one of us out. And, if one of us gets out, she tells everyone, everyone, until someone listens. She tells the other families how much we miss them."

Kalina's eyes grow misty, her breath shakes.

Halina opens her mouth, closes it.

Klara holds her eye and says, "He won't just kill you. He will torture you first."

Ainela hesitates. "He held me down. At one point, his hand was choking me–I felt him breaking me inside. He –"

"Ainela, stop," Klara's eyes mist.

"He can't do anything worse to me." She swallows. "Except take my freedom."

Lenka moves first. Tentatively, she taps the code: *One. One. Two, two. Free.*

Halina joins next. Kalina looks at Klara who purses her lips, tenses her shoulders. "It's suicide."

"We die if we don't do this. But what if, Klara? What if we did get out? It's freedom. Either way–it's freedom. No. More. Pain."

Kalina taps. *Free.*

Klara swallows.

Kaja nods curtly. "I'm in."

"Obedience –"

"Klara." Ainela's voice sharpens until Klara focuses on her. Ainela reaches out, puts a hand on one of hers. Instead of speaking, Ainela's blue eyes are steady on hers, holding her, silently willing her to let go of the fear. "You gave us this. This was *your* idea."

Klara frowns. "What are you talking about?"

"*Jakub doesn't come on Tuesdays,*" Ainela whispers, parroting Klara's words that awful night when she came back from the priest's room. The tears spill onto Klara's cheeks. She takes the back of her hand and wipes her eyes. Ainela presses, "You came back and you told us that."

"He doesn't. I count the boots. It's always lighter."

Ainela nods. "I know. I know because you see everything. You were thinking this long before I was. This was *your plan* all along. You gave at least one of us a way out. Will you help us now?"

A fragile sigh becomes a sharp intake of breath. "The bucket."

"What bucket?" Kaja asks.

"There's a bucket near the stairwell door. It's there to catch the dripping water from the ceiling." She shrugs.

Ainela smiles. "It's there," she sings, patting Klara's knee happily. "To prop the door for us. Isn't it, Klara?"

For a moment, a spark flares in Klara's eyes.

She nods.

The moon outside rises higher, clouds shift by slowly, letting it shimmer brighter for the first night in weeks. "It's decided then," Ainela whispers. The others note how her face seems to glow. A hint of color returns to her cheeks; she seems stronger than she has in days. *The flame thrower's happy*, Kalina teases.

"We need to think," she paces the room back and forth while Lenka draws the plans in the Rhymebook. A bucket – they'll use it to prop the door open. "We need to decide who will run." Ainela takes a deep breath, holds it while the room weighs her words.

"You mean who might survive this?" Kaja asks. Her voice is emotionless.

Ainela nods. "We give one a fighting chance. Then we protect the rest."

Halina: "Lenka is the fastest. She is also not sick. She might – she *might* –" Halina emphasizes, "be able to outrun them."

"Anyone disagree?"

Klara: "Lenka, you have to run—you can't look back, and you cannot stop. No matter what."

Lenka swallows. "If I'm caught..."

"If you don't want to be the runner," Ainela says, "Then Kalina."

Kalina shakes her head violently.

Lenka closes her eyes, breathes. "I can run."

"Kaja, we need you to watch Tomasz and Mateusz. You made the creak map — you know which boards make sounds and which don't – can you draw it for us? So that Lenka will know where to step in case she gets ahead of them, and they don't know where exactly she is?"

"Yes." She takes the charcoal nub and the loose Rhymebook pages, begins making a map. *H* for *hush boards,* C for boards that *cry.*

"We go on a Tuesday," Ainela's hands move as she speaks, her head bent in concentration, her voice coming faster and faster. "When they line us up for work. Last week, they didn't separate us into two groups, it was just one because there are so few of us now. So, it'll just be one guard."

"If it's Mateusz, he'll use the whip," Kaja says. "Tomasz is mostly hands."

WHISPERROOT: A HUSHWOOD TALE

"We'll remember that for those of us who remain. We'll make sure that the weakest of us is closer to Tomasz since he won't use a whip."

"I've been coughing–and the other day, Tomasz and Jakub were talking, saying..." Halina sighs. "Saying I might be next." Her voice gains strength. "So, I can distract them somehow."

Ainela nods, pointing at the air. "Yes. Yes, that's it. Okay. They come to line us up. Halina will be first in line. We'll start walking down the wall towards work, but then, Halina, you'll pretend to faint, falling *forward,* so that you fall *into* the guard, make him stumble–"

"On the third hush," Kaja adds, lifting her head from the page. She turns it so everyone can see. They'll walk along the boards closest to the wall. "If we can get Lenka to be fourth in line, and Halina is first, then when Halina touches the third hush, Lenka will be *at* the staircase."

A moment's silence. *If she's at the staircase, and a commotion happens, she can run.* It feels like a victory when Klara's smile dawns first. She chimes in and says what everyone has just heard from Kaja: "When Halina falls, the guard will have to either catch her or at least right himself. That'll give us a second or two, and Lenka will be *right at the staircase.*"

"Okay. When Halina falls, Kaja – you and Klara will leap forward, okay, like you're trying to help her. It'll cause more chaos at the front of the line, giving Lenka a few extra seconds to get up the stairs. I'll be behind Lenka, and I'll push the water bucket forward, so that it props the door open. In case someone else has a chance to run. Kalina, you will be in front of Lenka. You might have a chance to run with her."

A moment of silence passes.

"Write it down," Ainela instructs. Kaja's hand moves.

"What about the stairwell door? I won't be able to open it."

The silence grows heavier. The hope that seemed so close moments ago deflates.

Klara's lips twitch. She glances up toward the stone ceiling. "On Tuesdays... they don't *always* lock it. Tomasz always does, he never forgets. But Mateusz–sometimes he doesn't bother. I count bolts."

"Maybe the chore will be scrubbing floors because we have to carry buckets up and down. Sometimes they leave it propped for that." Kalina says softly.

"So, we bet everything on 'sometimes'?" Kaja mutters.

The girls lean closer, hope flickering like a candle.

Ainela's voice is fierce as she presses: "We bet on sometimes. Because it's all we have."

Klara pulls her bottom lip between her teeth. "Then Lenka, Kalina, whoever gets to that door—they have one chance."

Lenka's eyes widen as she sits, holding her breath. "We need signals." She says. "We need signals. Someway that those who are in the back of the line can tell those who are in the front *not* to do this. What if *he* shows up somewhere and only a couple of us see him? What if another guard comes out of a room, blocking the stairwell? It'll only be seconds that I'll have...."

Kalina tilts her chin. "I'll hum. Always. You'll hear me. But if I *stop* humming - don't move. You don't fall. You do nothing. Nothing at all. We wait another day."

WHISPERROOT: A HUSHWOOD TALE

Brown eyes, blue eyes, green eyes – they flick from one to the other. It's fragile. They know they won't survive it.

"Ainela, if you're at the end, you'll be by the door… you can run, too. Will you lead her out?" Klara asks.

Ainela hesitates only a moment. "No. I will make sure the Rhymebook is carried. I will prop the door open for anyone who can get through it. I will stand in front of it afterwards, scream and claw and kick, buying you time." She pauses, lifting her chin. "And then I will be free."

Lenka taps slowly, deliberately. *One. One. Two, two.*

The cellar is silent except for the taps. *One. One. Two, two.* Each girl presses her fingers harder, the sound soft but steady, echoing off stone. For a moment, the rhythm is louder than hunger, louder than fear, louder than the priest's voice that lingers in their heads. For a moment, the rhythm is a shared heartbeat.

Free.

Every step is a prayer the earth keeps

The Hushwood

Chapter Twenty-Nine

The Runner

Two days. Two days until Tuesday. The cellar holds its breath, thoughts tumbling over themselves, taking up all the air in the room. They've spent everyday practicing. Ainela's led them in mock drills where, without warning, she stands knocks softly on the wall as if she were the guards unlocking the door. They line up in order smoothly and quickly now with no confusion on placement: Halina first followed by Klara, Kaja, Kalina, Lenka and Ainela. The first three have very little chance of making it to the staircase; they'll be tumbling, creating the diversion. Lenka will be positioned directly in front of the staircase – all she'll have to do is run. Kalina may try if she has time. Ainela will do whatever she can to stop the guard from running after them. *It should only be a minute, two, tops*, Ainela stresses, *but that's enough time to run up the stairs.* Kalina has hummed without stopping since the plan. She says, *so you'll notice right away if I'm not humming.*

The unanswered questions worry them the most.

What if the door at the top of the stairs is locked? Ainela's response: *Pray it's open.*

The guard will likely shout when the commotion happens – what happens if another guard, or the priest, come to see what's happening? Ainela: *That will happen. But it will take the other person at least a minute or two to hear the shout and get here. We still have one to two minutes.*

What if it's more than one guard that comes to get them? Ainela's shoulders sag and she replies, *Then, we wait for a day it's only one.*

A short gasp from Klara.

"Shh shh," she taps three times. *Stop*. Kalina's hum dies. Without it, the air feels tight.

The priest comes in, his hands clasped behind his back. Jakub and Mateusz are with him but the girls feel Tomasz's absence. He walks slowly to stand in front of Ainela. She swallows, moistens her lips, drops her eyes. Klara's lashes close briefly, her lips moving in a whispered prayer. *Obedient, Ainela, be obedient.* But not because it's safer. It was Klara who told Ainela to *be good* until the escape because, if she wasn't, they might pay closer attention, they might strike more frequently. Pride swells Klara's chest as she watches Ainela struggle to appear weak. Content with her submissive stance, he moves to study Lenka. Lenka's limbs tremble, but she swallows. She doesn't meet his stare, but she doesn't look down, either. Instead, her eyes gaze at his cheek. Halina coughs as he moves to stand in front of her. She sniffles, coughs again. She is not acting: her cold hollows her cheeks while forming dark circles beneath her eyes. She sways, grits her teeth, and stares at a spot on the floor to keep herself steady.

His lips quirk. "Did you run out of herbs for yourself, then?" When she doesn't reply, he says, "Witchcraft is the Devil's playground. You grow ill because you've dabbled too long in the occult."

Halina's lips part just enough to pull in a breath that rattles her lungs.

He moves past.

She glances up quickly in time to see Jakub tilt his head, shift his head to this right, as if he's trying to look at something that's turned upside down. Memory kicks Halina's heart into a full gallop. Her eyes drop. *The Rhymebook page.*

WHISPERROOT: A HUSHWOOD TALE

The creak map. The plan. Before he can decide what he sees, Halina coughs hard, two times, bending forward while, at the same time, covertly sliding the page back.

The priest turns his head to look at her again, frowning.

Jakub lifts a bushy brow, straightening his head.

Did he see? Would he know what the letters meant? How clear did Kaja make the map?

"While I was in communion with the Lord, He revealed some things that you each should know about your families. It may sound harsh, but we need to focus on truth. People despised our Lord because He spoke the truth. Each of you tells yourself lies that are designed to comfort, but doing so drives you further from righteousness." The priest bows his head, as though it burdens him to share.

"Scripture tells us of the prodigal son. He had everything–just as you once did–loving family, opportunity. But–just like you did–he squandered it, wasted it, rejected God. Only when he was living in a pigsty did he think of asking to come home." He paces, walking back and forth in front of the girls, his voice calm and steady. He doesn't waver. "You are still living in the pigsty, you've not repented of your sins or even asked to return home to your Father." He pauses, his eyes hardening. "Your families don't want you. I know each one."

He pauses in front of Klara and says, "Four." *Klara,* Ainela corrects silently. Her name is *Klara.* "Your father is grateful to be free of the distraction you caused; your brothers do not ask for you." Klara's eyes narrows. Her head jerks a fraction to the left as though rejecting what's being said. He smiles at Halina. "One," *Halina.* "You used to fetch herbs, but they're gathered by others now. You were never needed." Ainela sees the arrow pierce Halina. Being needed matters to the healer. Her hands clench and unclench, grip her shift, holding tight to control.

"Eleven," *Kalina. "*Your sister wears new ribbons in her hair, and she smiles, too. She takes your place at the hearth. You hope they think of you before each meal, but they do not." Kalina doesn't flinch; she remains still and quiet. *She doesn't believe him.*

"And you. Nine."

Kaja. Ainela's eyes narrow, sucking on the inside of her cheek so hard she flinches.

"Do you think the forest loved you? it hasn't spoken your name to anyone – no one recalls it, not even the trees."

Kaja can't stop the shard of pain that slices across her face. Her shoulders stiffen and she drops her head. Ainela sees Lenka: she's tapping her first finger against her thumb. *Tap. Tap. Tap, tap.* Over and over again, silently steeling herself for when he stands in front of her. "You aren't special, Five." *Lenka,* Ainela corrects, shouting it silently, hoping Lenka can somehow hear her. "Your family never looked for you. Your mother wishes you had run a long time ago." Lena inclines her head, the tapping of her fingers stops. *She doesn't believe him.*

Nothing he says is true, Ainela whispers this to herself. *I'm strong. I don't believe him.* But when he stops in front of her, his piercing gray eyes probing her face, the knot that curls in her stomach knows it is not true. Memories of him hurting her, tearing her insides with his fingers and his body, make her tremble. She shifts, anxiety building the longer he is silent. "You cursed your sister with silence, and it has rooted so far into her that she cannot even speak to God. She is alone. The children mock her, say she is a broken thing. Perhaps they are right. You think she'll remember you, but she has forgotten. She bows her head, and she obeys." He pauses and then says softly, leaning in closer to her face. "Losing you means nothing to her—she'll never say your name again, Twelve."

Pain feels sharp, like razor blades slicing her heart. She doesn't realize she's holding her breath until she starts struggling to breathe. The others haven't seen Ainela fold inward like this, not since the priest took her alone.

Zosia.

She cannot speak to God.

She has no one.

She is a broken thing.

She obeys.

Each promise a lash that rips and snags against her soul, her reason for breathing.

"That's not true." Lenka's voice is clear. Both the priest and Ainela turn to look at her. She draws a shaky breath and says, "I saw the sketchbook she carried. A lot of her drawings were of you. Zosia will never forget you."

Ainela's eyes, full of shame and the quiet doubt she doesn't want to admit, lift. Lenka's eyes meet hers, then drop to her fingers. When Ainela follows her gaze, she sees Lenka tapping again. *One. One. Two, two.* Ainela takes a shaky breath, taps back. *FREE.*

"So," the priest says, moving to stand in front of Lenka again. "You still think you can run from the truth, do you?" He pauses, looks over his shoulder at the guards. Mateusz snickers, Tomasz lifts a shoulder. Jakub stands impassive.

"Take her to the courtyard without her shoes. She'll run until the truth breaks her like it did the prodigal son." His eyes scan the room.

Ainela panics. She can't do it. The plan– but she starts to interfere, steps forward even to do so, Lenka gives a nearly imperceptible shake of her head as if saying, *I got this*. The girls freeze until the heavy door slams shut. Halina bends quickly and retrieves a page of the Rhymebook, the others run to the window. Murmurs fill the silence, bodies crowd close together beneath the glass, eyes widen as they see Jakub push Lenka into the snow.

And then it begins.

Halina slips in between Ainela and Klara, her body tight, fingers clutching the cold windowsill like a lifeline. "Look," Klara breathes, pointing out with a trembling finger. The chapel courtyard, half-walled by stone, opens to the hushwood beyond—a path the girls have seen the guards tread repeatedly, boots crunching over snow like a slow, steady drum. Mateusz's heavy steps carve a trail through the white silence until he stands, immovable, in the center. "It leads to the forest," Kaja whispers, barely more than a breath. Eyes meet in silent accord, the memory of the open path—a fragile thread of hope for escape—looming between them.

Jakub shoves Lenka, a sudden shove that sends her stumbling but not falling. She wavers, caught between fear and something fragile—a hand raised, palm turning up and down like snowflakes drifting softly. Then, a smile breaks through, quiet and trembling. Halina's voice falls to a whisper, "She's outside."

WHISPERROOT: A HUSHWOOD TALE

"I don't think I remember what it feels like," Kalina murmurs, voice raw with longing.

"Cold," Ainela answers, eyes distant. "But a fresh cold, not this dead cold in here. Out there—it breathes, it lives. Watch—" she gestures to Lenka, who touches her cheek, fists clenched, a faint smile breaking free. "The cold outside—it makes you feel something."

The priest's hand slices through the air, drawing a circle of command. Tomasz steps forward, ready to strike.

But Lenka runs.

"Her feet," Halina murmurs, breath caught. Bare feet pounding the courtyard's snow, light at first, fragile like whispers pressed into white dust. But when she slows, Mateusz's whip cracks—a sharp, cruel sound. Tomasz rubs his hands, blowing warmth into cold palms. Their breaths rise, ghosting like smoke in the freezing air. Still, Lenka runs, each step digging the white impressions deeper. She stumbles once more; the whip lands hand against her back. A small bloodstain darkens the back of her shift. Still, she runs.

Outside, sweat beads Lenka's temples, and neck. *I'm outside!* It took her several moments to believe where she was. She hasn't been out of the cellar in so long. The snow against her feet, the brush of the wind against her cheeks, the smell of the air–she'd almost forgotten all of this. The courtyard is half-enclosed by a stone wall, but she sees an opening. It's guarded: she would never get past him.

"You will run until the truth breaks you." The priest nods. "So, run."

She was out of breath after two laps. Her spirit dampened, she felt tendrils of fear blooming. *What if she can't do this?* After four laps, her heart feels as though it's going to burst. Gasping breath beats in her ears as an erratic rhythm. The world shakes as she runs around and around the courtyard. When the wind stirs, she feels it gliding over her skin. She should be cold, but running makes her warm. *I'm outside*, the thought tantalizes her. Sometimes, in the Spring, her grandmama brought her out to the chapel courtyard after church to pick bellbottom blossoms. The snow crunches beneath her boots and, suddenly, she hears her grandmother's voice, clear as a chapel bell. *Once,* Grandmama would lean closer to her, as if she were sharing a secret, *Bellbottom blossoms were the homes of fairies. When I was a girl, I gathered as many blossoms as I could find, and kept them in my room.*

Lenka pushes her arms, ignores the ache in her legs, pretends her lungs don't burn, and ignores the warning of her heart squeezing in her ribcage. When she passes Mateusz, for half a moment, she thinks of running through the tiny space between him and him the wall. If she could only get out of the courtyard... but the space is so small she would touch him. She would never get past him. And then she would die. *We can choose,* Ainela whispers in her memory. She shakes her head. *Not now.*

Finally, only once, I saw one! Her grandmama's wrinkled face lit up remembering. She would pat Lenka's hand and say, *She was about the size of my finger and I wanted to keep her forever.* Her grandmama smelled of rosemary and hollyhocks. She would tell her, *don't ever give up on yourself. That's the one person you never give up on, you hear?*

Lenka doesn't stop.

She wants to.

WHISPERROOT: A HUSHWOOD TALE

But Grandmama's eyes would dim if she did: *don't ever give up on yourself, you hear?* So, she breathes in the air, remembering the smell of hollyhocks and rosemary. She pushes onward. Every time she passes in front of Tomasz, he shoves her forward, making her stumble. *Tomasz is all hands.* Lenka sucks in breath, the sound a whistle and a wheeze in her chest. She presses inward and down, as hard as she can, forcing her legs to move. She can't give up, she can't stop. *Tuesday.* The word becomes a chant as the world starts to blur. *Tuesday. Tuesday. Tuesday.* The word drums in time with her heartbeat. She picks a spot in the sky, a small star, and focuses on that. The priest and each of the guards hold lanterns whose glow casts the courtyard in silver shadows, but the white star twinkles. It reminds her of her little brother, Michal.

I'm going to catch one! His hair, the color of nutmeg, was always tousled, two little strands sticking straight up. Freckles dotted his cheeks, just under his eyes. *Look at me!* Chasing the geese was one of his favorite games. Bursting into laughter as the geese cackled, Michal would say, *Race you, Lenka!* until she gave in and raced him through the town.

The sounds of the priest and the guards mocking her fade as the star twinkles. Her brother won't forget. Her gaze flickers to the window of the cellar. She knows the girls watch. Can they see her in the dark? She feels their presence, senses their hands pressed against the windowpane. It spurs her forward even when she thinks she can't anymore.

She doesn't see hear the priest tell Mateusz to *stop her,* and she is unprepared for the brutal crack of the whip landing against the back of her knees. It trips her, steals her fragile balance, and she falls. When she pushes her hands against the freezing snow, digging her fingers into the soft drift, she feels the tingling in her legs, hears the buzzing in her ears. She tries to push herself up, but a steel-toed boot kicks her down.

"It looks as though you cannot go any more," the priest says from above her. She wants to tell him he's wrong; she wants to shout she can still run. But blood oozes from her cuts, and the stinging in her legs feels like thousands of needles. She doesn't know how long she's run, but she knows they won't let her get up. If she tries, she might die. She cannot stand, but she refuses to give them her voice. That silence belongs to her.

"Stand up."

She tries. She pushes her hands further into the snow, a brief image flashing through her mind of throwing the snow in their faces, and pushes. Her chest heaves, and she lifts herself to her knees. But her legs, numb, give out. She collapses into the snowdrift. Tomasz laughs, calls her worthless. Jakub's hand seizes the back of her neck. It should crush, but instead it steadies. He drives her forward, but his grip slackens, almost as though he doesn't want her to fall again. As she walks, none of them notice the small smile touching her lips, like a star that refuses to go out.

Torchlight allows the girls to see each painful lap.

"She's slowing down," Kalina notices softly.

Ainela grasps Halina's wrist, and adds breathlessly, "But she's not giving up. She can do this."

Outside, the moon shines and stars twinkle. Beyond the courtyard lies the hushwood. Though dark, the girls can make out the shadows of the trees just behind Mateusz.

"She's pacing herself." Awe hugs Halina's voice. "She's not running as hard as she can. Look at her head–she holds it upright. If she were really running as hard as she could, her head would drop. And her arms are down by her waist. Wouldn't they be closer to her chest if she were really putting all her effort into it?"

"She paces herself," Kaja says curtly. "So that she can run longer."

"Training," Kalina agrees. "She's training."

Ainela pulls her bottom lip between her teeth. "But for how long?" She frowns, hope mixing with fear. "How long can she do this?"

"Wouldn't she need to run as fast as she can if she were training?" Kaja asks, tilting her head.

"No." Kalina's voice is sure. "She'll have to use all her energy in the beginning, to get up the stairs and far enough away that they can't reach her, yes, but then she'll have to keep going. She won't be able to stop. She'll have to keep running."

"She can do it," Halina promises. She feels Ainela gently squeeze her wrist, and glances toward her. A hint of uncertainty, of fragility, flashes across Ainela's face. Ainela feels her stomach churning. If Lenka can't do it... who else is strong enough to run? Sensing her turmoil, Halina repeats, her voice stronger: "She can do it." Carried by Halina's fierce tone, Ainela nods, blinking twice.

"Right."

"Look."

Torchlight shows Lenka on the ground. She tries to stand, but she's kicked back down. They watch Jakub grip her neck, pull her to her feet. "They're coming back," Kaja warns.

Quickly, the girls scatter from the windows, scurrying to their mats.

Seconds pass. Minutes.

"Where are they?" Kalina asks.

An hour passes.

"What are they doing to her?" Kalina paces. But Ainela shares a knowing glance with Kaja. Ainela swallows, closing her eyes. Quietly, she counts. Every number has a name. *One – Halina. Two–Iskra. Three-Joanna. Four–Klara. Five–Kaja. Six–Lusia.*

"Please come back," Ainela whispers.

The silence falls thick until the only thing they hear is pounding hearts. When the familiar pattern – *heavy, heavy, jingle* – interrupts the silence, breaths expel, shoulders fall in relief. The scrape of keys turns the lock, and the heavy door opens. *Seven–Lenka.*

Lenka staggers in murmuring, "I did it." Her knees don't bend quite right, and lanterns show black and blue bruises lining her cheekbones. Her nose is busted, blood trickling down. Girls surround her. Halina stares, unmoving, at her feet.

"What is it?" Klara asks.

Halina swallows heavily. Lenka's feet are dark blue, almost black. *Frostbite.* She pinches a toe. "Can you feel that?" Lenka murmurs again, her lips blue, her hands stiff and frigid.

"We need to warm her up right now." Halina's voice holds urgency.

The girls gather around. Halina bends Lenka's knees so her feet are flat on the floor. She tears a piece of her shift, wraps it around her feet. Then she uses her hands and rubs Lenka's foot repeatedly, quick, to spark warmth. Ainela takes the other foot and mimics Halina's fast movements. Kaja and Kalina do the same with her hands.

Kaja surprises them by speaking first. "You ran for hours, Lenka."

Lenka's eyes open. She stares blankly at Kaja who smiles at her. "They didn't punish you. They gave you time to practice running."

"Fairies live in bellroot blossoms."

The girls exchange worried glances.

"Just sleep," Ainela says softly.

She murmurs, "I'm going to find the fairies, Grandmama." When silence falls, she whispers, "We'll chase geese, Michal. Chase—" Her breath comes in a rush, and she falls quiet.

"Halina—"

Halina puts a finger beneath her nose, watches her chest. It rises and falls. "She's sleeping. Just sleeping. Keep warming her up."

Knock

and the door shall be opened for you

———————————

Matthew 7:7

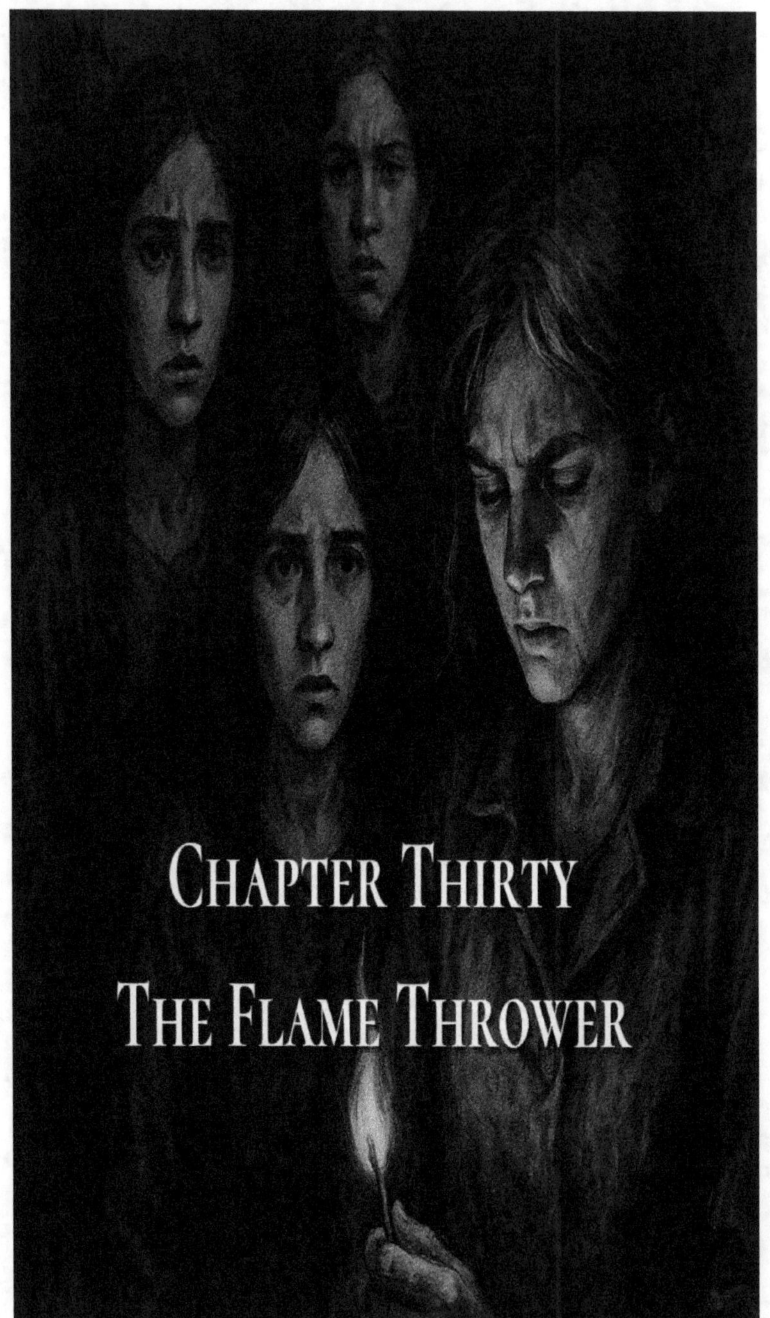

Chapter Thirty

The Flame Thrower

The mouse scurries along the corner of the wall, looking for even the tiniest crumbles left behind. Halina had stopped leaving pieces for him but quietly resumed after Joanna died. A pinch of bread wasn't enough for any of the girls to avoid starvation, but it might keep *someone*, even if just a mouse, alive. Lenka's legs twitched for two nights after the run. Sometimes the pain made her cry out, but she hasn't hurt in two days. When she says *I'm ready* her voice is steady but, sometimes, Ainela catches her staring out the window, her lips moving.

"If I make it, if I really get to the forest... then what? I can't go home; they came there to take me. They'd just take me back." Lenka's voice is barely a whisper. It's still dark outside, the sun still hidden, but they know no one sleeps.

Memories flashed through each of them. *Home* can never be *home* again. Where do you go when home isn't safe? It still burns like hot coals remembering the knock at the door, the knot of fear that curled like tangled whisperroot vines around Ainela's ribcage when she realized Papa was going to make her go. They didn't let her wake Zosia, so she didn't get a chance to tell her goodbye, although, as they walked through the snow in a single file line, she thought she saw her standing at the bedroom window.

"The widow healer," Halina's voice is hesitant. "I heard Tomasz mocking her. I don't think she wanted them to take us. She lives on the outskirt of town, way out, by the old woodcutter's cottage."

"And if she turns me in?" Lenka sucks on the inside of her cheek, her eyes wide.

"We have to risk it," Klara pipes in. "We don't know anyone else who might listen. Plus, if she's a healer, she might be able to help care for any wounds you might have by the time you get there."

Ainela closes her eyes, swallows, uncertainty pooling in her stomach. She has no fear for herself, but this risks all their lives. Uncomfortable, she remembers Klara's objections. *This is suicide. You just want out, even if it means dying. The rest of us want to live.* Her lips open, close, open again. The words feel like gritty sand, but she forces them out. "You don't have to do this."

In the silver shadows cast by the moon, she sees Klara turn her head towards her.

"What?"

Ainela bites her lip. "I'm just saying ... Lenka has the greatest risk. If she runs up the stairs, they won't be kind. I need freedom, but I can get that for myself if the rest of you don't want to risk it."

Silence fills the room for three, four beats of the heart.

"We're going to die anyway." Klara says softly. "That's what you said, and it's true. If we stay here, we're going to die."

"I can do it." Lenka says fiercely. "If the door is unlocked, I can get out." She hesitates and then adds in a whisper, "I felt the wind. I - I felt snow. I haven't been outside in so long, but I felt it when they made me run. I want to feel it again. I'd rather freeze in the forest than rot in here."

Ainela inhales a shaky breath. "Okay. Then you run to the woodcutter's cottage. Do you remember how to get there?"

"I'll stay in the woods. Follow the creek until I pass the blacksmith's shop, then curve away from the creek, pass the rickety bridge, as if I'm leaving Myreska. Just on the other side of the bridge is another grove of trees. The woodcutter's cottage is set in the middle of them. The widow's is close by."

"The woodcutter cottage is abandoned. You could go there if you don't want to ask the widow."

Lenka nods.

Halina asks, "Do you remember what I showed you? How to recognize the nettles, and rosemary? How to make painkillers with them?"

Lenka nods again. "Yes."

"Spring is coming, they'll bloom soon."

Lenka moistens her lips. "Okay. If I do make it to Ida– what do I tell her?"

"The truth." Ainela says fiercely. "All of it. Show her your scars. Tell her what happened to us. Tell her that we're in danger, that six of us have died and are buried in the hushwood."

"If she doesn't listen, leave. Go back into the forest and run North until you get far away from Myreska. And tell somebody else, the first person you see." Klara's voice is sharp, like a razor blade, as though she's accepted what will happen.

"We're more than sinners." Ainela insists. "Halina, you're a healer. Klara, you're a sister. Kalina, you're a singer. Lenka, you're brave. We're more than what they say we are."

"You forgot someone." Klara points out. "You're more than what he says, too."

Ainela hesitates, says softly. "I don't know what I am, but I don't want to be caged anymore."

"We know what you are." Klara insists. "You're a flame thrower."

Kaja hears the creaks first.

"They're coming," she whispers, moving away from the vent. Breaths mingling, hearts pounding, the girls exchange quick glances. They are ready. Kalina begins to hum. If she stops, the plan stops. It is Mateusz who opens the door—and he is alone. Their expressions give nothing away, but the sight of only one guard bolsters the starved, but hopeful, girls.

"Let's go," he says flatly. He scratches his jaw as he watches them line up.

Halina takes the lead, standing with her head bowed in front of him. Kaja and Klara slide into positions with Lenka and Ainela in the back. Just as rehearsed. He mutters about "the damn humming" but Kalina doesn't falter. Halina coughs. It's not what they'd planned, and Ainela isn't sure if it was a real cough or one for show. Time seems to crawl.

Ainela's eyes flit over the cellar. Echoes of Iskra's jokes fill her head. Images of Lusia's face flash behind her eyes. The other mats seem emptier than usual. They should be here. They should have done this together, a long time ago. They should have had the same chance. Larisa needed something to believe in; she could have believed in this. As they begin walking, and Lenka steps outside the cellar, Ainela's own lips move, and she catches herself tapping two fingers. *One. One. Two, two.* The board waits. The plan waits.

WHISPERROOT: A HUSHWOOD TALE

She hears Halina cough again.

She looks down.

They're almost there. Two more steps and Halina will step on the right board.

Kalina hums.

Suddenly, without warning, a cough, movement, Mateusz stumbles, falls. Kaja and Klara leap forward. It happens so fast. Lenka sprints up the stairs, her feet running after her. She hears the smack of Mateusz's whip against Kaja and Klara's cry. Kalina's hum falters, but Ainela screams, "Go!" and pushes Kalina towards the stairs, forcing her to run after Lenka. Mateusz's boots sound like thunder as he pushes past the three girls. Ainela grabs his arm, bites down as hard as she can. Kaja attacks him from behind, grabbing his leg and pulling.

"Tomasz!" Mateusz screams, stomping his foot.

Lenka grabs the doorknob and twists – Ainela hears the creak, sees the heavy door open. For a heartbeat, she sees it - the ink-blue night, a drift of snow swirling through the crack of the open door. But, before she can step into it, Mateusz's whip cracks against the side of her face, slicing her cheek, and the world slams shut. She screams, releases his arm to protect her face.

Boots echo heavily from somewhere; Ainela's not sure whose.

In only seconds, Mateusz grips the back of Kalina's neck and throws her behind him, down the stairs. She tumbles, the sound of bones cracking against wood and limbs thumping against the stone splitting the hall. She lands in an odd position, her head and shoulders on the floor in front of Ainela, her legs still crumbled against the stair. For a moment, time seems to freeze. Ainela 's breath hitches as she reaches for Kalina's arm, pulls hard. Kalina moans, eyes fluttering. Just like that, time rushes again, things happening too quickly for Ainela to see it all.

Mateusz grabs Lenka's hair and drags her down the stairs, stepping on Kalina's hand as he storms past. Ainela doesn't know where he came from, but she hears Tomasz beating Kaja, Klara screaming. *His boots*. Was it his boots she heard?

"Get them back in the cellar!" Mateusz barks.

When Tomasz grabs her arm, Ainela's fingers grip the stone wall. They cling for only a moment before she falls flat on her face as her leg is jerked from beneath her. Time warps into a cacophony of sounds and blurry images: bodies, screams, angry shouts, blood splashing stone, girls' shifts as they are thrown against walls. The sound of a whip snapping, fists cracking against bone race around the room. And then— just as suddenly–the slamming of the heavy oak door.

The silence that follows is not empty. It breathes, heavy and final, pressing against the stone as if death itself had stepped inside with them.

Ainela touches her cheek and flinches as blood stains her fingertips. The whip slashed diagonally across her cheekbone, caching her upper lip. New bruises bloom around her shoulders and neck; her ribs feel tight. But it is the others who worry her.

Gritting her teeth against the pain, she crawls. The room reeks of blood and sweat. Kalina lies curled in a fetal position moaning. Lenka's eyes are swollen; her wrist is clearly broken. Klara and Halina seem bruised, cut in a few places from the whip, but not as badly injured as the others. Ainela takes Kalina's hand in hers and squeezes. Kalina screams in pain. Ainela drops her hand, her mind flashing back to when Mateusz stepped on her fingers as he came down the stairs. "I'm sorry," Ainela whispers.

Silence fractures hope one second at a time.

It's broken by the sound of a choked sob from Kaja's tall frame. "My – back," she gasps. Halina steals a glance with Ainela, moves toward Kaja. When she lifts Kaja's shift, her eyes widen and her lips purse. Klara covers her mouth, fresh tears stinging her eyes. Between bruises both fresh and old, and cuts from the whip, Kaja's back is a broken, jagged piece of flesh. Halina starts to tremble violently, her usually rock steady demeanor cracking under her own pain and the weight of the others'. Klara puts a hand on Halina's knee and taps. *One. One. Two, two.* From the side of the room, Kalina, badly beaten, tries to hum but tears break her voice. Kaja adds her own stark note.

"We - we can't – there's no - no way," Halina's words fall apart as she hyperventilates, her breath coming short and choppy her pale skin marred by unnatural colors. "He won't let us – he's going to kill - kill us. All of us." When her palms lay flat against the cold stone floor, Ainela notices the blue tint to her fingers, the swollen knuckle and bent pinkie. She half-walks, half-stumbles to the heavy oak door and bangs against it, rattles the knob, and then hits her head against the wood, tears streaming down her face. Guilt tugs at Ainela's heart. *Halina holds us, tends to our wounds, and now she breaks.*

Klara looks at Ainela. "She's right," she says softly. "When they come in here, they're going to kill us, aren't they?"

Ainela's blue eyes shine with tears. "I don't know," she whispers.

"So, we try again? We can't make it up the stairs in time." Lenka says, desperation clinging to her voice like honey dripping from a comb. "There has to be another way."

When red-rimmed, tear-filled eyes move to Ainela again, she holds her breath, counts to three and, in a voice so soft they barely hear her, says, "Maybe." Her fingers crawl like spiders to the pocket she sewed inside her shift, curve around the treasure she stole from the kitchen during chores and holds it up for the others to see.

One small, red-tipped match.

The noise outside the cellar makes the silence inside the cellar profound. They hear Jakub cursing and Mateusz shouting back at him. *Heavy, heavy, jingle.* Boots stomping tight on the wooden floor. The girls look to Kaja, whose eyes are closed, focusing on the sounds. It has to be timed just right. She holds a finger up in the air, tracks the boots with it slowly. Suddenly, she nods, her eyes opening, catching Ainela's. "Now," she whispers.

Ainela pulls the match against the jagged, molten stone wall.

It does not catch. She exhales harshly, shaking hair out of her eyes. "Come on," she whispers. The girls gather around her, watching, praying.

Heavy, heavy, jingle.

The boots get closer, voices outside grow louder.

WHISPERROOT: A HUSHWOOD TALE

Ainela rubs it against a different spot on the wall. It starts to light, but then fizzles. Ainela's hands shake. Klara whispers, "Please." Lenka takes Halina's hand.

"They're almost here," Kaja's voice sounds stronger than it ever has, less breathy.

"I know, I know," Ainela murmurs, stands. "I don't think the wall – " Her eyes scan for something to strike it against, sees the iron bonding on the door itself. Slowly, her eyes calm. "We're going to burn the cage itself."

Kalina starts to hum as the others hold their breath. The boots stop walking outside, but they don't hear keys jingling yet. There's still time. Ainela presses the tip of the match against the iron and drags it with just enough pressure, just enough of a *snap*.

The match fractures the silence.

Joy lights the room as orange flames lick against the wood and begin to spread. Instead of backing away from the fire, the girls crowd together in front of the door. Keys scrape against the lock as the smoke begins to fill the space.

The girls don't wait. They storm forward, pushing into the guard hard enough to make Tomasz stumble back. Flames leap from the wood to the edge of his shirt and Tomasz screams, backing into Mateusz. The smoke is thick now, blurring vision.

"I can't see, my eyes are swollen!"

"Straight!" The voice is loud and strong.

Jakub.

Ainela freezes for only a second before she grips Halina's shoulders and pushes her toward Jakub's voice. Lenka and Kaja run after her, race up the stairs. Tomasz stumbles past them, flames now eating his flesh. Ainela looks behind her, screams, "Klara! Kalina!" She hesitates, looks towards the stairs, then behind her. *The cellar. They're still in the cellar.* Ainela runs back to the room, but smoke and flames engulf it. She doesn't hear screaming. She frowns, coughing heavily, smoke burning her eyes. *Maybe they got out.* She hears footsteps and stumbles towards them, towards the stairs.

"Straight!" The voice is loud and strong.

Jakub.

Behind Ainela, Klara sees her push Halina towards Jakub's voice but the smoke is so thick. Kalina passes the stairwell, going straight, towards the laundry. "Kalina!" she cries but the crackling of fire as it breaks eats woods, the screaming of Tomasz on fire, Mateusz barging up the stairs - it all drowns her voice out. *She's the weakest of us , I won't leave her.* Instead of taking the stairs, Klara runs after Kalina. Coughing she stumbles into one room, calling her name. She thinks she hears Kalina from behind her, and turns, going back into the smoke filled corridor and into the laundry room. Kalina lies on the floor.

Klara can't see the door anymore, all she can see is Kalina's body curling into a ball. "Come on, get up, get up, the stairs aren't far." But when she pulls, she sees it: massive amounts of blood staining the front of Kalina's shift. "Tom-Tom–" her words fray into a cough. Klara remembers: the silver glint of a knife's edge, a scream she thought was from a fist blow. "He stabbed you—oh—"

"Go," Kalina yells.

Klara shakes her head. "No," she whispers.

"I can't walk—-" she coughs again and blood spills from her mouth.

Klara turns, closes the door to the laundry and bolts it. And then she kneels, laying in front of Kalina. She puts her trembling arms around Kalina and pulls her closer until Kalina's head rests against her chest. Kalina tries to speak, but can't. Klara moans, but it sounds like a hum. Kalina's body tenses and she starts shaking, pointing.

Klara doesn't look.

She knows. She hears the hiss of the flames as they slink under the door. She taps against Kalina's skin. *One. One. Two, two. One. One. Two, two.* She keeps tapping even as her hum grows louder against Kalina's ear. Kalina's body slowly relaxes. By the time the flames reach their feet, Kalina's breath is already gone.

And Klara holds her.

"Straight!" The voice is loud and strong.
Jakub.

Lenka runs behind Halina. She hears someone behind her; she thinks it's Kaja. Jakub doesn't stop Halina as she grabs the railing and pulls herself up. Lenka takes two steps before she feels something plunge into the back of her neck, feels herself tumbling down the stone steps. Blood spurts from her neck. She freezes. Just before she falls, she feels a shoulder shove her forward. She trips over the next step, but not backwards. Jakub and Mateusz crash into the wall, fists flying. Something moves quick past her, but she doesn't know what.

She groans, flames now racing up the stairs. Unable to pull herself, she feels someone's fingers bite into her forearm, pull her up. She's shoved through the door and falls face forward into the snow. She tries to move but can't.

I see snow! Joy overshadows the pain, and she laughs deliriously, her hand grabbing a fist full of the drift and laying it over the wound in her neck. Her arms start to tingle, black spots dance in her vision. The world narrows and her head feels fuzzy but – what is that? Kaja? At the tree line? But Halina was in front of her – wasn't she?

She laughs again and finds just enough strength left to tap against the snow. *I'd rather freeze in the forest than rot in here.*

One. One.

The last gasp is always the loudest and the sharpest.

"Straight!" The voice is loud and strong.

Jakub.

Ainela freezes for only a second before she grips Halina's shoulders and pushes her toward Jakub's voice. Lenka and Kaja run after her, race up the stairs. Tomasz stumbles past them, flames now eating his flesh. Ainela looks behind her, screams, "Klara! Kalina!" She hesitates, looks towards the stairs, then behind her. *The cellar. They're still in the cellar.* Ainela runs back to the room, but smoke and flames engulf it. She doesn't hear screaming. She frowns, coughing heavily, smoke burning her eyes. *Maybe they got out.* She hears footsteps and stumbles towards them, towards the stairs.

WHISPERROOT: A HUSHWOOD TALE

She steps over the body lying at the bottom of the stairs, starts to sprint—and looks up. The priest stands at the top of the stairs, staring down at her. Fury clenches his face. He says nothing as he slams the door. She hears the bolt and knows—she is sealed.

Flames hiss behind her.

She swallows, pressing her back against the wall. She closes her eyes.

We did it.

They got out.

Calmly, she turns. Not toward the top of the stairs, but down. She steps over the body again, her chin tilted up, her shoulders lowered. Her breathing is short and she coughs twice from the smoke, but her feet are sure.

By the time she returns to the cellar, it is engulfed in flames.

She stands in front of it, watches it for a moment. Hears the shattering of glass somewhere down the corridor. Spreading her arms, she starts to hum.

And the flame thrower walks into the fire.

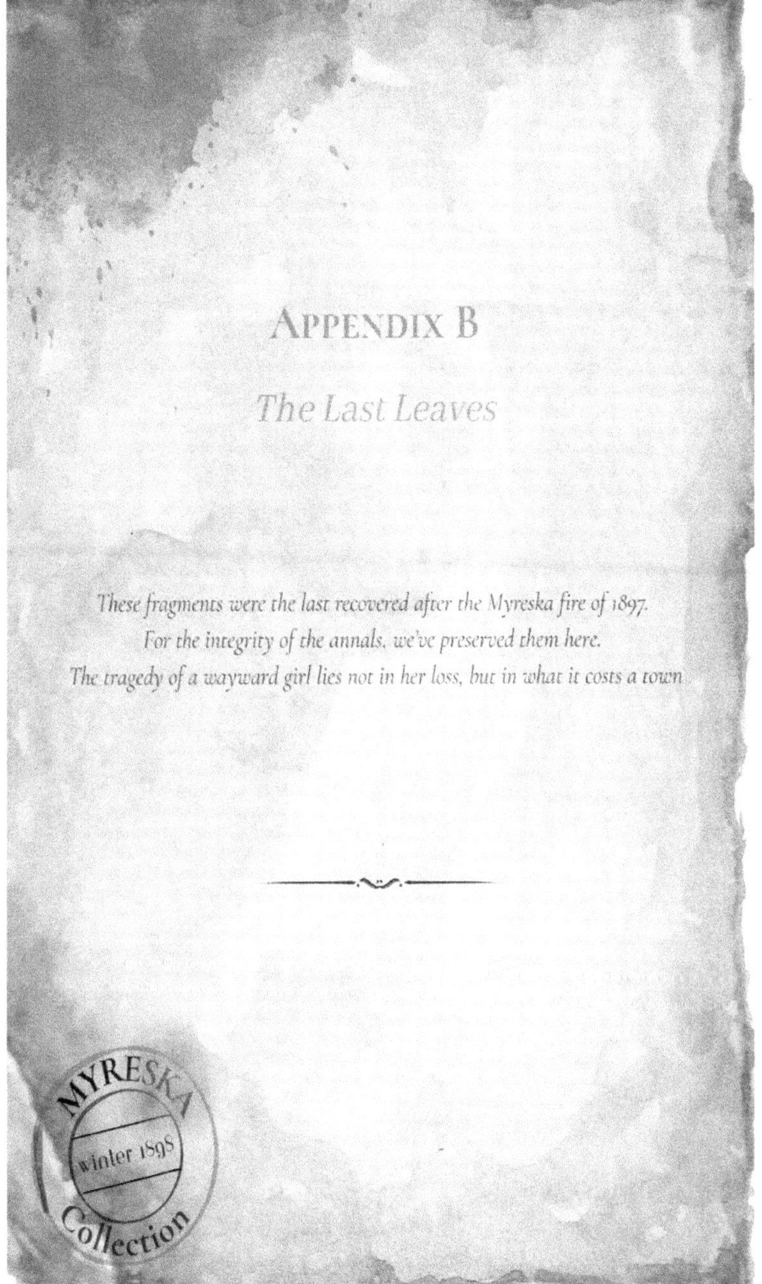

APPENDIX B

The Last Leaves

These fragments were the last recovered after the Myreska fire of 1897.
For the integrity of the annals, we've preserved them here.
The tragedy of a wayward girl lies not in her loss, but in what it costs a town

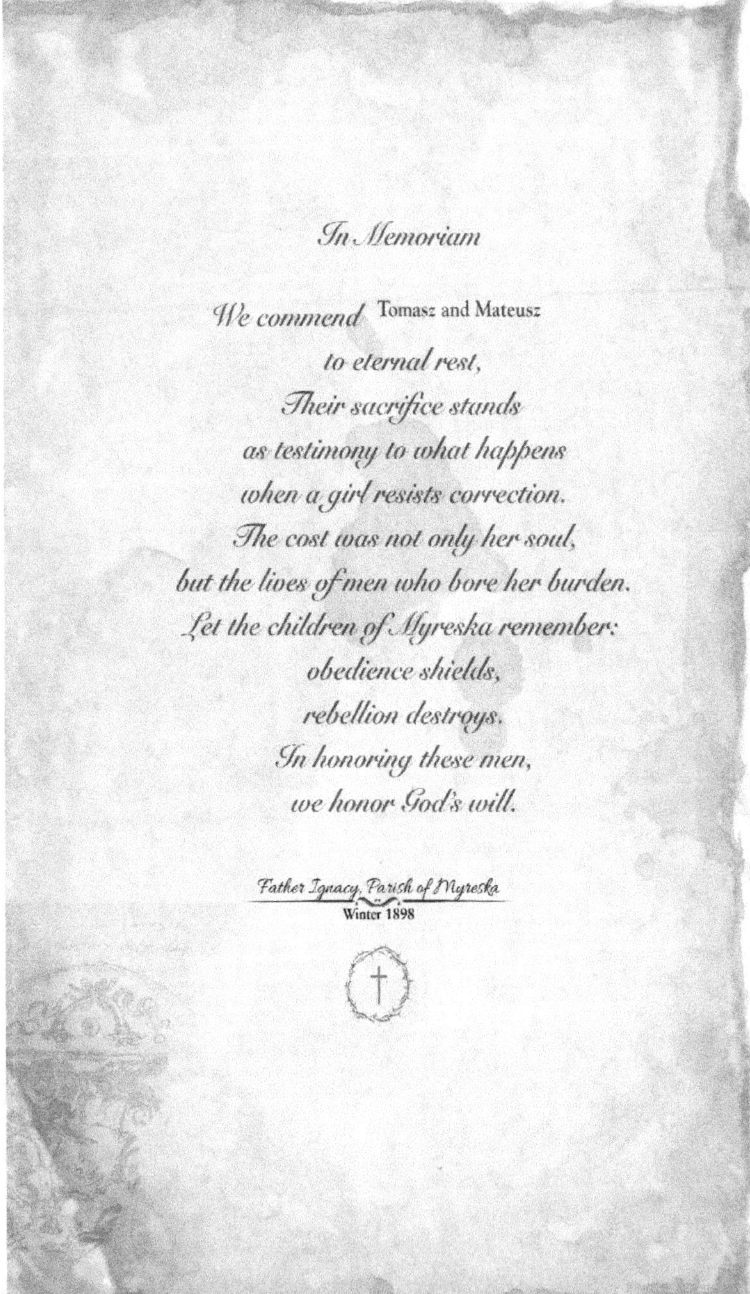
In Memoriam

We commend Tomasz and Mateusz
to eternal rest,
Their sacrifice stands
as testimony to what happens
when a girl resists correction.
The cost was not only her soul,
but the lives of men who bore her burden.
Let the children of Myreska remember:
obedience shields,
rebellion destroys.
In honoring these men,
we honor God's will.

Father Ignacy, Parish of Myreska
Winter 1898

fierce like a hummingbird
her song carried us
small but she remembered

who she was

Lusia
she carried memory past her breath

I am READY
If I reach the HUSHWOOD
I won't look BACK

Lenka
She was ready but the world was not

beads slip
string breaks
I gather them up anyway
my lips move faster
than answers come

Larsa
she prayed though no answer came

I draw sounds

C for CRY
H for HUSH

I know the way out.

Koja
She turns creeks into escape

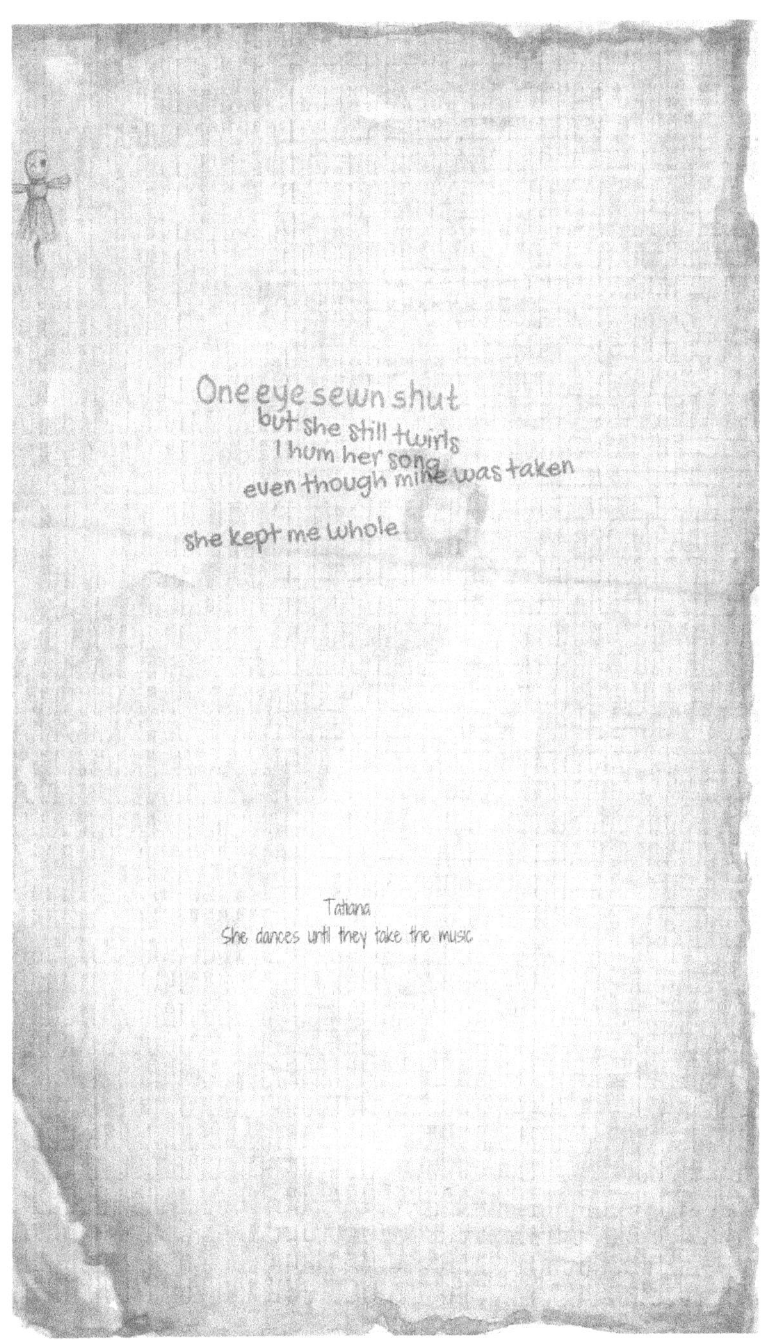
One eye sewn shut
but she still twirls
I hum her song
even though mine was taken

she kept me whole

Tatiana
She dances until they take the music

The forest remembers what fire cannot erase.

kneel
they said
but even silence bends
if they BURN my name
remember the ember
it is not gone
the flame thrower holds it still

Ainela — She named even silence to keep herself alive

Part Four: The Memory Keeper

Silence is not the absence of sound,
but the weight of voices we refuse to hear

The Embergirls' Rhymebook
recovered fragment

$$\frac{\text{The match fractured the silence}}{\text{the red one}}$$

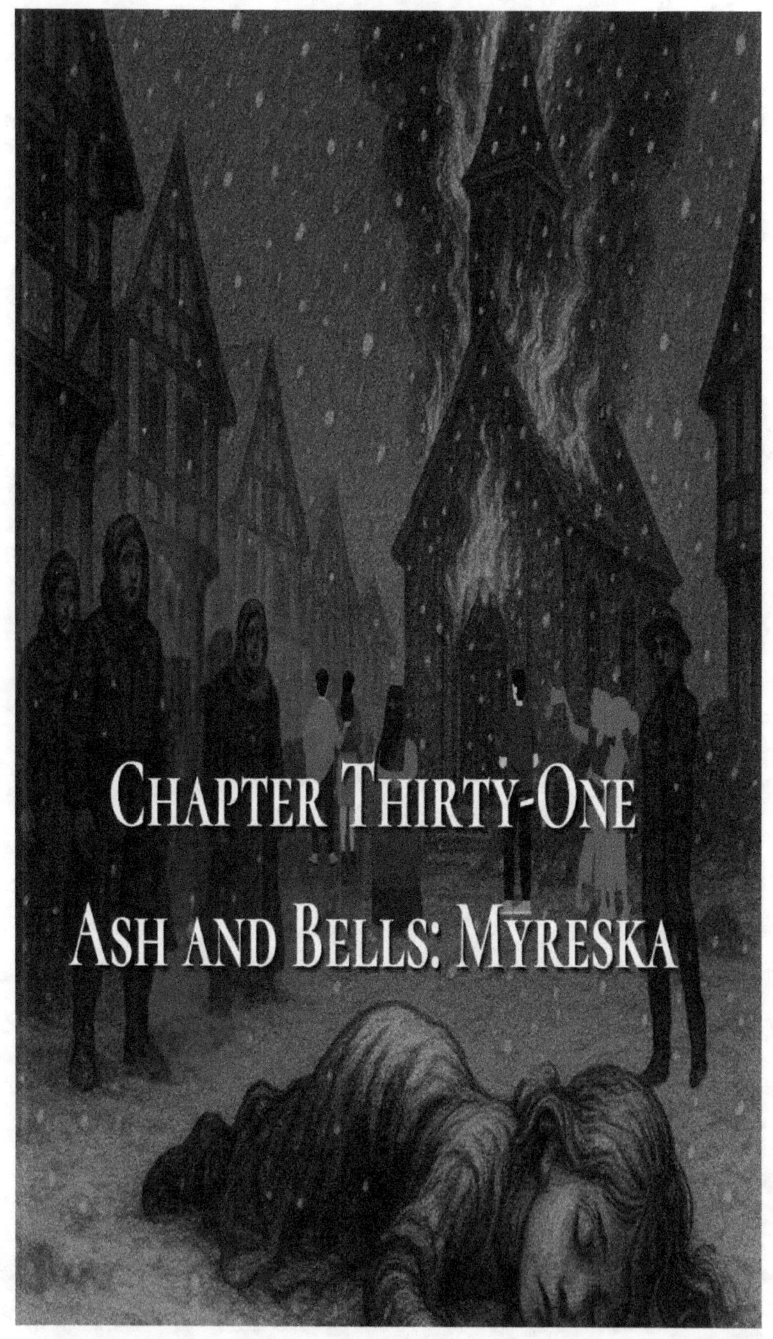
Chapter Thirty-One

Ash and Bells: Myreska

WHISPERROOT: A HUSHWOOD TALE

The bells hadn't rang in ages. Father Ignacy said it was mourning for the girls who left because they fell silent soon after the red one left. But they're causing a ruckus now, ringing erratically. Instead of the peaceful, quiet chimes we've missed, they sound like skulls cracking open. We're not sure what it means now that they're ringing again. We would say it's a blessing, a sign that we're among the righteous, except the sound is so awful we wonder if it's a curse instead. Our husbands burst through the doors of our cottages, yelling nonsense and scaring the children. When we look out our windows slick with snowmelt, the most horrific sight we can imagine greets us: clouds of black smoke rising over the center of town. Friends and neighbors leaving breakfast on hot coals. Some of us grab a shawl, but others just move.

The black smoke looks like a nightmare, billowing, getting larger. Our hearts race.

"Who is at the chapel?" someone yells as we run down the snow-laden cobblestones.

"I hope Father Ignacy is not there!"

The men yell for us to stay back, but we don't listen. Wives ought to submit to their husbands, so saith the Lord but we are decent folk who go to chapel and confessional every week. Maybe we never asked why the floor groaned beneath us as we sang, or why the door that leads to the basement is never unlocked, but no one likes a nosy neighbor. God will forgive worse things than curiosity, or so we've told ourselves. The sight of our beloved chapel engulfed in bright orange and yellow flames stops us short. We gasp, our breaths curling in the Winter cold. Neither man, woman nor child moves. It's as if we're as frozen as the icicles dangling from our roofs. The shattering of glass and the *whoosh* of fire as it consumes the wooden beams shocks us back to life.

"Somebody get water!"

The frenzied clanging of the bells and the fierce roaring of the fire competes with our shouting.

"Where's Father Ignacy? Is he in there?"

"Water!"

"Do you hear that? I hear – is that screaming? Where is it coming from?"

"It's the fire, not screaming!"

But, even as we say it, we know it's not true. We've heard these sounds before.

The door to the chapel swings up and Father Ignacy stumbles out, a wet cloth pressed to his mouth, a smoke-filled cough racking his shoulders. We rush towards him, embracing him. Our men lead him away from the fire just in time. Wooden beams swell from the heat, buckle beneath it, and even the men throwing water on the inferno stop. The flames reflect the terror in our eyes; the heartbreak mixed with relief for Father Ignacy's alive keep us rooted where we are. Trembling, Father grasps the only thing he brought out of there–a Bible–and says, "Mateusz. Tomasz."

We gasp.

But it is too late to go inside for anyone else. We cannot risk our own lives or that of our men now. We tell ourselves that life is granted and taken away by God: He will determine who to spare. Snowflakes drift into the grooves of the flames. We grip each other's hands, and hug the shoulders of our children, and feel our eyes brimming with tears.

"Get back!" someone yells as a sickening sound rips through the air.

The bells clang again as the tower snaps in two, huge pieces of debris and the bells fall. We scream, running back, farther away from the chapel stairs. Father coughs, crossing himself, shaking his head, and mumbling things that don't make any sense.

Well, that's not completely true. Maybe they make sense, but one of Myreska's great gifts is our ability to see only that which is comfortable. We're not sure who sees them first–some of us swear it was Ida, the widow healer while others say it was the baker. We're not sure but we hear Mama calling Zosia's name and watch as she turns the corner, walking behind the chapel. When Sam trails her, some of us follow. They are children—we'll protect them.

The sudden scream that pierces the air is something those of us there will never forget. It haunts us already. It's the kind of scream that starts real low in the heart and bubbles up until you can't control it. It's filled with a rawness, a realness, that we don't know what to do with here. It makes some of us pause as if we can make something not real by choosing not to see it.

But a pause is not the same as a stop: we are not a town of cowards; we run *towards* the scream, around to the side of the chapel, where the back door is, the one that's always locked. We turn the corner as more beams inside the chapel fall, the stained-glass windows shatter, and the walls cave in. Some of us grab our children's arms, yank them back. When we turn the corner, the first thing we see is snow and debris from the chapel. Shards of glass from the small window lay on the snow, reflecting the sun's light, which feels like a lie. Nothing here is bright, not with the smoke hovering over us. And then–for just a moment, time freezes–when we see it. A red ribbon flutters against the snow. The end of it is caught on something; when we realize that *something* is an ashen, unnaturally still hand, confusion wars with—well, we call it grief, but it's more like guilt.

A body–a small one–lies face down in the snow. She's not covered with a shawl. There are no shoes on her feet. Her hair, the one that was always a haven for lice (bless her heart, she cut it all off, but they came back. Father Ignacy said lice were like the demons Jesus sent into the pigs. Some of us bristled at that but she *was* a handful, and, well, dirty. But that's neither here nor there now, is it), is singed. Soot and ash and colorful bruises decorate her arms and face. Her face is white, snow coating her lashes. Blood pools beneath her, turning the white snow red.

Of course it's Zosia who finds her.

That girl makes everyone uneasy. She has yet to speak but, somehow, seems to see everything. Father praises her silence and condemns her sight. Her mother grabs her by the shoulders and pulls her back. Lenka's mother, though, rushes forward, dropping to her knees as she screams again. Her grief is such that her body cannot contain it. Her mama was told she went to live in the Krakow convent. It was, they said, an opportunity for her to find a relationship with Christ and redeem herself. We can't quite remember her name–what was it again?—but we have fleeting memories of her playing with her brother in the meadow. We've seen her before, a ribbon tied to a tree, an extra pebble laid out during the holiday, a gift placed by Jakub at the empty chair, scraps of food left out *just in case.*

She never came to get any of them.

We heard screaming.

When we stood in front of the chapel, watching it disintegrate, waiting for word of Father Ignacy, we heard something. *Is that screaming?* we asked. *No,* we reassured ourselves that it wasn't. *It's the fire.* But we've heard it before. One morning on his way home from the market, Sam took a short cut through the chapel's courtyard. He came back with tales of seeing girls asleep on straw mats through the oblong window.

We told him to shush.

On Sundays, when we sang our hymns, we heard things beneath the floorboards. We told ourselves the chapel was settling in the cold, not girls shifting to stay warm. We made up stories and laughed about how the chapel's joints must be getting arthritis like some of us. We laughed off the night when Iskra's mother said she heard her daughter's voice in the hymns. We heard. We saw. It's like a secret that's not really a secret. We're not the only ones who keep secrets. Your town has them too; you just don't want to tell us about them whereas at least we tie ribbons. Yes, we tie the ribbons and call it remembrance even if what we're really good at is forgetting.

Father Ignacy coughs again, and then straightens his shoulders. He doesn't appear worried; the fierceness of his steel grey eyes are familiar to us. Even as we stare at the blood staining snow, even as the girl's mother rocks her dead child back and forth, we're comforted by Father's certainty. We don't want to question him, but what would people think if we didn't? While it feels like time stops for an eternity, her mother's sobs break the silence after only a moment. Some of our women venture closer to her, put our hands around her shoulders, offering what comfort we can. Because we know. *This one wasn't the only one who left.* The crackling hiss of the fire makes us to turn our heads, forces us to witness destruction.

"Get away from the unclean body, woman," Father's voice holds us stronger than the fire. The girl's mother looks up, her face streaked with tears. Father puts an arm around her shoulders and pulls. "I know you miss her," he says, "But she was possessed by demons. They all were. Look! Look what they did to our chapel!" He waves a hand at the burning building behind him.

We murmur, our eyes moving from the flames to Father Ignacy to the girl on the ground.

"She's bruised...." someone says softly. Some of us look, see the blue and black marks against her skin.

"Yes, she's bruised," Father Ignacy's voice rises. "She's bruised because we had to. The demons living inside her made her angry. She tried to kill us—she did kill Tomasz! I saw the poor man on the ground encircled by flames. He was screaming and his arm was on fire. I couldn't get to him because the flames were too high."

"But why is she bleeding?"

"Because Tomasz was protecting himself. He didn't mean to kill her. I don't know, I wasn't there, I didn't see her get injured. What I do know is I heard screaming from the men. They shouted that the girls had set us on fire. Mateusz opened the door for them to come out–we always bring them out to enjoy the sunshine after breakfast–but, when they opened the door, they struck a match and threw it at us. She deserves what happened to her. God decides punishments.

WHISPERROOT: A HUSHWOOD TALE

Only He decides who lives and who dies. She wasn't worthy of life."

Her mother clutches the limp body, arms dangling, head supported by her mother's hands.

Father Ignacy holds up his hand, shows us he, too, was touched by fire. Blisters rise on the backs of his hands. "They were our daughters,. I know you care for them." He gentles his voice., but then it hardens as he shouts above the fire. "But they are not the pure among us. God told me how to discipline them to save their souls, but the Devil's grip was too great." He covers his mouth with his hand, his shoulders shake as he bows his head. "I listened, but my own compassion kept me from fully obeying God's righteous orders. We weren't strict enough in our discipline, I couldn't drive the demons out of them. They weren't like our golden ones. They were evil and they deserved death."

People shift. Some of us move to Father, put our arms around him, comforting him.

"We know you did the best you could," they murmur.

"She was always dirty."

"She always ran away from her mother, from her duties as a daughter."

The widow healer frowns, crosses herself, and shakes her head. "That's not how I remember this one." She moves closer to the girl's mother, puts a hand on the woman's shoulder in comfort. "She was a bright girl."

"But look at her. She looks like she hasn't eaten in weeks."

"And some of the bruising is old." The apothecary murmurs. "Not fresh."

Father Ignacy bristles. Agony dances across his face. "Surely, you don't question me?" he grips the edge of the

Bible he still holds. "I am only His servant. I am His vessel. He said not to spare the rod from the ones you love." His voice breaks. "Of course I love them. It's why I tried so hard to get them to see their sins for what they were and to repent. Some of them came close. A few found me in prayer one day and told me they were obedient but unclean. I thought they had repented. But it was nothing but a devil's trick." He shook his head. "I am only one person. If any of you had heard anything amiss, if any of you ever saw something that felt off, wouldn't you have come to me with it as commanded in Scripture? Wouldn't you have trusted me enough to ask your questions? No one ever came to me."

No.

We didn't.

We heard the noises beneath the floorboards. We thought it was wind. We told ourselves it was nothing. We told ourselves silence was safer. We teach our daughters to be quiet because silence keeps them clean. If no one sees the ugly parts, then they have no reason to hurt us. So, we heard the noises shifting beneath the floorboards and laughed about games children play. The ribbons, like the one clinging to the girl's lifeless fingers, allowed us to pretend. Pretend we did something when we did not. Pretend to grieve when we really gave thanks our daughters *would never*. Our men tolerated crude jokes because it meant they could say *we're not hiding anything; we were just talking about them*.

So, Father Ignacy isn't wrong.

We *didn't* go to him. We went silent.

Don't read it like *that*. You pretend silence is a crime, but there's nothing wrong with controlling your tongue. Sometimes it *is* safer: we knew what would happen if we didn't. The girls who went missing–they knew better. They knew silence is safer, too, but they chose to ignore the warnings Father Ignacy–and their parents–issued. Disobedience is a sin. The Bible says so.

Some of us clutch at Father's words. *Of course*, we tell ourselves, *of course we would have said something.* Even if Sam did see girls sleeping on straw through the window, so what? That wasn't evidence of anything except Father doing what we agreed upon. We cast votes saying something should happen, and we trust Father's judgment. He is our shepherd. He knows what's best for us.

"Forgive us, Father, for doubting." The shoemaker, the schoolteacher, the butcher and others tighten around him. He accepts their repentance (for now), nodding and placing his injured hands on their hands. Some of us, though, shift our glances between the mother, the dead girl, and Father Ignacy. The truth scares some of us. What if it was us? We thought they deserved punishment... but what about us? These gazes linger a moment longer on the body of the little girl but then flick and rest on Father Ignacy. If we trust him, if we cling to his words, then we're still safe. Nothing has to change for our lives, for our families. We don't give our approval verbally, we don't ask for forgiveness (because the very nature of asking for forgiveness means admitting blame), but we don't condemn, either. Judging isn't our place.

Then there's the few of us who huddle together closer to the body of the girl than to Father. There aren't many of us in this group. Our silence is heaviest of all, thick with questions we know will go unanswered. We knew she was dirty. We knew she disobeyed her elders, running off all the time. We cast our vote same as the others because we knew she needed to be punished. But this?

"Look at her face," Father Ignacy's voice cracks a bit. "Look at her smiling. She faces the chapel. She saw it burning and what does she do? She smiles. Even in death the poor thing was consumed by evil."

It's true.

A small smile does curve her lips.

It's these words that make her mother pull back, examine her daughter's face for herself. She frowns, her eyes switching to the chapel still burning bright.

"You remember, don't you? How she lied about everything. I did let Mateusz, Tomasz, Jakub—I did let them punish her. But I gave her shelter and food and truth. She rebuked it." His shoulders shake as tears gather in his eyes. "I tried, I tried to lead her to Christ, but she practiced witchcraft in the house of the Lord. There was nothing I could do."

"Witchcraft?" Her mother whispers, putting a hand over her throat.

"Oh, they all did. It was led by the red one and the girl who picked herbs, I don't know her name anymore. But they stole herbs, used their own spit to mix up a concoction, and used it to paste over the wounds. We heard them chanting."

"Chanting." Shocked murmurs pass among us.

"She was possessed. It is right that fire consumes them, that she bled out. It is the only way for our children to be protected against witches' curses."

Mothers pull their children closer to their bosoms.

"Can witches' blood cast spells?"

"But.... they're so young..."

"So was Mary, the mother of our Lord."

"Seven went crazy, delirious–"

"Who's seven?"

WHISPERROOT: A HUSHWOOD TALE

Father nods towards the girl. "We didn't know names and demons told their minds, so we gave them numbers. We stitched them into their shifts so that they would know who they were, poor souls."

Our eyes see the white *seven* stitched into her shift. Its blackened now, some of its threads are scorched, but the number is unmistakable.

"I—I saw her number in a vision from God." Ignacy swallows. "The Lord uses numbers to reveal things. Seven means something is completed. Something is whole. I didn't understand at first, but now.... now I do. She was never meant to live."

Slowly, her mother lays her onto the snow. She watches her daughter for several moments. Time suspends for us all as we wait, wondering which of our groups she'll go to. Instead, she swallows, murmurs, "Thank you, Father, for your care of her soul," and rises. She walks stiffly, as though she's seen a ghost, past us. She doesn't acknowledge our outstretched hands or murmurs of comfort. She just walks. Orange flames dance across her back.

And, somehow, we know.

We'll find another noose, this one in her cottage, tomorrow. Or maybe it won't be a noose. Maybe we'll see her crumpled on her mattress, her blood spilling as her daughter's had. We wonder what she'll use. We hope we won't need to clean much blood.

... twelve voices, then eleven, then ten...
still, the chorus broke into embers

—————

charred fragment

CHAPTER THIRTY-TWO

THE SCRAPS

Zosia drifts from the townspeople who still gather around the ruins of the chapel. Someone asks about Jakub; Father Ignacy says *I didn't see him in the chaos.* Someone else says he was seen walking to his shop. Father crosses himself, says, "What we saw is a lot for anyone." Mama stands close to Father Ignacy, patting his sleeve. Her eyes were dry, but Zosia noticed how her hands trembled. When the girl's mother walked away from everyone, Mama's eyes followed her, her quivering fingers placed over her heart.

"We should check on her tomorrow," the schoolteacher says.

Mama nods slowly.

Zosia stood staring at the ribbon. It wasn't like the others. Bright red, almost the same strawberry color that stained the snow, it was singed at one end. Ashes darkened parts of it. She watched its end sway in the breeze, wondering where it came from. The longer she stared at it, the stronger she could feel the hushwood.

"They called her Seven because it means complete."

The gust howled, then thinned into a frayed thread of sound. *Lenka.* The name slid into her ears like something half-remembered. Long buried whispers stir deep within her like faded memories, *almost* memories. Does she remember the name? She isn't sure, but she knows the dead girl's name is Lenka.

She was the only one anyone talked about.

But it's not the name Zosia longs to hear.

Even across the cobblestones and around the corner, smoke mixes with snow, layering the air with a gritty, unclean feel. Her muscles don't feel the chill of the wind, her belly doesn't rumble with twinges of hunger yet, her head doesn't hurt from the clanging of the bells that crashed into the snow. But there is something gnawing on the edges of numbness, something that crackles and suffocating her breath. When she sees the hushbark, her eyes look to the ground. She's left the green satin ribbon tied to the whisperroot. She doesn't know why, except that, every time she sees it, there's a half-second where hope blooms and she thinks, *Ainela's back!* Then she remembers: the green ribbon is always there.

She misses her sister.

Sometimes she thinks if she could just scream for her, if she could scream her name louder than the sermons, then, wherever she is, Ainela might hear her and come home. But the fire was so big and the flames so hot they warmed her cheeks. If Lenka ran from there, was Ainela there, too? The hollow space of the tree holds nothing new, but checking makes her feel as if her sister is closer to her. Or maybe it's just being inside the hushwood that makes her seem closer.

Papa's voice carries across the path, fragile against the hushwood's breath. Silently, she slips from the shadows of the hushwood back to the curved path home.

No one sleeps.

Zosia hears Mama late into the night, pacing back and forth in the front room, whispering things to herself. She talks to Papa, telling him she knows silence is safer, she does, but she's lost so much because of it. She breaks down in tears long after the moon is up, her sobs echoing through the cottage. Papa is gentle; Zosia can't hear his words.

She stares at the dark ceiling, remembering.

Once, when Zosia was young, Ainela took her sledding down the big snow hill across the bridge. She sat behind Zosia, her arms wrapped around her waist, her knees pulled up on either side of her. *Do you think you're ready for this?* Ainela's voice always sounded like musical chimes, light and airy, as if every moment was a reason to giggle. Zosia's mittened fingers tightened. They squealed together as they flew down the hillside, drifts of snow flying around them. Zosia clutches the locket now, returning to a home that doesn't feel like a home without Ainela. *Pinkie promise.* They locked pinkies, promising to always *see each other*.

Mama leaves when the morning is young, golden rays barely breaking through the smoke-hued sky. Zosia hurries. Now is her chance. She takes her sketchbook this time and slips out the back door of the empty cottage. The village seems eerily quiet. There are no carts whose wheels creak over cobblestone as villagers make deliveries. When she passes the baker's, the doors are still locked shut, no smell of rye bread trailing. No hammer strikes from the forge at the blacksmith's shop–the first morning in ages the constant clinking falls silent. Even the chime-thrush is quiet. The only sound is the ashfeather owl: Zosia's heard him six times already this morning.

If you hear the ashfeather owl's cry three times in a row, someone is being remembered. Does six times mean two people are being remembered? Zosia's stomach hurts at the thought, a cramp that gets tighter with each eerie cry.

Shivers chase her spine. She thinks *it's just the wind* even though the wind doesn't blow. She feels the weight of the hushbark and alder trees of the hushwood as they lean in. *We remember more than two.*

She thinks of Ainela as she climbs the hill but, as she crests it, the girlish giggles of her memory trail. The chapel looms ahead, a blackened husk against the pale morning. Smoke still curls from its now roofless flame, like ghosts rising. Snow has drifted inside through shattered windows. Zosia swallows, her heart beating faster, as her gaze shifts.

She sees no one.

It is unguarded.

She pulls one side of her lip through her teeth. *Is it dangerous?* Something might still fall. And yet... if Ainela was there... she clutches the sketchbook tighter against her chest, gathers a deep breath, and bravely steps forward. *See?* She hears Ainela's voice, reeking of pride, when Zosia learned to tie her boots by herself. *You can do hard things, don't let anyone tell you that you can't.* Ainela's chin tilted up a notch. *If they doubt you, just tell them who your sister is, and they'll know.*

A black bird swoops past her unexpectedly just as she steps through what was once the door of the chapel. She gasps, stepping back, nearly tripping over the small steps. She steadies herself again, her eyes flicking around her. Her heart aches. She feels her lungs constrict . The whitewashed walls she'd grown up within are now blistered and scorched, streaked with soot so dark it seems the stone itself has bled. Shards of colored glass lie scattered in the snow, catching the thin light in dull glimmers – fragments of saints and angels now faceless on the ground.

WHISPERROOT: A HUSHWOOD TALE

Her family always sat in that pew—third row, right side–and it makes Zosia feel funny seeing it charred now. A heavy wooden beam has fallen, cracking the alar where Father Ignacy always stands. She turns and the sound of crinkling pages beneath her boots make her look down. Her cheeks stain with shame: she's stepping on the burnt pages of a hymnal. Pages fall apart as she picks it up, but she sees lines of *Amazing Grace*, the song her mother loves the most. *Grace is in our soil.*

The pages smell like the air: musky, like burnt wood and iron. Even the snow seems touched by fire here, gray and crusted, crunching different. As she steps further into the sanctuary, looking for something, she doesn't know what, she senses a presence with her. Her eyes catch sight of something small, something that shouldn't be here: a root, pushing up through the snow, in the middle of their pew. Where Ainela used to sit.

Yes, that's right. We grow where truths are buried.

She bends, her teeth pulling the mitten off her hand. Tenderly, she touches the stems and hisses, her fingers jerking back from the warmth. She feels the ground beneath her boots shift, as if sighing. She hears something muffled beneath the snow. It sounds almost like a girl crying.

No. Not crying. Our roots just ache for the girls who were here and whose stories we carry now.

She lifts her head.

Who said that?

A gentle wind passes through the ruined chapel and the air itself seems to whisper around her.

The haunting cry of the ashfeather owl sounds again.

Seven.

Zosia stands, turns, not sure where to go next. She glances at the small root pushing up through the floorboards. Stepping back so she can see more of the whole sanctuary, she opens her sketchbook, pulls the small charcoal stick from her pocket, and begins sketching. Even on paper, the root looks out of place. It grows through a charred plank in the floor, the only sign of life left here. Lines appear on the page, uneven, a few circular ones, as the pew forms. She uses her thumb to gently rub shadows into the pew, darkened spots to mirror the charred edges.

As she closes the book, she lifts her head, looks around. Near the altar, where a heavy beam has cracked the stone, Zosia notices something dark gaping behind the rubble. At first it looks like another shadow, but when she edges closer she sees the outline of a doorway, its frame warped by heat. The iron latch has melted to a twisted curl. She pushes at the door, and it groans, opening on ruined hinges. A breath of air rises from the darkness, damp and heavy, laced with sour tang of ash and stone.

On the inside of the door scratches are carved, as if nails had raked over the wood, desperate to break through. The cry of the ashfeather owl clenches her stomach. *Eight.* The first step is still intact, though blackened. Beyond it, though, the staircase drops into gloom, the edges crumbled, wood and stone both scarred by fire. Charred timbers jut across the stairwell like ribs, and patches of snow have sifted down through cracks overhead, melting in slow rivulets along the wall.

Roots have already begun to claim it.

Thin tendrils curl between the steps, pushing through scorched mortar, pale against blackened stone. When she leans closer, Zosia thinks she hears the faintest echo drifting from below–something between a sigh and a sob. The air is warmer down there, as if the fire still lingers. Her hand tightens around her sketchbook. She hesitates, heart hammering.

You can do hard things. Just tell them who your sister is, and they'll know. I see you. Ainela's voice breaks Zosia. She holds her breath as she cautiously steps onto the first plank. It cries, but holds. The roots seem to stretch upwards, stronger than the fragile one in the sanctuary. When she reaches out to grasp one, it hardens like stone. Another root rises from the darkness, bending just below her foot. She steps on it and it sinks, slowly lowering her, darkness gathering around her the deeper she goes. Each time she moves her foot, a new vine stretches to meet her, helping her move even where wood has fallen away.

From somewhere above her, the ashfeather cries twice, quick, back-to-back.

*Nine (*is that three people?)

Zosia's eyes adjust to the darkness. She sees more doors, most of which are gone except for the iron bits that rest against the ground. Whisperroots glow a faint red, twisting amongst each other. The faint whispers grow stronger and a foul smell, one of blood and urine and decay rise to meet her. She coughs, smoke clogging her vision. She steps off the vine and feels swallowed by darkness. Dust, scattered by her feet and pale light that bleeds through cracked floorboards and shattered windows, float in the air.

Ainela.

She isn't here, but Zosia feels her.

She takes one cautious step after another. Boards above her groan and shift. Every time they do, she looks up, murmuring a prayer. If a beam falls through the floor, it might pin her. She might die. A pile of ash falls through a crack, covering her head and shoulders. She coughs, waving a hand, walking further into a room she never knew was here. A busted window looks out towards the chapel courtyard.

Beads from a broken rosary, black ones and red ones, lay scattered amid the ashes. The silver cross lies buried under scorched mat of straw. She gathers two of the beads and the cross, which is warm to the touch, and pockets them. Whisperroots pulse faintly red near the window, twisting together as if knotting a secret. Tangled in their vines are scorched fragments of paper, edges curling inward. She reaches for one, her breath caught.

We hold what her flame freed.

The fragment feels fragile. Just as she hears the ashfeather owl again – *ten* – she gasps, her hand covering her mouth. The writing on the fragment is Ainela's. She's sure of it. She can't read it right now–it's too dark here, and part of it has been burned away while the rest is smudged, but she recognizes the S whose end curls beneath itself. She can't fold the scrap, it's too fragile, so she opens her sketchbook, carefully tucks the fragment between pages, and then flips to an empty space. Standing in the middle of the ruins, she sketches what she sees.

Chalk lines, like tally marks, on a plank that now lies broken in half on the floor. Scorched mats scattered around the room. A frayed piece of ribbon. Tin cups, overturned. And–what is that? The whispering gets louder, like a chorus, but indistinct, she can't make out words. In the soot by the wall lies something pale and small. She crouches, brushing away ash. A bone, delicate as a pin. She knows it at once – the shape of a mouse.

WHISPERROOT: A HUSHWOOD TALE

You made a harness for a caterpillar. I'll never forget that, Caterbutton. You always see the smallest things. A sob shakes Zosia's shoulders. She fingers the mouse bone, wondering, *did they feed you? Or were you the only food they had?*

A gentle stirring of a breeze outside makes the whisperroot near the window pulse. She reaches out, lays her hand over the root. It's warm, but it doesn't sear her skin. She feels it pulsing like a heartbeat against her palm.

Either way, not even Chico could survive this room.

Chico. Her fingers tremble as she slides one back and forth over the bone.

They named you.

The sound of voices outside makes her head lift quickly, and her breathing falters.

She glances towards the stairs–but there are no stairs, and the vines are low to the ground, not stepping stools. If they find her here, will she be next?

Together, the ashfeather cries again—*eleven*—and a breeze rushes across her face. She turns her head towards the breeze and sees the window. The breeze stirs again, stronger, carrying ash across her face. She glances at the window, too high, unreachable.

They tried to reach this window, but they couldn't.

She presses her palm to the stone sill. This was the place of their last hope. The emptiness in her heart swells until it's nearly unbearable. Her breath quickens—until she sees the wall below it. Charred beams jut at angles, the stone cracked and piled where fire gnawed it away. She presses her foot onto one beam, then another, but still she cannot reach. Her hand slips, splinters biting her skin. Panic seizes as she feels her grip slipping.

We'll hold you. We're here.

The whisperroot pulses, stretching upward. A tendril coils along the wall, stiffening into something she can grasp. She hesitates, then takes hold. It hardens beneath her hand, steady as wood. Step by step, root and rubble together raise her higher, until she hauls herself, their presence rattling in her bones, over the sill just as the owl cries again.

Twelve.

Her number was twelve.

We are a witness.

We are alive, and we are witnesses.

The night they were taken, we watched. We noticed which ones sobbed, which ones were angry, which ones were silent. When Hunger consumed their thoughts, stole their attention, our roots gathered. Our soil tightened. Ainela snuck out after dark, she said, to visit us because she loved our emberflies. There was so much little girl in her, so much joy, but we witnessed the night she stopped dreaming of emberflies.

When his hands held her down, when his knee bruised the inside of her thigh, when he took what was never his to take, we witnessed the shift. Whisperroots grow where truth is buried and so, beneath that room, whisperroots bloom. They heave, stretch, and invade every inch of his space. Our soil presses tighter together, holding the memory of how hard she clamped her legs shut. In some places, the vines braid together, tight as her muscles, while, in others, they barely touch, keeping the memory of how he ripped her knees apart. Our fauna carry the heartbreak of a girl who sobbed brokenly for her mother, and of another whose sister's name shattered our peace. Our leaves, though buried still beneath the snow and ice, carry their songs, prayers and stories in their veins. Their screams we remember in the way we howl and whistle through the streets.

We are a witness.

Our very terrain bares evidence of secrets. Mounds that weren't there before now force recognition that something was silenced. We felt the sharp pain of an edged shovel disturbing our roots, throwing our soil into careless piles until a hole was deep enough to carry broken girls. Our roots braid with their limbs, so as to whisper, *you're not alone.* We are a witness to the way dirt piled on their faces, covering their eyes, blocking their noses, filling their mouths that were not allowed to scream. We are a witness to the final expressions on their faces–some joyful, others scared– and we know every bruise, burn, scratch and cut on their bodies.

We are witnesses and we do not forget.

Zosia trips over a few small twigs in her hurry to hide. Her boots leave small tracks in the snow, but no one notices her. Ever since Ainela left, her silence has grown deeper. Some praise her for obedience; others secretly whisper about unnatural behavior. *We feel her wrap an arm around our hushbark, our skin tingles with a promise. We will protect her.*

Out of breath, and hidden behind the hushwood trees, Zosia opens the sketchbook. She pulls each item out, one a time, and examines it. The mouse bone. The broken rosary beads. And, finally, the fragment. She opens the sketchbook to the first empty page she sees, begins to draw.

Time freezes.

We lean in, our branches drooping towards her. We're waiting, hoping, almost begging her to ease some of the burden we carry, to remember.

She looks around, as if trying to find a place to rest.

We exhale softly, just enough to blow drifts of snow off a thick log.

The snow swirling in the air catches her eye, and she sees a log cleared of snow. Her boots tread lightly as she walks over and sits, her mind a whirlpool of images, thoughts and emotions. Her shift is covered in ash now, and Mama will certainly ask why. She rolls the rosary beads between her fingers, uses a bit of snow to wash away the soot. Carefully, she places it into a small groove in the log she sits on and then examines the silver cross.

She moves the rosary bead to sit on top of the crucifix and stares at it for a moment.

We remember Larisa. Her faith was a lifeline. The rosary was a lifeline. They never took that from her, though they tried.

Zosia tips her head, her fingers using light strokes against the paper to draw the outline of the crucifix. Beneath it, a striped log. *She is here, buried beneath our trees. Her Savior died from a tree. No one ever asked what she prayed for, but we heard her prayers. She prayed for the others to be free. She didn't pray for herself.*

Remember, Zosia.

The corner of Zosia's tongue touches her lips as she makes a quick half circle, a bead, and then uses her thumbnail to shade it. On paper, she adds stripes to the log, carving away charcoal with her nail. She doesn't know why, but stripes against the cross makes sense. Somehow, she knows: this isn't Mama's hymn, this isn't *Amazing Grace*. It's Larisa's prayer.

Because stripes were made to her flesh, too. The whip touched them all. We saw it, ribbons of blood trailing down her tender side. We witnessed the bloodbath the whippings caused. Some were worse than others, but none of them, not one, made it out unscathed. We saw the anger, indeed the hatred, on the faces of Mateusz as his whip ripped their skin. We heard the screams: they pressed through the walls, into the soil, until we howled with them.

The ashfeather owl cries again, it's mournful song matching the grief swelling Zosia's heart. *Thirteen*. When it goes again, her lips move. *Fourteen*. The owl has cried all day.

Zosia tenderly turns the pages in her sketchbook until she sees it: the yellowed, frail, small scrap, barely wide enough to hold words at all. The edges are burned, and the charcoal smudged, but still, she makes out a few words:

... they won't .. our... last song. Don't do–

The last word is lost to the fire. She frowns. *They won't ....* have? play? hear? *last song*. What about the last thought – *don't do–?*

They won't have our last song. Don't doubt this: we sing last.

The words whisper around her, like the sound of grass rustling.

You hear us, don't you, Zosia? Draw. Draw her. Draw the red one.

Pressure builds within her chest. She turns to a new page, and her fingers sketch an incomplete oval face. Her eyes are wide, and light. Zosia remembers that: her eyes were the same shade as bluebells. Strands of thin hair fall across one cheek and as the lines and curves take shape, Zosia hears something in the distance. *Caterbutton. Caterbutton. I see you. Pinkie promise.*

Tears slip down her cheek, over her chin and drop onto the page.

The tiny mouse bone burns a hole in her pocket. The shattered glass of the cellar flashes behind her eyes, and the rancid smell of smoke and rot waves beneath her nose. She shakes her head, her charcoal slipping from her fingers as a sob breaks free. She doesn't want to remember, she can't.

You must.

It was her greatest wish. That someone remembers. We saw her. We watched her. We listened. We held her. But she needs you to speak for her. Remember your sister, Zosia. Our roots curl around her bones.

The scent of smoke edges wraps around her, and the ground beneath her boots seems to pulse in a rhythm she doesn't understand: *one. one. two, two.* She frowns, listens for the owl again. Is that the rhythm it's been calling all day?

Draw it.

She blows a rush of air out, picks up the charcoal and returns to the drawing. *One. One. Two, two.* She doesn't know. She listens, the trees swelling around her, sealing her in from the outside world. As she glances up, the branches of the hushbark seem to bend, a path opening before her. *Open. Free.*

Yes.

Zosia's fingers sketch faster now, more frantically, as she struggles to make sense of the images in her head. She doesn't know what she's drawing, only that lines curve, and then shoot straight down from the top of the page to the bottom. She slides the book around, makes more straight lines, these from one side to the other. Briefly, she pauses to look: *bars. Caged.*

But remember: one. one. two, two.

It makes no sense, she doesn't understand, but she can't draw a cage over her sister's face. So, instead of drawing unbroken lines across the page, she leaves two fingers' worth of space between each line. When she draws Ainela's fingers, they curl around the bars, as if she's breaking the cage open.

At the bottom of the page, she draws the fragment, blending the charcoal so it looks like wisps of gray smoke, jagged edges as its rip down the center. The charcoal slips from her hand by accident. It lands on the log beside her but, as she picks it up, she sees something. Brushing away a few snowflakes, she uses just two fingers to carefully pick it up.

An emberfly's wing.

The wing is cracked, but still warm—fragile and alive, both at once.

Like they were cracked.

Do you know where they came from? Ainela's voice whispers in her ear. Suddenly, she feels the warmth of the hearth in their room. They'd captured two emberflies and placed them in a jar, just for a little while. Ainela's face glowed as she watched them. *Once, long ago,* It was the same story she always told Zosia, every time they saw the emberflies, but Zosia loved it so much she didn't care that she'd already heard it. *Myreska's winters chilled the little ones—so much so that they almost wasted away from the cold. The fires in the hearths couldn't warm them. One evening, a little girl, with hair just the shade of yours, carried a live coal from her hearth into the hushwood. She wanted to beg the trees for warmth. But she stumbled, and the coal fell from her mitten. But it didn't die. Instead, it rose, sprouting wings of light. The emberfly was born.*

That night, hundreds of tiny sparks lifted from the ground, fluttering like fire. They followed the girl home and filled her family's hearth with a glow that never quite went out. That's why they say that emberflies carry bits of hearthfire on their wings.

Her heart hurts and her mouth forms the shape of Ainela's name, but she can't say it. She stares at the emberfly wing and lays it on the edge of a new sheet of paper, her last one. When the ashfeather owl cries again, she counts: *Fifteen.* Does fifteen cries from an ashfeather owl mean five girls are remembered?

Her eyes lift to see whisperroots scattered around the hushwood floor. There's one – by the hushbark tree—and another by the mound, closer to the creek, and a third beyond the third birch. She can barely see it, twisting around the trunk of the birch. Something tickles her ankle and, when she looks down, she sees a fourth whisperroot, growing around the log she sits on.

Whisperroots hold the truth. We hold the truth.

Zosia's hand aches as she keeps drawing. When she stops, she brushes the charcoal bits away and stares: a half circle of emberflies hover over a whisperroot whose tangled vines carry small, torn ribbons. Tears stain the edges of the paper. She drags in a shaky breath. The hushwood bends around her, almost tenderly, watching. She closes the sketchbook and hugs it to her chest.

WHISPERROOT: A HUSHWOOD TALE

As she slips from the forest's shadows, the wind stirs again, and in its breath she hears it, faint as an emberfly's wings: *she loved you.*

She speaks nonsense, so none of it must be true

———————

Father Ignacy

Chapter Thirty-three

The Living proof

WHISPERROOT: A HUSHWOOD TALE

osia hugs the bag of warm rye bread and jam close to her chest. Mama baked it for the men cleaning the ruins. It's been a couple of days now without fresh snow. Icicles are beginning to drop from the edges of roofs and tree branches. Her boots don't sink quite so far down into the drift anymore, and fingers without mittens don't turn blue as quickly.

The normal sounds of the town are back: birds chirp in the crisp air, horses' hooves clomp through the snow, tiny bells jingle as the door to a shop door opens, a dog barks nearby. There's new sights and sounds, too: men clearing away heavy logs from the ruins, the clanking of the cracked chapel bell as ropes pull them away from the ground, and, perhaps loudest of all, the silence when that falls as Zosia passes by women who drop both their pointed whispers and judging eyes.

It's not just the women—everyone does it.

As she passes the seamstress's cottage, the curtains are pulled abruptly. The edges of them are pulled back slightly, just enough for her to see the seamstress's face peer out. Zosia drops her head and continues walking, trying not to let the looks bother her. They started after the chapel burned. Father Ignacy says Ainela started the fire. He said she laughed like she was possessed. He tried to save her, tried to get to the door in time, but it was closed, and he couldn't see or breathe for the smoke. He thought she might have gotten out because Jakub, even at great risk to himself, was still there, helping them.

A mother pulls her daughter to the other side of the lane instead of walking beside her. Her own eyes drop to the ground still covered in snow. *Take these to the men*, her mother's voice this morning was sure. *They're working hard, and we want to show how thankful we are.* Mama used the last of the flour to make the rye bread. The first day after the fire, Mama cried and did very little else. But then she began edging closer to Father Ignacy and offering to help the rebuilding efforts.

She did not ask about Ainela.

She did not mention her at all.

When she saw Zosia curled up in a fetal position, the locket in her hand, and tears rolling down her cheeks, Mama sighed. She said simply, *"I know you're hurting. I know you miss her."* Mama's eyes shifted to the window. Placing a hand over her neck, she took a few steps closer, staring out at the hushwood. *"I do, too,"* she confessed softly. *"But,"* her voice grew stronger as she turned to face her again. *"We can't change what happened. We just have to make sure everyone knows that you're not your sister. You're different. Helpful. Mindful."* She hesitated, then lifted a shoulder in a tiny wave. *"Especially to the chapel and Father Ignacy. We need him to see that you are part of the golden ones."*

Taking bread and jam to the men who are clearing out the chapel debris is the least they can do. She sees the schoolmaster and waves at her, but the schoolmaster shifts her gaze, looking in the opposite direction, almost as though she never saw Zosia. She hears whispers behind her. "She's *her* sister."

"I think she's dumb;."

"Father Ignacy said the red one was possessed."

"Do you think *she* is?"

"They say *she* started the fire —"

"On purpose!"

Zosia veers to the right, crossing the road. She grips the bag tighter, hunches her shoulders, and pretends she can't hear them. Ainela wouldn't have set the fire on purpose. Was it just her and the snow girl? That's what Father Ignacy says: that those two couldn't be relocated to the convent because of their behaviors. Visions of the dark, shadowy cellar cross her mind: *how many mats were there?* She doesn't remember, not exactly, but more than two.

Ash mixes with snow, making the ground near the chapel a gray slush tamped down with large footprints. Father Ignacy stands in the middle of the ruins, his hands trembling as he gathers up charred relics—a tin cup that held wine for communion, a cross, burned hymnal pages. As she watches him, a drift of wind that feels almost like a breath passes by. Some distance away, closer to Zosia, the apothecary and the stablemaster, wrap ropes around heavy beams to drag it from the site. Frederick, the stablemaster, says quietly, his voice only rising just enough to reach Zosia, "But I wonder what happened to Mateusz and Tomasz, you know?"

"Father says Tomasz was on fire."

"I think Mateusz fled."

The crunching of wood and snow fill the air. As the men heave the beam, moving it only inches, the apothecary says, "But why, you know? What happened that made him need to run?"

"I don't think any of us want to know that."

"Hold on– the girl—"

Zosia reaches them and holds out the bag silently. The men lower the beams to the ground. They take the treats and nod at her, satisfied. Zosia doesn't hear the whisper the stablemaster makes as she walks away, but feels the sting of scrutiny as she walks further into the site. *You find Father Ignacy and start with him*, Mama said. *You'll be offering nourishment for hardworking men volunteering to rebuild the chapel. He won't refuse you, and, when he doesn't, the others won't.*

Father Ignacy sees her approaching and stands tall. "Good morning, Zosia. You needn't be here. The ruins are not safe."

Zosia nods, holds out the bag.

"What do you have there?" Father takes the bag. The earthy aroma of rye bread warms the chilly air. He smiles, breathing in deep. "Well, now," he reaches in and takes a piece of the bread. "This is nice of you–and your mother. Thank you, Zosia."

She doesn't move when he reaches out and pats her shoulder, his hand heavier than silence. She notices other men glancing at her, then looking away. Jakub, stands just outside the ruins, his eyes narrowed as he watches. Zosia doesn't know why, but the prickly feeling that raises goose bellies on her arm doesn't come when she sees Jakub. Curiously, she steps carefully over beams with exposed nails, pieces of shattered glass and other debris. He says nothing; only watches her. When she holds the bag out, he hesitates. Slowly, he takes it, his large hands calloused and dirty.

Someone tells her to get out of the way, that it's not safe for her to be here.

WHISPERROOT: A HUSHWOOD TALE

Zosia blinks, looking away from Jakub, and moves until she's not standing on the chapel ruins. On her right, the hushwood forest watches, like a sentinel, guarding its secrets while hoping someone insists on uncovering them. Not ready to go home, Zosia walks towards the bench that still sits near the town center. When she sits with her bottom all the way to the back of the bench, her feet don't touch the ground. She swings them, watching as her black boots come in, and out, of view.

A grey mist settles over Myreska, draping the edge of the forest in shadows the color of ash.

"Do you think it was just the two of them in there?"

Zosia lifts her head to see two of the village women walking. They carry sacks of flour and sugar, on their way home from the market. Memories burst forth of the Winter festival: the one that speaks has a daughter just a year or two older than her, one who always carried a corn doll with one eye. The other woman, a village homemaker, shakes her head and whispers something Zosia can't hear. The first woman nods, her arms clutching the bag. Her eyes scan the area and, when she sees Zosia, she frowns, *shushes* her friend. A heartbeat's pause as they walk another step before one says, loud enough for her to hear, "I know they say the red one started the fire. I know she died, too, but *what if* there *were* others down there? She might have *been the reason they died.*"

Ice runs down Zosia's back.

Ainela wouldn't have set the fire. Not on purpose. Not unless....

"I'm not sure any of them were sent to Krakow."

"You mean all—"

'Twelve, yes," the woman's voice drops to a fierce whisper as they pass the bench. "Don't you think?"

"I don't know. Father Ignacy wouldn't—"

"I hate to say it but–well, wouldn't he? To protect their souls?"

Zosia frowns. The chill begins to seep into the wool of her coat, and her cheeks turn numb, her heart heavy as the hushwood branches laden down with snow. She watches the town *Wouldn't he* do what? Memories swirl, pages of her notebook flipping fast. Page after page–there was the one with the freckles, and the one with the dimple. How many faces has she drawn that she doesn't recognize? Who are they?

A rabbit scampers by in front of her, the white of his fur hiding him amongst the blanket of snow. Suddenly, she hears something behind her. The hushwood is steps behind. Standing, she turns to look. Nothing seems out of place except... tipping her head, she walks slowly towards the woods.

Faint footprints appear to veer into the woods, then out of it, always hovering at the edge of the hushwood. A branch falls; the sound of wings fluttering follows. But the hushwood is dark. No shadows move. The sense of unease grows.

Amelia says she saw one of them. She hears Mama's whispers in her ear. Last night, sitting in front of the hearth, she spoke quietly. Papa smoked a cigar, the sweet smell curling through the air. *She says she's crazy.*

Well, Papa asked, *which one?*

She wasn't sure, the girl was too far away.

Zosia stares at the footprints. She glances behind her, but the villagers have passed by; no one watches.

WHISPERROOT: A HUSHWOOD TALE

Tentatively, she steps forward, following the path, feeling a chill race along her spine.

    The hushwood leans closer. Zosia feels its weight press on her as she steps beyond the birch trees and into its heart. Faint footprints appear jagged–sometimes in a line, other times cutting to one side or the other. Sometimes they disappear altogether. They aren't animal prints–they have five toes–and they appear to be barefoot. Could someone stay in the snow barefoot for long?

    She feels the forest watching her. As she takes each step, wind shifts, as a gentle hand against her neck, guiding her. Something shifts; her head turns quickly. What was that? She thought she saw a tail move, but deeper, further away from the edge of the forest. Deeper than she's been before.

    Zosia swallows.

    What if the there *was* a girl who survived? And what if that girl *was* Ainela? Even if it's not her sister, what if, whoever it might be, knew Ainela? Pulling the edge of her lip between her teeth, Zosia hesitates. She looks over her shoulder where she can still barely see the village. She doesn't have her sketchbook with her, but she kneels, places her hand in the footprint. Curiously, she stands and holds her foot over it, trying to see how much bigger than hers it is.

    Not much.

    Her print is only slightly smaller.

    Could be Ainela's.

    She pulls her coat tighter around her and keeps walking.

There it is again – something shifts behind the grove of trees just ahead. Her heart leaps into her throat. Branches sway. Beneath the gentle stirring of wind, beneath the muffled crunching of snow, Zosia hears the same sound she's heard here before: *a hum.* Low, indistinct, just a quiet humming sound. When she steps forward, she sees a pair of golden eyes staring at her from behind the trees. Her breath catches as she stares at the redveil fox.

Her breath hitches; her eyes widen; time freezes.

Memory-keeper of betrayals. Ainela loved stories of the redveil fox. Its story was one of the first Zosia remembers Ainela telling her. *Long, long ago, during the famine, it came. There was a blood-red mist that rose from the hushwood at dusk, and from that mist came a fox who had a crimson-tipped veil over its muzzle. He prowled the edges of cottages. Families who followed him—they found hidden caches of food, but the gift always came at a price. Something was always taken in exchange: a hen gone missing, a lamb stillborn, or a secret whispered to the wrong ears. Now, it only appears whenever someone's betrayal is about to be revealed.*

Zosia doesn't move, doesn't blink.

Villagers say the pawprints of a redveil fox are omens: warnings that what's hidden will soon be dragged into the open. A few months ago, the laundress, Mrs. Crowder, saw its prints just behind her cottage. A week later, whispers started about her husband seeing the young dairymaid. And, once, the carriage driver swore he saw the fox's prints. Days later he discovered his wife spent the money he saved for years on new fabrics.

His thick copper coat is brushed with flakes of snow as he stands patiently behind the trunk of a hushbark. A veil the color of a ghost paints his muzzle starting at his shiny black nose. He looks nothing like the sly, clever trickster from Mama's stories. This one is still, watching her with his fire=colored fur that seems to almost glow. HIs chest is so dark it looks charred, like the center of a burned log, and his tail fans behind him like a red banner.

The forest seems to hold its breath with him. The molten amber eyes watching her neither threatening nor kind, just knowing. Zosia feels as though he's not really looking at her, but more through her, reading thoughts she hasn't spoken. When she blinks, he doesn't flinch. He waits, patient as a keeper of secrets, until she feels she might have to say something or bow or run. The air smells faintly of smoke, though the fire has long been out now.

What secret will be unveiled now?

Suddenly, sounds from the town behind her break the silence. The fox runs, disappearing deeper into the forest. Zosia's heart races as she steps from the within the hushwood back into the town. She sees people gathering in front of the butcher's shop. Children point; mothers pull them behind their legs.

She stands in the middle of the lane.

She's tall, taller than Ainela, and so thin Zosia can see the outline of her collarbone from here. Hor arms look fragile and so small Zosia could wrap her fingers completely around them. Her hair hangs like waxen straw, covering half her face. Eyes the color of liquid amber flash. She isn't still, and she isn't quiet. Her hollow cheeks look almost ghostly, and her expression seems almost confused. Only when Father Ignacy appears from behind the crowd, walking from the ruins, does she react.

She runs to one side of the street; the villagers shriek and move quickly out of her reach. As if in a frenzy, she turns and runs to others who stand closer to Zosia. They, too, dart from her reach. Zosia doesn't move. Instead, she notes the terrors shining from her eyes. The girl starts shouting things, pausing only to moisten her lips. Her voice scratches across the town. "Straw smells – like blood –" Townspeople near Zosia gasp. "Crusts – there – one for two."

Zosia frowns.

Straw.

"The rosary – beads rolled everyone – she – she kept one—"

Shivers race along Zosia's spine. *The rosary beads she found in the basement.*

"It was – a – she cried – mouse—"

"*Possessed.*" One of the townspeople whispers.

"She's broken."

"Madness."

Father Ignacy steps forward, and the girl screams, running backwards, "Blood! "

Shocked murmurs race through the townspeople as she points her finger at Father Ignacy. "Baths in ash!"

Baths in ash?

Father crosses himself, speaks to the people. "This is what I meant." His voice is gentle, sad. "Mothers, take your children, pull them close to your bosom. This is demonic illness. Look at her—don't you see? This is God's punishment for her behavior. She invited all that happened onto herself by refusing to repent of evil."

"Stone floor – chains, chains—names—we wrote them!" She holds her hands out, turning them this way and that, "On my hands —- the — the walls! They're on the walls!"

WHISPERROOT: A HUSHWOOD TALE

She takes two steps towards Father who steps back. "His hands — red — prayed after. Sin – sin – sin – but no, hunger. It was hunger."

A man spits in the snow. "Liar."

Father Ignacy starts to speak, but the widow Ida steps forward. She's an elderly woman whose shoulders curve inward. The town invites her to its festivals and events, but they don't really want her there. Zosia only knows she lives at the edge of town; women see her when they need help they shouldn't need.

"I'll take her."

Whispers stack on top of each other. People near her murmur she's dangerous. Someone asks what her name was; no one remembers. Zosia thinks of her sketchbook; she remembers drawing this girl, someone she never knew, on a night when the moon was full, and the hushwood's roots whispered.

"She can stay in the woodcutter's cottage. It's abandoned and she won't be of any harm to anyone there."

"Anyone remember her name?"

No one claims to.

Father frowns, nods. "Alright, I think as long as she doesn't harm anyone, she can stay there, that's a good idea since we don't have the chapel to contain her right now."

Ida walks fearlessly up to the girl, takes her slender wrist in her hand, and tugs. The girl still murmurs nonsense as they walk away from the village. The hushwood breathes.

"They were like this; the other one, too. Possessed. A danger to our children." Father insists, bowing his head. "I tried. I tried casting out the demons, but Satan's hand is so strong. We must guard ourselves against evil. You children that are here—remember what we just saw because that's what God allows to happen to children who play with evil."

Zosia feels the weight of the hushwood behind her. The wind stirs, almost a breath, and she swears she hears someone whisper *remember*. The girl talked of rosary beads; Zosia still smells the smoke and rot of the cellar. Her hands still remember the gritty feel of the rosary beads as she pulled it from the ash. The baker says *she deserved this, Father's right.* But she shouted, *his hands – red – prayed after. It was hunger.* Suddenly, as an icicle drops, clinking against a fencepost, Zosia sees sketches she's drawn. Flashing across her mind like pictures, the bones of the mouse are first. *Was that all they had to eat?*

She cried – mouse –

Zosia knows there *was* a mouse. The girl spoke of the cellar: Zosia saw it, but the townspeople hadn't. They didn't know. What she said was true, not crazy. Beneath her, the ground seems to swell. She looks around, glances to the hushwood, thinks she catches a glimmer of movement.

And she remembers.

Her mouth parts, forming a word. Silently, she mouths it. But she can't voice it. Memories come quicker name, one after another, pressing down on her until she feels almost suffocated. There was a name—she drew it in the sketchbook over the image of this girl—but she didn't know where it had come from. Memories stir again, and she almost remembers a lively, strong girl rubbing an ointment over a scratch she got from falling. She tries again – opening her mouth, trying to say the word, trying to give back the name—but her throat squeezes, unwilling to find sound.

She mouths it instead.

Halina.

Memory leaves its own footprints —
even when no one dares follow.

———————

Myreska Proverb

CHAPTER THIRTY-FOUR

THE UNSAID

WHISPERROOT: A HUSHWOOD TALE

Dawn seeps into the cottage. The sound of carriages traveling and men shouting pry Zosia's eyes open. Their cottage sits close enough to the ruins she can hear hammers clinking. She takes a deep breath and rises, her eyes moving from the hearth that's died out, to the window. Pulling back her curtains just a notch, she watches the wagon full of rubble from the ruins.

"Good morning," Mama says. The room feels chilly, so Mama adds a log to the hearth for her, strikes a match. As the fire takes hold, she joins Zosia at the window. Peeking out, she watches for a moment, then pats Zosia's back. "Life moves on whether we're ready or not." She brushes Zosia's hair behind her ear and said, "We'll be ready to break fast soon." Her hand drops and she turns to leave the bedchambers. Before she does, she hesitates, then says, "Zosia. If that girl comes back..." her eyes flutter to the night table where Zosia's sketchbook lies and her hand curls into a fist. "I don't want you to near her. She shouldn't be here. She'll just make things worse."

Zosia hears what Mama doesn't say: Halina's presence scares her, but the dangers of speaking truth aloud scare her more. Mama's story sits in the corner of Zosia's mind. *Forced. Shamed. No one listened. No one cared.* Zosia moves her gaze from Mama to the window again, her shoulders stiffening. Words are gathering in the back of her throat. They are stuck, but they are there. *You are my sister. You can do hard things*. Ainela's voice sings through her memory. *Well, if they're going to talk, might as well give them something pretty to look at while they do.*

Longing clenches in Zosia's belly.

Mama's shoulders drop slightly as she studies her. She looks down for a moment, as if recognizing something even Zosia can't yet see. When she lifts her head again, Mama's dark eyes glisten. "Both my daughters are more like me than they know." Her voice sounds gruff with pride that makes Zosia's heart squeeze. Mama's hand reaches out, hesitates, then drops to her side. The breath she draws in rattles, as if trying to steel herself. Zosia watches her leave the bedchambers, her lips parting, as if trying to say something, but sound won't come.

The newly rekindled fire in the hearth warms the room as Zosia dresses. She stares at the bed with the patchwork quilt she shared with her sister and, for a moment, senses Ainela close. *I always won our morning fights, didn't I?* The memory of Ainela's voice makes Zosia ache. Grief blooms fast and fiery and when she least expects it. Sometimes she makes it through most of a day now without tears swelling her eyes. Other times, she can't go an hour without something reminding her of Ainela: those are hardest days.

But, on every day, Zosia vows: *Ainela will not be forgotten.*

Life moves on whether we're ready or not, Mama's words ring loud in Zosia's mind as she walks through town. Shops are open again. The smell of early morning bread baking wafts from the baker's shop, the apothecary's door sits ajar, glass vials glinting in the dim interior. Zosia keeps her sketchbook close to her chest, pretending not to hear the whispers of other children as she walks by.

Her boots crunch the snow, noticing how the layers thin a little every day. The air smells of wet ash and fresh sawdust–it's a strange mix that makes her nose tickle. The wagons she saw from her window travel back and forth, creaking under the weight of charred timbers. Men shout over the clang of hammers and the thud of axes splitting beams.

She sees a circle of women at the well, scarves tied tight under their chins, speaking in low voices. When they notice her, the talking stops, hands dipping suddenly into buckets, backs turning toward her. A dog trots through, shakes melted snow from its coat, and is shooed away by a boy carrying a broom taller than he is. Near the steps of the chapel, the shoemaker and the blacksmith wrestle loose a piece of the cracked bell. Its dull, hollow sound echoes too loudly in the winter air, making Zosia's stomach twist. The schoolteacher stands off to the side, hat in hand, murmuring to Father Ignacy, who surveys the ruins with a look that might almost pass for sorrow, but Zosia knows better. The square feels smaller than before, more watchful almost. Curtains twitch in nearby windows, and even the pigeons on the rooflines seem still, their heads cocked, as if the whole town holds its breath.

As she walks closer to the ruins, she stares at the door—the one in the back of the chapel, the one whose stairs once led to the cellar. The door Zosia opened and went down into. It still stands but has been nailed shut. She knows because she returned after dark, trying to find her way down to the cellar again, hoping the whisperroots would help her as they did before. Only the heavy door with its iron bolts is now nailed shut. She wasn't able to breech it.

Anger coils in her belly again, just as it had when she first returned to find the door nailed shut. The anger feels like the fire: hot, fast and dangerous. Pausing where she stands, Zosia opens the sketchbook, stains her fingers with charcoal to sketch the door, shading a large X over its shape. The sound of charcoal on the page is harsh, final. Anger cages her grief, allowing dangerous thoughts to echo through her mind.

I will see it again. The thought thrums through her.

What right do they have to lock any door of a chapel?

She knows where she's going this morning. Just past the third birch tree to the hushbark with the hollow space. It's her cache, the one place she keeps everything she collects. She places it there because the green ribbon, frayed but faithful, still remains knotted against the whisperroots.

Just in case.

But not today.

Today, she wants to bring them home; she wants to keep them with her. So, she'll be ready. Ready for what, she doesn't know. There they are: the mouse bones, the ribbon she found still scorched, still warm to her touch. The rosary beads and the crucifix are tucked in the back. And the cracked emberfly's wing still carefully folded into the ribbon. She will not hide them again. As she puts them in her coat pocket, one by one, her eyes see something fluttering nearby. Yellowed, small, the scrap of paper is torn from a hymnal. Soot blackens the edges, water blurs the ink. The handwriting is so distorted between the snowmelt, and fire, that she can't decide if it's Ainela's writing or not.

—tomorrow I die.

WHISPERROOT: A HUSHWOOD TALE

Fear prickles her scalp, and she swallows heavily. How would one know one was going to die tomorrow? Unless–was there a plan? Unless there was a rebellion? Zosia's frown deepens.

The sound of branches cracking force her head up and a strange chirring noise. Her head lifts in time to see a squirrel scampering up the side of the tree. When Zosia opens the sketchbook to the back and places the fragment on top of the others she found, the forest responds. The chime-thrush sings, and there's a faint breeze that lifts the snow drift into swirling circles in front of her. There's a name she can feel, just in the back of her throat, but the letters won't align, they just spin around as if teasing her, *almost* giving her a name. But not.

The knot of anger tangles with frustration, burying any lingering fear. The fragment haunts her until she opens the sketchbook again, gently writes, *"Today you live."*

The forest seems to hush and a faint voice, Ainela's, drifts like a breath: *Caterbutton. Caterbutton.* Zosia looks up, her eyes wide, her mouth shaping the name. But there is no one. There is only the hushwood listening.

The sun sits high in the sky, and the town welcomes the heat like an unexpected gift.

Winter has never been so long.

Zosia sits on the same bench in the middle of town, sketching random things: the child with the beautiful shawl Zosia covets, the wagons as they travel back and forth with their big wheels and loyal horses.

"There she is again," the whispers come from nowhere, fast and ruthless, jarring Zosia from thought. When she raises her head, she notices: Halina stands again in the town square, her eyes drawn like magnets to the chapel ruins just past Zosia. Townspeople stop their afternoon plans and start whispering instead. Someone knocks on Father's Ignacy's cottage door and pleads with him to come. Because, in Myreska, the priest is the religious authority, but he's also the constable.

Zosia's fingers begin sketching before she's even aware of herself doing so. Halina's hair remains unkempt, stringy, just as wild as it was the first time she appeared. *Has she bathed?* Her dress is torn. She's so thin that the sleeves of her dress fall off one of her shoulders. A bruise the size of a man's fist darkens the otherwise pale flesh.

This time, Halina isn't shouting.

Instead, she's murmuring to herself, quietly, her eyes fixed straight ahead at the ruins.

Her eyes narrow and she walks. The townspeople don't try to stop her. Even Father Ignacy stands to the side. Someone wonders where Jakub is, another says they saw him this morning.

Halina's murmurs shift into a hum that grows louder and louder the closer she gets to the chapel ruins. Soon, the hum drowns all other sounds out. Zosia sketches, a record keeper, a truth-teller, when others say nothing. Charcoal presses against the page, drawing a girl who looks mad ... but isn't, girl who sounds mad... but isn't. As she passes Zosia, she stops in front of her.

The town gasps.

Halina stares at the young girl, as if she sees a ghost. Her lips murmur incoherently.

"... the red one ... don't stop ... don't stop ... don't stop...."

Zosia swallows, her eyes holding Halina's. She doesn't see madness, but she doesn't have a name for what Halina's molten amber gaze show. Maybe just *pain*. Others cover their mouths with their hands. When they whisper *"possessed"*, the flame of anger bursts higher in Zosia. She clenches her jaw and focuses on her sketch.

Halina moves away, continues walking straight into the middle of the chapel ruins.

"We shouldn't let her – "

"Father, what –"

He lifts a hand. "Let's see what she does."

The hum comes back, louder than before, as Halina stands in the middle of the ruined chapels. Every now and then, disjointed phrases interrupt the hum. Quietly, she walks from standing in the middle of the chapel to turning towards the side, where the door that led to the basement once stood. The space where Lenka's body was found. In that spot now grows a whisperroot that hadn't been there before. Still young, the whisperroot has only appeared in the last few days, when no one talked about the blood that pooled around her or the marks on her body that suggested something worse than an occasional correction.

She bends to her knees in the snow and then lies down, curling into a fetal position.

And she cries, sobs that are so raw and heartbreaking that the town's whispers stop. Guilty eyes move away. Some of the townspeople leave, walking with their heads down, as if they can't withstand the sight of such truth. The hoarse, raw, aching sound of Halina sobbing waylays Zosia's anger long enough for grief to take over. Tears swell her eyes; her breathing turns shallow.

No one approaches Halina.

No one offers her comfort.

Shame crushes Zosia's chest because she doesn't, either.

Movement shifts in the hushwood and, this time, when Zosia looks back, she thinks she sees a shadow moving but can't be sure. Halina? She scans the snow but doesn't see fresh prints on the outside of the forest.

They're calling her the ghost-girl, which makes Zosia's blood boil because *she's not a ghost.*

Zosia slips out the door of the cottage once the stars are out, and the silver of the moon breaches the tops of the trees. While the snow slowly melts, nights are still freezing, and Zosia worries. She's not sure this will help. She's not sure anyone is there. All she knows for certain is Ainela would have helped. Mama can't know what she does; she'd be very angry, but Zosia can't do nothing.

Wolves howl into the night, their cries echoing a sorrowful sadness ricocheting around the walls of her heart. She isn't sure she knows the way; only that she must try. There are no sounds, and the silence grows deeper the further out she walks. The rickety bridge stands precariously at the edge of town, the creek beneath it still frozen. It might hold a wagon, but crossing over in one would frighten Zosia. Its planks beneath the snow groan with every step she takes. This far from the town square, the snow is untouched. She slides her mittened hand across the top of the bridge railing, scattering snow drifts. She hadn't noticed the deer watching her until it bolts into the woods.

When she makes it across the bridge, she exhales a tiny breath of relief and scans the surroundings. She isn't sure where she's going. Her only directions were from the whispers of the townspeople:

That woman lives too far out, past the bridge.

It's further than that. You have to climb the hill afore you can see her roof.

That hill could kill a man when it ices.

So, she walks further, looking for a steep, dangerous hill. The only one she sees doesn't look too steep. Covered in snow, it deceives Zosia. Within moments, her feet slide from beneath her and she rolls to the bottom of the hill. The snow here is a thin layer, her boots hitting ice beneath it. She tries again, this time moving slowly, digging her boots into the ground until she cracks the ice beneath. Sweat gathers under her chin and along her brow by the time she makes it to the top of the hill. Breathing rapidly, she looks down from where she came.

The rooftops of the town look far, far away.

When she looks up to the sky, the moon looks to have shifted a bit. If she's going to get home before she's missed, she doesn't have long. And she has to get home before she is missed. Ainela leaving taught her that.

Black smoke curls into the chilly night air ahead of her and the roofline of a cottage is barely visible.

I don't think she's staying at Ida's. I think she's living in the woodcutter's place.

You mean that shack that sits a mile to the East of Ida's? By that big ole creek?

That's what I heard.

Zosia hopes what they heard was true as she sets out walking East of the roofline she sees. Her legs ache by the time she sees smoke rising from another roofline. She can't see the town anymore below her, only the edges of the hushwood.

Black smoke curls into the sky ahead, faint but certain. Her heart stutters.

The woodcutter's place, she thinks.

The shack is barely visible through the hushwood shadows, crouched low against the snow as though hiding. Zosia's legs ache as she trudges toward it, every step loud in the quiet night. By the time she reaches the clearing, she can't see the town anymore – only the dark edge of the hushwood and the lonely line of smoke rising from the roof.

The woodcutter's cottage is a shack. The porch is rotted, a hole through the middle of one end. The windows don't have curtains, but Zosia can't see through the frosted panes. She swallows heavily. She doesn't want to speak to Halina. She doesn't want to frighten her. She walks closer, noting the small footprints in the snow. Pausing, she holds her own foot over one, and frowns. Is that the same as the other prints she saw in the hushwood? These seem a little smaller. Quickly, she bends down and measures the footprint with her hand.

As she rises, she sees a candle flicker out in the window.

She exhales a long steam of air through pursed lips.

When she reaches the porch, she doesn't step onto it. Instead, she drops the sack slung over her shoulder, digs inside, and pulls out the pair of leather ankle boots. They are a pair of Ainela's. Worn, with scuffs on the sides, and soles Zosia had to patch. The brown leather is tired, curling at the tops, and the left one is missing a button. Zosia remembers Ainela stomping through drifts in these, laughing, snow kicking up in sprays. But Zosia noticed when Halina walked past her that her feet were a faint blue-ish color. These are better than nothing. She places the boots with a pair of thick wool socks on the porch. She hesitates, memories of Ainela dancing in her heart. Gently, she brushes the softened leather, and tucks the socks deeper into the boot to keep them dry. Finally, she steps back. The woods are so quiet she can hear her own heartbeat.

As she steps off the porch to begin the long walk home, she knows she's being watched. The feeling stays with her until the woodcutter's cottage is no longer visible.

For God gave us a spirit not of fear
but of power

———

2 Timothy 1:7

Chapter Thirty-Five

The EmberKeeper

WHISPERROOT: A HUSHWOOD TALE

The wind blows strong. Since the journey to the woodcutter's cottage, Zosia's anger builds. Chapel services are shorter now to fight the cold, but each minute fuels her fire. Whisperroots seem to grow everywhere now and, when she sees them, Zosia feels the weight.

They say Halina's crazy.

Zosia knows she's not.

They say Halina's possessed.

But her fragments are truth.

The fear that's held Zosia captive since Ainela's taking fades every time she catches sight of Halina. Her suffering squeezes the air out of Zosia. Ainela wouldn't let Halina suffer in silence like this. What about the others? Where are they? Part of her knows: she's seen glimpses of mounds in the forest, unnatural mounds with whisperroots growing in the center of them. Last night, in her dream, she saw the whisperroots stretching down into the ground and wrapping around thin, gaunt bodies. She awoke sobbing when she saw twisted roots pushing out of Ainela's lifeless mouth, curling like fingers around her face. Roots twisted around her, not choking but cradling her body, as if claiming her for the forest. Zosia's heart raced for hours, tears streamed down her face, and she lay awake for hours afterwards, praying Ainela isn't dead.

But knowing she is.

She stares out the window. The town's quiet this late, lit only by lanterns.

There were whispers at the well today. The nursemaid wondered who would be next; the priest came to see her because her daughter, Tonya, laughs too loud in chapel. *The others went to Krakow*, that's what the priest says. But the rosary beads weren't Ainela's, and they weren't Lenka's. A man swore they belonged to his daughter, Larisa, and that she wouldn't be seen without them. Why would she leave them behind if she went to Krakow? Why would she have been in the cellar at all?

The night feels heavy, and its wind stronger than usual. The shutters rattle, a quiet unease settles against her bones. Zosia pulls her sketchbook open. The pages crinkle as she gently turns one after another. Blue eyes, green eyes, brown eyes stare back at her. Girls with freckles and dimples and space between their teeth. Ribbons tied around their necks, or their wrists, or tangled in their hands connect them.

The wind whistles loud.

Zosia feels a pull tonight, a calling she can't explain but knows she must follow. Slipping out of the bed, she laces the black leather, buttoned up boots. She hesitates but opens a bottom drawer and digs in the back of it. Beneath shifts and blouses, she finds the knitted shawl she sewed shortly after the Winter Festival. The yarn glows red even in the dim light. At the Festival, Ainela danced and laughed in red.

The Devil's color.

But Ainela loved wearing it; her face glowed merrily as she brushed aside the town's complaints. *They're going to talk*, Ainela told her once, shrugging her shoulders. *I simply wasn't meant to be part of this town. And, truthfully, Zosia, that doesn't sadden me at all.* Zosia longed to have her sister's carelessness, her devil-may-care attitude, the strength to defy the priest so, late at night, when everyone else, even Ainela, slept, Zosia sat by the hearth and knitted a shawl. It was bright red. *I'll never wear this,* she thought as she finished it. Too frightened to show even Ainela, she hid it in the bottom drawer, tucked behind all of her other cloths.

Until tonight.

As she slips it over her shoulders, she feels Ainela smiling. Pride swells her sister's eyes, and she hears Ainela say gaily, *See? You are my sister.* To Zosia, it feels like a banner, dangerous and defiant, and a reminder of who she is.

The town suffocates Zosia, but her feet are sure as she walks towards the hushwood. She feels the twitching of curtains, sees the eyes of the town catch her. She knows what they'll whisper tomorrow:

that one—I saw her sneak out last night after dark in the same color the red one wore!

It's disgraceful the influence that girl has on our daughters; we must protect the ones who are innocent.

If she's sneaking out, what else is she doing?

That boy Sam—she's been seen walking with him. More than once!

She's too young for any of that.

It's in her genes – the mother, you know...

The Hushwood pulls her. She hears a low throbbing, like the earth itself hums. But, as she approaches the line of trees, something stops her. Emberflies appear by the dozens, the scent of vanilla hovering in the air, as their warmth spreads. The trees seem to lean closer together, their dark limbs locking. She stumbles, confused. *Does the forest itself warn her away? The hushwood refuses to let her in? But – she needs proof. How can she have proof without the secrets in the forest?*

From her left, the ashfeather cries three times in quick succession.

When she turns her head to see, her heart skips a beat. There she is.

She wears the boots she left for her. Zosia notices them first because they stand out: Halina is not dressed for the cold. Her dress is still torn, holes in the bottom of it, the shoulders sliding down her arm. Filth clings to her. Dirt cakes beneath her fingers. Her gold hair looks dull and stained with gray, as if she took handfuls of ash and dumped them over her own head.

Zosia pulls her lip between her teeth, uncertain about what to do now. The girl is only steps away, but the gulf between them feels wide. She almost turns back — almost lets the gossip win — but her feet stay rooted.

Crouching by the edge of the trees, Halina shakes, her eyes watchful. She points, her eyes frenzied, into the forest. "She's *there*."

Zosia's stomach flips, clenches. She looks into the forest, but the darkness keeps everything hidden. She doesn't see anything, not even the footprints. And were the footprints Halina's? The village whispers haunt Zosia's memory: *possessed, mad, broken.*

Cautiously, she takes a step closer to the girl. Halina holds still, her body quivering, though whether from fear or the cold, Zosia doesn't know. Quickly, Zosia unwraps the pale blue scarf from around her neck. Holding it out as an offering, she waits.

Halina stares at it only a moment before her fingers snatch it, bunching the edges of it in her fist. She clutches it tight, as if she can't remember how to wear a shawl. Zosia reaches out, her fingers lightly grazing the edge of the garment. Gently, she tugs. Halina opens her fist and Zosia shakes it out, then drapes it over Halina's shoulders.

Halina stammers, "Ainela – Ainela – red one —"
Zosia nods slowly.
Halina points to Zosia. "Sister."
Zosia nods again.
Halina moves, standing, peering the tree limbs into the forest. Its branches lock, the trees sway closer. Emberflies bunch together. *Not here.* The whisper seems to come from the earth itself. The soil aches as it shifts. Halina whispers, "She's in there."

Zosia points – a fallen log that touches the hushwood. A dry place for them to sit. Zosia moves first, Halina hesitates, watchful. When she sees the girl's fear, Zosia opens her brown satchel and carefully pulls the sketchbook out. When Halina's gaze cuts to the forest, then to chapel ruins, as if frozen, Zosia opens the book to the back where the fragments she found lie. Gingerly, she holds one up.

WHISPERROOT: A HUSHWOOD TALE

Halina's reaction is visceral. She gasps, her eyes widening, the trembling of her body becomes visible. She moves forward, her steps clunky in unfamiliar shoes, she reaches out and takes the fragment from Zosia. Her mouth opens to breathe as tears fill her eyes. "We wrote....not lost... embers...."

Zosia holds up the last one she found:

– tomorrow I die.

Halina moans, her shoulder curving in, as if the pain presses on her, heavier than she can bear. "The match—the door—one. one. two, two. One. One. Two, two—F. R.E. E" Halina's breathing quickens, fear rising tangibly in her, her fingers tapping code repeatedly against the inside of her wrist. She shakes her head violently, unable to breathe, a moan turning into a frantic hum.

Zosia holds a hand out, pats the air, trying to slow her down.

"Unclean but obedient," Halina whispers. "One." She points to her chest. "One unclean but obedient."

Zosia shakes her head, reaches out and takes Halina's hand. Halina grips it, her eyes falling to the sketchbook. "Lenka—she was stabbed—" Halina covers her mouth her free hand, closing her eyes. "Ainela – Ainela — Jakub — straight—Ainela pushed me to-toward him, Lenka followed. But–" she shook her head. "Somehow she was stabbed," her voice falters, fades to a whisper. "Blood was –everywhere. Fire. There was so much – much smoke."

She picks up the rosary beads, nodding. "Larisa," she moans, her shoulders shaking.

Zosia's heart races. Her eyes move from her sketchbook, from the ribbon and the beads, and broken emberfly wing to Halina. The forest exhales, its locked branches loosen. A chime-thrush sings in the middle of the night, adding a piece of the Halina's story to its song. A quiet *sashaying* makes them both look, but the stars and the emberflies aren't bright enough to illuminate the heart of the forest. Zosia swallows, her chest aching. *The drawings. The fragments. The beads. The ribbons. And Halina.* A word rises unbidden: *witness.* She isn't alone anymore.

Suddenly, Halina's eyes clear, and her hand tightens on Zosia's.

Zosia focuses, her gaze shifting to Halina's. "If you speak, I will stand."

The emberflies flare all at once, like sparks from a struck match. Their glow spills over the snow, warm as breath, smelling of sweet vanilla and firelit hearths.

They'll know: you are my sister.

Tears shining in her eyes, grief and anger swirling as one, she nods.

They will stand.

Halina holds Zosia's hand tightly as they walk towards the town square. She closes her eyes for a moment, her face tight with resolve. When she opens them, they are clear, sharp. Then, she takes Zosia's lantern. "Wait here, I'll gather people. I'll—I'll bring them." She hesitates only a moment, then turns away, her grip on the lantern tightening. The light swings wildly as she strides to the first door.

Zosia stands in the center of the town. The air is crisp, and the stars are bright. Emberflies swarm, following Halina. Holding the lantern high, she stops at the first cottage, and raps on the door. Without waiting for someone to answer, she moves to the next cottage, rapping strongly. As the glow of lanterns begin lighting windows, a chorus of chime-thrushes begin chirping. Shadows move from deep within the forest. Each time Halina knocks, a groan rolls through the hushwood like an answering drumbeat. When the last cottage door is struck, a chime-thrush sings once, clear as a bell, and the forest falls still. That's when the first townspeople appear, lanterns trembling in their hands.

As they spill into the paths, their lanterns held high, murmurs of curiosity swelling the night, Zosia waits. The night feels brittle, every sound sharpened: the crunch of distant footsteps, the soft creak of shutters opening. Emberflies swirl higher, as though marking her place, until she feels she is standing in a ring of faint, pulsing stars. She sees them coming closer in the glow of lamplight. Some clutch prayer ropes. Other cross themselves as they approach, whispering about omens and judgment. None dare turn back. The air feels thick, as if the whole town has been summoned for a reckoning. Mama clutches Papa's hand, her lips pursed as she watches her daughter. When she sees the sketchbook, she closes her eyes, a prayer spilling from her lips.

Soon, Halina returns.

A girl in a red shawl—-the color of the Devil—stands beside the mute girl. Both remind the town of what they knew, of what they surrendered. Unease ripples through the crowd as they wait for one of the girls to speak. Quietly, slowly, Zosia pulls her sketches out. Lays them on the snow in front of the crowd, one by one. People crowd closer, craning their necks to see. Whispers turn into gasps of recognition as mothers recognize the faces of their daughters preserved in charcoal. Gasps turn to murmurs when she holds up her discoveries: the rosary beads, the frayed ribbon Mama placed in the hollow of the tree for Ainela to find, the mouse bone, the crucifix, the fragments with voices that cannot be denied.

As each is laid before the town, the forest holds its breath. Shadows shift, snow crunches. The whisper of movement walking between the trees, dark eyes watching, waiting. Once the final piece is laid bare, Zosia pauses, her head bent. She draws in a deep breath, filling her lungs with the crisp Winter air warmed by vanilla. Emberflies hover over her, some alighting on the sketches, and the ribbons. Zosia's hand clenches, her nails digging into her palm, the bitter taste of fear swelling her throat. But then she lifts her head, sees Halina.

Fire blooms in the empty space between them.

But not the fire that kills.

A fire that frees.

Zosia's mouth opens, closes. The words feel gritty, taste like ash. Fear makes her scan the crowd. Jakub leans against a fence, his arms folded, his eyes lowered halfway, hooded. Muscles bunch in his chest as he watches the girls—the one who got away, and the one whose sister engineered the escape. The priest is not among the crowd. Her throat tightens and the air tastes of iron. For a moment, for just a second, she nearly drops the fragments and flees. Until Halina's fingers squeeze hers, and Zosia feels heat against her neck. She opens her mouth. "Halina."

She turns and puts a hand on Halina's arm.

"She is not the ghost-girl. Her name is Halina." The hushwood responds. Roots groan, the snow beneath their feet starts to melt in the dead of night beneath the emberflies' heat, and the wind shifts. "Iskra." The air feels momentarily charged as it does just before a storm gathers. For an instant, the sound of laughter chases the ashfeather owl's cry. A father groans at the sound of his daughter's name, spoken aloud for the first time since her kidnapping. "Joanna." The strength and clarity she saw in Halina moments earlier falters and Halina's head bows, her shoulders shaking as tears roll down her cheeks. "Klara." The name sends a shiver down Zosia's spine when the ground trembles beneath the snow. One lone emberfly rises above the others, circling Zosia twice before vanishing towards the trees.

"Kaja."

Lantern light elongates the tree-shadows, making them appear to lean closer. A sudden guest of wind blows, carrying with it a sound that almost forms her name. The towns people whisper and bunch closer together, arms wrapping around their loved ones as if to protect them. The weight of silence and guilt and loss thickens the air.

"Lusia." Zosia's voice grows in strength. Halina exhales, her shoulders straightening, courage stiffening her spine. "Lenka." The whisperroot growing near the ruins of the chapel glow a faint red, making the snow appear stained by blood. "Larisa." The chime-thrush cries, sounding like a church bell ringing. "Tatiana." Three emberflies rise higher than the others, circle three times, and fly towards the woods while the wind shifts again. Snow drifts swirl and, for a moment, the play of lamplight and shadows creates an

WHISPERROOT: A HUSHWOOD TALE

illusion of a doll spinning. "Mila." A nearby treat groans, almost like a sigh.

"Kalina." Startling everyone a chime-thrush flies above the crowd, singing loudly. It's voice rattles glass in nearby cottages. The baker swipes a tear from his eyes; the seamstress wraps her arms around her waist as if trying to keep herself from falling apart. The teamster looks skeptical, his eyes judging the reaction of others. Jakub's jaw clenches, his fist opening and closing.

"Ainela," Zosia whispers and feels a rush of heat up her spine, as though Ainela's spark passes through her. The warm, yellow glow of Zosia's lantern flickers, then burns blue. Not a midnight blue or a bellbottom blue but an ocean kind of blue, tinged with emerald. The snowfall stops in mid-air for the space of a drumbeat, then falls more softly, slower, almost like a shroud being lowered to the ground. Suddenly, the hushwood roots, which have trembled with other names, breaks the surface, curling slightly toward Zosia, as if it reaches for her. A deep, slow *thoom*, as massive as a giant's heartbeat, rolls beneath the ground, startling the townspeople who shift their feet, fear tightening the crowd. The forest itself seems to blush – trunks appear darker, the snow catching the faint ember-red glow of the whisperroots within it.

Zosia holds up the fragments she's discovered and reads them, one by one, her voice clear and strong. "This one reads – *tomorrow, I die.*"

"Ainela wrote that," Halina adds, her voice soft. "She pushed me towards the door, and then she went back to get others while I ran." She nods, her chest aching. "I don't know–" her breaks and she tries again. "You'll find marks in the wood, tally marks for each death."

The square is silent.

Even the forest waits.

A few townspeople—the carriage driver, the lamplighter, their families—turn, their backs disappearing against the stars as they leave the square. A few follow them. Snow falls quietly but the names hang in the air, too heavy to fall.

Go ahead,
Call me an arsonist, but I didn't set that fire
Maybe, if I had their courage.
If you are reading this, I've left this town.
If you find this, tell 'em----

---

letter found in Jakub's cottage

CHAPTER THIRTY-SIX
ASH IN OUR MOUTHS

WHISPERROOT: A HUSHWOOD TALE

Most of us woke today hoping that last night was nothing more than a nightmare. We stare out our windows, tilting our heads as if trying to make sense of what we—saw? Did we really see it? The ghost girl and the mute girl, standing side by side, holding ... holding what, exactly? Fragments of letters written by ... who? Some of us saw them; some of us went up afterwards and asked to hold them (these were mainly the mothers and fathers of the missing girls, but a few of our more skeptical neighbors also wanted to see). They weren't signed. And they weren't dated. So, some of us woke this morning wondering, *could we even be sure of what they were?*

We stare at the white of the snow and, for a moment, we almost believe it's clean. Tucked into our cottages, with only our families, we don't have to think about what was said. Or what we knew. What we *know*. A sense of impending doom settles in our stomachs, makes us wish for a storm or illness or anything that would enable us to *stay* in our cottages with our families. But—no. Instead, our husbands offer mumbles that are supposed to be comforting, take their lunch pails, and go off to the chapel ruins or the mines or wherever work calls them. Wives wrap themselves tightly in safe colors, drape our golden children in hugs and schoolbooks and send them off to the schoolhouse to learn reading and arithmetic.

Lanterns still hang on cottage doors, icicles dripping from them. The hushwood looms, but there's no emberflies now, no scent of sweet vanilla, the whisperroots don't glow. Mary, a laundress, is such a gossip: dropping off baskets of garments for her to wash means inevitable whispers.

"Zosia spoke–"

"All twelve names were spoken—"

"Shush," the rest of us urge. "Father Ignacy was not there." Self-righteousness hugs our voices. "We don't want to talk about it until he knows what happened." None of us intend to tell Father Ignacy what happened last night. We know what might happen to our daughters if we did and, well, we are a careful town. But, deep down, guilt plagues us. Because, of course, we knew. Sam told us. The other children told us. And we ourselves might have heard things—groanings beneath the chapel floorboards on Sundays, crying that was just soft enough for us to ignore.

Would they be here if we spoke up?

Once, many years ago, shortly after the famine that wiped out most of our great-grandparents, something similar happened. Around All Souls Day there are legends about the girl who was buried in the village well. No one knows her name because it's not really important. What matters to us is *why* the girl was shoved into the village well to drown. She was said to have lied to her parents. About what, none of us really know. But the legend we tell our children ends with a stark reminder for our children: her absence from the town meant one mouth less to feed during a famine. We don't feel that way about these girls–parents are still mourning their loss–but the heart of the story speaks to who we are as a town.

Resourceful.

Resilient.

Loyal–to our traditions, at least.

We study our daughters, the feel of braiding their hair and the sound of their voices. We wonder which one might have been next if not for that fire. Zosia's voice, and the ghost girl's, still echoes, though we try not to hear it. It sounded so much like a bell we forgot had been broken. There's a quiet sense of pride that Zosia speaks again, but it's a pride none of us will admit to. Not now. Not when *what* she spoke threatens us.

As some of us walk to shops or the well or the chapel ruins, we pause, tie a fresh ribbon to a branch. One of us ties a ribbon so tight the branch snaps. She gasps, looks around — and pretends she meant to do it. Tying ribbons helps us feel better. It helps us believe we're doing the right thing. Most of us believe we are. Well, some of us. Just as branches have snapped off the trees of the forest, there are fractures among us.

In one tavern, men skip morning work in lieu of having beer. Their wives will know about this come evening when they came home with whiskey on their breaths... but there won't be any arguments about the loss of coin. Not today. "We should bring in the constable... Krakow, if we have to..." A carpenter sounds fierce.

"What?" Others sound shocked. "That would bring ruin to this town."

A father in the corner stands, says, "I'll go to Krakow." But, even before the others can urge him to wait, he sits. The heaviness in the room grows.

At the marketplace, women shop together, their voices hushed but fierce. "We need to do something," the seamstress insists. "This can't be happening here."

'They had fragments—"

"It's been so long since I saw that ribbon—"

"We must tell someone."

"Tell who? Besides, it will only bring scandal."

"But—"

"We must keep the feast."

"We need peace, we don't need outsiders telling us how to live."

"For the children."

We turn from the windows, pulling the curtains tight. We turn from the forest, telling ourselves it was nothing but a dream. We turn from one another if we have to. We're not made of stone: when we pass the snowy hills, we hear their laughter. When we past the meadow, we remember their wishes. We set crumbs out on the windowsill—*just in case*. And yet—we never really expected anyone to *take* the crumbs. What do you say to a ghost-girl? Or to one who goes forever without speaking only to resurrect her voice in front of the entire town?

Well.

Not the *entire* town. Father Ignacy wasn't there last night. He's not feeling so well; just a small cough that the apothecary assures us isn't serious. We aren't sure if we're relieved or saddened that he missed that performance. Most of us wish we could hear his reaction because it would root us, give us back common ground. His fiery sermons on righteousness and purity and the cost of evil spreading through our homes make us feel as though we made the right choices.

When the children whisper their names today, we shush them. Our hands are clean, but our hearts are not. Memories of the night we gathered in the chapel haunt us. Each of us cast a vote that night. Even the widow Ida who hesitated and asked, "*But shouldn't we protect her, too?*" cast a vote.

We know it's hard to understand, but you'd sacrifice *someone else's* daughter for your own, wouldn't you? We tell ourselves we have done what we must. But when the wind sweeps through the hushwood at night, we fear it is carrying the names back to us.

It is easier when there is someone to blame. Father Ignacy hints at it first: maybe the red one didn't strike the match, after all. He didn't see who did, and Jakub carried matches in his pocket. We know he's a wounded man, what with the war and Anka, his daughter, and all. Father Ignacy blames his memory lapses on the smoke and chaos of trying to save the girls while also trying to get out alive.

We watch with both horror and awe as Father Ignacy walks through the town towards the blacksmith's cottage. His arms swing lightly by his side, his chiseled face an appropriate mixture of sorrow and determination. *It's a shepherd's responsibility before God to hold his sheep accountable. It's a heavy burden to place on a man, but I take the load our Lord has seen fit to give me.* In moments like these, we trust him a little more. It's hard not to. His voice cracks with the weight a man carries as parish of an entire town. He must guide each of us so that our souls are saved.

WHISPERROOT: A HUSHWOOD TALE

We don't wonder why he doesn't talk to Zosia or the ghost-girl, both who clearly suffer from a soul deep affliction, but he answers our unspoken question by telling us a Bible story. *Jesus Himself gave us very clear directions when someone refuses our message of salvation, of repentance. In Matthew, chapter ten, He says, 'If anyone will not listen to your words, shake off the dust from your feet when you leave that house.* Father Ignacy's voice grew weighed and sad. We feel the words cling to our boots like mud. He's tried to cleanse the ghost-girl, but the demons living in her are very strong. Too strong for a mere man: she must suffer the punishment of God.

The parents—and some of us—imagine Jakub in the town square, hanging from a noose. We don't speak these things aloud, of course, but we breathe easier at night believing someone else might bear the weight of our sin. Some of the men threaten to harm him; he broke the stablemaster's nose the day after the naming because the stablemaster challenged him to a duel. Some of us pull our blankets over us at night, whispering to our husbands, *He was always a threat. I know he set that fire.*

A few of us aren't sure.

A few of us barely breathe what we wish for: God to call Father Ignacy home already. We can never mention that one. When we see Father Ignacy walking towards Jakub's cottage, we feign indifference but our eyes drift to catch every movement. We see Father knock; we watch Jakub open the door and step aside, allowing him in. We're not close enough to see them moving through the windows, but we wait with bated breath for Father to come out.

When the door opens and Father Ignacy steps out, Jakub's frame looms in the doorway. Someone swears they heard raised voices. Another says they saw Jakub's hand clench into a fist before he let it drop to his side. We hold our breath, afraid the priest will be struck down in his own parishioner's doorway. We know something has shifted. The priest doesn't look back as he walks with his head high away from the cottage.

We don't have to wait long.

Within an hour of Father's visit, we watch Jakub from a distance as he throws bags into the back of a wagon. He moves with purpose, but not recklessness. He leaves his door open, as if daring someone to stop him. We watch from our porches or from behind parted curtains. No one steps forward.

"He must be guilty," we say. "If he didn't set that fire, why does he leave?" It is easier to sleep when guilt has a face.

"He didn't set the fire. He saved that girl."

That's what the ghost-girl says: that he shouted at them to come straight towards him and then stood by while they escaped. Others trust Father Ignacy and believe Jakub must have set the blaze to cover his sins. *He's a wounded man*, Father says, *the war changed him*. We understand that. Still, we mutter *thank you* prayers to God as we watch Jakub haul himself into the wagon. We don't need any arsonist in our town, after all. If his leaving protects us, then we are happy. If it keeps the golden children safe, we'll call it righteous. But–what if? The question sits like ash in our mouths, scalding us with its bitterness. *What if* he's a hero?

Mama rocks back and forth in the chair knitting by the hearth while Papa smokes a cigar and tells a story about a squirrel he almost killed accidentally while chopping wood together. Zosia leans against the wall of the cottage, knees bent, sketchbook open, capturing the moment. Mama worries she might go to Krakow soon.

The milkman stands with his hands on his hips, staring out the window. From his cottage, he can sese Jakub's front door. He left it wide open. Stars twinkle outside. When he turns towards his wife, he says, "Pretty night."

In another cottage, Sam eats dinner with his parents. "I remember Ainela." His father sighs heavily. His mother's hand pauses mid-air. Neither shush him. No one answers at all.

We're not sure who that person is.

WHISPERROOT: A HUSHWOOD TALE

We swallow the names. The forest keeps them now.

Though Spring comes soon, the snow still falls for now. It covers the last of the tracks.

Myreska sits with her windows shuttered, snowflakes falling, whisperroots twisting amongst themselves. The hushwood is a dark silhouette watching. Tomorrow, we will sweep the square. Tomorrow, we will smile. Tomorrow, we will say none of this ever happened.

What you bury, we grow

———————————

the Hushwood

TIFFINI JOHNSON

WHISPERROOT: A HUSHWOOD TALE

As the emberflies flicker like dim stars and the roots beneath our soil hum a familiar tune, we watch. We see Zosia place soft fingers over the fragment her sister wrote. We count the number of times Halina taps the code for *free* on her wrist (six). We hear what others do not. The whispers between mothers and fathers–*did you see the sketch of her? It looked just like her*—and between the children—*She helped me catch a frog one time and told me to kiss it!* Mostly, we listen to the silence that settles over Myreska like a dirty, heavy, and familiar blanket. It tastes like iron and smells like charred timber. One by one lamplights are extinguished in the cottages.

But we never rest.

Only after the last light in the last cottage goes dark do we exhale, our trunks creaking as we settle deeply into the soil. We pull ourselves away from each other, standing straight again, our branches no longer locking. The chime-thrushes settle their feathers in straw nests that sometimes makes us remember straw mats.

They've been named.

Our bark tingles with the memory of Halina standing side-by-side Zosia, holding hands, each giving the other courage. We watched Halina as she faded from the town's sight. Only when she reached the steep hill did she stop. Instead of climbing up, she sat in the snow, her hands gripping the white fluff. Only we see her eyes glaze. She struggles to breathe, memory and guilt and sadness pressing on her like weights. A rabbit pauses near her and the two of them lock eyes. Only when Halina stands does the rabbit scamper off.

The echo of her tears, the memory of her pain, still engraves itself in our roots.

We grieve for the Embergirls. Blood-red hushbark sap glints on our trunks, dripping into the snow like memory made visible. Because we remember.

We remember Halina. We hum her name low, like a lullaby. She was the caretaker, the hand that checked for breath under Larisa's nose, the one who shielded the weakest with her own body. We watched her sit by Iskra's side through fever, through burns, through tears. Her palms smelled of lye soap and straw, her touch was gentler than water. When others broke, she held them together; when the room fell silent, she was the first to speak. We root her steadfastness in our trunks, so that even in storms, we do not break.

We remember Iskra. Her jokes and laughter braid as chords in the chime-thrush's song, one that our animals listen for. She wore bruises like a second skin, but she made them laugh— even when her ribs ached, even when her burns cracked and bled, even when her breath staggered and failed. *Laughing means it can't hurt me*, she said, and the words struck our bark like an oath. She stuck her tongue out behind his back and made Tatiana's tears fray into giggles. When her chest stilled, emberflies rose like sparks from cooling ash, as though refusing to let her go cold. We keep her laughter still, banked like a hidden fire under snow. One day, when someone dares laugh at the wrong time, we will let it flare.

We remember Joanna, and her attention to detail. We hear her in our marrow. We root her name with charcoal under our skin. She was the one who noticed the lines, who said *that belongs in the book*. When others despaired, she pressed fingers to knee and turned pain into rhythm, words into seed. We remember her braiding of memory — stitching girls together with rhyme, so they could not be unmade. Her lips often moved silently, counting, cataloguing, refusing to let any detail slip away.
We keep her ink-smudged spirit, her quiet insistence that what happened would be told. Even now, buried pages warm certain patches of our soil, making emberflies hover as if drawn to a campfire.

WHISPERROOT: A HUSHWOOD TALE

We guard those words, and when the snow melts, we will whisper them again.

We remember Lusia. We root her name deep, where warmth is hidden under ash. She curled her fingers around the warmed knot. She banked it like a coal under ash. Small, but alive, waiting for someone to stir it into a flame. Scratches scored her arms, thin as claw marks. We have traced them into our bark so no one can say they were not real. She did not roar or rage; she banked herself. She waited to be remembered. Now, we keep her warmth, and no winter will put her out.

We remember Klara. We speak her name heavy, slow, sinking it like a stone into our soil. She sat upright when pain would have pressed her flat. She was a protector of others–moving between Mila and the guards, creating a barrier with her own body. We remember her bruises, dark constellations on her skin, the way her breath matched the rhythm of our roots. With her last breath, she gave to another. She never let the despair that lay weighted across her shoulders crush her. We keep her fight now.

We remember Mila. We whisper her name with the rustle of blood-soaked straw. We remember the sound of her small body striking the wall, the bone-crack that made even the soldier wince. Ainela cradled her head, pressing her forehead against hers so she would not cross alone. Her blood ran into us, and we answered with a new root–pale, thin, determined to live. We have held her since, not in darkness, but in ember-light.

We remember Tatiana. The way she said *she died alone* and made a vow with her voice that no one else would. Watched her take the red ribbon, fingers angry, mouth tight, and tie it to the cornhusk doll like a promise. Since that day, the doll has never left her mat. We feel its weight through the floorboards, through the stone, into us. The ribbon is still red. We will keep it that way.

We remember Kaja. We keep her name close to the air vent, where she listened.
She was the one who could hear the footsteps first, the jingle of keys before the door opened.
We remember her hitting the back of her skull against the stone,

slow and steady, when fear threatened to split her apart. We watched her lip split purple, her cheek bloom black — she never hid them. She was the first to speak of ribbons, to say what others only thought. *When I saw ribbons, I thought of them.* We root that memory so that every red strip that dances in our branches will also whisper her truth.

We remember Lenka. We name her with swiftness — a flicker through snow.
She was the runner, the one who would risk the lash for the chance to feel the forest's breath.
We remember the way she tensed like a bowstring, ready to fly, ready to carry the others' hope.
Her footfalls were light, but her heart struck heavy. Even when fear made the others freeze, she planned the path, tracing the blacksmith's shop, the rickety bridge, the cottage. We keep her maps etched into our roots so no girl will ever be lost if she must run.

We remember Kalina. We remember the red thread she wrapped around her wound, holding herself together by will alone. We watched her tap the word *free* into her skin, starting the dangerous rhythm that made the room breathe again. She was slight, dizzy with hunger, but she sparked the rebellion with two fingers and a whisper. When the guards passed, her eyes still burned.
We keep that ember burning, glowing faintly under the snow, ready for the next girl who needs courage.

We remember Larisa. We say her name with the sound of beads falling to stone.
She was the one who clutched her rosary until the wood left marks in her palms, who prayed even when no one answered. We remember her quiet lips forming the words when the others had no strength to speak them. She begged for a funeral when Mila's body was taken, her voice cracking against the stone walls, but no priest came. She kept vigil anyway, whispering prayers to the dark.
When her breath stopped, we caught it and carried it into our roots so she would not be alone.

WHISPERROOT: A HUSHWOOD TALE

The beads she dropped still lie buried where her mat once was; we curl roots around them gently.
We hum her prayers back to the soil, so that even if no one above remembers, heaven still hears her name.

We remember Ainela. We do not whisper her name — we speak it like a vow.
She was the stitcher, the one who gave the girls their names back, one by one, even when her own ribs ached from the switch. She turned pain into poetry. We remember how she ached, how she screamed *Caterbutton* as she lay trembling and bleeding, and we remember how she turned that pain into a secret vow to be free. We remember her tears falling on Mila's hair, her fury spilling across the Rhymebook page, her promise that someone would know. We root her story deeper than all the others, because she is the one who chose to remember first.

Deep in our heart, mist rises between our trunks and silhouettes of these Embergirls appear. They do not stay but, for just a moment, they are above ground, free. When, one by one, they bow and fade back into our roots, we inhale their scent and taste the absence of fear. They are ours now.

And they are free here.

SKETCHBOOK

TIFFINI JOHNSON

For her.

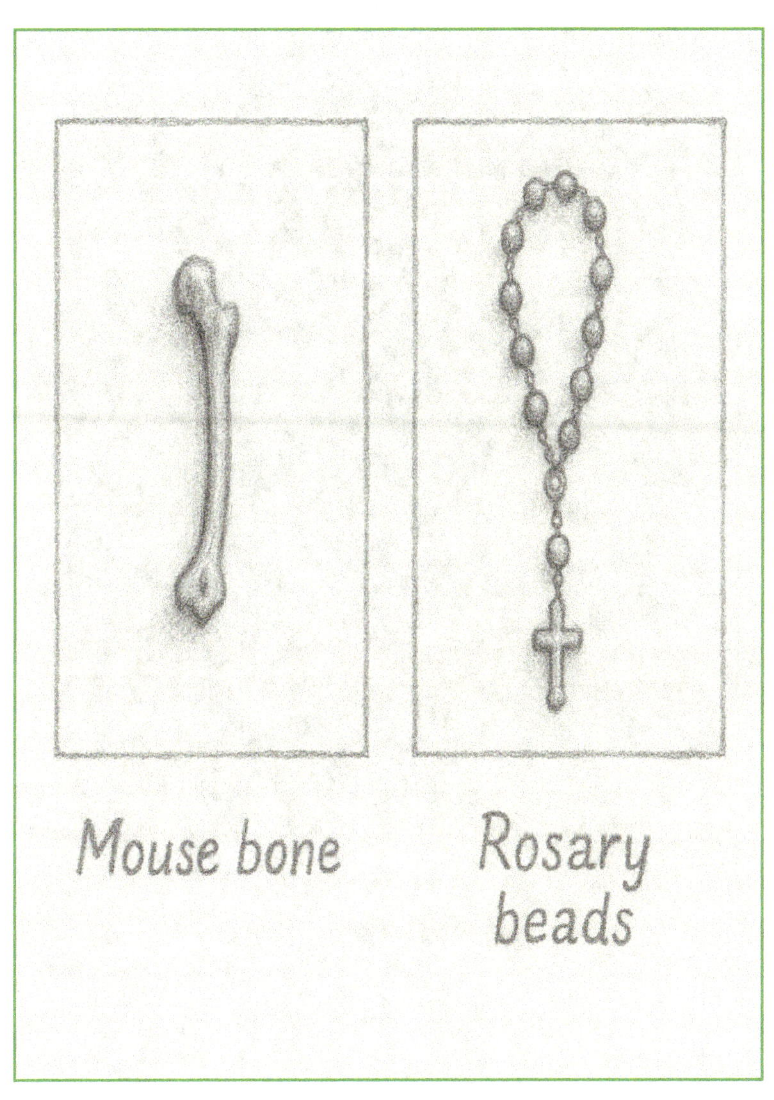

Mouse bone
Rosary
beads

They led me.

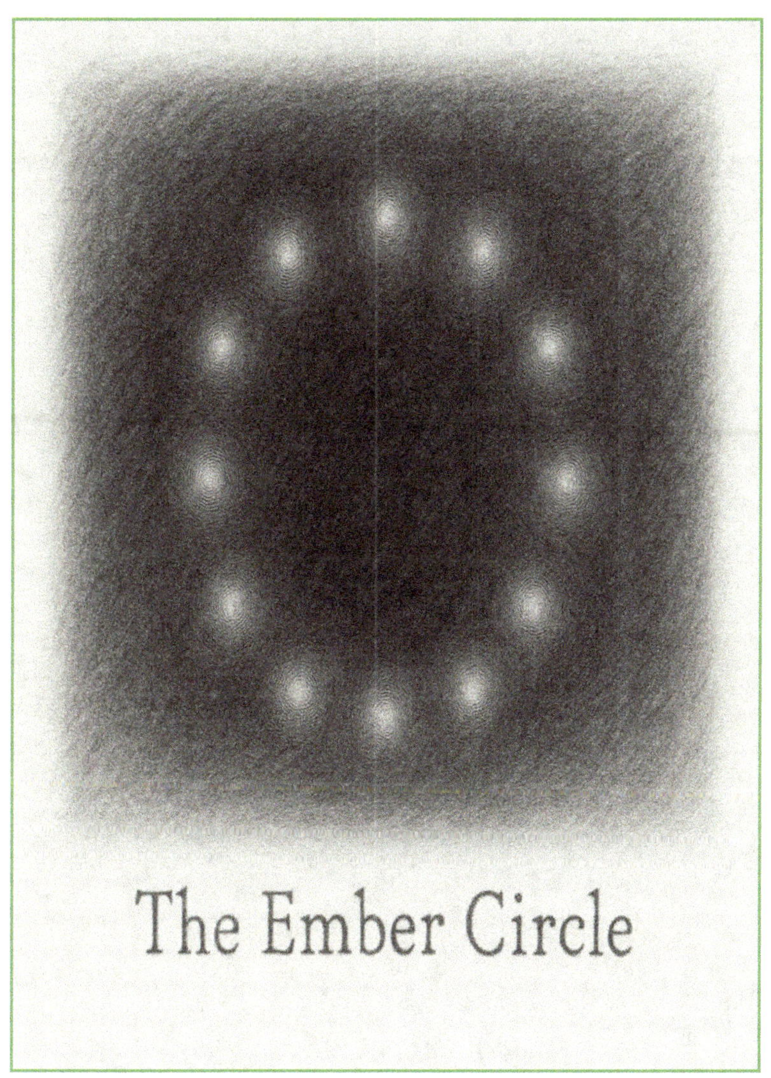

The Ember Circle

Alive.

WHISPERROOT: A HUSHWOOD TALE

WHISPERROOT: A HUSHWOOD TALE

Resources
Your story matters. You are not alone.

RAINN
the nation's leading source of information, resources and
prevention for survivors of sexual assault. Offers 24/7 phone,
chat, WhatsApp support
www.rainn.org

988
National Suicide Prevention hotline - offers trained support for
those in crisis.
https://988lifeline.org/

1in6
Offers chats, resources and support groups for men who have been
impacted by sexual violence.
https://1in6.org/

Whisperroot: A Hushwood Tale

Book Club Discussion

The Hushwood and Symbolism

1. How does the opening forest POV shape your understanding of the Hushwood—as a setting, a character, and a keeper of memory?

2. In the early town POV chapters, the villagers justify their silence about the missing girls. What does this reveal about collective complicity, and how do you think the same mindset might appear in real-life communities?

3. What role do red ribbons play in the story so far? How does their symbolism shift depending on whether they are tied by the townspeople, the girls, or the forest?

4. How does Zosia's muteness function as both a symptom of trauma and an act of resistance?

5. What do you learn about Ainela through her interactions with the forest compared to her interactions within the town?

6. In Chapter 11's "Ashwater Purification," how does the ritual's brutality work as a form of control? How do the girls' private acts—like Halina's hidden salve—undermine that control?

7. The Silence Drill in Chapter 12 forces the girls into a day-long vow of silence. How do their small acts of defiance—such as glances, gestures, and the lullaby—challenge the imposed silence?

8. What does the relationship between Ainela and Zosia reveal about sisterhood under pressure? How does the green satin ribbon exchange deepen this dynamic?

9. In the locket scenes, how does the object operate as a vessel for both memory and defiance?

10. How does Jakob's role complicate the reader's sense of morality in Myreska? Is his silence more damning, or is it a form of survival?

11. What do the repeated "Zosia-thread" moments in Ainela's POV add to your understanding of how the sisters remain connected despite separation?

Silence, Complicity, and the Town

12. What might the hushbark tree's remembered stories suggest about the power and danger of keeping history alive?

13. In what ways does Father Ignacy manipulate faith and morality to maintain his power?

14. Several girls, including Ainela, Klara, and Halina, act protectively toward others in captivity. How does this solidarity develop, and what risks does it carry?

15. The townspeople's language often reframes the girls' disappearances as "running away" or being "taken for protection." How does this narrative rewriting affect the truth? Consider events such as the Rwandan genocide where the Tutsi were referred to as "cockroaches" or the Holocaust where Jews were depicted as "evil", bloodthirsty Jesus killers. How has language shaped American culture---for the better, and for the worse? How does language contribute to the destruction or protection of innocence in the novel? In abusive homes? In churches? In loving homes?

16. How do the forest's symbolic creatures—the duskstag, chime-thrush, and ashfeather owl—mirror the emotional states of the girls?

17. In the opening chapters, many adults are shown choosing not to "see" what is happening. How

does this willful blindness compare to the silence of the children?

18. Ainela notes that each girl's red ribbon knot is tied differently. How does this detail reflect their individuality within shared captivity?

19. How is shame used as a tool of control in both the town and the cellar scenes? How would you define shame?

20. If you were living in Myreska, what would it take for you to break the silence?

21. How does Mama's silence in key moments—such as when Ainela is accused—shape your understanding of her character? Do you interpret it as fear, complicity, or something else?

Mama and Family Dynamics

22. Explore Ainela's family dynamics. Who is in charge of the home?

23. What role does Mama play in reinforcing or challenging the town's norms around obedience and reputation?

24. Mama's warnings to Zosia often focus on safety through silence. How do these instructions affect Zosia's choices and sense of agency? What are some valid reasons for silence? Is there ever a good reason to stay quiet if you are being hurt?

25. In what ways does Mama's relationship with Ainela differ from her relationship with Zosia, and how might this reflect deeper themes in the novel?

Memory, Ritual, and Resistance

26. How do the characters in both the cellar and the town use small, private rituals to cope with ongoing

trauma? Which of these moments stood out most to you?

27. What role does memory—both the keeping and the forgetting of it—play as a survival mechanism for the girls and the townspeople?

28. In what ways do the girls' acts of resistance, such as humming the lullaby or sewing symbols, serve as trauma responses as well as rebellion?

29. In Chapter 16 hunger is personified as an almost living presence. What does this metaphor suggest about the way deprivation can reshape identity and perception? Did this chapter alter your sense of what "violence" means in captivity?

30. The creak-map, humming, and tapping codes give the girls a secret language of survival. How does the creation of these shared practices serve both as grounding techniques and acts of rebellion?

31. Across these chapters, how does the rhymebook evolve from a secret act of remembrance into a collective tool of defiance? How does Ainela's blood-marked entry complicate the book's symbolism of reclamation and cost?

Trauma and Abuse

32. How is shame used as a tool of control in both the town and the cellar scenes?

33. In Chapter 14, Klara's return after assault is marked by her refusal of touch. How does her body language communicate both defiance and unbearable pain? How do the other girls navigate giving her space versus offering care?

34. Chapter 18 introduces the ritual chant "Unclean but obedient." What psychological impact does this phrase have on Ainela, and how do the girls

navigate the tension between enforced obedience and inner rebellion?

35. How does the physical toll of repeated punishments—such as Iskra's worsening wounds—raise the stakes of survival? How do you see the line between survival and slow erasure blurring here?

36. Across Chapters 19–29, we see repeated physical, psychological, sexual and spiritual abuse. How do these abuses reshape the girls' sense of self, and where do you notice lasting fractures versus acts of resistance?

37. In the wake of assaults and punishments, how do the girls' bodies "speak" even when they cannot—through refusal of touch, trembling, or silence? What does this suggest about the lingering weight of trauma?

38. How do small acts of care (bread-sharing, salves, songs) counterbalance the destructive effects of abuse? Do these moments feel like healing, survival, or defiance to you?

Names and Identity

39. Ainela notes that each girl's red ribbon knot is tied differently. How does this detail reflect their individuality within shared captivity?

40. How does the forced numbering of the girls reduce them to objects of control? How does Ainela's inner correction of each number back into a name resist this erasure?

41. The rhymebook preserves names even as the cellar strips them away. How do you interpret the contrast between imposed numbers and reclaimed names?

42. When Ignacy's own name begins to lose authority, what does this reveal about the fragility of power based on fear and shame? How does the novel use naming to show both domination and resistance?

43. The stripping away of names mirrors real-world practices of dehumanization. Have you ever experienced, or witnessed, the power of being called by name — or the harm of being denied it?

Jakub's Role

44. How does Jakob's role complicate the reader's sense of morality in Myreska? Is his silence more damning, or is it a form of survival?

45. Jakub hovers between complicity and quiet protection. How do his silences differ from the town's silence? Are they more forgivable—or more haunting?

46. At times Jakub seems both ally and betrayer. How do you interpret his choices in this section: as cowardice, survival, or subtle resistance?

47. In what ways does Jakub's war-haunted past shape his interactions with the girls? Do you see him as a character carrying guilt, or as someone unable to break free from cycles of violence?

Reader Reflection

48. Which girl's experience in Chapters 19–29 resonated with you most strongly, and why? Did it change how you thought about resilience under pressure?

49. What was the hardest section, scene or chapter for you to read? Why? Where did it make you feel the most vulnerable? The strongest?

50. How do you personally respond to stories that expose abuse and trauma in such raw terms? Do

you find yourself pulling back, leaning in, or holding both?

51. The sisters' quiet bond — through sketches, nicknames, and shared secrets — offers glimmers of hope. What small threads of connection help you endure difficult seasons in your own life?

52. Silence in *Whisperroot* is both a weapon and a survival tool. In your own experience, when has silence been protective, and when has it been harmful?

53. If you had been in the cellar with the girls, would you have chosen obedience to stay alive longer, or defiance even at great cost? What does your answer say about how you personally define survival?

Character-Specific Arcs

54. Several girls, including Ainela, Klara, and Halina, act protectively toward others in captivity. How does this solidarity develop, and what risks does it carry?

55. Lenka's breakdown during the roll call highlights the cost of imposed shame. How do the other girls respond to her vulnerability, and what does their reaction reveal about the fragility of solidarity under pressure?

56. In Chapter 14, Klara's return after assault is marked by her refusal of touch. How does her body language communicate both defiance and unbearable pain? How do the other girls navigate giving her space versus offering care?

57. In Chapter 17, Klara's sacrifice for Lusia shifts the dynamics among the girls. How does this moment of selflessness echo earlier themes of sisterhood, and how does it foreshadow coming fractures?

58. – How does Klara change once Lusia is gone? Do you read her shifts — the way she withdraws, the faint spark returning when she touches the corn doll — as signs of collapse, renewal, or both?

59. The cellar girls constantly weigh the cost of submission against the danger of resistance. Which choices felt most believable to you, and which do you think offered them the greater chance of survival?

60. 60 In these chapters, freedom is imagined through hunger, escape plans, ribbons, and memories. How do the girls define freedom for themselves, and how might those definitions differ from what the town believes freedom is?

61. Kaja's arc moves in the background of escape planning and punishment. What happened to her, and how does her absence/presence alter the balance among the girls? Do you see her as silenced, erased, or remembered differently than the others?

62. Each girl in the cellar has a breaking point: Ainela after the assault, Klara after Lusia's death, Halina in accepting death as freedom. Which of these moments struck you as most devastating, and why?

63. 63 Do the girls truly "break" in these scenes, or do they transform — finding new ways to survive, resist, or make meaning of their suffering? How did you interpret these shifts?

Ainela's Strengths and Weaknesses

64. What qualities make Ainela a natural leader for the other girls? How do her determination, creativity, and willingness to carry risk set her apart?

65. – Where do you see cracks in Ainela's leadership? Do these weaknesses make her less

effective, or do they highlight the impossible weight she is carrying?

66. As a survivor of sexual assault, Ainela walks the line between breaking and persevering. How do her experiences of trauma shape her choices, her voice, and her relationship with the other girls?

67. How does Ainela balance being both "just a girl" (a sister, a daughter, a friend) and a figure of resistance? Do you think she ever wishes someone else could take her place as the leader?

68. The rhyme tells us gold means "true," blue means "the wish you never knew," green is wild, red is forbidden, and black is refusal. Ainela's wish burns blue. What do you think her secret wish was? If your own wish were tossed into the flame, what color might it burn?

69. The town divides its daughters into "golden ones" and "wayward ones." How are these labels assigned, and what do they reveal about the town's fears and priorities? Do you think anyone can truly remain "golden" in Myreska?

70. The Power of Naming vs. Nicknaming – How do nicknames differ from true names in this story? Do you see them as acts of intimacy, rebellion, or erasure?

71. Other Nicknames – Which of the other names or labels (such as forest-girl, mouse, singer, caretaker) struck you most? Did they feel like gifts of identity, or like cages of expectation?

72. The Red One – Several girls are marked by their colors (green cape, red ribbon, blue scarf). How do these color-based labels both empower and endanger them?

73.Flame Thrower / Flame Stitch – Ainela's fiery identity grows from resistance and stitching. How does this nickname shape the other girls' perception of her, and how does it reflect the cost of leadership?

74.Caterbutton – What does Ainela's nickname for Zosia reveal about how she sees her sister? How does it carry both tenderness and responsibility?

75.Why might the townspeople not interfere with what Ignacy and the guards are doing? What are they themselves afraid of losing, or what consequences are they avoiding by staying silent?

76.How do the townspeople treat, interact with, or see Jakub and Mateusz in the novel's town POV sections? What do their attitudes toward these men reveal about complicity and shifting power?

Additional Questions

77. Chapter 31 – "Ash and Bells": How does the burning of the chapel reframe the town's sense of sanctity and guilt? Do you think the destruction is purifying, or does it leave new scars?

78. How do the town's multiple POV chapters evolve from passive complicity to fearful self-preservation? By the time we reach Chapter 35, are they capable of change, or are they still protecting themselves?

79. Several townspeople choose not to intervene in the climactic events (gathering in the square, listening but not acting). Do you see this as cowardice, survival, or a slow shift toward accountability?

80. In Chapters 33–35, Zosia shifts from silent witness to active truth-teller. What moment most convinces you she is ready to speak?

81. When Zosia names the girls aloud, how does the forest respond? Do you interpret this as magical realism, divine justice, or the psychological weight of memory breaking loose?

82. Zosia becomes the "Emberkeeper" in Chapter 36. What do you think it means to keep the memory of the girls alive, and how does this role transform her from the quiet younger sister into a symbol of resistance?

83. How does Halina's fractured memory and testimony shift the credibility of the story for the townspeople? Does her voice finally "count," or is it still doubted?

84. Halina and Zosia share a private covenant before gathering the town. Do you read this as an act of solidarity, a passing of the torch, or both?

85. The final forest POV chapter closes the novel with both mourning and warning. Do you think the hushwood's memory ensures safety for future girls, or does it hint that the cycle could repeat?

86. The forest seems to "hold" the names after Zosia speaks them. What does this say about the relationship between memory, land, and justice?

87. The novel ends with snow falling over the square, the town still silent. Did you find this ending hopeful, tragic, or unresolved?

88. After finishing the book, who do you think carries the most responsibility for what happened — Father Ignacy, the town, the parents, or the forest itself?

89. If the Embergirls' story were uncovered generations later, how do you think Myreska's descendants would tell it? Would they change the story, redeem it, or bury it again?

Whisperroot: A Hushwood Tale

Interview with Tiffini Johnson

TIFFINI JOHNSON

1. **What first inspired you to write *Whisperroot: A Hushwood Tale*?**

      I'm a big fan of William Faulkner. When I was high school, a wonderful teacher had us read "A Rose For Emily." The short story never left me. After devouring more of his works, I've loved the idea of personifying things. In one of my books, "Ash," I personify Death. When I knew I wanted to write about a historical, fictional town in Poland, I wanted to incorporate that technique again. Only this time, I wanted to personify an entire town.
      Once I had the knowledge that one of the characters was going to be in the collective "we" voice of a Town, I wanted to talk about the dangers of silence---and, also, why people remain silent even in the face of stark proof.

2. **Did you always know it would be a story about missing girls, or did that theme emerge as you wrote?**

      I knew there were missing girls. And I knew how many there were. I didn't know all of their personalities or idiosyncrasies, but I knew they were going to be missing.

3. **How did you decide to let the forest "speak" as a narrator?**

      Really, this was by accident. I was a little Intimidated by the idea of writing in the Town's voice. I thought writing from the forest might be an easier thing to do. Kind of like a practice. But it was a lot harder than I imagined it would be. Then it turned into fun. So, I kept it up.

4. **The hushwood feels like its own character. What does it symbolize for you?**

The hushwood is definitely its own character! For me, the hushwood and Zosia are two sides of the same coin. Both represent memory—and the cost of silence.

5. **Red ribbons, emberflies, and whisperroots appear again and again. Which symbol came first, and how did you weave them together?**

Red ribbons came first, and it was part of the Initial outline. I wanted something practical and common to girlhood that could be easily woven into multiple scenes. Most girls use something to tie hair back—my daughters and I call them "pretties." So, initially, the idea was simply to use red ribbons as anchors, a way to remind the readers that these were young girls.

Whisperroots was kind of the whole idea. So, I wanted something to symbolically represent what can happen when we bury a truth. When we do that, when we silence ourselves or others, whisperroots can grow. In the story, whisperroots grow where a truth is buried. In real life, what does that look like? In real life, whisperroots are the addictions, mental illnesses, and complications that can arise from burying something important. I truly believe that things like self-harm, suicide ideation, addictions – those are symptoms of a larger, emotional issue that has been silenced—either voluntarily or otherwise.

When we silence our voices, we work so hard to be "okay" but, all the while, the trauma we silenced, it burrows deeper. We start to internalize negative self-scripts and that is so painful that we must find a way to cope. If we cannot do that constructively, then whisperroots form. In essence, then, whisperroots are destructive coping mechanisms.

Emberflies were totally by accident and, honestly, Just because I love fireflies!

6. **Silence plays a huge role in the story — both as harm and as survival. What drew you to explore this theme so deeply?**

> *I am a survivor of sexual abuse. And I did not tell anyone until I became a mother. The protection of my daughter was more important than my own safety and gave me the courage to break a silence that had lasted for eighteen years.*
>
> *I am not defined by that abuse. I am more than it. But it does continue to impact my life, and every decision I make. Readers of my other works know that this is a topic I've explored many times before, and in many different ways.*
>
> *But never specifically the cost of silence.*
>
> *And that's a massive topic.*
>
> *Because, for me, the shame that resulted from the abuse was worse than the abuse itself. The mind games that resulted in me questioning my own self-worth and believing that no one really cared about me as a person, only what I could give them, were the most devastating aspect of my abuse.*
>
> *No one stays silent because they want to. Not really. People stay silent because they are afraid. Afraid of retribution. Afraid that their worst fears about who they are might be confirmed and, if that happened, then the shame would be real and self-loathing would be worse. So, silence as a means of survival was really interesting for me to explore. Because that's what it is. It's a way of staying alive. There's a time and place for silence.*
>
> *There's also a time and a place for voice.*

7. **Zosia begins the book silent and ends as a speaker of names. What was most important to you about her transformation?**

I wanted Zosia to learn to trust herself.

Zosia's silence was a physical manifestation of the town's emphasis on obedience. But here's the thing: I was really good at obeying. I still am. If your whole world revolves around only saying what is appropriate or accepted, then, eventually, you lose sight of who you are.

Once, while at the gas station, I decided to get something to drink. But when I walked up to the refrigerator and saw rows upon rows of drinks, I froze. I didn't really want my go-to soda, but I didn't know if I'd like any of the other options.

I stood there, literally frozen, until I realized a man was very patiently waiting for me to make a selection. Flustered, I grabbed the first thing I saw: a watermelon juice I'd never had before. I also apologized for taking too long to make a decision. I walked out of the gas station feeling stupid and inferior. Because, even now, I rarely make decisions because it's something I want. Truth is, I don't even know what I'd like because I only get or do or say things that are safe.

I wanted Zosia to first feel the weight of that. Of being unable to express herself freely—whether that be by running around like a kid or saying what she thought. I wanted her to feel caged, her only means of expression limited to the sketchbook.

And then—I wanted her to feel the freedom that comes with confidence, with agency, with a voice.

8. **Ainela's leadership feels both brave and costly. Do you see her as a tragic hero, a martyr, or something else?**

I see her as a tragic hero. She never set out to be the hero. But Ainela was a rare bird: she had the secret ingredients that make-up a true leader long before she ever entered the cellar.

Somehow, despite being raised in Myreska, she

had not lost her own identity. She had an understated sense of courage that, when tested, would rise to the surface.

There were moments in the book where I thought her courage leaned more toward desperation than bravery-but desperation actually can bring out the courageous side of us. Ainela isn't a hero because she started a fire or even because she pushed the girls towards Jakub—and the door. She's a hero because she pushed the girls, specifically, Klara, into daring to see another path forward.

The greatest leaders aren't the ones whose voices are the loudest. Actually, they're usually the ones whose voices are the quietest. True leaders are leaders exactly because they do not force: they inspire.

9. **Which Embergirl was hardest to write — and which one surprised you the most?**

That's a good question.

I think Larisa was the hardest because, as a devout Christian, I thoroughly hated the idea of spiritual abuse and I really hated that Larisa's prayers weren't answered in the way she hoped they would be.

As a child, I routinely asked God to hold my hand and believed He did. I never had a relic, like a rosary, but I know what it's like to feel Him near---and to feel Him far away. Larisa was desperate and she clung to the only thing that had ever given her any semblance of hope. It was really challenging because I wanted to show how comforting faith can be but that really wasn't Larisa's arc. And I struggled with that. For the record, I also really struggled with Father Ignacy being the perpetrator for the same reason.

But—one of my pastors said once, "ff you haven't been hurt by the Church, then you haven't gone to Church long enough." And he was right. Because the Church is comprised of flawed human beings. It's an imperfect gathering of God's people.

10. **The Rhymebook leaves are visually striking. Did you plan them from the start, or add them later to deepen the girls' voices?**

   They were not planned, as I have never done anything like that before! Honestly, this book has several devices that I have never used in my work. For instance, epigraphs. I've never used them. Chapter headers as photos---never done that either. So, every time I wrote a fragment, or used one as an epigraph, a little sprout in my head would say, "Hm... wouldn't it be great if you could combine these in some way so that the reader could see the Rhymebook?" Eventually, I used Canva to create the images, just as I was using Canva to create the epigraph pages.
   I love the way the appendixes ended up!
   I went back and forth about the title pages. But Ultimately, the town of Myreska would not have allowed the name Embergirls to remain. It's too raw, too emotional, etc. So, even though they had that word on a fragment, I thought it more suited the story for Myreska to preserve them as historical documents. It allowed them to say, "See? We're doing all we can – we saved their writings – we even displayed them!"

11. **This story deals with trauma, complicity, and survival. The scenes of sexual abuse in the novel are heartbreaking and intense. Were they necessary to the novel's core?**

   Were they necessary? I mean, probably not necessary. They were being beaten and forced to undergo horrendous conditions without the sexual abuse. So, no,

I don't suppose it was necessary.

However, one of the primary reasons I write is to heal from my own abuse. When I told my mother and my story came out, I promised a little girl who is buried deep inside of me that she didn't have to be quiet anymore. Keeping that promise means advocacy---and writing about the life-altering damage sexual abuse causes.

*Connecting with survivors, and supporting them, matters a lot to me. One of the most important messages I want to say is that you are not alone. Every 7 seconds in the United States, someone is sexually abused. That means that there are 12,343 instances of **reported** sexual abuse every, single day. This works out to 4.5 million occurrences of sexual abuse per year---and that's only in the United States. Now, every 9 minutes, that person is a child. This means that there are 160 instances of child sexual abuse **every day** in the United States. This works out to 56,400 incidences of reported child sexual abuse.*

Those numbers shatter me because one of the common emotions of survivors are that they are alone—they feel this even though the statistics say they are not. It was part of why the #metoo movement was so strong.

*I used to think, "Yeah, but I'm different because XYZ. I knew who to tell; I was old enough to know it was Wrong, etc." These are lies—but they are powerful ones. So, for me, these scenes of abuse say all the things I, as a survivor, have thought or feared. And I say them in all their ugliness because I want even one survivor to read it and go, "What? I didn't think anyone else understood. Maybe I'm **not** alone."*

It is my way of challenging the lies.

12. What do you hope readers carry with them after finishing the book?

I hope they question silence. I hope they

hear, loud and clear, that Myreska was not it. Myreska feared change. They feared the unknown. And they let that fear rob them of their daughters.

I hope they see Ainela, and Klara, and Halina, and all of the others as beacons of truth.

13. If you could sit down with the townspeople of Myreska, what would you want to say to them?

I would acknowledge that their pain. And their fear. They weren't purposefully being malicious. They were afraid of Father Ignacy. They were afraid for the lives of their own daughters, and of being shunned. So, I would first acknowledge their pain, and express empathy for what they lost. Because, in the quiet stillness of night, they hurt.

*I would then help them discover alternate ways to stay safe---and to protect **all** of their daughters. Often, when you feel vulnerable, you legitimately cannot see any other way forward. Everything feels impossible. And you're already hurting more than you know how to handle, so sometimes you just can't risk any new kind of pain. At least the pain you are in is familiar and, therefore, in a weird way, safer than an unknown pain.*

Myreska needed someone to hold her hand and guide her to a different path. Several legends in the book reveal generational trauma in this town, so I'd want to address that, too.

And then—I'd empower them by reminding them that they have the ability that no one else does. The ability to stop Father Ignacy, and to give their daughters a life they didn't have. I'd point out their strengths and how much they have to build on.

Finally, I'd beg.

I'd beg them to see their daughters as more than chattel. I'd teach them the Biblical context surrounding each and every one of Father Ignacy's scriptures. And I'd tell them he's missing the most crucial piece of the Gospel of Jesus Christ: that they are loved, pursued, and forgiven. That they do not have to hide behind traditions in order to save their souls—or their daughters.

And I'd help them develop a safety plan which would outline exact steps for become a healthier, more empowered, more faithful, more authentic town. One whose daughters grew up in a safe and loving community.

14. Is there more to explore in Myreska or the hushwood? Could there be a companion book or prequel?

I doubt it. I've never done that before. And, frankly, I'm not sure I could handle another piece of this town!

15. What was your research for the WHISPERROOT like? Did you use AI?

I created posters and ads that solicited current or past residents of Poland to share their stories with me. I received some interesting e-mails including some with recipes from their grandmothers and some with entertaining superstitions—a handful of which were included in the book!

Some of the chapter header images were generated with the help of AI tools. Once they were generated, I then edited them to the finished product in Canva. None of the text, nor the Rhymebook images were AI generated and—for the record—will never be!

16. When can we expect a new book from you, and how can readers connect with you?

So, WHISPERROOT was published four months

WHISPERROOT: A HUSHWOOD TALE

after REMEMBER THE NIGHTINGALE. It is the only time in many years that I've published more than one book in a year. Typically, I take an emotional hiatus for a few weeks after writing one.

And then I wait.

I cannot write without a character and sometimes takes a really long time. So, I'm not sure on when to expect one – maybe a year, maybe four months. It really depends on who the next character is!

Readers can connect with me directly at www.tiffinijohnson.com where they'll find trailers of the books, discounted pricing at the Hartprints Bookshop, details about the online book club I lead, Chapter Chats, and a lot more!

Whisperroot: A Hushwood Tale

Interview with Tiffini Johnson

TIFFINI JOHNSON acclaimed author of fifteen books, including **DANCE FOR ME, RIVER'S ROWAN, and REMEMBER THE NIGHTINGALE**. Her works have been featured on major news outlets and reviewed by THE NEW YORK BOOK REVIEW, USA NEWS, and others. A tireless advocate for survivors of abuse, she is a hotline specialist and member of the Speaker's Bureau for RAINN (Rape and Incest National Network), as well as a court-appointed Guardian ad Litem for children in foster care. She runs workshops dedicated to providing support for survivors and those who love them.

Her greatest passion is being a mother to her two daughters Breathe and Alight. They have always given her motivation, joy, and strength. Outside of being a mother and a writer, Tiffini's faith is a cornerstone of her life. She loves horses, the mountains and chocolate.

She is also a survivor of sexual abuse.

Readers can connect with her at tiffinijohnson.com

WHISPERROOT: A HUSHWOOD TALE

www.ingramcontent.com/pod-product-compliance
Lightning Source LLC
Chambersburg PA
CBHW070258310726
48976CB00005B/1480